THE STORMBRINGER SAGA

UNRAVELED

BOOK ONE

KIT ALDRIDGE

AZALA PRESS

To my 18-year-old self:
Thank you for staying.

FROZEN WA
CAER SAVALIER
CRAVENWOOD
TORRE DIUR
DREAD CITY
WEST GLEN
DRACONIS
THE DRAGON'S SPINE

VER SIGNIA
S
RILONNE
THE DRAGON'S NEST
N

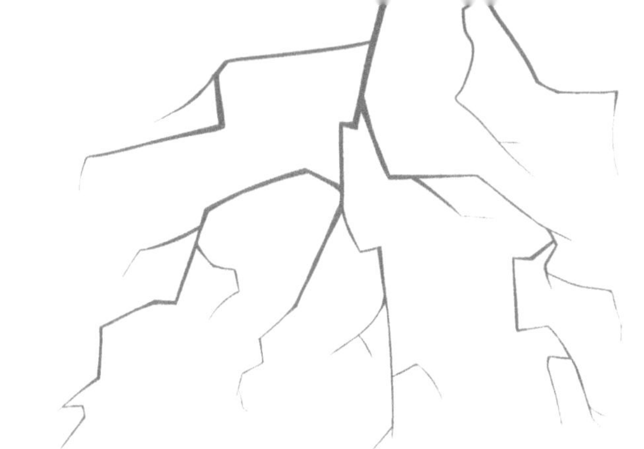

Act I

All That is Unseen

I. REINA

This man wasn't dying fast enough.

Reina drummed her fingertips against her knee. She and an entire amphitheater of spectators leaned forward, eager for bloodshed.

The raging dragon in the ring kicked up a cloud of dust and sand in pursuit of its prey. Murmurs of excitement and intrigue rose from the crowd when the fighter suddenly slipped. His crude steel sword fell from his hand, and he flipped to his back just as the dragon shadowed him. Powerful jaws muffled his panicked shriek. And with a final *crunch* of bone, the fight was over.

A light smattering of applause showered the dragon as it feasted.

Reina sighed through her teeth, her heartbeat calming.

In the commentator's box, a man shouted into a horn that amplified his voice. "The odds for the Infernal continue to rise!" He beckoned with a wave of his hand. "Trainers, please."

At his behest, a group of men—each clothed in fire-resistant armor and equipped with chains and noise-makers—

jogged out into the arena to contain the dragon while another team cleared away the gory remnants. Curious spectators leaned over the sides of the barriers to get a closer look at the carnage.

Continuing with a grand sweep of his arm, the announcer called, "Our next fighter graces our presence from the shining jewel of Caer Savalier. Please welcome to the ring Ser Demerin the Valiant!"

Reina tore her eyes away from the littering of blood and bones. Her head swiveled toward the champion's corner—just a darkened box from this distance. "Did he just say 'ser'?"

As the trainers cleared the area, the iron gates of the champion's box opened, and a mountain of a man sauntered into the ring, wearing spotless silver armor. He wielded a heavy broadsword and carried no shield. His face was concealed behind a helmet, but his battle cry was as clear as a war horn.

At the opposite end of the ring, the Infernal dragon snarled, licking its lips. Ser Demerin did not flinch.

Reina scoffed. "And here I thought that dragon fighting was beneath the Kingsguard." She elbowed Meiryn, frowning at her hunched shoulders and bowed head. "How long do you think he'll last?"

Meiryn peeked at the fighting ring through her fingers. "Hopefully longer than that last man, if he's actually a knight."

"He is," Reina said, pointing at the shimmering silver figure. "Armor like that only comes from Caer Savalier."

"Well, let's just hope it lasts him a while, then."

"You're forgetting who we've placed our bets on," Reina muttered.

A broad ring of at least a couple hundred spectators roared with excitement when Ser Demerin brandished his sword.

Reina joined the battle cries. The Infernal lashed its tail back and forth, chains rattling like bells.

Ser Demerin charged. He dodged the dragon's spiked tail with a gallant leap that brought the crowd to their feet. Reina hopped up on the bench just in time to catch the knight's blade carving a deep gash in the dragon's thigh. Blood sprayed his armor. The Infernal gnashed its teeth, and the knight rolled under its belly, dragging his sword through armored scales.

The dragon's shrill cry rattled through the air. Reina raised herself on tiptoe, staggering when the benches wobbled. Meiryn steadied her and cast her an exasperated look.

"Sit down—you'll fall and get hurt again."

Reina ignored her, craning her neck. She tracked the knight's path between raised fists and bobbing heads. "I think this'll be the last one," she gasped. Anxiousness churned her stomach. She glanced toward the betting table, where all of her and Meiryn's shared gold sat in a small coin purse. "Ser Demerin is holding out."

Meiryn, eyes low, shared a cautious look with Reina. It would be safer to pull their winnings out now; they'd already tripled the amount they'd thrown in. But if they sat through this fight, and the dragon won again, they'd be even better off for their journey tomorrow.

So Reina waited, and she watched as the knight rolled to his feet and delivered a hard kick to the dragon's ribs. The Infernal careened sideways, wings shooting out for balance. Ser Demerin lifted his sword high and tore the blade clean through the leathery wing.

A piercing cry erupted from the throat of the Infernal. The crowd was practically jumping in their seats as the dragon clawed at the sands, trying to drag itself away from Ser Demerin.

Its eyes followed the knight's movements, and he glared back, teeth bared. He marched around to the dragon's opposite side and tore through its second wing. The Infernal was flightless.

Pain kept the dragon down as Ser Demerin rushed forth with an onslaught of attacks. Blood spewed from every incision; his sword sang a brutal song of death and triumph; and the crowd began chanting Ser Demerin's name when he finally brought the beast to its knees.

The shouting rose to deafening volumes, drowning out the Infernal's shuddering wail. Reina could barely hear her own thoughts. Ser Demerin tore his helmet off, revealing a greying head of hair and a smug face. Trails of crimson trickled down his sword when he lifted both arms in the air and roared.

"Ser Demerin won!" Reina cried.

Meiryn's hands were clamped over her ears, but she snapped her head in Reina's direction. "He *won*?"

Reina's vision tunneled on the knight. The cheers slurred into a thick drone. A slow fire crept into her chest.

Everything they had—all the gold they had saved up—was gone. Lost in a reckless gamble.

Reina started to reply, but a shrill scream cut through the cheers, followed by horrified gasps. She turned back toward the arena just in time to see the dragon lift its head and unhinge its jaws.

While Ser Demerin bathed in praise, a great, roaring fire built in the back of the dragon's throat. Warning cries lifted— but too late.

Ser Demerin had barely spun before the Infernal released a swirling vortex of flame. People shrank back in their seats. Reina's mouth fell open as Ser Demerin's armor melted into his skin. His scream split the air like a knife. Silver bled into crimson, and the scent of burning flesh stifled the air. Smoke billowed from his body as he sank to his knees, then collapsed in the sand. Unmoving.

Dead.

A stunned hush fell over the crowd. The dragon pawed at the knight and gave a satisfied huff, fangs sinking through charred flesh and warped silver.

The announcer rushed to the stand. "Well," he called, chuckling uneasily, "that was quite a finish! Another mark for the Infernal, please."

A group of four or five men rose from their seats, grumbling and muttering. They cast a nasty look toward the dragon. As they exited the arena, they dropped handfuls of gold into a betting stand.

Reina exhaled heavily and sat down again. Hope loosened the tension in her shoulders. She leaned close so Meiryn could hear her over the roaring stands. "See? I told you that Infernal is strong."

Meiryn peered at her through her fingers. "And if the next fighter happens to kill it instead, then we've lost everything. Let's just go."

Reina, still exhilarated by the fight, waved a dismissive hand. "You saw how it took out that man in the end." She paused. "Well. No, you didn't. But it was fantastic." It was just like the fights she heard stories about when she was growing up. Dragon fights were a poor man's form of entertainment, her parents had sneered, but Reina found them utterly enthralling. Riveting, fast-paced, not a moment to spare looking anywhere but at the bloodbath in the middle of the arena.

Meiryn just groaned and rolled her eyes.

"Now," the announcer said, "we have one last fighter for

this evening. Hailing from the rippling emerald fields of the Ashuman Empire, I welcome to the ring—Nona!"

Reina frowned as a tiny figure strode out from the champions' corner. The woman—who looked more like a child from this distance—couldn't have been much older than Reina herself, and she carried only two whips.

When the crowd caught sight of her, mixed reactions met her one-handed waves. Applause was scattered. Lighter. But from one corner of the arena, a group of burly men erupted into a fit of boos and hisses. Reina sat back when someone shouted, *"Malduna!"* Another urged that the fight was rigged so that Nona—a little Ashuman woman—could finish off a nearly dead dragon and go home with all the winnings. It had happened once before, and since then, no one trusted any Ashuman who stepped into the ring with a dragon.

Nona held her head high, as if the accusations and outrage could not reach her.

Meiryn finally dropped her hands. Her voice was hard, her tone wary. "Reina, maybe we should leave."

But Reina shook her head. "I want to see how this woman plans to take down a fully matured dragon." And what she planned to do if things didn't go her way. To admit defeat would be to brand herself a coward, but standing her ground could very well lead to her death.

"No—look." Meiryn nodded at the group of men who had made their way to the barrier of the ring. They shouted insults and slurs, which were met with either silence or uncomfortable laughter.

Nona's brow lowered. She turned her back to the crowd. Her lips moved, but whatever she whispered drowned beneath the chanting of *"Malduna."*

Deceiver. Trickster. Enemy.

It was an insult that people had spat at Reina's own feet, so she was no stranger to this mistrust. But even still, she tugged her hood up.

The bell announced the start of the fight, and Reina gasped when Nona darted to the dragon's side, as swift as the wind. With a resounding *snap-snap, snap-snap*, her whips pierced through every insult thrown her way. She tapped the Infernal's tail, then leaped away when it swiveled. Her voice was a thin cry, egging the dragon on and taunting it around the fighting ring.

In a mere few seconds, Nona had managed to captivate the audience with her strange tactics. Even Meiryn lifted her head to watch the fight.

Nona dodged every spitting ember, snaked between every tendril of flame. She danced mere feet from the Infernal's jaws, whips snapping with an almost rhythmic cadence that put the dragon in a trance. At one point, Nona reached out to it, and she appeared to coil a rope of flame around her arm. But when she leaped away from those razor-sharp fangs, her skin was unmarred. The only fire lighting up the arena was the excitement in her eyes.

The spectators were enchanted, forgetting that they'd come for bloodshed. But it was only when Nona swept around to their side of the arena that Reina finally realized what was happening.

Without laying a hand or a blade on the dragon, Nona was provoking it. Urging it to attack with the flames it had been trained to stifle. Her whips were not weapons to inflict harm; she was directing the Infernal's attention—directing its fire past the barriers of the ring.

The dragon growled a low warning. Weary eyes flashed like

diamonds. Against the broken armor of blood-spattered scales, Reina saw a dull, flickering glow. Dread gripped her, and she gripped Meiryn's arm. "We need to go."

Meiryn cast her an alarmed look. "But you wanted to stay—"

"And now I am saying we must go."

Reina pulled Meiryn to her feet right as Nona darted to the far end of the arena, where the men still jeered like dogs. Reina's heart pounded as the Infernal stretched its jaws. Nona rocked on her feet, whips snapping on either side of the dragon's head. "Come on, you! Light it up!"

With a bellowing roar, the dragon unleashed its fury.

The audience shrieked as fire swept into the stands, stretching thirty, forty, fifty feet back. The men's taunts turned to screams of fear.

Meiryn gasped, clasping the back of Reina's shirt. Reina twisted and grabbed her wrist, pulling her forward.

Nona was still darting about the ring. She wove between pillars of smoke and fire—untouched by any of it. Chaos broke out when another breath of flame scorched the arena.

The announcer was shouting furiously, his voice drowning beneath the clamor of panic. He waved his arms, and two men broke into the fighting ring. Nona's back was to them, but before they reached her, an arrow shot from somewhere in the crowd.

Reina whipped her head around and found a redheaded archer at the furthest corner of the spectator stands. Another arrow was already nocked in their bow. Reina blinked—and the second guard crumpled at Nona's feet.

Nona whirled. Her eyes went wide, and she ducked when

the dragon tossed its head, spewing embers and scoring trails of fire into the fighting sands.

Reina grabbed Meiryn and yanked her down. Fire raged over them, then swept in a wide arc.

"What does she think she's doing?" Meiryn shrieked. "She's going to get everyone killed!"

"No," Reina gasped. "She's setting the dragon free."

And if that were true, then that could only mean—

"It's the Hunters Guild!" a voice screamed.

No sooner did the words tear through the chaos than a stream of armed fighters flooded into the ring. Half of their numbers swarmed the dragon, gripping its chains and slamming their weapons against the steel. Someone drove an axe through the wooden barrier that kept the dragon's leash tethered to the wall. The other half stormed the stands near the champion's corner, dousing the benches and stairs with oil. The flames grew hotter. Higher. They stretched up to the ceiling, emitting a pungent odor.

The stands shuddered as spectators trampled over one another. Once seated in neat rows, the people now pushed and shoved in a formless mass, keeping a wide berth between themselves and the dragon.

Reina held fast to Meiryn and led them closer to the fighting ring, where fire surged but the path was clearer. The heat drew sweat to their brows. Smoke shrouded everything from view. Reina had lost sight of Nona—and the archer who had saved her—but she shuddered to a halt when the dragon screeched. Crippled wings flailed in desperation; jagged and rotted teeth snapped dangerously near, splintering the stands just behind them.

"Reina!" Meiryn screamed, shaking her by the shoulders. "We need to go!"

Startled, Reina scrambled forward. Meiryn kept their hands clasped tightly, and Reina was merciless and unapologetic as she shoved through the tunnel and out into the city.

People scattered like rats. The place was already swarming with guards shouting for reinforcements and water buckets. Reina dodged around them and ducked into the nearest alleyway, dropping into the shadows.

Smoke billowed upward, and firelight burned within, giving the arena the look of a massive forge. Guards rushed inside, swords whining.

"Six hells," Meiryn swore breathlessly. She raked a hand through her full head of gold hair, pale hands shaking violently. "I will *never* let you get me that close to another dragon again."

Reina gasped and leaned her head back. Despite everything, she managed a flicker of a smile. "They're amazing, aren't they? And that's just an Infernal. I can't imagine what a Hibern might do... Seeing them up close—it's different than just hearing stories."

It was *enthralling*.

"Well, I think I've had more than enough encounters," Meiryn retorted. "If that's how an injured dragon fights, then it's no wonder the Order hasn't made any ground on the Nest."

Reina shrugged. She knew that the Silver Order sought to exterminate dragons forever, but it was fights like these that gave cause to her admiration for the beasts. They were untamed and uncontrollable. Their existence alone kept the entire kingdom of Ver Signia on constant alert.

Their ferocity was the reason the Order so often failed to eradicate dragons, and why independent organizations like the

Hunters Guild were so dangerous. Unleashing something as unpredictable as that...

Those huntsmen were more insane than the agents of the Order who sought to slaughter what the Ashumans called *kaeli rekks*—rulers of the sky.

Reina jerked her head up when the sound of creaking wood and rattling chains grew louder. She peered around the corner of the alleyway—just in time to see the Infernal tear through the walls of the arena.

Wood splintered. Stone crumbled in a cloud of dust. Meiryn screamed, and Reina silenced her with a tight hand over her mouth.

The dragon was no more than fifty feet away. It sniffed the air and opened its wings, but Ser Demerin had stripped it of its ability to fly. The ground trembled and stone walls shuddered as the Infernal set off at a sprint. Reina watched, mouth agape, as the dragon raced toward the eastern gates, leaving a trail of ruin and fear in its wake.

Stragglers poured out of the arena. Like wolves, the huntsmen clashed against city guards—a few slipping free to chase after the dragon, more falling at the hands of their enemy.

But Reina stilled when she saw a small figure stumble out of the chaos.

"Look," she gasped, "it's Nona."

The woman only had one whip left, and she was coughing violently, each step staggering and lilting. When she emerged from the flames, the guards pointed, lifting their voices in alarm.

Reina sank back as they swarmed the Ashuman fighter. They disarmed her and chained her wrists behind her back. A wave of huntsmen surged forward, the redheaded archer the first among them.

The battle didn't last long, for the fire swelled to a deafening roar, and the walls of the arena caved. Ash and soot tainted the air. Embers jumped from the wreckage. Reina was so transfixed on the battle that she almost forgot about Meiryn until she felt a harsh tug on her arm.

Meiryn's eyes were wide and terrified. She looked pale in the glow of the firelight. "We need to go," she breathed, tearing herself free of Reina's grip. "Please."

Reina glanced back, where the guards had just managed to pry a kicking and thrashing Nona off the ground. The archer shouted, her voice hoarse and frantic, but one of her companions held her back.

"You can't do anything to help her," Meiryn insisted, pulling on Reina's arm again.

"No." Reina shook her head. It wasn't Nona's capture that rooted a cold dread into her stomach now. It was the sinking realization that she had forgotten something vitally important. The whole reason they'd come here and risked everything.

"All our gold," she breathed. "Everything we saved—it's all gone."

And the woman responsible had just been captured.

II. MEIRYN

One moment, Reina was a statue at Meiryn's side; the next, she was a blur in the darkness. Meiryn scrambled after her, hurtling through unlit backstreets and slipping through puddles of sewage.

"Reina!" Meiryn panted. Her lungs were as hot as the flames that had scorched the arena. Her legs threatened to collapse at any second. And yet, Reina kept running. "Reina, stop. Where are you—I can't—I need to breathe. *Wait.*"

Meiryn doubled over, nearly crashing over a pile of wooden crates. Rats scampered at her feet, but she was too fatigued to jump back. Every breath speared ice through her chest, and she grimaced when a stitch in her side kept her bent at the waist.

Several blocks away from the arena now, sleeping homes shielded them from harm. The roar of fire was a distant crackle; the darkness was still again.

But Reina's eyes were stormy when Meiryn caught up with her. Blacker than midnight, glinting with untempered fury. She barely looked winded, as if anger alone fueled her.

Meiryn sank to her knees. Her hair fell over her shoulders

and grazed the grimy cobblestones, and as she heaved in full breaths, she swore she could feel the ground shuddering under Reina's pacing.

"Six *fucking* hells," Reina fumed. "That girl just ruined the whole match."

Meiryn was trying not to think of it. Of what it meant for them. She lifted an open hand, trying to soothe Reina. Even here in the alleys, anyone could be listening. Watching. "Give me a moment. We'll move someplace safer—then we'll talk."

But Reina ignored her—typical, when her fury took over. "I can't believe that happened. Of all the gods-damned things—"

"Reina." Meiryn threw every ounce of desperation she could muster into her voice. The oxygen in her chest was thin; her head was spinning. "We'll worry about it in the morning—"

"We weren't even supposed to be here by then," Reina interrupted. "The winnings from that fight should have taken us to Ashuma."

"I know, but—"

"We lost *everything.*"

"There's nothing we can do," Meiryn snapped. She forced herself upright, and in the least accusatory tone she could manage, she ground out, "This was your idea. You knew the risks, yet you took them anyway."

Reina halted. Her arms had been folded tightly across her chest, but now she let them fall. If looks could kill, Meiryn would have been six feet underground. "I did what needed to be done."

"No, you—" Meiryn stopped herself. *You did what you wanted. Like you always do.*

She took a deep breath and swallowed her words.

Starting again, this time with forced calmness, she said, "Neither of us could have known what would happen." *But if you had just listened to me from the start, we wouldn't even be in this situation.*

Reina's mouth pressed into a thin line. An oily strand of ink-black hair fell over her eye. "I messed up. I know that."

"I'm not blaming you," Meiryn murmured. A tense silence settled between them, and Meiryn scrambled to fill it. "Why don't we just rest here until morning? We'll go back to the arena, see if we can get the guards to tell us what's happening with the bets. You saw the crowd; we won't be the only ones who lost money tonight."

It was as much hope as they could grasp, but the next day, when they tried exactly that, the guard out front laughed in their faces.

"Do you know how many of you have already come crawling at my feet today?" He scanned them with a look of disdain. His eyes narrowed at Reina, but he addressed Meiryn in a clipped voice. "Tell your Ashuman friend here that gambling is a fool's game."

Meiryn glowered, and Reina snapped, "I *know*. And I can understand you."

The guard clicked his tongue impatiently. He regarded her as if she were a roach creeping along his polished leather boots. "Then you'll understand this perfectly: get lost."

Reina's eyes flashed. Before she could say or do anything that might make their situation worse, Meiryn jumped in with a pleading, almost groveling tone. "Please. Can't you just talk to the sponsors from the fight? What about the man who was collecting all the bets?"

"That man was killed half a mile outside West Glen for

attempting to flee with all that coin. Turns out this wasn't his first time scamming a bunch of gamblers."

So it didn't even matter that Nona had ruined the match; even if the fight had been fair, anyone who placed bets would have lost money.

Reina pressed, "You didn't recover anything off his person?"

The guard gave her a flat look. "Why? Hoping to fill your purse with someone else's hard-earned gold?" He smirked at the jab, then gestured to the smoldering wreckage behind him. "The Guild got to him first, but our guards scared off those greedy bastards before they could loot everything. What wasn't stolen is being used to rebuild what those huntsmen tore down. And to pay the Silver Order for their services."

Reina stiffened. Meiryn frowned and asked, "Why bother summoning the Order? Wouldn't they be occupied with the dragon campaign?"

Reina answered her in a strained voice. "Agents of the Order are sent where they're needed—wherever trouble with dragons arises. They don't confine themselves to the Nest, so if a cadre was notified of last night's fight, they'll be here before the day is over. They can deal with huntsmen swifter than any amount of common city guards." Her arms tightened around her chest, and she chewed her lower lip, oblivious to the guard's indignation.

"If you already know," he barked, "then why are you still here wasting my time?" He marched forward, forcing Meiryn and Reina to retreat. A smug grin tilted his mouth when Reina's feet scuffed through dirt, and he lowered his voice as a pair of his colleagues approached. "Heed my words and get lost. Or else the Order will be dragging two *maldunas* and a street rat out of here."

He spun away when one of the other guards called his name, and Meiryn jutted an arm out, stopping Reina from following him.

Reina shot her a look. "We need—"

"To leave," Meiryn finished. She glanced at the guards; all three were eyeing them suspiciously, and her skin prickled at the way they studied Reina. She closed a hand around Reina's arm. "Come on. Before they decide we're worth more than nothing."

Her heart pounded in her ears long after she and Reina slipped out of sight. She couldn't shake the feeling that they were being watched, but each time she turned back, she found nothing but a waking city.

Though the forest enveloping West Glen was dense enough in some areas to conceal sunlight altogether, a broad street led them beneath an open sky, further into the city. The market district was bustling with vendors and shoppers caught in haggling battles; wealthy traders from northern Ver Signia—and a sparse few from Ashuma—flashed their wares beneath curious noses; shopkeepers polished their storefronts and hollered out their sales.

Six months ago, when she and Reina stowed away on that farmer's wagon, Meiryn had gazed upon West Glen with a quiet sense of hope. Unlike other Ver Signian cities she'd been to that fed off underpaid labor, West Glen breathed with the life of the surrounding environment. Winding through the city was a clear, twinkling river that powered the watermills. Flora decorated the street corners and gave even the most industrial buildings a natural feel, as the forest itself played a hand in constructing the lumber mills. She was enchanted by the simplicity of the stone townhouses, all unmarred by a dragon's rage, and though she never confided in Reina, Meiryn had sunk into the dream of living in a place like this. It wasn't perfect, and it wouldn't bring back either of the families they had lost, but it could be home, if they wanted it to be.

Now, when she gazed at it all, she only felt trapped by the towering wooden walls. Though this area of West Glen hadn't been touched by last night's dragon fight, the treetops still crept at the corners of the sky, and the cracks between the cobblestones grew longer with each passing day. Beds of grimy stone made for stiff backs; taking shelter under the stars had long since lost its appeal. It was as if the city itself were whispering, *None of this belongs to you. None of it ever belonged to you.*

Meiryn's paranoia from the morning followed her like a second, darker shadow. She thought she was hiding it well, but eventually, Reina gave her a look and muttered, "You're making me look more like a criminal than these people already think I am."

Meiryn blinked, finally noticing the way she was gripping Reina's wrist; the way passersby eyed Reina with mistrust and gave her a wide berth.

"You're not a criminal." Meiryn released Reina and clasped her hands behind her back. "You've done nothing wrong." *Except lose everything we've saved up.* She shook the thought from her head and offered, meekly, "We'll figure something out. We always do." Meiryn squeezed between two people, nearly losing sight of Reina in the process.

Reina tugged the hood of her thin, tattered cloak over her head as the heart of the city grew more congested. Shadows crossed half her face as she turned and hissed, "If your plan is to stay here another six months, then forget it. We might as well just smuggle ourselves across the border."

The mere thought twisted Meiryn's gut, and before she

could stop herself, she griped, "Haven't you gambled enough already?"

Immediately, she regretted her words, but Reina had heard. She halted, and not a heartbeat later, a sharp voice yelled, "Look out!"

Reina grunted as someone shoved her out of the way of an oncoming wagon. As it sped past, Meiryn caught a glimpse through the bars. The Ashuman fighter from last night, Nona, was stuffed into the jailer's cage, hands bound behind her back. About four or five other faces flashed by before the carriage was gone.

Meiryn looked up at Reina's savior. His face was young, dotted with freckles and framed by short waves of coppery hair. Even in the summer heat, he wore a leather hunting jacket, and strapped across his chest was a baldric that looked like it might fall apart at the slightest strain. Peeking over his right shoulder was the leather-wrapped hilt of a sword.

"You saved her," Meiryn breathed. She met a pair of warm hazel eyes. "Thank you."

The man said nothing. His brow lowered as he stared after the jailer's wagon, and he merely straightened his jacket before trailing after it. He slipped from view the moment Reina positioned herself in front of Meiryn.

Her hood had dropped. Anger blistered her face, and she didn't even seem to care that she'd nearly been trampled. "I don't need you telling me everything I did wrong. I know this is my mess to clean up, and if you'd rather not be a part of it, then you can stand by and watch—like you always do."

Meiryn gaped. "What—"

"One way or another, I'm going to Ashuma," Reina interrupted. Her eyes were glassy, but her voice was thick with rage.

"I've spent my entire life being called *malduna*, answering to people who thought they could control me. You've never known how it feels to be so trapped, like nothing you do matters because someone else has already decided what you're going to do or say. So even if I have to sneak my way through the Dragon's Spine, even if you're too afraid to come with me, I am leaving this kingdom."

The words pierced Meiryn like knives. "Reina—"

She was already gone. Meiryn's heart jumped, and she scrambled to catch up. Reina wouldn't truly abandon her—of that, Meiryn was certain—but her anger often blinded her to her surroundings.

No sooner did Meiryn call Reina's name again than a small part of the crowd let out a surprised yelp. Meiryn diverted her attention just long enough to see a pair of street performers launching themselves at one another on a tiny, raised stage. One was clothed in black and wielded a long wooden sword spotted with faded silver paint. Flowing from his shoulders was a black cape trimmed with grey threading, and upon the left side of his chest was a crude outline of silver flames—the emblem of the Silver Order. Facing him, dressed in ragged clothing stitched from moss and leaves, was his opponent: the top half of this man's face hid behind a wolf mask, and he had soaked his mouth in garish crimson paint to mimic blood-soaked fangs.

Reina stopped short as the audience blocked her path. Meiryn squeezed in close. Curiosity turned her head, and she peered over several pairs of shoulders to catch a glimpse of the show. The performers danced around each other, taunting and teasing, building anticipation.

Reina leaned back just enough for Meiryn to hear her

mutter, "If it's second-rate performances you're looking for, the king's court is full of them."

Meiryn bit her tongue. Those "second-rate performances" were what fed her imagination as an orphaned child. Even if they weren't the most sophisticated form of entertainment, they took Meiryn back to a time when she was little, when stories were the only thing to keep her company on cold winter nights.

Reina's fingers curled around Meiryn's wrist, though she still would not meet her gaze. She tugged lightly. "Let's go."

But the audience had multiplied, and the pair found themselves trapped among eager and curious spectators. The performers battled on, their exaggerated gestures attracting an even larger crowd.

"Down, you monster!" the swordfighter shouted. "Cower at the sting of my blade. Crumple beneath the might of the Silver Order!"

The man in the wolf mask released a haunting wail as the black-clad performer jabbed with his wooden sword. Red cloth streamed from a fake wound, and the crowd cheered for the victor.

The masked performer keeled over, howling and writhing on the ground. His limbs jerked grotesquely, but just before his eyes rolled back in his skull, another wolfish cry erupted from somewhere in the crowd.

Meiryn gasped as a third actress sliced through the audience. Her hair flew like a wild mane, and concealing her face was a similar wolf mask. On all fours, she pounced onto the stage and bared her teeth.

"The Hunters Guild protects its own," she snarled. Behind the mask, her eyes flashed as she glared down the length of the wooden sword. Every word struck like venom from painted lips. "May the Wolf King take you, poacher of the forest and sky."

The audience hissed. Cries of "heathen" and "rogue" pounded the actress's arched back. She pawed at the ground with a curled fist, covering her fallen companion's body with her own. Her head tossed like an animal, and her voice turned thin as smoke.

"All those who tread on false comfort, hear my words and take heed: it is the arrogance of power that brings even the strongest to their knees." She circled the swordfighter while staring out at the crowd. For a heartbeat, her eyes found Meiryn's. "A clever mind cuts deeper than the sharpest steel, and in the shadows of all that is unseen, the Wolf King's guild outlasts the Order's relentless zeal."

The performer lifted her head and howled. Meiryn, still transfixed, jumped when Reina tugged on her wrist again. She ground out through clenched teeth, "*Let's. Go.*"

Meiryn blinked twice. If it weren't Reina—if it weren't her *friend*—Meiryn might have shrunk away. In the three years they'd known each other, Meiryn had never seen Reina so high-strung.

Cautiously, she asked, "Are you alright?"

Reina didn't answer. She tugged her hood over her head again and motioned for Meiryn to follow.

Meiryn shut her mouth, but as she let Reina drag her away, she noticed people staring again, watching Reina with suspicion. Baseless accusations, cries of *"malduna"* echoed in Meiryn's mind. Reina seemed not to notice or care about how people looked at her—she never did. But Meiryn saw the stiff anticipation in the people's shoulders; she noticed them looking Reina up and down, taking in her bedraggled appearance; and she pictured that jailer's wagon carrying Nona away. The performer's words narrated some hazy image of the battle just outside the arena last night: all those huntsmen clashing against the guards, all that bloodshed, just to get to Nona.

Meiryn could not let that happen to Reina. Not after all they had been through together.

Meiryn came to a sudden stop, pulling in a sharp breath.

Reina spun around impatiently. "What now?"

Meiryn winced, but a daring—perhaps even deadly—plan was weaving itself together in her mind. She saw it unfold as if she had already lived it, and amidst her rising excitement, all she could muster was a quiet "I know how to get us out of West Glen."

Reina's shoulders dropped. Meiryn could already sense her dismissal, so she pushed her words out before Reina could speak. "Nona was in that wagon. If the Guild truly protects its own, then they'll be back for her, especially if the Order is coming to take her."

"You're basing your plan on the words of a child's play." Reina folded her arms over her chest, eyes narrowing scornfully. "Besides, why would we bother ourselves with the Guild when Ashuma is just beyond the border?"

"Because we're returning something valuable to them." She prayed Reina could decipher what she was too excited to express in more coherent terms. "The southern woods are dangerous, but if the huntsmen deal in trades like the stories say—and if Nona is guiding us—then I'd bet they'd pay handsomely to have her back."

And if the huntsmen had looted the announcer's body, as the guard had said, then they were at least richer than she and Reina.

For once, Reina was quiet. Meiryn watched, with no small amount of satisfaction, as Reina caught on to the wild scheme. A slow grin spread across her lips, melting away the bitterness from before.

"A jailbreak?" Reina mused. "That's risky, especially for you."

Meiryn tossed a lock of hair over her shoulder. "It can't be much riskier than betting away all our coin."

Reina's smile flickered, but she made no comment.

Breathing an inward sigh of relief, Meiryn continued, "I don't know exactly how much time we have before that cadre gets here, but if the guards sent word about the Hunters Guild, then I can't imagine it'll be long."

"We can make time," Reina said, shrugging. Her grin turned fiendish. "This might just be one of your best ideas."

"Don't sound so surprised." Meiryn scoffed. "I've had ideas before. You just—" *Never listened.* "You always had a plan of your own."

Reina waved a hand. "You're too cautious. We wouldn't even be in West Glen now if it weren't for me."

"Whatever." Meiryn let her smile drop. "I know this isn't the best option, but it seems better than staying here for another six months."

Reina shook her head. Her voice dropped low, like it always did when she was talking seriously. "It's better than waiting around. And if it goes well, I promise never to doubt you again."

Meiryn flashed a tight grin. "I appreciate the confidence."

Reina dropped her hands by her sides again. Her posture straightened with reborn determination. For a moment, as the sun outlined her form in gold, Reina appeared as regal and elegant as a highborn lady. It was that trademark air of confidence that reminded Meiryn of why she had decided to follow Reina in the first place. Beaten and worn as they both were, Reina was the one who led them from that dingy little corner tavern. Reina was the one who directed their feet down paths Meiryn would never have dared to traverse.

"That's it, then," Reina decided. "We're getting Nona out of that prison, taking her back to the Guild, and then we're getting out of this kingdom."

It seemed so simple when she stated it that way. As if every danger were a mere obstacle they could walk around, like a felled tree in the middle of a forest path. How, in the face of everything that could go wrong, Reina remained so self-assured was a complete mystery to Meiryn.

Still, it was that confidence that drew Meiryn to Reina's side. To go where she led, no matter the risk. And though she'd had enough of life-threatening gambles, Meiryn was willing to throw herself into fire—for Reina, for herself, and for the life they dreamed of beneath star-speckled skies.

III. REINA

NO SCHEME HAD EVER BEEN SO simple yet so prone to failure. At least, not one that Meiryn devised. Reina had executed her own escape plan years ago, but she'd had the advantage of knowing exactly when the guards changed shift, where her clearest routes lay, and who might turn her over to her captors.

This plan had developed in a matter of hours, and factoring in Meiryn's involvement proved more tedious than Reina anticipated. She needed her out of harm's way in case things went awry, and her only solution was to utilize Meiryn's charm.

Perched atop the wall of a stone bridge that arched over the river, Meiryn listened attentively. The evening sun danced across the water and painted a warm blush across her cheeks, setting a heavenly glow within her flaxen hair. With those honey-brown eyes and long brass lashes, she would have no trouble catching the attention of a few impressionable stable hands.

But when Reina said as much, Meiryn interrupted with a vehement complaint. "Why am I always the diversion?"

Reina lifted a brow. "You'd rather endanger yourself?"

"It's dangerous no matter how you look at it," Meiryn pointed out. Her narrow, pointed nose scrunched in a telltale sign of trepidation; her gaze crawled along the path of the river and peered into nearby homes, where families were gathering around tables set for dinner. She flicked a pebble into the river. "I don't know if I can do this. I'm not a good liar."

"Well, you're no good with a lockpick, either." Reina fell silent as a couple joined them on the bridge. They were smiling, holding hands, murmuring sweet nothings against each other's necks.

How simple their lives must be. How plain and quiet.

Only when they crossed to the other side, out of earshot, did Reina continue in a lower voice, "We only have a couple hours before the cadre gets here." She glanced at Meiryn—brows knit, hands fidgeting nervously—and heaved a sigh. "This was your idea. Don't tell me you're backing out now."

"I'm not." But the worry in Meiryn's eyes said otherwise. She pinned her stare on Reina. "I just want to make sure you know what you're doing. I'll do my best—you know I will. But you still won't have much time. You need to get in there, get out, and find me as soon as you have her."

"I know the risks." She didn't need Meiryn reminding her of their failure from yesterday, nor did she intend to repeat her mistakes. Bitter sarcasm arose from the shame she stifled. "Besides, if it goes to shit, then we'll just steal a boat, sail east, and find our new home someplace far away from here."

Meiryn snorted. "Now who's the one basing their plan on the words of children's stories?"

None of the maps—Ver Signian or Ashuman—extended beyond the Nest; however, night-tales of a distant land beyond the black storm of the Veil enticed daring—or foolish—sailors. Countless had set out on grand quests of discovery. None ever returned.

Reina almost succumbed to the daydream of freedom preluded by open waters. It might be nice to discover a new continent, or even claim a deserted island for herself. No one would know her name. No one would know any part of her. The ghosts haunting her past would never reach her. She could fabricate another persona if she so desired.

But her fantasies were just that—fantasy. The sun had set; it was time to act.

She committed the city's layout to memory as she and Meiryn made their way toward the jailhouse. The river snaked latitudinally through West Glen; Reina's road to freedom led her eastward, toward the city gates. Night would provide enough cover for all of them, and so long as she kept her bearings, she would find her way out of West Glen, out of Ver Signia, for good.

"Don't let Nona slip away from you," Meiryn nagged for the fourth time. "We've dealt with petty thieves and drunken gamblers before, but the Hunters Guild won't be like any of them. For all we know, the rumors could be true. And if Nona is armed, keep an eye on her weapon. The minute you turn your back, she could split you open like that Infernal did to those fighters last night."

Reina held up a hand, mostly because the streets were emptier now. Anyone could be eavesdropping. "She won't get away, and if she was carrying any weapons, they'll have been confiscated."

"Right," Meiryn said, "but you can't underestimate her. We can't afford it."

Anxious as she was, she spoke true, but Reina wasn't going to let her have the satisfaction of knowing so. "I've got it," she assured. "I'm fairly good at getting myself into places I'm not supposed to be. It's you I'm worried about."

Meiryn lifted a brow. Half her face was concealed in shadow as she turned away from the flickering firelight of a streetlamp. "What do you mean?"

"You have to keep those guards away long enough for me to get in and out. If they suspect the truth, then..." *Then they might hurt you. And I'd never forgive myself.* "Then everything will have been a waste," Reina finished. She swallowed thickly when Meiryn rolled her eyes.

"You act like I can't look after myself."

Reina curled her hands into fists behind her back. "You did well before we met. I've heard the caretakers are cruel, so I know you're capable. Just...be careful."

Meiryn stilled. Reina would have apologized for bringing up Meiryn's past, but they were nearing the prison cells. Their paths diverged here.

Parting words failed Reina when Meiryn pulled her into a tight embrace. They were both trembling—or maybe it was just Reina—but for a moment longer than necessary, they held each other there, teetering on a delicate balance between the hope for a new life and the end of everything they held dear. Reina closed her eyes and inhaled deeply.

"I will," Meiryn promised. She stepped back and held Reina at arm's length. "I'll give you as much time as possible."

Reina flashed a quick smile that she hoped masked her worry. "I'll see you soon."

Meiryn searched her face for a moment, then nodded once. She squeezed Reina's shoulder. "Be quick, Reina."

"Be brave," Reina answered.

And with that, Meiryn turned down the adjacent street, toward the stables reserved for the guardsmen. Reina counted sixty seconds in her head before continuing along the path that would lead her straight to the cells.

In darkness and solitude, she drummed each nervous fingertip on her thumb and slowed her steps as a group of townsfolk walked past. They paid her no mind. She might as well have been invisible.

Meiryn would have reached the stables by now, but it would take her another minute to lure away the hands and set all the horses free. Reina quickened her pace; she needed to be there when the guards fell for the diversion.

As night stretched over the earth, the city warded away the creeping shadows with hazy orange glows that emanated from every lantern lining the street. Reina dodged each pool of soft light, as if touching them would scorch her like the breath of an Infernal.

She ran a hand over her pocket, checking for the third time that she had her lockpicks. Her hands were clammy, shuddering with anticipation. She clenched and unclenched her fists, willing her heartbeat to steady as she neared the jailhouse.

It was a simple, unassuming building made of the same stone as every bridge in the city. Firelight danced through a small window. The cells sat belowground so that if any prisoner attempted to flee, they would have to fight their way up the stairs and through a host of armed guards. Luckily for Reina, West Glen was a city of little crime. Prisoners were thieves who stole bread for their families, or drunkards who got too rowdy. There wouldn't be many guards to fight through—and once Meiryn set the horses loose, there would be even less.

Creeping along the back wall, Reina's view of the street was obstructed, but she could hear well enough. Right on time, the wail of a frightened horse sounded. An alarmed cry rang out from the stables, and another called for help. Not a second later, at least ten stallions, all branded by West Glen's horsemaster, thundered past the jailhouse.

Nearby guards swore, ducking inside to call for backup. Reina shrank into the safer folds of the surrounding darkness as a team of five guards chased after the horses and the stable hands.

The bait had lured its prey.

When the last guard disappeared from view, Reina waited five seconds before darting out from her hiding place. Anyone still in the street ogled after the horses, so she slipped unnoticed into the jailhouse.

The first room was dimly lit. A wooden table of questionable stability sat in one corner, tankards and playing cards abandoned. Weapons and shields bearing the crest of West Glen hung precariously on the walls, and rusted instruments of torture occupied the bookshelves.

Reina stopped just inside the threshold, stifling her breath and straining to hear. The guards might have been gullible, but they weren't stupid. After a moment, a pair of voices drifted up from the lower level, where the prisoners were held.

"My brother's out there, slashing dragons to bits," one said, his voice slurred, "while I'm stuck here on guard duty. Imagine —he's younger than me, less experienced, and yet he gets to see the Nest and defend our shores."

"It's honorable work," the second guard said.

The first laughed bitterly. "Oh, yes—honorable, indeed. So honorable, in fact, that he'll not deign to tell me a single word of what he sees on that archipelago. Though, just between you and me"—he lowered his voice—"I've heard talk of another beast—different from the others. Black as night, they say, and deadlier than any dragon we've yet seen."

Reina's interest piqued, and she leaned forward.

"Some claim it carries the weight of the sky on its back. That with a mere blink of an eye, it can summon enough rain to flood an entire city. Others think it might be the reason for the storming seas beyond the Nest. They think it's protecting something."

"What do you make of that?"

The sound of spit pelting stone—then, the first guard answered with Reina's exact thoughts: "Horseshit. Probably just a night-tale woven by the bards to frighten children, or an overworked bastard was hallucinating."

"Hm." The second guard took a moment to formulate a reply, and in that time, Reina tightened the reins on her focus, scanning the room for every possible exit.

There was only one side door, but it was barricaded by trunks full of spare armor and weapons. Moving everything would take too much time—not to mention the sheer amount of noise it would create.

She made it two more steps before the second guard finally spoke again. Somber now, he said, "The Nest isn't like the Dragon's Spine. I lost my arm to a hatchling not a day after I set foot on those islands. If there's word of a worse monster than we've already faced, then you'd better pray the Order doesn't enlist us all."

His companion muttered incomprehensibly, but Reina had already stopped listening. Her boots landed silently. She kept her eyes on the stairwell that led down to the lower level, swiping a dagger from one of the trunks. To her right, an abandoned pile of gambling coins glittered in the firelight. Reina snatched a handful, pocketed all but one, and tossed the spare coin down the stairs.

The guards went silent as the coin clattered to the bottom and rolled across the stones. A confused pause—then, "What in six hells?"

Reina launched herself into darkness. Landing hard, she grabbed the nearest guard and slammed the pommel of the dagger against his temple. He crumpled instantly.

Five prisoners leaped to their feet, chains rattling, and Reina caught a flash of Nona's wide-eyed gaze before the second guard reared back, sword gleaming in the torchlight.

Reina ducked. Sparks flew as the sword clashed against iron bars, and he recoiled on unsteady feet. He was the one who had lost his arm.

He cast an alarmed glance at his partner before charging forward again, blade swinging. Reina feinted right and darted left at the last second. She hissed as the tip of his blade sliced into her arm, but she whirled and kicked hard against his lower back.

He stumbled, grunting, into the bars of the nearest cell. Reina lifted her dagger to strike, but the prisoner behind the bars had grabbed the guard by the neck.

Nona.

Reina watched, simultaneously impressed and intimidated, as Nona wrestled the guard's weapon from his hand. It clattered, forgotten, at her feet. She grabbed him by the ears and yanked his face through the bars of her cage. He screamed, his arm flailing and grasping at whatever he could find. With a wild shout, Nona slammed her head against his. He fell, uttering only a quiet groan before Nona delivered a swift kick to his temple.

Reina started forward, but Nona kicked the guard again, this time hard enough to crack the skull. Nona spat on the blood that seeped from his wound.

"That's for calling me a *malduna*," she said, a bitter smile tugging at her lips. Her eyes snapped to Reina, narrow and discerning. "Who are you?"

"No time. I'm getting you out of here." Reina's hands trembled with nervous energy as she knelt in front of the cell and worked her tools into the keyhole.

But Nona reached through the bars and grabbed Reina's wrist. She bared her teeth like a wolf. "Who. Are. You?"

Reina blinked. "Rinh," she lied quickly.

"Why are you here, Rinh?"

Reina huffed and threw a glance over her shoulder. The guard she'd struck first was still unconscious, but gods only knew how much longer he'd be out. "I saw you last night, in the ring. You did nothing wrong." When Nona only blinked, Reina added hastily, "And because your friends are waiting for you."

It was only half the truth. But it was enough to wipe the suspicion off Nona's face. She dropped Reina's hand and clung to the bars, as if she could force an opening. "What? They're still here?"

Reina nodded, unable to face the hope that softened Nona's features. She was pretty; she had a quick mind, too, which might prove troublesome once she realized that Reina wasn't telling the whole truth—but that was a concern for later.

The lock clicked, and Reina held her breath. She gave a slight push, laughing with relief when the door swung open.

Nona slipped out, and Reina unfastened her cloak. "Here," she said, shoving it into Nona's hands. "Wear this."

"You have my thanks, Rinh." Nona took the cloak and secured it around her shoulders, shadowing her face beneath the tattered cloth. She nodded at the other cells. "Now open their doors."

Reina halted. She'd tailored every step to allow for one unlocked cell, not an entire prison. She barely glanced at the others. "Are they with you?"

"No," Nona said, crossing her arms, "but they only stole to make ends meet. They have loved ones waiting on them, too."

One of the prisoners threw himself into Reina's narrow periphery. "It's true, girl!" he called desperately. His face reddened between the iron bars. "I've a daughter and a son— both not a day older than ten years."

"I'm the only one my grandmother has," another chimed in.

Suddenly they were all clamoring over each other, pleading for Reina to unlock their doors. She cast a dirty look at Nona. "We don't have time. The guards will be back soon."

"Then you'd better get to work."

Reina shook her head. "You would stay here, even though your little Guild friends are waiting for you?"

Nona glared. Firelight crept under her hood, burning in her pupils. "If they found out I left these people behind to save my own ass, I'd never be able to look them in the eye again."

Reina suppressed a groan. Were all huntsmen this annoyingly noble?

"Fine," she snapped. "Watch for trouble, then."

Reina worked as quickly as she could. With each passing minute, her anxiety only grew. Meiryn had played her part and would be waiting at the gates now, but if the guards tracked her down, they would hang her from the gallows.

More blood on her hands. More ghosts to run from.

So Reina hurried, and one by one, the other prisoners bolted from their cells. When the last door swung open, the final prisoner scurried up the stairs without so much as a thank-you.

Reina scowled, pocketing her lockpicks, but Nona nodded tersely. "You did a good thing."

"Congratulate me later."

The two made their exit. Nona equipped herself with the dagger Reina had used to incapacitate the first guard, who still lay unconscious; Reina snatched the gold coin she'd tossed as bait. Nona burst through the front door, and Reina pushed after her—only to slam into her back.

"What—" She choked on her words when she spotted the guards.

All five of them, eyes raging and furious, hurtled around the corner, raising an alarm. The newly freed prisoners had scattered in every direction, attracting terrified stares—and leaving Reina and Nona in direct sight of the guards.

"*Shit*—run!"

Reina had barely blinked before Nona sprinted. Reina chased after her. They took the backstreets and alleys, and Reina noticed Nona constantly glancing toward the rooftops. There was no time to question her. She heard the guards splitting their numbers, covering more ground. Heard their clanging armor, their taunting jeers.

"How fast are you?" Nona panted.

Reina cast her a bewildered look, and Nona let out a maniacal laugh, pushing herself even faster. Reina forced her legs to keep pace.

She'd only flown this fast once before, but she'd never forgotten the feeling of near weightlessness. The feeling of the wind in her veins, of her heart beating like frantic wings of a hummingbird. The world became a blur of light and shadow, the onlookers like stones in a stream.

Her legs burned more with every block they cleared. One bridge crossed, then two. Down the main street, past all the shops. Through neighborhoods, between townhouses. People leaped back, crying out in alarm. The guards stayed hot on their trail.

Were they any closer to the eastern gates? It was impossible to tell.

Ducking into an alley, Reina's heart dropped when Nona yanked her down into the open mouth of a sewage tunnel. Darkness consumed them, along with a horrible stench. She gagged on a desperate inhale just as a pair of footsteps stomped overhead.

"They went down this way!" the guard shouted, too near for comfort.

Torchlight spilled across the cobblestones. Shadows flashed along the walls as the guards sped down the alley, their footsteps as loud as thunder.

Lungs burning, Reina loosened a tight breath. Her nostrils flared against the pungent scent of the sewers, and her lips curled in disgust when the heel of her boot squelched into something soft.

Nona peeked up into the alley, unperturbed. A thin chuckle rattled out of her. "That was beautiful," she whispered. Her eyes glittered in the faint strips of light from above. "For a second there, I thought you'd get caught."

Reina just shook her head, too winded for words.

"Come on. I think we're clear." Without waiting for Reina's response, Nona slithered back into the alley.

Reina clambered after her, swallowing the bile that rose in the back of her throat when her hands slipped along wet walls. Nona was already on her feet by the time Reina emerged. Head tilted back, she scanned the rooftops again. It was quiet here, but a few streets down, a commotion grew louder.

"I don't see my friends anywhere." Nona frowned, pushing her hood down. "You said they were waiting for me."

"They must have run when the guards sounded the alarm," Reina rasped. She prayed that Nona wouldn't see through this lie. "If they're as loyal to you as you are to strangers, they're around here somewhere."

Nona's brow furrowed deeper. She gave a short, three-toned whistle.

Reina, hands braced on her knees, jerked her head up. "What are you doing?"

Nona ignored her. Whistled again. When silence met her signal and the shouting in the city grew more desperate, she snapped her eyes to Reina. Her voice hardened as she repeated herself: "You said my friends were waiting for me."

"They are," Reina insisted. "They're probably just in the woods—"

"'Probably?'" Nona echoed. "You mean, you don't know where they are, or you never met them at all?"

Reina glanced at the dagger in Nona's fist. She was treading thin ice. "Look, you don't need my help to find your friends, but I need to be with you when you do."

Nona's eyes narrowed. Her knuckles were growing pale. "Who are you? Really?"

"I told you—"

"And I don't believe you." Nona marched forward and trapped Reina against the wall, her hands bracketing Reina's head. "What do you have to gain from breaking me out? Are you with the Order? Or are you one of those bounty hunters?"

A bounty hunter? She looked Nona up and down, brows drawing close. "What have you done that—"

Nona shoved the tip of the knife under Reina's chin. "You have ten seconds to answer my question."

"Only if you tell me how you walked away from an Infernal without a single burn."

The blade broke through her skin. Reina winced, and Nona pressed herself closer.

"The answer would cost you your tongue." Her words were merciless, but in her eyes, Reina found the tiniest seed of hesitation. Of *fear*.

She had no intention of killing or even harming Reina.

But before either woman would get another word in, a sharp whistle pierced the tension: three-toned, but different from Nona's, like a delayed response to her call.

Shock and recognition flashed across Nona's face. For an instant, her grip loosened. "The Order," she whispered.

Reina went rigid. Her stomach clenched, and she tried to lean away from Nona's blade. "Listen—"

"No," Nona snapped, whirling back. "You're going to tell me what you were doing in the jailhouse tonight, or I'll let the Order take you instead. What's one *malduna* in exchange for another when they can't even tell us apart?"

Seized by panic, Reina blurted, "Gold. We—we needed gold, and I knew that if I took you back to your allies—"

"You freed me just to demand a ransom?" Nona sounded more affronted than angry. She shoved herself away, shaking her head as the thundering hooves grew closer. She tossed a final glance toward the rooftops. "The Guild doesn't deal in petty trades. You have my gratitude for my life, but that's all you get."

Her blade gleamed beneath a cold silver moon as she raced down the alley and dodged out of sight.

"Wait—"

Reina chased after her, but a stitch in her side flared. She swore and slammed a fist against the bricks as her steps faltered and Nona fled beyond reach. Reina clawed her hands through her hair. She'd lost everything—*again*. Once Meiryn found out—

Oh, gods.

Where was Meiryn?

Fear like ice spiked through Reina's chest. She heard people in the streets—screaming, calling for their loved ones, begging for mercy. Louder voices tossed commands like cards on a gambling table. A high-pitched song of steel joined a chorus of nickering horses.

The prisoners had attracted too much attention when they fled. Between guardsmen hounding their trail and the Order's arrival, Reina was out of time. She needed to find Meiryn and get out of here. Now.

Against her better judgment, she peered into the street. Her eyes widened.

A small group of fighters—huntsmen, Reina realized with a jolt—clawed through a flock of guards. Even with only four of them, they carved a wide path. They were looking for Nona, but so were the guardsmen, who were now overshadowed by the five riders who drove their horses through the street.

Agents of the Order—assigned to take Nona. But with the Guild standing against them, things would only get bloodier.

Reina ducked back into the alley and set her sights eastward.

Find Meiryn. Get out. That was all that mattered now.

Her mind was still buzzing from her catastrophic failure, trying to scrounge up some explanation to give to Meiryn once she found her again. She wasn't masking her presence well, and all too late, she remembered to silence her steps.

Darkness clouded her, and with a horrible, sinking feeling, she paused and looked over her shoulder.

At the end of the block stood a large male figure. His imposing frame was backlit by orange light. He held a war axe in one hand, shackles in another. His black uniform was reminiscent of an executioner's, and Reina's heart sank when she spotted the silver flames embroidered on the left breast of his uniform.

He was with the Order.

The man inclined his head and gave her a slow, chilling smile. "There you are."

"What's one malduna *in exchange for another when they can't even tell us apart?"* Nona had seethed.

She was right.

Reina bolted. She ran faster than she'd ever run in her life. Faster than she'd fled the streets of a place that had never been home. Faster than she'd flown through fields of sun-scorched grass and wilting wildflowers. Faster than she'd run with Nona mere moments ago.

If this agent caught up to Reina, he would capture her

without question. Never mind the fact that Reina hadn't faced the Infernal, nor was she allied with the huntsmen.

None of that would matter if the Order caught her.

She snaked through the labyrinthine backstreets and sewers. Chains rattled as her pursuer closed in. Reina's heart pulsed a thousand beats per second.

She skidded around the next corner, but her boots were slick. With a pained yelp, she crashed against the cobblestones.

The agent in pursuit appeared just as she staggered to her feet. She cried out as he closed a tight hand around her bicep. He yanked her back, slamming her hard against his chest. Reina fisted her free hand and swung wildly, sorely regretting letting Nona get away with that dagger. The agent dodged her blows and swept her feet out from under her. The wind *whooshed* from her lungs.

She might as well have been a child compared to him. Reina snarled and thrashed, but this man had at least fifty pounds on her—nothing but muscle and bone.

"Stop moving," he growled, pinning her arms with his knees.

Tears flooded her eyes. Her captor gripped her wrists and clamped the iron shackles around her. Tightly.

Reina swore and spat. She'd never let him see her fear. Never let him sense the utter panic that coiled in her chest.

No sooner did the thought cross her mind than a second male voice spoke. "Ah, Raiko, there you are."

Reina froze. Horror and disbelief seized every fiber of her being and plunged her into the frozen lakes of the northern mountains. She *knew* that voice. It was a voice that slithered from the depths of countless memories she'd buried and tried desperately to forget. One she thought she'd never have to hear again.

Footsteps approached—familiar in that lazy, arrogant gait.

No. Please, no—

"Have you secured the girl?" the second voice asked, its speaker still out of view.

Reina's captor, Raiko, nodded. His eyes narrowed. "She is not as cunning as they warned." His accent was heavy. Ashuman. "She is sloppy and careless."

Reina spat in his face. He slammed his knee against her gut. Agony cracked through her body, and she coughed, tears sliding from the corners of her eyes.

Raiko frowned. "Weak, too."

She wanted to scream. To bash her head against his nose. To sink into the earth. But her prayers fell on deaf ears—as they always did.

Over Raiko's shoulder, a face loomed into view: young, sharp-featured, and mirroring her own in nearly every way.

Her brother—Aaron Rhysanthe, second son to Lord Dante and Lady Rinh Rhysanthe.

He blinked when he saw her. It was the only surprise he let show. A disbelieving laugh burst from him, the sound as chilling as the terror that clawed into Reina's chest now. He crouched and peered at her like she was plucked straight from a child's fairy tale.

"Well," he said in a voice like smoke, "this is certainly a twist. Wouldn't you agree, Athira?"

Her vision blurred as she began to weep.

IV. MEIRYN

MEIRYN HAD CHEWED her nails down to the quick, and sweat beaded at her brow. She darted from alley to alley, keeping to the shadows the way she'd seen Reina do so naturally.

Something was wrong. People were screaming, and commanding voices boomed above the sharpness of breaking glass. If things had gone according to plan, there wouldn't be so much chaos. An air of terror followed Meiryn all the way to the eastern city gates, where she was supposed to reunite with Reina and Nona. There she found a handful of frazzled and agitated guards—but no sign of her companion.

Meiryn held her breath. Counted down sixty seconds. She listened for two pairs of footsteps, a whispered call—anything.

Sixty more seconds passed, and Meiryn began pacing. She glanced at every street outlet, jumped at every noise—hoping, praying that Reina might be one of those flickering shadows dragging Nona in tow.

But by the third minute, West Glen was wailing, and Reina was nowhere in sight. Meiryn's throat ached with an overwhelming urge to cry. Her feet carried her in frantic circles until, finally, she forced herself to leave the safety of darkness. She couldn't soothe the wrenching twist of her gut as she crept along the walls, making her way back toward the jailhouse.

Locals cowered as she staggered past their doors. Curtains flitted shut. Homeless travelers took cover in the shadowed alleyways or peered down from the rooftops.

What happened? What were they so afraid of?

"Reina!" Meiryn called, voice cracking on the last desperate syllable. Hope bled out with every wandering step.

Further in the city, she heard several whistling calls overlapping with the shouted orders of the city guards, all accompanied by the chilling song of steel blades. It was all too familiar—this paralyzing fear, the ice settling into the marrow of her bones, clashing against the stubborn instinct to survive. To outlast.

Where would Reina have taken Nona, if not to their rendezvous point? Had they even made it out of the prison? What if they'd been captured? What if—

Stop.

Meiryn inhaled sharply, then exhaled heavily. She clenched her hands into fists. She couldn't panic now. Not when Reina could be in danger. How many times had Reina used herself to shield Meiryn from scorn? Where would Meiryn be now if it weren't for Reina's guidance and courage?

Reina had told her, as if sensing that something would go wrong, "*Be brave.*"

And so, Meiryn swallowed her fear. Blinked hard to dispel the tears from her eyes. She quickened her pace, hair slapping against her back as she scurried past black windows and locked shutters.

The streets blurred into streaks of plaster and wood and stone. Shadows writhed at the corners of her vision, and her heart hammered like a fist on the doors of a church. The guards she had diverted were gone, preoccupied with whatever had infiltrated the city. Maybe she could slip past their notice and—

"Move!"

Meiryn screamed as something hard crashed into her. She sprawled out on the cobblestones. Her head banged against the ground, and she shook stars from her vision. She winced, focusing on a redheaded woman on all fours, who was swearing profusely and scooping up armfuls of arrows that had fallen from her quiver.

It took Meiryn a moment before the familiarity hit her: it was the archer from the arena. A member of the Hunters Guild.

Meiryn gaped at the second figure that bounded around the corner. His face was splattered with blood, as was the bronze sword he wielded, but there was no doubt: this was the man who had pushed Reina out of the way of the jailer's cart. He wore no armor of the city guards, nor did the crest of the Silver Order sit proudly upon his chest.

He was one of them, too—a huntsman. His eyes widened as he bent to help the archer. "Faun—"

"Not now, Lukas," she snarled. "I need to find Nona."

Every hair on Meiryn's body stood on end. She snapped her head toward the archer, but her tongue lay useless in her mouth, refusing to call out even as her mind reeled.

Nona. Find Nona—find Reina.

Before Meiryn could even begin to collect herself, the archer had already shoved herself to her feet and taken off at a breakneck pace, not even glancing once at Meiryn.

The man—Lukas, she'd just barely caught—looked at Meiryn with only a vague hint of recognition. "Are you alright?" He offered her a hand, which she took after a moment's hesitation. He lifted her to her feet like she was made of air and steadied her with a hand on her shoulder.

He looked Meiryn over, concern tightening his features. "You're hurt," he said, nodding at her temple. His hand went white around the hilt of his sword. "You need to get out of here. Find shelter and stay low for a while."

He started to run after his companion, but Meiryn halted him with a strangled "Wait!"

Lukas paused, and Meiryn rasped out Nona's name. In three strides, he stood mere inches away. Meiryn could smell the sweat and blood on his face. Eyes gleaming with hope, he panted, "You know where she is?"

Meiryn shook her head, grasping for words amidst a throbbing headache. "My friend and I—we were going to save her. But she—"

"What?" Confusion furrowed Lukas's brows. "Why would you want to save her?"

There was no time to explain. "Please," Meiryn implored, throat tightening with emotion, "you have to—"

She broke off when a scream split the air. Before she could blink, Lukas was gone, heading after Faun's invisible trail.

Meiryn's head spun as she sprinted after him. The air whistled in her ears, and she could feel the blood trickling down the side of her head now. She could barely keep pace with Lukas's stride, but she managed to follow the heavy pounding of his footsteps.

She rounded a corner—then skidded to a halt just before slamming against Lukas's back.

At the end of the street, half-lit by fading lamplight, was Nona—pale-faced and wearing Reina's cloak. Her chest was impaled by a terrifying blade that extended on the steel tail of a whip. Her feet dangled an inch off the ground, and she stared into the eyes of a smaller woman with hair like snow and eyes like ice. Dressed in sleek black material, the woman's high-collared uniform bore the fiery crest of the Silver Order.

If the Order was here, then the plan had failed.

Halfway down the street was Faun. The muscles in her arms went taut as she fired a desperate arrow, but her shot went wide. The Order agent leaped back. With a *click*, her whip-sword retracted toward a crossguard shaped like a crane's wings. Blood sprayed from Nona's chest. The agent smirked, sheathed her weapon, and spun out of sight.

Meiryn lifted her hands to her mouth as Nona crumpled. Faun dropped her bow and dove forward, clutching at Nona's limp body. Arrows spilled from Faun's quiver, but neither woman paid them any mind. Faun pressed her hand against Nona's chest as if she could staunch the bleeding, but even from this distance, Meiryn knew that Nona's wounds were too great. She saw the blood pooling, seeping into Faun's pants; saw the tears rolling down Nona's cheeks as she cupped Faun's face with a trembling hand.

Lukas swore under his breath. He whirled, eyes watery, but his voice was steady. "You're not safe here," he told Meiryn. "That cadre will take down anyone they think is inhibiting their mission. Stay out of sight until it's over, understand?"

Meiryn didn't even have the chance to speak before he took off after the agent, sword flashing under garish orange light.

A sickening sort of dread cemented Meiryn in place. A slight ringing in her ears drowned out whatever words Nona murmured—words that made Faun smile, despite the fear and desperation twisting her face. Nona's lips moved weakly. The warmth drained from her face, and her hand fell to her side.

She was dead.

Faun shuddered. Her hand curled into a fist, and with a hellish, inhuman cry, she pummeled the ground beneath her, blood splattering upon impact.

Meiryn couldn't watch any longer. Her mouth was dry, and she could feel her courage disintegrating into ashes and smoke.

If Reina wasn't with Nona, then where was she?

The night blurred as Meiryn ran on burning legs. She shouted Reina's name, throwing caution to the sewers. Her voice broke as tears spilled over her face, and she abandoned the cover of the backstreets as she staggered into the main square.

Broken glass crunched beneath her boots. Crimson pools reflected fire that spat from shattered lanterns. Bodies—some barely moving, others eerily still—littered the street. A few huntsmen lingered, but they were retreating. One of the city guards had ignited a beacon in the south tower to summon reinforcements.

But where was that cadre? The woman who killed Nona slipped away so quickly that Meiryn barely had time to process what happened.

The thought had just crossed her mind when five horses thundered past, each carrying a rider clad in black armor. Among them was the white-haired agent from before.

Meiryn wheeled back, but her heart stopped altogether when she spotted a small figure pinned between the second rider and his saddle. A head of dark hair bounced wildly against the horse's flank.

"Reina!" Meiryn hardly recognized her own voice ripping from deep inside her chest. She chased after the horses, stumbling over lifeless forms and broken glass. She pleaded for the cadre to stop, but they did not hear. They did not stop.

They'd taken the wrong woman and killed the one they actually came for. They'd taken Meiryn's best friend, her *only* friend, her only family left in this world.

Meiryn crashed to all fours. Glass sliced into her palms, and her head throbbed—but all she could see was the cadre storming through the city gates and into the open jaws of the forest. She gasped for a shred of air amidst the sobs that wracked her body.

Reina was gone. Taken for a crime she did not commit. And if they took her where Meiryn feared they would, they would kill her.

It took everything Meiryn had not to let her head fall. She scraped her fingers against the ground as she tried to steady her breath, but panic and a sudden, overwhelming sense of loss constricted every muscle in her body. She crouched there for what felt like hours, staring after the cadre, but she knew it hadn't even been a full minute when she heard a voice snap, "I'll run that stable boy through with my sword. I don't care. Incompetent bastard."

Meiryn's blood ran cold. Pushed only by pure fear, she dove behind an overturned wagon just as a pair of city guards, looking worse for wear, trudged by, three horses in tow.

The taller of the two shook his head at the carnage littering their path. "Damn shame. The king ought to just set the whole forest ablaze. Weed out those damned huntsmen."

His companion shot him a look. "And risk burning down all of West Glen in the process?"

"At least the Guild wouldn't be an issue anymore."

"He'd lose half his lumber supply," the shorter guard said. "Not to mention the hundreds of families he'd leave stranded."

The taller one snorted. His voice drifted as they walked

further out of earshot, but Meiryn caught the bitterness of his words. "If you think the king cares about anyone who lives beyond the shadow of his castle, you're deluding yourself."

The shorter guard snapped out some sharp-tongued reply that Meiryn did not hear. She peeked over the side of the wagon, waiting for them to disappear from view. Only when she was certain that no one else was approaching did she dare to step out from her hiding spot.

Through the tightness in her chest and the ache in her head, the tiniest fragment of an idea took form. Meiryn made her way to the place where Nona had been killed. The heavy, metallic stench of blood lingered, but Nona's body was gone—as was Faun. Had she not overheard the guard mention the southern woods, Meiryn would have admitted defeat right there in the silence and darkness.

Though the flickering hope of a starting point pierced through the fog in her mind, dread still tugged at Meiryn's stomach. The southern forest of Ver Signia was riddled with dark rumors: wolves were said to lurk around every jutting boulder; vultures and crows nested in the treetops, waiting to feast on carrion; thieves and spies of the Guild robbed every errant traveler of their belongings and—if they were unfortunate enough—their lives. No one knew where the Guild made its home. No one had even met the dreaded Wolf King and lived to tell the tale. The stories alone were enough to keep the illustrious Silver Order from trespassing too deep.

But Meiryn had no other choice. She had met one of those huntsmen—albeit briefly. She'd seen Lukas fight for one of his own people; she'd seen the way Faun mourned for Nona. Surely there was some shred of humanity amidst the feral rumors.

And if she wanted to save Reina, she needed to leave West

Glen. Now. The safety of these wooden walls had been burned to ashes, and there was nowhere left to go but forward.

Still bleeding from her temple, Meiryn sneaked out of West Glen. She dodged stray guards and avoided looking for too long at the lifeless bodies in the streets.

She didn't spare a glance over her shoulder when she left the city behind. She couldn't afford to, lest she turn around and admit defeat without even trying. The only thing she knew about the Guild's hidden base was that it was located somewhere in the heart of the woods, where the trees were thick enough to block out the sun on a cloudless day. The only path to follow was overgrown and thin, as if the earth itself were trying to warn her away.

Reina's words echoed in her mind like a tolling bell: *Be brave.*

Meiryn breathed deeply, stepping out of a patch of silver moonlight and into the black forest. Thick treetops covered her. Hot summer air wrung the sweat from her body. Shadows stole the courage from her heart, and yet, Meiryn pressed on into the dark night.

V. REINA

REINA KEPT her eyes squeezed shut, lest she vomit from being jostled about. That she was empty-stomached now provided a rare moment of gladness. She felt the horse's muscles shifting against her body, the heavy fall of every hoof; heard the breathless snort as Aaron led the cadre beyond the walls of West Glen.

She had tried to wriggle free, but Raiko's hand was an iron clamp on her back. He'd not uttered a single word since slinging her over the back of his horse. His silence was unsettling—strangely more so than the danger that ensnared her now.

Aaron called for an abrupt halt, and Reina lurched as Raiko yanked up on the reins. She snapped her eyes open and blinked to adjust to an all-consuming darkness.

The forest offered no clear or beaten trail this far from West Glen, but something had trampled through this area. Something massive. Tree branches hung by mere splinters from their trunks. The horses stood on terrain gouged by deep claw marks, and the faintest scent of smoke—fresh, nearby—tainted the night air.

"Why are we stopping?" someone demanded.

Reina strained her neck in the direction of the voice. Barely discernible from the dark forest were three other horses, each bearing the weight of an agent. The speaker was the last rider: white-skinned and silver-haired, he wore an irritated expression, as if the delay was a personal affront.

But Aaron silenced him with a quick wave of his hand, sliding off his horse with an easy grace. His gaze was locked on a point somewhere off the path; Reina gasped when she found what had captured his attention.

Roughly the size of a house, the Infernal dragon lay prone atop a bed of shrubbery. Its head alone was larger than Raiko's horse; that thick collar of iron still squeezed around its throat, and the chain lay tangled around a couple of trees whose bark had been scraped away by the leash. Half-shut blue eyes emanated a weak light. Wings, shredded and bloody, were strewn like a ruined dress across its body. Each breath seemed to shorten what little life the dragon had left.

Reina marveled at how anyone had even managed to transport it so far from the Nest; how anyone could have fought it alone and survived longer than a few seconds.

Her heart clenched when Aaron unsheathed his sword. "Raiko," he said without taking his eyes off the dragon, "bring me my sister."

Reina protested uselessly against Raiko's grip, which was rough and terse, as if touching her disgusted him. He dismounted and dragged her from the back of the horse. Reina could feel the other agents watching. Their eyes burned into the back of her skull.

When she stood beside her brother, Aaron clamped a cold hand around the back of her neck. "Is this the beast you so bravely liberated?" he sneered.

"It wasn't me." She'd lost track of how many times she'd said it in the past half-hour.

"Stop talking," Aaron barked. "And stop talking like *that*. You sound ridiculous." He was referring to the southern accent she faked, the one she spent years perfecting by talking for hours on end with Meiryn.

Aaron yanked her out of Raiko's grasp and shoved her to her knees, right in front of the dragon's fangs.

Reina bit back her scream. She was certain the others could hear her pounding heart. Surely the dragon did, for its eyes slid to her, flashing with some weak sort of defiance, as if she were in any position to cause it more harm. Steam scented like burning coals billowed from its nostrils. Reina didn't move a muscle. She hardly dared to draw in another breath.

"It seems your efforts were in vain," Aaron continued. His words fell from a tongue as sharp as his sword. "It would have been a mercy to kill this Infernal. Think of all the gold you could have taken home. That is—if you had a home to go back to."

Reina twisted her neck and glared. Every inch of her body bristled. "Shut up."

Tears sprang into her eyes when Aaron dug his fingers into her windpipe. His voice was dangerously quiet and revoltingly close. "No. You don't get to speak here or tell me what to do. I'm the captain of this cadre, in case you haven't pieced that together yet."

Wisely, Reina kept her mouth shut.

Aaron's blade lowered into her line of view. He pressed the tip of his sword against the dragon's skull and smirked when it groaned softly.

"This Infernal's scales are fireproof, which means if I do

this…" He pressed a button on the hilt of his sword, and Reina flinched as the entire blade erupted into flames. Aaron held her fast. Too close to the fiery rope that writhed around blazing steel. A quiet fascination crept into his voice as he watched the fire hiss and crack—but never burn. With an eerie calm, he finished, "Nothing happens to the beast."

The dragon's eyes were locked on the flame. The heat of the sword drowned out Reina's every thought. Even if she could escape Aaron and his cadre, fear would be her downfall.

"Now," Aaron continued, pressing Reina closer to the dragon, "watch what happens when I do this."

His blade sank through leathery scales. Blood trickled from the center of the dragon's skull, sizzling on the steel.

A pained groan rattled in the Infernal's chest. The earth churned as the beast dug its claws into the ground, trying to pull away. But the wounds it had suffered in the arena rendered it an easy target, and Aaron leaned his full weight on his sword. With a final grunt, a push of effort, he broke through the bone and pierced the brain.

There was no spray of blood. No surge of flashy triumph that usually accompanied a dragon's death by Ver Signian blade. There was only the dragon's stiff grunt, the final shudder of its wings. And then it fell still.

Aaron sighed and dragged his sword back. He was smiling, eyes like pools of ink. Blood hissed on the hot steel of his blade, and he held it under Reina's nose.

"Look here, Athira." He extinguished the flames, plunging them into darkness once more. "Do you know how many dragons have bled out on my sword?"

Reina stared into her brother's eyes. His expression was guarded. Unmovable as stone walls.

She saw straight through him.

"You've never even set foot on the Nest, have you?" she challenged, donning her northern drawl—the longer vowels, the clipped Rs—like an old dress she once favored. Aaron remained silent, and Reina grinned. "Of course you haven't. Why would they let a loud, bumbling agent like you wander—"

She blinked back tears when Aaron pressed his blade, still hot from the flames, against her neck.

"I could do it, you know. I could drench my sword in your blood. Leave you here for the crows." He chuckled in a low tone. "But perhaps it's too easy. Too swift a punishment for what you've done."

Reina ground out, "I told you. I didn't do this."

Aaron scoffed, tossing an oily strand of black hair from his face. "I wasn't referring to the beast."

Sixteen years of memories flashed between them. Sixteen years of resentment, of framing one for the other's mistakes, of vying for their parents' approval, of never knowing a moment of peace in the stifling golden halls of their family's mansion.

But even now, hatred was quick to fill the four years of separation that ended so abruptly tonight. It was heavy—and loud. A roaring defiance against the other, like two stones colliding beneath the current of an unrelenting river.

Reina set her jaw and raised her chin. She stared into the face she despised, the one that haunted her darkest memories. "I did what was best for everyone. You know that."

Aaron shook his head slowly, his expression becoming as flat and hard as stone. "What I know is that you betrayed House Rhysanthe."

The very sound of their family name brittled Reina's bones. She steeled her gaze. "What would you do with me, then, now that you've captured me? Expose me in front of every courtier in Caer Savalier? Tell them exactly what happened, so that our house can fall even farther than it already has?"

"I am sending you to Verilonne. Father can deal with you as he pleases."

No.

Fear—true, immobilizing terror—rocked her to her core. Reina could only blink helplessly as Aaron rose, drawing away from her, and sheathed his sword. No sooner did his hand fall away from her neck than Raiko swooped down to chain her again.

Overcome with a sudden desperation, Reina threw her head back and slammed her skull against Raiko's face. He swore profusely, staggering. In the time it took Aaron to whirl back, Reina was already on her feet, breaking through a wall of trees.

Hands still bound, she ran, unbalanced and erratic. Her heart hammered in her throat. Branches clawed at her arms like knives, scoring long red lines into her skin, but she willed speed into her legs, strength into her lungs. Five pairs of leather boots thundered after her.

So close. Too close.

Reina dodged between patches of silver moonlight, clinging to the darkness like a moth to flame. No amount of fatigue could slow her now; she'd run herself to death if that was what it took—but she would never, ever go back to that mansion.

She splashed through a thin stream and caught a flicker of white light in her periphery. Too late, when her feet squelched into damp earth, did she realize that it was not light—but hair.

A long, snakelike sword lunged from the shadows, and Reina shouted as plated blades struck her thighs. She jerked away from their venomous bite, toppled, and crashed against the ground.

A face, young and female, stared down at her with a dull, unimpressed look. Dark spots that Reina barely registered as blood dotted a thin line across one pale cheek. White skin framed round eyes as cold and blue as the Frozen Wastes of the north. For a moment, Reina halted, struck by a vague sense of familiarity.

That moment shattered when Raiko threw himself on top of her. His hands squeezed around her arms, and he dug his knees against the insides of her elbows.

Reina's eyes watered, but even through the tears and darkness, she could see a trail of blood trickling from his bottom lip and dripping off the rounded edge of his chin.

"Get off," Reina snarled, still thrashing.

Raiko chuckled, panting shallowly. "When will you give this up?"

"I don't surrender."

"So much good that has done." He smirked with a chilling likeness to Aaron. Reina writhed in his grasp, and he held her fast, his words falling like plumes of smoke on her neck. "If that is your wish, then by all means, *my lady*, do not give up so soon. I do love a good chase."

A biting remark nearly shot from her tongue, but heavy footsteps bounded near. An alarmed voice called, "Iliana! Are you alright?"

The girl who had struck Reina sheathed her sword and wiped her face. Annoyance flashed in her eyes. "I'm fine, Evren."

A man stepped into view—the one Reina had glimpsed from the back of the line. At his hips hung a pair of twin daggers; strapped to his back was an ironwood crossbow. He swooped over Iliana like a ghostly shadow, inspecting her for injuries, but she waved him away as two other figures marched up.

Aaron was accompanied by the last member of his cadre: a taller, burlier man with skin as deep and brown as rain-soaked earth. His left eye was clouded with blindness, but his attention on Reina was sharp and focused. He gestured to her, brows raised.

"This is your sister?" He sounded incredulous, as if it were impossible to find any semblance of relation between Reina and his captain. "I thought you highborns were more..."

Dignified—just like a Rhysanthe.

"Poised," the man finished.

Reina shook her father's resonating words from her mind as Aaron sighed. Disapproval stretched every syllable. "I'm afraid that Athira was never truly cut out for that life. But you had no trouble finding your own way out, did you?" He crouched near her, and humiliation brought a scorching heat to Reina's face. "Accept defeat, Athira. You've brought enough disgrace upon us all. It's time to answer for what you've done."

The man at his side said, "We have orders, Rhysanthe. There's no time for another one of your excursions."

"Oh, don't you worry, Korris." Aaron looked back at him, his smile unwavering. "We're still going to Draconis."

"But you said—"

"That we were sending her back to my parents. Verilonne strays too far from our path, and I'd rather not spend more time with my dear sister than I need to. I'll send a notice to the Lord and Lady Rhysanthe; once they hear of Athira's miraculous return, I'm sure they'll be eager to send an attendant to fetch her."

"And who," Korris pressed, arms crossed over his chest, "do you expect to watch her until she's been retrieved?"

"I've heard the wardens of Morturrim are quite proficient at their jobs."

Images of bloody shackles and torture chambers lit by a single, dying torch flashed in Reina's mind. She'd heard stories of the Tower of Death—that infamous prison rooted like a thorn in the heart of Draconis, named for its constant smell of decay and rot—and the brutality that its inhabitants endured within impenetrable walls of obsidian-forged brick. Centuries of weathering and time failed to shake the foundations of that tower, even as its architects stacked the cells higher and higher to accommodate more prisoners. Some believed that the stone itself was indestructible, for not even the summertime hurricanes that rolled in from the eastern sea could dent the outer walls; others claimed that its infallibility was the result of some ancient, forgotten magic. A ridiculous thought, since the only magic ever to touch Ver Signian soil belonged to the dragons.

But regardless of which stories were true, this was certain: not one prisoner in the whole of Morturrim's reign had ever escaped. Those who entered never saw the light of day again.

Reina glared through her fear. "If you're doing this just to make Father love you—"

She hadn't so much as blinked before Aaron struck a hand across her face. The sound of impact came before the stinging pain. Fresh tears brimmed, but she blinked hard. She wouldn't let these agents see her cry. Not when they already thought so little of her.

She held Aaron's stare and challenged, "Do it again. I know

you've been holding back a lot of those since we were children. If it pleases you, *Captain*, then go on. I'm sure that when our parents see me, all bruised and bloody, they're going to be so proud of you. Maybe you'll finally convince them to hand over Alexander's birthright. Then you wouldn't have to be out here, wandering through the forest, just to make a name for yourself. Maybe Father would finally notice you."

She'd struck a sensitive nerve.

Their elder brother, Alexander, was first in line to inherit the fortune and responsibilities of House Rhysanthe, but Aaron had spent a lifetime trying to prove himself the worthier son. For as long as Reina could recall, Alexander had expressed nothing but disdain for noble life. He thought the entire caste system was outdated and cruel—that power ought to be granted by merit rather than blood—but he might as well have been screaming against the surging tides of the Abyss. His reluctance to claim the title of Lord of House Rhysanthe drove Aaron to near madness, because despite Aaron's willingness to take over Alexander's duties, their father refused him.

Aaron inhaled deeply, rolled his neck, then exhaled slowly. When he spoke, he sounded like he was struggling to keep his voice quiet. "I have spent these last four years rebuilding everything you destroyed when you left. You will not mock me here —not when you are the one lying on your back, defenseless against me. I won, Athira."

"Reina," she barked.

He blinked. "Excuse me?"

"I don't use that name anymore."

Aaron exchanged an amused glance with his agents. His mouth split into a twisted grin. "Is this how you've evaded us? By using a false name?"

Reina cocked her head. "I didn't realize you cared enough to look for me."

"You're a Rhysanthe whether you accept it or not," Aaron said. He pushed to his feet and gave Raiko a one-handed cue. Reina grunted as Raiko lifted her to her feet. Aaron watched her carefully. "As a Rhysanthe, you have a duty to your house. It's time you grew up, *Athira*, and realized that you are bound by the same contracts as I."

"And how is that working for you?" Reina strained against Raiko's grip, spitting as Aaron turned his back. "What does it feel like, knowing that each day you spend out here, you're fighting for something you'll never truly earn?"

Aaron did not look at her again, nor did he deign to respond. He merely motioned for his cadre to follow, and like mute dogs, they obeyed.

VI. MEIRYN

Halfway through the night, Meiryn's exhaustion caught up to her. She hadn't meant to fall asleep—only to rest her feet and still her pounding heart—but the instant her head hit the earth, a wave of fatigue dragged her into a deep slumber.

When she awoke, the night had yielded to day. Shadows fled from blinding strips of light; birds sang and flitted from branch to treetop; the forest was already steaming and hot.

Meiryn scrambled to her feet. She brushed twigs and dirt from her hair and took in her surroundings, grimacing at the way the foliage stung the abrasions on her hands. With the dawn of a new day, she had hoped to find a trail to follow—footsteps left in the earth or spots of blood on the shrubs—but the forest was thick. Undisturbed. Even the ground where she'd slept was smooth again. It was as if the woods had been trained to shield the Guild from outsiders. As if it were a living, sentient being.

Her gaze darted about as she suddenly remembered the stories of travelers being mauled by feral wolves. Some believed that the mangled bodies strewn across the beaten paths were left by the Hunters Guild. Meiryn didn't know what she believed—only that the longer she wandered here, the closer Reina came to meeting a darker fate.

"Stop it." Her voice was raw and weak, but she forced the words out, if only to pierce the silence. Scaring herself wasn't helping anyone, least of all Reina. And if the roles were reversed, Reina would have already found Meiryn and snatched her from that cadre. Reina was the strong one; she was the one who always knew what to do, where to go, what to say to get them out of tense situations.

But Reina wasn't here. She was trapped, and it was Meiryn's duty to save her. To make up for all she had failed to do to save her own family.

Meiryn looked skyward, trying to gauge a sense of time. The sun blazed at its peak, glaring down at the forest below, but ferns and shrubs crowded any path she might have followed.

She cursed herself for oversleeping and started walking anyway. The southern woods stretched over hundreds of miles of Ver Signian territory. Surely, if she trudged through enough of it, she would stumble upon the Guild within the next day. It would take the cadre at least another two days to reach Draconis, and if Meiryn found the huntsmen in time, they might be able to intercept the cadre and help rescue Reina.

So she walked.

And walked.

The day went by at a snail's pace. The forest looked the same at every turn, and the sun smeared like honey across the sky. Needles of amber poked through the trees at sundown, then gave way to the shadows of the night, and the second dawn found Meiryn shivering. Her stomach had started rumbling too loudly to ignore. Hunger ached deep. Every abrupt movement sent her head spinning. Without even realizing it, she had stopped watching for wolves and started searching for food.

Brightly colored berries dotted the sides of the untrodden path, but Meiryn strayed from their enticing gleam. Vague memories from her mother's apothecary told her that one bite would render her breathless and feverish.

She was no hunter, either. She carried no weapon and alerted critters to her presence with every step. Even if she knew how to rig up a snare, she had never started a fire. Reina was always the one who made sure they had something to eat, whether she caught it herself or stole it from a vendor's stall.

It was a cruel joke, to be in a forest as lush and green as this, and to be utterly helpless.

The days were unforgiving in the summertime heat, but it was the night that struck true fear into Meiryn's heart. She ignored the boot that lay off the trail, lone and bloody; ignored the hunter's trap that someone—or some*thing*—had disarmed. The chirps and chitters of unseen wildlife kept her senses alert, and at every snapping twig, she swiveled, half-expecting to find a wolf peering at her through the bushes. Sometimes, when the winds blew stronger, Meiryn swore dragons flew over the forest; swore she could hear their bone-rattling cries echoing across starry skies. But beneath the cover of the trees, she spent the dark hours fighting off sleep. Every time her chin dropped against her chest, she'd jerk upright as if shocked by lightning. Images of Reina locked away in a cell in Draconis threatened to drag her into sweat-inducing nightmares, and so she refused to let herself rest.

By the third day, she was breaching her limit.

Her lips were dry and cracked. Hunger and thirst made her clumsy, and on more than one occasion, she nearly tripped over her own feet. Individual leaves and blades of grass flattened into solid green canvases. A figure in the distance—*human or animal?*—flitted from sight before she could piece together a clear picture, and fatigue convinced her that she had seen nothing at all.

The sun had long since crested its noontime peak. Pale daylight would turn golden soon, and when it did, Meiryn would have wasted half a week wandering.

She could have melted into a puddle of tears. Was the Hunters Guild even still here? Or were the rumors old, and the elusive huntsmen that raided villages and pillaged cities had moved on from these woods?

A fragment of the street performance replayed in Meiryn's mind. *In the shadows of all that is unseen, the Wolf King's guild outlasts.*

They were here somewhere. There was nowhere else for them to hide, not when the whole of Ver Signia saw them as threats to the kingdom.

Meiryn stifled her hunger and thirst, carrying on into the woods.

By some mercy of the gods who had abandoned this world, the soft trickling of a freshwater stream reached her ears, and it was all too easy for Meiryn to forget her mission. She trampled through the underbrush, mouth watering even before she caught a glimpse of light shimmering along clear waters. She could already imagine the feel of earth softening beneath her feet, the water sliding over her palms and washing the sweat from her skin—

Something *snapped*, and barbed steel wound itself around Meiryn's right ankle, stringing her ten feet up into the air.

Meiryn screamed. White stars dotted her vision; tears

flooded her eyes and soaked her cheeks. The wire's teeth dug deep into her leg, tapping the bone. Blood was already flowing like water spurting from cracks in a dam. It was pain unlike any she'd ever known. A broken, panicked sob rattled her chest. Her arms flailed uselessly as she tried to reach up for the wire.

She spun slowly, limbs stretched wide like a tiny dancer encased inside a music box. But her face was growing red and bright as the blood rushed downward. Her right leg felt like it was burning inside a forge.

Through the pounding of her heart in her ears, she heard the sharp sound of a three-toned whistle.

The Hunters Guild.

This is it, she thought, letting her hands fall against her ears. Tears struck her trembling fingers. *They found me. They're going to kill me.*

She blinked. A streak of red hair blurred in her periphery, and her heart jumped as an arrow shot through the wire.

Meiryn crashed to the earth. Her head narrowly missed a sharp rock jutting out by the stream. She'd just caught her breath when the archer from West Glen, Faun, descended upon her with a coil of rope clutched in two white fists.

"No, wait—" Her words were severed by Faun's wild shout. Faun grabbed the metal wire and yanked hard.

Steel pierced through bone. Meiryn shrieked and begged for mercy, reaching forward.

Faun backhanded her. The force was strong enough to send Meiryn sprawling again. Another pair of footsteps bounded near, and a deep male voice demanded, "Who is that?"

Faun did not respond. She was busy tying the rope tight around Meiryn's wrists—an easy task, since Meiryn was dazed and winded, and losing blood fast.

Meiryn gasped as the ropes bit into her skin. She glanced up as the second figure approached. Familiarity struck them both at the same time.

"You," Lukas gasped, eyes wide with shock.

No sooner had he spoken than Faun pulled a dark hood over Meiryn's head. Plunged into sudden darkness, Meiryn panicked. She sobbed and pleaded for Faun to stop, but Faun gripped her shoulders in clawed hands. Her voice sounded dangerously near to Meiryn's ear.

"I'm going to use this wire to sew your mouth shut if you don't quiet down right now."

Meiryn wept harder.

There was the sound of scuffling footsteps, and for a moment, the pain in Meiryn's leg subsided. Lukas had unwound part of the trap.

Faun swore. "What are you doing? She has to be the one Elder spotted. We can't trust her."

"She's unarmed!"

"She's trespassing."

Meiryn choked out, "I was trying to help my friend," but her voice was broken, her words incomprehensible. She bit back a sharp cry as Faun yanked her upright.

"We're taking her back to the Guild," she growled. "They can decide what to do with her then."

"You know what they'll do. Besides, she's bleeding too much. She won't make it that far."

No. No, you have to take me to Draconis.

"It's her own fault for trying to follow us," Faun replied sharply. "Just because she's unarmed doesn't mean she's innocent." She tugged on the barbed steel again.

Meiryn groaned. She feared she might vomit from the agony

pulsing up from her leg and seeping into the rest of her body. Exhaustion and fatigue heightened the fear in her heart, but she could not admit defeat now. She'd come this far. She would not give up on Reina.

"Help me," she managed. "Please, I just need—"

Something hard slammed against Meiryn's head, and she heard, saw, felt—nothing.

VII. REINA

The trip to Draconis took an additional two days. Aaron drove the cadre hard, ordering them to travel at a gallop despite Raiko's warning that the horses would tire too quickly. As a compromise, Aaron allowed for brief lunch breaks during the day.

Reina swore she could feel the cadre studying her like she was some anomaly dragged off the Nest; that the hushed whispers at her back were laced with wild speculations about her mysterious and scandalous disappearance from House Rhysanthe.

The truth behind her eventual escape was a complicated one. So complicated that, should she attempt to explain, the agents would be left with more questions than she could bear to answer. It wasn't like Aaron would allow for that kind of conversation, anyway. He had made himself perfectly clear: *"Athira is nothing more than a package to be delivered. You are not to speak to her."*

And so they hadn't. Not a single word had been uttered in her direction, and Reina could scarcely complain. Silence offered her some shred of comfort from the impending fate that awaited her in the depths of Morturrim, but fear and anxiety tore holes in every escape plan she devised.

On her last night with the cadre, Reina was jumping at every slight noise, flinching at every sudden movement. Aaron took notice and made no effort to hide his cold satisfaction.

Seated around the small campfire, Aaron bit into a roasted quail's leg. He announced around a mouthful of food, "I don't want to waste any more time than we already have. Raiko— you've been a sufficient keeper thus far. I trust you to take Athira to Morturrim, then meet the rest of us at the compound. In the meantime, I'll write a notice to the Lord and Lady Rhysanthe and send out a courier. Once Athira is off our hands, we'll head out with new orders."

Reina sat in silence. She watched the cadre gorge on their hunted meal while her stomach ached with emptiness—yet she spoke not a word. Aaron met her eye, grinned, and made a show of taking his next bite. Reina slid her gaze to Raiko's axe, imagining how it would feel to sever Aaron's head from his shoulders and watch it roll across the forest floor.

Korris gave a low, grumbling chuckle and grinned at Reina. "What did you do to make him hate you so?"

Reina scowled. "He hates everything."

"Did I not forbid you to speak to her?" Aaron barked. He wiped the back of his hand over his mouth and cleaned the meat off the bone, tossing it into the darkness of the woods.

Korris ducked his head, but not before Reina saw the dirty look he threw Aaron's way.

Raiko cleared his throat. He hadn't touched most of his portion—which wasn't much to begin with. He picked at it prudently, as if trying to make it last. "Far be it from me to question your orders," he said with a nod in Aaron's direction, "but what, exactly, do we have to gain by dumping your sister in a prison cell?"

Aaron seemed to have been waiting for this question. Eagerly, he responded, "It'll take at least a week on horseback for the courier to deliver the message to Verilonne. Another week for someone to come retrieve Athira from Draconis. Unless you'd rather be the one watching her for all that time, I'll entrust her to the wardens."

"Morturrim was made to keep murderers off the streets," Raiko said. "Contained within those walls are the most dangerous criminals in the kingdom."

"And attempting to unleash an Infernal upon an entire city isn't dangerous?" Evren piped up.

Reina rolled her eyes, but residual fear spat out her protest: "It wasn't me."

"Silence." Aaron glared between his agents and Reina, but he addressed no one in particular when he said with a tone of finality, "You would do well to remember that I am your captain. My word is your law."

A tiny snort disrupted the tension. Five heads swiveled in Reina's direction.

Aaron raised a dark brow. "Something humorous, *sister*?"

Reina knew she was treading thin ice, but if Aaron truly meant to deposit her in Morturrim, nothing she said now could worsen her luck.

She tilted her head at Raiko and crooned, "How does it feel being Aaron's little bitch?"

Before she could even laugh at the taunt, Aaron was flying toward her, fist already swinging.

Reina awoke again sometime in the middle of the night.

Her ears were ringing, one side of her face pressed against the earth. Someone had tied a gag around her mouth—a punishment likely deserved, but one that she no less resented.

The campfire was out, and most of the cadre was asleep. Reina lay motionless on her side—mostly to ease the ache in her head, but also because she'd just processed the hissing whispers of a pair of voices.

Raiko and Aaron. Arguing.

Reina strained her ears, catching her trueborn name falling from Aaron's tongue like sewage into backwater. But the two were speaking the Ashuman common tongue of Mal'dhi. Reina frowned.

When they were still children, Reina and her brothers had Ashuman tutors who offered lessons in Mal'dhi. It was Lady Rhysanthe's sole request in terms of her children's education: to retain a sliver of her heritage, to have someone to talk with outside of the Ver Signian courts. Lord Rhysanthe all but forbade it, claiming that it would appear suspicious to courtiers outside of House Rhysanthe if his entire family was speaking "the language of the enemy"—so when Reina fled from home, it was all too easy to forget what little she had learned. Her ears lost the ability to distinguish each tone and her tongue forgot how to let the language flow like water, but Aaron was nearly fluent. Reina recalled that part of his acolyte training in the Order included language lessons—to better sway the hearts of potential Ashuman recruits. Despite the scattered syllables he stumbled over, he sounded no less arrogant in Mal'dhi than he did in Vers. Conversely, Raiko sounded more comfortable speaking Mal'dhi—though his tone was clipped, his sentences short and terse.

Their hushed whispers clashed like rain against embers.

Reina lay in silence and listened, hoping that she might somehow understand some fragment of their words, but her eyelids were growing heavy again.

She had nearly succumbed to another restless sleep when Raiko snapped, "Let me say this in a language you understand, *Captain*." Reina blinked at the anger in his voice. "You are letting your emotions get in the way of reason. Whatever happened in the past cannot overshadow the opportunity that faces you now. You would be a fool to—"

"*Enough.*"

Reina held her breath. If the rest of the cadre hadn't been surrounding them, she was almost certain Aaron would have had Raiko's head by now. But Aaron's next reply came in a resigned, almost remorseful tone, as if it bothered him to oppose his second. "I don't need your lectures, Raiko. You think I haven't weighed the consequences of Athira's return?"

Consequences?

"I think Athira is right in that you are desperate to prove something," Raiko said.

Reina could practically see her brother bristling, feel the rage boiling beneath indignation. That Raiko was bold enough to say such things surprised Reina more than anything else she'd witnessed during her time with the cadre.

Aaron sniffed deeply. "And I think you should get some rest. You're taking Athira to that dreadful tower tomorrow; you'll need your energy."

"You are not my keeper."

"No; I'm your captain, and you will do as I say."

And so, dutifully, Raiko said nothing. Even after the night bled into a grey, misty dawn, Raiko and Aaron seemed separated by an invisible gap that they were both too stubborn to bridge. Whether the other agents could sense a rift between them was beneath Reina's concern. She was silent when Raiko removed her gag and offered her a meager breakfast of stale bread, and silent still when he loaded her onto his horse for the last leg of their journey.

She noted how Raiko left some distance between himself and Aaron's horse; how the rest of the cadre seemed more willing to maintain Raiko's pace than Aaron's. The silence hanging over the five agents was as thick and heavy as the fog that shrouded their path until the searing midday heat dispersed the mist. When the flat horizon grew staggered and took the form of a city, the tension only stretched tighter.

Raiko agitated his horse with an iron grip on the reins, and Reina narrowed her eyes at the way the other agents sat stiffer in their saddles. Even Aaron seemed on edge. His lips thinned in the way they did when he was buried deep in thought.

It didn't make sense. Draconis was home to the Silver Order. Aaron himself made it seem like returning would provide them with much-needed rest after dragging her along. But as the city came closer into focus, he gradually slowed his pace until he and his cadre formed a dense unit.

Reina glanced at him sidelong, wary of another fight, but Aaron looked past her, as if she weren't even there. He addressed his cadre. "We won't spend more time here than necessary. Be sure to restock your supplies as needed. I'll notify you all when we have our next orders."

"If we get them," Korris muttered.

Reina craned her neck to look at him. "Why wouldn't you?"

"Because—"

"It's none of your concern," Aaron interrupted. He shot a

warning glare at Korris, who duly shut his mouth. Aaron glanced at Reina, and for a heartbeat, she could have sworn she caught a flicker of worry in his eye. But he blinked, replacing it with that cold, impartial stare. "Perhaps the wardens of Morturrim will teach you not to speak out of turn. Gods know no one else could."

"Maybe I'll befriend the wardens instead," Reina retorted with a cold laugh. An old, bitter wound resurfaced, and she stared daggers into her brother's eyes. "Would they befit me more than another nobleman's son? Or does everyone I talk to fall beneath your standards?"

Aaron's fists went white around his reins, and he faced forward again. Reina waited for a response—some feeble explanation that might justify why he wanted her miserable, going so far as to sever her connection to the only friend she had growing up—but he said nothing. It was a pain he relished, she knew, as were all the others he'd caused.

"One day, Athira," he sighed, rolling his neck, "you will realize that everything I did was for your benefit."

Reina might have laughed if Aaron weren't being completely serious. She glared with all the fuming hatred in her heart. "Everything you did only made my life harder. I couldn't rely on anyone but myself."

Even Alexander, kinder and gentler than all the Rhysanthes combined, was too fearful of their father's anger to be of much help. He might have never wanted his sister to suffer, but neither had he done much to offer her comfort and safety from the torment—especially in her last year at home.

Aaron mirrored her expression. He dug his heels into his horse's flank, pulling ahead of the cadre. Without looking back, he called, "Then you should be well-prepared for what awaits you at House Rhysanthe. After what you did, only the gods can save you from Father's anger now."

———

Draconis was renowned for its resolution throughout the ages. Stories of the fortress-like architecture that housed common civilians attracted travelers from all across Ver Signia, but, fearing an encounter with Aaron, Reina neglected to see it for her own eyes.

Now, standing beneath the silver flames waving on black flags, she understood why this city, out of every historical landmark in Ver Signia, brought in tourists from all corners of the kingdom.

The outer walls reached at least a hundred feet into the air, with watchtowers standing twice as tall at each of the cardinal directions. Uniform lines of armed guards patrolled the perimeter like ants marching along the ridges of tree bark. Great steel spikes, dulled by the grey clouds gathering in the sky, were bolted into the stone walls, giving the impression of metal teeth meant to clamp down on any enemy who dared to threaten the inhabitants within. Giant crossbows peeked out from the watchtowers, and if Reina squinted her eyes, she could just make out the steel-tipped arrowheads of the bolts loaded into the weapons.

Rumors of the ruthlessness within pushed to the forefront of Reina's mind: that the Order was enlisting children into their ranks; that agents were now taming the dragons they captured from the Nest instead of merely harvesting their corpses for armor and weapons; and that these dragon tamers had been appointed by the king himself to finally stake a firm claim over the valley of the Dragon's Spine.

How horribly naive she'd been to scoff at such claims.

An abrupt metal clanging within the city's forges pierced holes in her mask of courage. Billowing clouds of smoke rose from the belly of the city, but not even the smog-stained air could conceal the black spire of Morturrim from view. Reina blinked rapidly, clenching her jaw to keep her mouth from falling open.

Looming over every watchtower and stretching wider than the Grand Arena in Caer Savalier, the prison was a black thorn piercing straight through the heart of Draconis. Anchoring the tower were six metal chains, each stretching all the way to the city's outer walls.

Ironic, Reina mused, that Draconis's notorious prison was, itself, a prisoner in its own home.

That was the only thing to settle her mind as the cadre approached the grand front gates. City guards dressed in stiff armor snapped to attention. Aaron acknowledged them with a shallow nod, but as he led his cadre onward, Reina noticed the way the guards counted their numbers—five agents in total, carrying one prisoner—and cast each other sly, knowing glances. Whispers were exchanged behind callused hands.

The cadre noticed, too. Iliana shrank in her saddle, and Evren drew close to her side. Korris straightened his spine, but he wouldn't—or couldn't—look away from the path ahead.

"What—" Reina started.

Raiko muttered some irritable command, prodding her with a finger. Reina turned forward obediently and caught the quickest glimpse of Aaron's side profile.

His ears were scarlet, his mouth parchment-thin.

The tunnel consumed them one by one. Stretching several meters long and lit by a few sparse torches, the entrance to Draconis was as eerie as the catacombs beneath House Rhysanthe's mansion. Navy banners, almost black in the dimness, displayed the city's crest: a snarling dragon skull pierced by two crossing swords. A steady *drip-drip-drip* echoed against the soft *clip-clop* of the horses' hooves, and as they neared the faint glow of the first torch, Reina squinted at the carvings on the walls.

Six agents of the Order stood in solemn vigil: three men, three women, all radiating power and command in their stone-silent forms. The sculptors had gone so far as to carve out the minute details of their hands curling around the pommels of their swords, the wrinkle of cloth at the elbows. Reina half-expected them to spring to life. Each bore the fire emblem of the Silver Order on their chest, and stretching over their eyes was a long banner inscribed with words that Reina recited into the quiet:

"I AM THE FLAME IN THE DARKEST NIGHT; THE STING OF AN UNYIELDING BLADE; THE EYE THAT SEES THE UNSEEN."

She tilted her head. Vague memories of Aaron sulking around the mansion, muttering these words under his breath, resurfaced. "Those are your vows, aren't they?"

Neither Aaron nor anyone else responded, but he tensed in his saddle.

Emboldened by his discomfort and the gaping silence, Reina pressed, "Why are there only five of you? Are all cadres—"

"Enough." Aaron pulled on his reins. His horse stopped, and the rest of his cadre followed suit. Shadows covered half his face. "I told you not to speak out of turn."

"An order I've yet to follow—but here you are, wasting your breath again." She jerked her chin at the carvings and asked, "Where is your sixth agent?"

Aaron inhaled sharply, like he meant to berate her again, but Raiko cleared his throat. Reina froze and watched Aaron force out a slow, calm breath. The fire in his eyes faded when he looked past her and addressed the rest of his cadre.

"You have your orders. Make no detour, waste no time—and speak not a word of Athira's imprisonment."

She glared through narrowed vision. Aaron was ignoring her. Dismissing her presence before she was even gone. It was nothing she wasn't accustomed to, so why did it sting so much now? And what was it about Raiko that persuaded Aaron to act more rationally?

In a hardened voice, Aaron continued, "Should anyone ask you what became of the rogue huntress, tell them that it is a matter only for the cadre involved."

Iliana sounded doubtful. "But the commander—"

"Cannot be bothered with such trivial matters," Aaron finished with a warning tone. "I'm sure she has plenty on her hands with the Nest. One traitor to the kingdom is beneath her concern."

"You mean *we're* beneath her concern."

"Do not forget your place in the Order." Everyone jumped at Aaron's booming command. "We operate under the same laws as every other agent; we fight together as any other cadre. Our place here is earned—just as anyone else's."

Reina stared, but he didn't spare her a second glance. He turned his horse away, leading his cadre out of the shadows and into the muted grey light that covered Draconis.

VIII. MEIRYN

Upon awakening, the first thing Meiryn heard was the soft lull of voices, then the sizzle of a nearby flame. The air was cooler, though the night itself was still warm. A deep, earthy scent reached her nose. Meiryn lifted her head and winced. Was it her imagination, or did she smell blood? She blinked against rough cloth. Realizing that it was a blindfold, she tried to tear it away from her eyes, but her hands were bound to a stake that prodded her spine.

"Lukas," she groaned. She remembered the fleeting glimpse of his face just before Faun yanked the hood over her head. He had tried to stop Faun. If he were here now, perhaps he could sway the Guild to release her.

She called out to him again, her throat straining against dryness. All at once, the dull chatter fell silent, and Meiryn's skin prickled. She was being watched.

A moment passed, and a heavy pair of footsteps stomped toward her. Meiryn flinched as someone tore away the blindfold.

Night shadowed her surroundings, but dim firelight flickered under a smattering of hooded torches. The forest encroached on a small encampment, threatening to poke holes through the roofs of patchwork tents. A crowd of huntsmen faced her, each clad in rugged clothing and armed to the teeth.

Meiryn swallowed a knot in her throat. She spotted Faun at the front; Lukas stood beside her, blinking at Meiryn with a bemused expression.

Meiryn strained against her bindings. Her voice was a cracked, hoarse plea. "Lukas—help me. Tell them to let me go."

Curious murmurs rippled through the Guild, and Faun glanced at Lukas with a raised brow. "She seems to know you."

Lukas frowned and shifted his weight. He looked uncomfortable. "We ran into her in West Glen, remember?"

"Ah, yes." A bitter smile twisted Faun's mouth. With that expression and her slightly pointed ears, she appeared uncannily foxlike. "She's the reason Nona is dead."

The huntsmen behind her bristled. Meiryn couldn't make herself look at any of them. She grappled for an explanation. "I was trying to find my friend. We were supposed to rescue Nona and bring her back to you."

Faun's shoulders dropped. Her eyes glinted murderously, and her voice trembled as she spoke. "What in six hells did you want with Nona?"

Meiryn shrank back from Faun's rage. She cast Lukas an imploring look. "Nothing bad was supposed to happen. We thought you might be able to help us if we returned her to you."

"'*Returned* her'?" Faun echoed. "As if she were just some commodity?"

Lukas jumped in before Faun could erupt further. Something like sympathy softened his gaze as he addressed Meiryn. "I doubt you meant for anything bad to happen. Regardless, Nona is dead, and we caught you trailing us."

Fear consumed reason. Meiryn leaned forward, begging him for mercy. "You helped me in West Glen. Help me now."

Faun whirled in Lukas's direction. From somewhere in the crowd, an accusatory voice called, "You're bringing in outsiders again, are you?"

Lukas flinched, as if the piercing stares of the huntsmen were knives stabbing into his back. Redness crept into his ears, and he refused to maintain eye contact with Meiryn. Loud enough for all to hear, he said, "I don't know this girl—I don't even know her name—and I didn't tell her to follow us. I told her to get someplace safe because the Order was in the city." To Meiryn, he spoke in a gentler yet firmer tone. "The Guild has no place for trespassers. I can't help you."

"Then take me to someone who can," Meiryn blurted. "Take me to the Wolf King."

Silence. Lukas dropped his head; Faun's gaze went cold as winter's first breath. Meiryn looked out at a sea of blank faces—all of them strangers, all of whom wanted her dead. It was as if, by merely mentioning the Wolf King, she had breached some invisible boundary.

When no one spoke up, Faun responded with a derisive "And who are you that you think you deserve to speak with him?"

"I'm..."

I'm desperate. I'm lost.

Meiryn cleared her throat but still shuddered under the Guild's unwavering stares. "I'm willing to do anything to get my friend back. The cadre that came for Nona—they took my friend instead. They'll kill her if you don't help me."

An outraged voice cried out, "She's using us!" Another accused her of being one of the Order's spies. Restless murmurs accompanied the outspoken protests.

Faun lifted her chin, and Lukas's face was unreadable. Meiryn blinked hard to stop her tears from falling and bit her tongue to keep from uttering another heartbroken plea. Her heart rattled in her chest, and her hands trembled so badly that she barely managed to keep them clasped together.

If the Hunters Guild refused to help her, what other option did she have? Faun's trap had weakened her, so even if she did manage to escape from these bindings, she couldn't run. Lukas had dismissed her. She was a stranger among these huntsmen. An outsider who couldn't be trusted, much less helped.

"Take me to the Wolf King," Meiryn repeated carefully. "Help me, and I'll do whatever you ask."

A thin, cold smile played on Faun's lips. "You'll do what we ask—and then, if you've proven yourself, we'll take you to him. It'll be his choice whether he wants to help you."

Lukas and several other huntsmen pinned Faun with alarmed stares, but she either didn't notice or didn't care.

Meiryn's heart sank. "Reina is in danger."

"If the Order took your friend, they won't bother wasting their own resources to keep her imprisoned," Faun said. "They'll leave her in the cells of Morturrim, and they'll forget about her— just like they do with every prisoner they take. I'd be surprised if anyone even remembers to make her stand trial. In the meantime, you get to decide whether she's really important enough to risk your life for. You clearly have no remorse for the life you cost me."

"I didn't mean for anyone to get hurt," Meiryn breathed. Words seemed to elude her, and dread sank like a stone in her gut. "All I wanted... I just—look. Reina was captured. I don't have time to play squire, but if you help me now, I *promise* I will return the favor."

"Your crimes were against the Guild," Faun reiterated. "The huntsmen will decide what to do with you, since you're the reason we lost Nona."

Lukas muttered Faun's name, giving her a sidelong look.

Faun ignored him. "Your success or failure to fulfill our demands will determine whether you're worthy to stand before the Wolf King and beg for his help the way you've done with us tonight."

Meiryn tossed pride to the wind. "And what if I fail? What if I can't do what you ask of me?"

"Then I will personally gouge out your eyes so you can never again look upon this part of the woods," Faun said without missing a beat, "and I'll feed your tongue to the crows to ensure that you never speak of what you saw, who you met, or where you were."

Meiryn cast an incredulous look at Lukas, who continued to avoid her gaze. The huntsmen behind Faun and Lukas murmured their solemn agreement, and Meiryn had no choice but to bow her head and accept the terms of their impossible demands.

"It's settled, then." Faun seemed no less displeased than she had been when Meiryn first awoke. She approached on silent feet and crouched in front of Meiryn. Anger rolled off her in waves, and Meiryn held her breath when Faun's mouth grazed her ear.

"There's no room for outsiders here," Faun hissed. "If it were up to me, I'd have shot an arrow through your heart the second you stumbled into my trap. You might not be Nona's killer, but she's still dead because of you."

Meiryn yelped when Faun shoved her back against the stake and turned away. The huntsmen had dispersed, but Lukas remained where he stood. Meiryn caught his eye and found some emotion there too heavy for words.

He had shown her kindness before. Why now, when she needed him most, did he shun her?

The silent question lingered between them until someone called Lukas's name. He blinked, as if snapping out of a trance. Meiryn opened her mouth to call to him, but he shook his head. Without another word, he turned away and retreated into the darkness beyond the torchlight.

Before his shadow had even left her, Meiryn was already weeping.

IX. REINA

Smoke and coal, oil and grease—all embraced by the crackling embers of the city's numerous forges—stained the air. Behind a thick veil of smog, the sun was little more than a hazy glow bearing down on the city, and the wind blowing in from the sea only seemed to darken the overcast skies.

Draconis, like other major cities, thrived only because of its inhabitants. It drank the sweat from the backs of its workers; sank its metal teeth through the cracks in the walls; shouldered the weight of too many people crammed into one place. The city took everything from its citizens—then gave scraps in return. Every building stood at least three stories high, and wooden bridges stretched between them, wobbling precariously beneath the constant flow of foot traffic. On the ground, one street could barely fit two men walking side by side. And with that damned tower looming over it all...

Reina stifled a cough when she inhaled the smog. Only now did she acknowledge what a luxury it had been to spend any amount of time in West Glen, where trees breathed life into the woodland city, birds perched on every rooftop, and deer wandered through the nearby groves. It wasn't everything that she hoped for, but it was all that she wanted now.

Her heart clenched at the thought of Meiryn—stranded somewhere in the western woods of Ver Signia. Had she followed the cadre out of West Glen? Or had she let fear overtake her, admitting defeat once Reina had been captured?

Reina prayed it was the former, but she knew Meiryn. Too often, she was quick to trust anyone who showed her any amount of kindness, taking their words at face value. She wasn't bold or cunning—didn't even try to be. It was that innocence and naivety that had allowed Reina to conceal her identity from Meiryn for the past three years.

None of that mattered now, though. Reina was chained again, ensnared in the truths she so desperately tried to hide. And Meiryn…

She couldn't think of Meiryn now. It hurt too much, knowing that all they had worked for amounted to this. That Meiryn had likely already found some other stray traveler to cling to for safety and comfort.

Reina forced back unexpected tears, jerking in the saddle as Raiko pulled away from the cadre. Her heart lurched. She twisted, trying to plead with Aaron one last time. "Wait."

But her brother was already gone.

"Sit still," Raiko snapped, loud enough for the cadre to hear. He gripped the reins in one hand and clamped the other around the back of her neck, turning her around before she could even catch a parting glimpse of the others.

Reina choked on a gasp. Her spine went rigid when Raiko's lips brushed her ear.

"Do not look back," he whispered, as if the cadre could still hear him over the din of the city. His tone was dark, but his voice was warm with that fluid, soothing cadence distinctive of Ashuma. "Not until we are out of sight."

Reina's ears pricked, but she obeyed. She wrinkled her nose as they sank into the stench of sweat and grime. The street was barely wide enough for the horse, much less the foot traffic pushing around them. Buildings pressed in like walls of a labyrinth, and the webbing bridges overhead swayed against gusts of salted wind. Reina gripped the horn of the saddle, flinching as throngs of people shoved around Raiko's horse—all weary-eyed and stone-faced.

When the shadow of Morturrim darkened the street, Reina peered over her shoulder. "What were you discussing with Aaron last night?"

He blinked, barely masking his surprise. "You were supposed to be sleeping."

"Hard to sleep when people are arguing nearby."

Raiko rolled his eyes but asked, "Can you not understand Mal'dhi, like your brother?" Reina looked away, choosing not to comment, and at her back, Raiko heaved a long sigh. "I suppose growing up in Ver Signia limits your need for Mal'dhi. Still—it is a useful skill to have."

"What does it matter to you?" Reina snapped. She couldn't make herself look at Morturrim, though it was hard to ignore. Was it paranoia, or could she hear the wails of the prisoners all the way out here? "You're dropping me in some dingy little cell, and you'll go about your life, serving Aaron and the Order until the day you die."

Raiko chuckled humorlessly. "You must think so little of me." He pulled on the reins, jostling Reina with the abrupt change in direction. She tightened her grip on the saddle, confusion rippling when she realized that he'd turned away from Morturrim.

The streets were no less crowded here, but they widened as the land sloped down toward the coast. Lightning flickered in the distant clouds. If Reina squinted her eyes, she could just make out the jagged outline of the archipelagic Nest shuddering beneath the storm.

"Where are you taking me?" she demanded. "You had orders."

"Let me make something clear, *Athira*." His voice roughened like a whetstone against a dull blade. "I may be Aaron's second, but I am nobody's bitch."

So it did bother him, then.

"If you—"

"*Quiet.*" He prodded his horse, easing into a steady canter. People swerved to avoid him, but not before throwing him menacing glares that he ignored. Reina craned her neck as Morturrim slowly drifted out of view.

Angrily, Raiko continued, "I grew up in Ashuma, but I am well aware of how ruthless these Ver Signian nobles can be. They stop at nothing to get what they want. Land, power, or status—they always get it in the end. If you managed to evade your family all this time, then you are clearly cleverer than Aaron wants to give you credit for."

"What are you saying?"

"Aaron wants to punish you, but your potential is wasted in a jail cell. Regardless of what he wants, I will not let this opportunity go to waste."

The fight between Raiko and Aaron came back to her, as did the odd tension in the tunnel mere moments ago. Aaron was hiding something from her, but Raiko had just given her the missing piece.

"Your cadre is incomplete. That's why Korris doesn't think you'll get further orders from your commander. You can't operate without a sixth agent." And Raiko thought she might be their solution. He wasn't taking her to Morturrim; he was drafting her into their cadre.

The sky blackened as Raiko explained, "We were given special permission because Aaron is a nobleman's son, but no one wanted to take orders from a"—he scoffed bitterly—"*malduna*. Never mind that he is highborn."

Reina blinked. "But your cadre—"

"We all carry burdens that were deemed too cumbersome for other captains. Aaron was desperate for a cadre to lead, and this was his reward: a mixed bunch of glorified mercenaries harboring weak loyalties to the Silver Order." His eyes clouded and darkened. "If that were not incriminating enough, we are without a sixth agent and, therefore, perceived as weak. Unfit for work. It is a wonder that the commander has allowed us to operate as long as we have."

There was no time for questions. While Reina was distracted by Raiko's absurd plan, he had carried them halfway down the hill.

The Silver Order's headquarters stretched all the way to the shoreline, barring public access. Along the coast sat a uniform row of massive traps that could either ensnare or kill a dragon. Lookout towers protruded from the bay, no doubt equipped with terrifying weaponry, but whatever operations took place within the towers emitted a grey sludge that muddied the waters. Further out, sails of the cargo ships that ferried supplies between the mainland and the Nest rippled in a restless breeze.

A wild burst of imagination punctured the apprehension in Reina's mind: if she stole a ship from the shores of Draconis, who would stop her from sailing into open waters? What sailor was skilled or daring enough to brave the Abyss?

"None of this matters," Reina said, mostly to steel her nerves. A brisk wind blew in from the sea, and she spat her hair from her mouth. "I won't join you."

"Would you rather I let you rot in a cell?"

Reina started to reply, but Raiko dug his heels against his horse's flank, lurching them onward.

Rainwater dotted Reina's face. Churning clouds that sat over the Nest strained closer inland, joined by a steady rainfall that quickly drenched the coastline just as Raiko pulled his steed to a halt outside the Order's massive gates.

Terse nods greeted him. Agents on foot made way for his return, and as they passed through the gates, Reina fell into a mute stupor.

Every wall, roof, and stone in the ground was imbued with black obsidian, rendering the entire place fireproof. The heart of the fortress was a colossal, multi-storied building. A spiraling skirt of stone provided covered walkways between each level, and a bell tower crowned the domed head of the fortress. Narrow windows offered natural daylight without betraying the secrets within, but on the penultimate level, Reina discerned the unmistakable glare of a raging fire.

Here on the ground, there was some grim fascination to behold in every direction: cannons meant to shatter Hiberns' icy blasts glowed with eternal flames; the perimeter of the base —a broad, graveled path between the outer wall and the main building—sat beneath crossed bars of steel that defended the agents and acolytes from aerial attacks; slinking along the ramparts were black-clad archers, their eyes locked on the city as they marched in perfect unison. Through sleet and rain, they were mere shadows. But what remained clear was the row of white skulls pinned over the front steps of the fortress—massive and horned, jaws straining in a permanent roar.

Dragons. Trophies of the Order's conquest.

Reina spoke over her shoulder. "I think I *would* rather you leave me at Morturrim."

Raiko snorted and directed his horse toward a separate sector, where a frenetic, rigid sort of energy buzzed within a training yard. Younger acolytes, pale-faced and shivering from the rain, ran laps in uniform rows. Their seniors barked out orders, snickering to one another as they reminisced about their own days of drills and servitude.

"Training is rigorous," Raiko said, speaking above the rainfall. "Unless you are dying from a wound or illness, there is no excuse for absence or tardiness."

Reina scowled. "You sound like my—"

A flash of blue light to the left snagged Reina's attention. She dug her heels into the horse's flank, earning an affronted protest from Raiko, but the horse continued walking obediently. Straining in the saddle, Reina quickly found what was turning the air to ice.

In a sunken stone pit caged beneath that protective steel ceiling, wranglers armored in thick dragon hide leaped around a young Hibern dragon. Chains rattled; shouted warnings overlapped with one another. Clouds of frostbitten air billowed from the dragonling's nostrils, and Reina gasped as tiny fractals of ice shot from its mouth like arrowheads. Some agents leaned over the barriers to watch, while others passed by without a second glance.

"The rumors are true, then," Reina said. Blue and white lights flared, followed by a pained screech. "You're taming dragonlings for your own army."

Raiko frowned. "The details of the dragon campaign are only disclosed to those involved. Although, we could learn more if you were to join our cadre."

Curious, he peered into the taming pit. The dragonling reared its head back, and ice bolts shot skyward, spooking Raiko's horse. He swore as it lurched sideways.

The movement jostled Reina in the saddle, and a few acolytes yelled in warning, swerving out of Raiko's way. He jerked on the reins, righting his horse, but Reina lost her balance and hit the ground hard.

Pain cracked through her body just as a spectral golden light flashed within the clouds. Wincing, Reina squinted through the sleet. A pitiful wail rose from the taming pit, and though the shadows fled under a cloud-covered sky, a deeper, darker shape flitted over the fortress.

Reina jumped when Raiko landed beside her. He opened his mouth, but the clanging of the bell tower drowned out his voice. His face went pale.

"What is that?" Reina demanded.

The agents on the ramparts were running now, aiming their arrows toward the clouds. The acolytes abandoned their training and made way for their seniors, who snatched weapons from the armory and shouted at one another. Above it all, the bell in the tower reverberated a jarring *clang-clang, clang-clang.*

"Get up," Raiko urged. His hand closed around Reina's arm, but his grip was loosened by the rain. "Athira—"

She slipped and fell back just as another vein of lightning

ripped across the sky. Her mouth fell open as a pair of shadowy wings tore through the clouds.

Screams erupted from the acolytes. Reina's blood froze, as if she had been struck by a Hibern. Raiko swore as his horse bolted. Thunder crashed and shook the earth, and from within the blackened sky, two golden suns blinked at the city.

No—not suns. Eyes.

A cry rose from the back of Reina's throat, but the rain pelted her tongue, choked out her words as the clouds split open—

And a black dragon pierced through the heart of the storm.

Gold lightning writhed around the beast's body and surged toward the earth. With a mere shift of its gaze, pillars of electrifying power ripped apart the steel bars and struck holes in the training yard. Archers upon the ramparts windmilled into violent vortexes that surged from each beat of its powerful wings. The rain pounded the earth as the dragon descended upon the bell tower, and within its deafening roar, a male voice, deep and guttural and ancient as time itself, rumbled like thunder.

"You dare to control the will of the Ancient Ones? Heed my words: I shall rid this world of your kind, just as you have done to mine."

The veins in his wings glowed with incandescent golden light. He swung his head toward the taming pit. The Hibern dragonling strained against its captors, and with an explosive crack of lightning, the steel barriers split open.

Alarms rose as the black dragon dropped into the pit. Jagged gold waves jumped along obsidian scales. Agents stampeded to escape while the young Hibern lifted its head to the sky and waved its tail like a flag. Raging blue lights pierced through the black storm clouds, and a host of adult dragons—Infernals and Hiberns, all enraged and deadly—flocked to the Silver Order's base.

The coastal defenses had failed.

Chaos reigned. Desperate commands drowned beneath the bone-rattling chorus of rogue dragons. Voices clamored over one another until Reina thought her head might split.

She didn't hear herself screaming until their cries fell to a rippling echo. Ears ringing, face wet with a mix of tears and rain, she found the black dragon in the swarm. He was smaller, sleeker than his Infernal and Hibern companions, but as lethal as three of them combined—and faster than any eye could track. Cloaked in the darkness of his own storm, he might as well have been born from shadows.

Bolts of lightning bit at the agents' heels and shocked their weapons from their hands. The fortress shuddered as every cannon fired against the dragons, but the agents manning them were inundated by the storm. Plumes of fire turned humans to matchsticks. Ice gored through chests. With the steel barriers no longer standing in the way of the dragons and their prey, the entire fortress became a hunting ground.

The black dragon commanded them all, his threats and furious shouts shaking the teeth inside Reina's skull, and when he whirled in her direction, the rest of the world fell away.

She drew in a shuddering gasp, and those eyes that captured the sun glinted like pure daylight. He *saw* her. Amidst the rain, amidst the fire and ice, amidst the scrambling agents—the dragon found her wide-eyed gaze and held it with his own.

Restless energy thrummed between them. Time stood still. Reina swore she could sense the wind and rain bending to the dragon's will; could feel his heavy breaths as though they were her own. Her hands strained against her bindings, and her fingers twitched, as if jolted by the dragon's lightning. She watched his rage subside to suspicion, then soften to curiosity.

And something clicked into place when he spoke to her in a lethally calm voice touched by incredulity. His mouth did not move; his words existed only within her head.

"What are you?"

Reina's lips parted, and her breath caught in her throat. She pulled threads of cold air into her lungs—

Steel flashed in her periphery, severing her connection to the dragon as well as the ropes around her wrists. She jumped as Raiko gripped her shoulders and shook her.

"What are you doing?" he demanded. Rain plastered his hair to his forehead, and he spat out a mouthful of water. "Move!"

Reina blinked rapidly as he tore her off the ground. Hands unbound, she grabbed his arm to steady herself as he shoved her against the agents that flocked to the nearest shelter. The archers on the ramparts had fallen to the Infernals and Hiberns. Bodies littered the yard like hollow trees in a fire-eaten forest.

"Where are the reinforcements?" Raiko shouted. He looked around frantically, and through the storm, Reina heard the storm dragon's voice again.

"How are you possible?"

Reina shrieked, nearly falling to her knees. The ground trembled, but Raiko kept her upright. Reina glanced over her shoulder.

The storm dragon pounced from the taming pit, jaws unhinged, claws outstretched.

Reina dove, dragging Raiko with her. Together, they rolled through ice and rain, narrowly missing a zigzagging path of lightning. Gold flares lit up the darkness, and Reina flinched when a pair of boots landed mere inches from her nose. She cried out as Aaron yanked her up by her hair. His eyes burned with the fury of an Infernal, veins bulging in his neck as he bellowed, "What in six hells are you doing here?"

Raiko answered before Reina could choke out some feeble response. "We have larger concerns. Did you see that dragon?"

Aaron shoved Reina aside. He drew his sword, and for a split moment, Reina thought he might kill her right there. But he ignited his blade and waved a hand. Not a heartbeat later, the rest of his cadre surged forward, weapons drawn to defend the Order to which they pledged their lives.

Reina sheltered behind a weapons rack, mouth agape as Aaron cut a path toward the dragon. Other agents lunged forward, trying to hold him back, but he broke through their lines and led a hopeless battle against the deadliest beast Ver Signia had ever seen.

Watching him fight was like watching a starved animal ravage a carcass. He moved with the swiftness and agility of the wind, dodging the dragon's lashing tail with alarming ease. His agents were no less skilled or deft: the five of them together were a force to be reckoned with, and Reina dug her nails into her palms when the black dragon snarled.

"How arrogant you are to challenge the Rage of the Storm." A sinister chuckle reverberated through the space his voice occupied in Reina's head. *"Let us see how you fare against the power vested in me by the Clans of Old."*

He sent a volley of lightning after Iliana, who yelped as the ground splintered at her feet. Evren dove after her, throwing himself directly in the dragon's line of sight.

Korris shouted Evren's name, wheeling his arm back just as

the dragon's throat burned with an otherworldly glow. Lightning struck not a foot away from Evren, and Korris swore as the shock traveled up his blade and seized the muscles in his hand. His weapon clattered uselessly out of reach.

Reina slapped her hands over her ears. Her heart constricted, and her veins thrummed with an energy that was not her own. Every inch of her was trembling—yet she was paralyzed on her knees.

Aaron pressed harder with his attacks. Raiko mirrored his strikes, chipping away at the dragon's armored scales. As blood sprayed and the ground grew darker beneath him, Reina crumbled under a wave of agony. No one touched her, and yet a million tiny knives stabbed at her shoulders, her back, her legs and arms.

Bursts of lightning scattered across the battlefield. The storm dragon's power was slow to recharge, and Reina saw the toll it took on him to keep them all at bay. She peered through a curtain of soaked hair and saw him staggering. He kept his wings beyond the reach of Aaron's cadre, but his softer underbelly was left exposed. Summoning the storm had drained him. Even the smallest bolts of lightning cost too much time and energy. But through the fatigue, his rage grew. He snapped his jaws, lashed out with those deadly talons. But he could not combat the speed of his enemies.

Iliana's whip-sword sliced through the rain, coiling around the dragon's foreleg. Reina winced at a stinging in her wrist, and she bit down on her tongue as he roared.

With a wild thrash of his paw, he threw Iliana halfway across the yard. The cadre, now joined by other agents, charged again, but the dragon's chest glowed gold. His pupils narrowed into thread-thin slits, and his nostrils flared as he panted through the exertion. He scraped this power from the bottom of an empty well.

An unbearable scorching sensation pierced through Reina's heart, and she clutched her chest, gasping hard as a wave of uncontrollable energy overtook her.

Lightning arced down from the sky, blazed in the dragon's chest, then burst from his jaws. An explosion sent the cadre flying, and blinding light filled the yard.

Reina was burning. Every hair stood on end. Arms spread wide, her body convulsed as something in her *snapped*.

Her hands opened like claws. She imagined the storm turning back on its master, and the dragon's eyes widened as spears of lightning rained down around him. He found her through the chaos and bellowed, *"WHAT ARE YOU?"*

Someone shouted her name. She barely heard; barely saw or felt or tasted anything beyond this power, this untamed energy that coursed through her veins. All she knew was fear. Fear of imprisonment, fear of dying, fear of pain.

"This is impossible," the dragon said. *"How can you wield such power?"*

Reina's world turned to gold. Searing, glittering gold—like the walls of her family's mansion, like the frames of her bedroom windows, like the lightning that caged her now. Bitterness and hate coveted the power at her fingertips.

"Stop," the dragon commanded, his voice urgent.

I will not yield. Not to anyone or anything.

"You do not understand—"

Reina threw her head back and screamed. A massive pillar of lightning pierced through the storm, tearing the clouds and the sky asunder. The dragon shrieked, the earth itself buckled, and Reina fell through the world.

Act II

All That Binds

X. REINA

INKY BLACK CLOUDS roiled like waves of the Abyss. Rain pelted Reina's skin, plastering her hair against her forehead and soaking her down to the bone. Her feet were planted in thick, sludgy mud that sucked her down further the more she struggled to free herself.

This was a dream she'd had countless times before. One that left her sweating and shaking in the night, wailing for comfort from a mother who would impatiently send an attendant to her bedside instead.

The shadows around her were breathing, taking shape. She knew the face that would appear from the darkness: it was the face of the monster that haunted her childhood nightmares.

The clouds contorted into fangs dripping with dark blood. Twin suns glared from behind a veil of black smoke. A crown of horns bled into the storming sky, and the dragon's terrible, glowering face took form.

"What are you?" His demand rattled in the air.

Reina shrank. She lifted her hands to shield herself as the dragon swooped down to swallow her whole—

And from her palms burst a light sharp enough to sever his shadowy form in two.

His bellowing roar rocked her to her core. She had the sensation of free-falling into open space, and when she landed, nothing but starry skies surrounded her. The rain had stopped —though a lingering smell of petrichor filled her nose. Wherever she stepped, starlight pulsed like a million tiny heartbeats.

This was new. She had never shot the dragon away.

Reina lifted a hand to eye level, marveling first at the twinkling dust on her skin, then at the faint scarring in the center of her palm. She traced the webbing shape, taking note of how her skin tingled at the touch. A matching scar rested on the other palm, and just as the question of its cause crossed her mind, the dragon answered her.

"You wield such raw power," he said, *"yet you know nothing of what it means to be a conduit of such chaos."*

His words resonated in head-pounding waves. Reina searched for any sign of him, but she was alone amongst the stars. She let her hands fall to her sides and asked, "What power is this?"

"You already know." Cold wind brushed against her cheeks, but it felt more like claws dragging across her face. *"You fear the very truth you seek."*

Because the truth was impossible. Because the truth would paint a target on her back. Because the truth would challenge everything she thought she knew about herself.

"Find me," the dragon ordered, *"and you will recover all that was lost to greed and fear."*

"I don't understand."

"Find me."

A breath of hot air melted the stars until they were naught

but white streaks of rain. Ice pierced her skin, and Reina screamed as she plunged through freezing blackness.

A rough hand clamped down on her shoulder and yanked her from the dream.

Reina snapped her eyes open, fists already swinging. Her knuckles cracked against something solid and rough, and she gasped at the spurt of pain. Her vision focused—and then the panic set in.

Wedged between two massive chunks of cobblestone, only a few inches of space separated her eyes from the rocks that entombed her. She doubted she even had enough space to roll onto her stomach.

"Athira," came Raiko's nearby voice. She craned her neck. He was barely discernible in the dark, but he lay on his stomach with his hand still grasping her shoulder. "Calm yourself. You were dreaming."

"We're...alive?" It hardly seemed plausible. Her heart threatened to break free of her ribs. She turned her head, feeling the tip of her nose graze the low ceiling. "Where are we? What happened?"

Raiko coughed and drew his hand away. Reina restrained herself from reaching for him. "If I had to guess," Raiko said, speaking in a hushed tone, "I would say we were somewhere beneath the city."

"What about the others?"

Strained silence answered her. Unsure how to offer comfort, Reina wrung her hands—then froze.

The scars she felt in her dream, the ones nested in her palms, were real: webbed like lightning, mirror images of one another.

Reina swallowed hard against the dryness in her throat. She

searched for Raiko but could barely see a thing. "Can you move at all?"

A pause. Then, "There is some space behind me, yes."

"Crawl." The order came more forcefully than she anticipated, but Raiko obeyed without question. The sound of rustling clothes filled their tiny alcove, and around them, the rocks shifted. Reina's heart jumped. "Stop."

Raiko halted. Reina held her breath, dread building inside her chest. She waited for the rocks to collapse and crush them both, but a distant, muffled call broke the silence.

Reina's chest swelled with disbelief and strained hope. "Is that Aaron?"

Neither of them uttered a sound until they heard him cry out again. Raiko inhaled sharply. "He is near. We must find him."

"Raiko—" The rocks clacked against one another as he pushed against them. Reina used her feet to scrape backward, and she snapped, "Stop moving. You'll bring the whole thing down on us."

"If we are buried beneath the city, then the crypts must be near," Raiko argued. "They will lead us back to the surface."

"We won't make it back at all if you're not careful."

"Athira?" It was Aaron again, sounding surprised. "Is that you?"

She held her tongue, plastering her stare on the cobblestones above her. Raiko called Aaron's name, then spoke in hurried Mal'dhi.

"Raiko!" Relief flooded Aaron's voice, and he answered in Vers. "Are you hurt? Are you safe?"

"I am unharmed," Raiko assured him. "I lost my weapon, but your sister is here with me. Have you found anyone else?"

Aaron said something incomprehensible. A second later, the rocks around them shuddered again, but neither Raiko nor Reina had touched them.

Sediment sprinkled over Reina's face, and she shouted, "*Stop moving.* You're going to get us both killed."

"I think I found you," Aaron said. He sounded closer now. "I'm going to have to clear this debris to get you out."

"Don't you move a thing," Reina ordered.

At the same time, Raiko called, "Just do it quickly."

Reina scraped her palms against stone as she inched closer to Raiko. The tops of their heads grazed one another, and Reina turned toward the sound of Aaron's voice. "One wrong move, and we could die."

"If he does nothing, then we will die," Raiko argued. "We just have to create enough space to squeeze out of here."

Reina wanted to protest again, but a clattering noise paralyzed her. Aaron was already working on deconstructing the wall. Pinpricks of faint light dashed thin lines across Raiko's face. He blinked, reaching toward the opening Aaron was creating.

The ceiling trembled. Dust filled Reina's nostrils; little rocks and pebbles battered her face. She felt her heart beating in her throat.

But the men had finally pried away enough rocks to face one another. Aaron's voice filled the chamber. "Six hells—you'll never fit through. We need a larger opening."

"Wait," Reina called.

They both ignored her. Raiko pushed against the wall of the opening, and Reina yelped when the chunk of stone above her face dropped an inch.

"Are you alright?" Raiko demanded, looking back at her.

Shadows tore through the light when Aaron jutted a hand through the narrow gap. "Get out of there, Raiko. Now."

Reina was hyperventilating. She had to keep her feet pointed forward now, because there was no more room above her. If that rock fell any lower, it would pin her in place.

Raiko spoke into her ear again. "Answer me. Are you hurt?"

She could only shake her head.

Aaron waved his arm. "Raiko, I said *move*. That's an order." His tone was impatient, growing more urgent.

Raiko nodded shortly but kept his eyes on Reina. "I am going to crawl through now. Once I am free, take my hand, and I will pull you out with me."

A meek nod was all she could muster. She barely noticed him leave her side. Her eyes were glued to the ceiling, and with each second that ticked by, she felt death creeping up on her. She saw how loose the rocks were; felt the walls trembling around her as Raiko squeezed through the narrow tunnel.

He grunted when Aaron tugged him to safety. Reina turned her head, light spilling over her face, and Aaron pushed a hand between Raiko's shoulder blades. "Let's go," he said. "This place won't last much longer."

"No!" Reina's voice shook when Aaron darted out of view. A cold fear paralyzed every inch of her body. "Aaron, you can't leave me."

He spoke over her. "We've fallen into the crypts. Let's find the others and get out of here."

"*Aaron.*" She was fighting back tears now. Salt burned in her eyes as dust grazed her cheeks.

Aaron gave a wordless protest, and a second later, Raiko's hand reached through the tunnel, feeling around for Reina. She could have wept at the sound of his voice.

"Athira," he called, blindly groping, "grab my hand."

Reina took a shuddering breath. She had to contort her arm against her body in order to extend it past her head. For a moment, she and Raiko struggled to find each other, but Reina held on tight when she finally felt their fingers interlock. His callused skin pressed against her scarred palms, and she prayed he did not notice.

Raiko pulled on her, and the stones quaked. Reina gasped and pressed her free hand against the ceiling. "I can't move any further."

Aaron sounded angry now. "Just leave her, Raiko. She can get herself out."

Reina wanted to scream. She squeezed Raiko's hand like she never intended to let go. He held onto her with equal strength.

"Leave if you wish," Raiko snarled. "I will not leave her to die."

"She's none of your concern."

"She is your sister!" Without warning, Raiko yanked on Reina's hand. She cried out when pain shot down her arm, but she felt herself sliding out from under the cobblestone. The walls of her escape were narrow; her shoulders barely fit, and she could feel the rocks threatening to give way.

"You need to push your way out," Raiko said. "Whatever you can push against, do it."

"I can't move my legs." But she wriggled her body, blocking out the precarious *click-clack* of rocks tumbling around her feet. Her view of Aaron and Raiko was upside-down, but what she saw was unmistakable: while Raiko tugged on her arm with both hands, Aaron shifted ever backward, eyes flitting from Reina to the wall that was seconds away from collapsing. Torchlight at the end of the passageway outlined him in a fiery glow. His expression was dark and empty.

"Come on!" Raiko shouted through clenched teeth. He pulled on her arm, nearly popping the joint from its socket.

The walls pressed in. Reina pried her second arm out and clutched Raiko's wrist, watching his features screw tight with effort as he gave a final heave.

Reina slithered out on her back and scrambled away as the pit filled in. A pair of hands cupped her armpits and yanked her to her feet.

"This whole tunnel is coming down," Raiko said with alarm. He dragged her with him and trailed after Aaron, who had already sped away.

Reina found solid footing and ran beside Raiko. Her heart was pounding like a war drum, but still, a quiet voice whispered between her heaving breaths.

Aaron would have left you. He wants you dead. You are nothing to him.

She dashed the thought from her mind. The ceiling was buckling; thin cracks followed them like veins of lightning, and Raiko suddenly darted left.

Reina shielded her face as rocks spilled into their path and threatened to trap them both again. Half-blinded by the dust, she leaped over the debris and hit the ground at a full sprint. She scrambled around the corner, ears ringing and eyes watering.

Sweat beaded on Reina's brow and dampened her neck. The earth shuddered, and the cacophony grew to a thunderous level. Reina and Raiko chased the sound of Aaron's voice. The tunnel spat them out into a dark pit, where they landed on all fours just as the passageway behind them crumpled.

Not a heartbeat later, Aaron swooped down and seized Reina by the shoulders. His fingers dug into her arms painfully, and the cavern trembled when he shouted, "You could have killed us all! What in six hells were you thinking?"

Only one torch on the opposite wall illuminated the entire room. Reina could barely see her brother's face, but she raised her arm instinctively, blocking his swinging fist. She shoved him hard enough to send him sprawling on his back.

"Don't touch me," she spat. Dehydration dizzied her, but she stood her ground. She adjusted quickly to the darkness and met Aaron's bewildered expression with reproach. "I didn't cause that tunnel to collapse. That was you, throwing everything around just to get to Raiko."

Aaron opened his mouth to spit back some venomous retort, but Raiko shouted a violent command for silence. Reina and Aaron shut their mouths quickly.

Raiko staggered to his feet and leveled a hard gaze on both of them. "None of that matters now," he said, like he was chastising a couple of children. "What matters is that we are alive. Leave it be."

Aaron rounded on him. "Why wasn't she in Morturrim?"

Raiko crossed his arms. "You know why."

"I told you already," Aaron argued, "she is not an option." An accusing glare darkened his face, and the distant firelight only emphasized his anger.

Raiko said, "She is the *only* option if you want the Order to respect you at all."

"*She* is right here," Reina snapped. Her outburst echoed in the chamber, and she lowered her voice before it could cause another cave-in. "And for your information, I have no intention of joining you."

Aaron motioned to her. "There, see? She resents you for saving her, just as I do. We would have been better off leaving her trapped in the wall."

"She cannot die here," Raiko said with a harsh exhale. "These crypts are reserved for agents of the Order."

"Which I am not," Reina interjected. "But you both are, so why don't you just stop arguing and point us out of here?"

The agents shared a sullen look. Aaron stood slowly, and when he refused to speak, Raiko took it upon himself to answer her question. "The tombs are off-limits to the living—with the exception of those who are assigned specifically to handle the burials."

"To enter the crypts prematurely is to curse yourself with certain death," Aaron added in a rough whisper.

Reina eyed him strangely. Her brother was overzealous, too keen to prove himself, and oftentimes more arrogant than his prowess warranted—but superstitious belief was never a trait that she expected. Maybe she just didn't know him very well. Maybe years of being brainwashed in the Order's ranks had led him to place his faith in hollow vows and empty threats.

But such things were beneath her concern. What worried her now was that none of them knew how to get back to the surface. They didn't even know where they were.

Reina heaved a sigh and finally took in their surroundings: the chamber they'd fallen into was deeper in the earth. A wooden staircase led back up to the tunnel from which they had escaped, but there was no going back that way. Their only path forward was through a darkened hollow in the wall. Its arch was too smooth to have been carved out by any cave-dwelling animal, but evidence of a human's touch did nothing to calm her nerves. There was every chance that it would only lead to a dead end, and that they were trapped here with each other.

That was a fate almost worse than the one she'd nearly met moments ago.

She pointed toward the exit. "We should keep moving. If the rest of your cadre survived, we won't find them by sitting here."

No one argued as she pried the single torch from its brazier and let the light spill into the corridor. Stale air lingered in her nose, but the faintest breeze brushed her hair back from her face and cooled the sweat on her brow.

If there was a draft, there was an exit.

"Give me the torch," Aaron said. "You don't know where you're going."

Reina looked at him sidelong and held the torch beyond his reach. "Neither do you. We don't know what else might be down here, and unless you want to be the one who leads us into danger, I suggest you let me carry the damned torch."

Aaron shut his mouth, and Reina led them onward.

The crypts stretched into a network of dead ends, pointless loops, and locked doors. Without anything to mark which paths they'd already taken, Reina led them in two wide circles before recognition of the same double doors registered. On her third trip around, she tried to turn the knob, only for it to break off into her hands.

"Just as well," Aaron muttered, unimpressed.

"What do you mean?"

He nodded to a placard above the door that read *D-I*. Reina furrowed her brows. "What's that?"

"It denotes the tomb of First Division agents," Raiko explained, "which means that we are prohibited from entering."

"But no one else is down here." Curiosity nagged, and Reina bent at the waist to peer through the hole where the knob used to sit.

Aaron seized the back of her neck and hauled her away. She clicked her tongue in annoyance, but Aaron merely shrugged. "You're disturbing the dead. Let them rest. And give me this; you're not helping." He wrenched the torch from Reina's hand before she could protest.

Raiko said nothing, but the look on his face suggested that he was just as unpleased with this turn of events as Reina.

She trailed behind the men like a ghost. Her feet grew heavier, her mind foggier with each hour that passed. She couldn't remember the last time her stomach had been so empty to the point of aching.

Aaron managed to free them of Reina's circular path, but his choice to take a stairwell to a lower level spat them out in an equally confusing labyrinth. More wooden doors—cloaked in thick cobwebs or ravaged by termites—bore similar plaques to the one on the upper level: *D-II* and *D-III*.

"How many divisions are there?" Reina asked. Despite Aaron's association with the Order, the precise operations still eluded her.

Raiko held up four fingers. "We are part of the Fourth Division."

Aaron looked at him sharply, but Raiko kept his stare straight and did not acknowledge him.

"We haven't found the Fourth Division tombs yet," Reina noted aloud. "Do you think they're further below the city?"

Aaron shot her a withering glare over his shoulder. "They are none of your concern, Athira. Now, unless you've spotted an exit, keep your mouth shut."

Reina made a face, but she obeyed and fell into begrudging silence.

With as little progress as they were making, Reina was convinced they would never see daylight again. Exhaustion was creeping up on them all, but Reina knew that if she allowed herself to stop and rest, she might well never rise again.

They followed the same maddening pattern until a rancid, putrid odor tainted the air. At first, Reina thought nothing of it. They were gods-knew-how-deep into the earth, lost in a massive catacomb. But when her eyes started watering, she finally halted.

"We can't stay here," she groaned. Her aching feet begged her to sit; she ignored them and backtracked a couple of steps. "I'm going to be sick."

Aaron turned toward her, also covering his face. Fire streaked through the air when he gestured with the torch. In a muffled voice, he ordered, "Keep up. I'm not stopping just because you can't stomach the smell."

Reina glanced at Raiko for solidarity. He seemed to think the ground was more worthy of his attention.

"Something's not right if it smells this bad," Reina groaned. Breathing through her mouth was worse. She looked back in the direction from which they came, and Aaron stormed toward her.

"You're not going anywhere," he said, brandishing the torch too close to her head for comfort. "Don't forget, you're still my prisoner."

Sharp laughter crowed through the fabric of her shirt. "How could I forget? We can't keep Mother and Father waiting, now, can we?"

A muscle in Aaron's jaw twitched. He scoffed and shook his

head. "I wonder every day how I could be so unlucky to be related to you."

He turned away, but Reina circled around him and blocked his path. She met Aaron's coal-black eyes with her own. "Prisoner or sister—clearly it doesn't matter to you what I am when you're content to let me die anyway."

Some fleeting emotion passed over his face before Reina could name it.

"You endangered my agent," Aaron said with eerie calmness. "His safety is my priority, not yours."

"There was time to help me after you got him out. You just didn't care."

"I made a choice when the situation demanded it," Aaron said, voice rising.

Reina jabbed a finger against his chest, a deep-seated rage burning on her tongue. "You never cared what happened to me. As long as you made it out with your pride intact, what did it matter if I took the fall for every one of your missteps? It was the same then, and it's no different now."

Aaron pounded his fist against the wall and shouted, "Raiko was in danger!"

"And I nearly died!"

"*Silence.*"

Aaron and Reina froze. Raiko's face was carved with displeasure, and Reina found it impossible even to look in his direction. Aaron leaned away, looking only mildly ashamed, but when he opened his mouth to speak, Raiko hushed him.

Distant words echoed down the corridor. "Hello? Is someone there?"

It was a young woman: her voice was thin like smoke, but vaguely familiar. Reina watched Aaron's face drop in disbelief.

"Iliana?" he called. He was already following her call. "It's Aaron—where are you?"

Reina jogged to keep up. Iliana's response drowned beneath the pounding of their footsteps, but Aaron's torch was the beacon that guided them. They rounded the corner at the end of the hall and found not just Iliana, but the rest of the cadre, too.

Feet skidded to a halt. Voices fell silent. No one celebrated the reunion.

The lost members of the cadre stood in the archway of a darkened chamber. Where there should have been a door, there was only a gaping hole in the wall with a rickety wooden staircase leading down into a pit. Nailed above the entrance was a slab of rotting wood with crude, nearly indecipherable lettering: *D-IV*.

The tomb of the Fourth Division agents.

The chamber was small, lit only by the torch that Korris carried, and it reeked of death. Piled in neat little pyramids were corpses in varying degrees of decay. Ribs jutted out from half-rotted chests. Worms squeezed through empty eye sockets while maggots and other insects dragged themselves over what were barely recognizable as human faces. Rats gnawed on dead skin like it was dried jerky, occasionally letting out a dissatisfied squeak that bounced off empty walls.

Not a single casket lay in sight. These agents were deposited with no funeral, no identifying placard, no honor.

The torch slipped from Aaron's fingers.

Iliana approached in numb silence, Evren sticking close to her side. The pair of them were paler than a full moon. If they weren't both breathing in stifled, uneasy unison, Reina would have thought them walking corpses.

Evren glanced at Aaron's party and offered them a stiff nod. His blue eyes were dull and hollow, matching his sister's blank expression. He had lost his crossbow but managed to keep his twin blades after the fall. In a dry voice, he said, "Welcome to the Sixth Hell."

From within the chamber, Korris swore under his breath and leaped back from something. Against better judgment, Reina peered past the stairwell and watched two rats scuffling by, battling for possession over a rotten forefinger. The skin ripped like parchment and flapped against the ground when the victor scampered off with its spoils.

Korris grimaced. He gave a humorless chuckle that sent a chill down Reina's spine. "It's a good day to be half-blind," he deadpanned. "But the smell...that's never going away."

Reina dropped to the ground and vomited at Raiko's feet.

XI. MEIRYN

THE GUILD KEPT MEIRYN BLINDFOLDED, baking in the summer heat for what felt like an eternity. She could hear the sounds of a lively encampment—chattering voices, sparring swords clanging in violent rhythms, orders barking from impatient mouths—but her world remained dark. Waves of heat in the daytime or merciful breezes at night marked the passage of time. Someone dribbled just enough food and water into her mouth to keep her alive, but often their hands were brusque and never the same, as if the huntsmen were drawing straws to determine who had to take care of her.

Her wrists were raw and itchy. The wire that bit into her leg had been removed sometime before the huntsmen dragged Meiryn to the Guild, but her wounds were still open and exposed. She could practically feel the blood crusting, the skin blistering and welting beneath patches of white-hot daylight.

Perhaps, a cruel voice in her head whispered, *they have no need of you and are merely keeping you alive so they can take turns flaying you later.*

Her heart shuddered painfully inside her chest. Was the Guild truly that malicious? What about Lukas?

Meiryn reminded herself that he had not come to see her once since that first night.

But that still left the question of *why*. Why would the Guild bother to keep her alive if they never intended to release her?

Meiryn did not waste the breath to ask anyone—even if she could speak around the knots forming in her throat, she'd only make a fool of herself. They would hear her crying out, watch her writhing against her ropes, and think only of prey caught in a snare.

On the third night, just as she was drifting into another restless sleep, she jerked at the feel of a hand—small and soft—pressing against her shin, just above her injury.

Meiryn yanked her right leg close to her chest. Someone nearby gasped.

"Who are you?" Meiryn hissed. Her voice cracked.

"It's alright," a timid voice replied. Young. Female. "Don't be scared."

Meiryn smelled something sharp. Alcohol? She flinched when the girl's fingertips brushed her wound again and kicked wildly with her other foot. *"Don't touch me."*

She hit something soft. The girl squeaked, and liquid splashed over the grass. But before either of them could get another word in, someone from deeper within the camp called, "He's back!"

Meiryn snapped her head up at the sound of a flurry of tent flaps being torn open. Huntsmen flocked like birds. Voices—tired, annoyed, and excited—clashed in an incomprehensible murmur. Meiryn strained to catch a single word, but they were speaking in low tones.

"Who is it?" she asked. "Who's back?"

She wriggled in her prison, but the girl nearby hushed her. Desperation surged. Meiryn tossed her head until her blindfold slipped down around her neck.

The camp glowed with the orange haze of faint torchlight. Meiryn had a poor view from where she sat on the ground, but she craned her neck anyway. Her wrists protested when she leaned forward, trying to catch a glimpse of the excitement.

About a foot to her right sat a girl who couldn't have been older than thirteen years. Her eyes were big and doe-like, her hair woven into a braid that settled over one shoulder. She looked alarmed to see Meiryn's full face.

"Who's back?" Meiryn asked again.

The girl blinked rapidly. Her lips were parted, but she made no sound.

Meiryn groaned and turned her eyes back to the crowd. Her ears had deceived her earlier: only a handful of huntsmen had actually risen to greet the newcomer, and when Meiryn caught a glimpse of him, she froze.

He had to be fashioned from the night itself: clothed in black from head to foot, the only parts of his face visible behind his hooded cowl were his eyes—ice-blue, sharp and cold as a Hibern's breath. Hanging from his hips were identical short swords that looked far too refined to have been crafted by a village blacksmith. The blades glistened unnaturally, as if they were imbued with glass or some other material besides metal. Sitting in a neat line on his belt were at least five smaller throwing knives.

Meiryn searched for any sign that he was part of the Silver Order, but there was no insignia on his clothes. In fact, as far as she could tell, he wore no real armor. So, he either possessed none, or he was deadly enough not to need it.

Of the huntsmen who had gathered, Faun was the first to greet him. She reached out and clasped his forearm. Nodded stiffly. "I'm glad to see you again, Grey."

Meiryn's chest deflated. Dangerous as he looked, this man was not the Wolf King.

The man—Grey—returned Faun's gesture but skipped the pleasantries. His voice was the kind that demanded attention: full, deep, and, most notably, laced with a faint northern accent.

Northern... Highborn? No, that couldn't be—the huntsmen were already clinging to every word, so they clearly trusted him. "I hadn't anticipated being back so soon, but it was urgent."

"Too urgent for a crow?"

"And too dangerous in the hands of the wrong people," he added, "although, I'm sure news will spread soon enough." He blinked slowly against the firelight, and Meiryn could practically see the tension in his shoulders from her position.

A ripple of trepidation washed over the huntsmen. Faun seemed the only one brave enough to speak. "What did you see?"

"Something that should have been impossible." He sighed and reached up with a gloved hand, tugging down his cowl. He was younger than expected: he couldn't have been much older than Meiryn herself. The cowl had concealed intense features and a frown that she suspected was permanently etched into his face. "You wouldn't believe it if I'd sent a crow, and I doubt you'll believe it now."

"What," Faun repeated, crossing her arms, "did you see?"

Grey lifted a brow at her tone, but he said, as plainly as if he were observing a change in the wind's path, "Draconis was assaulted by dragons from the Nest. They were led by a black beast—one that summoned a storm into clear skies."

Though Meiryn had kept her silence to witness the commotion, her speechlessness now came from shock and disbelief. Her gaze became unfocused as her mind conjured images of a city under siege by some of the most terrifying creatures known to Ver Signia. One rogue dragon could cause mass devastation, as she knew firsthand—but an entire *fleet*?

Someone from the crowd broke the silence with a feeble protest. "What about the forces on the Nest?"

"I can only assume that the Order lost contact with them," Grey answered. "I wasn't keen on staying to find out what happened to the shipyard."

Meiryn went rigid. Without knowing what was happening on the Nest, there would be no way to anticipate the next attack. No way to determine how many Ver Signian lives were stranded out on that archipelago. If everyone had been killed, then the only forces that remained to defend the mainland were the survivors of this freak incident.

The huntsmen murmured with an air of uncertainty and disbelief that matched Meiryn's own.

A new, more outraged voice demanded, "What proof do you have? How do we know you aren't simply fear-mongering?"

Grey flicked his eyes upward before fixing the huntsman with a sneer. "You know what dragons are capable of, Rook. Is it really any surprise that they finally grew tired of being the ones forced to defend their territory?"

"I'd think the Order would at least be able to hold their ground," Faun interjected before the argument could grow hotter.

Grey grunted wordlessly and scratched at his jaw, lips thinning. His eyes were ringed by shadows, but he betrayed no other sign of fatigue. "This assault was different. They ravaged the Order's headquarters, but from what I could see, the Infernals and Hiberns came only to free their hatchlings from the Order. They left once they had their young back under their wings."

"And the storm dragon?" Faun pressed.

Grey looked at her as if to say, *What do you think?*

Faun swore. "If the Order captured a dragon like that, there's no telling what they could do. Even with their forces crippled, they've just secured an enormous amount of power..." She mumbled to herself, which only seemed to agitate the huntsmen further.

Grey cleared his throat. "There's more, but I think it's best if I talk with Nona about this. She might know..." He trailed off when the others shuffled. Tensing, he asked, "Where is she?"

Meiryn shrank against the stake, ignoring the way it prodded against her spine. No one dared to answer him, but another fire ignited within Faun's stare. She set her jaw and refolded her arms tightly over her chest. "Nona's dead."

Grey's shoulders dropped. His eyes dulled, and before anyone could do or say anything more, Faun pointed straight toward Meiryn. "You can ask *her* how it happened."

Meiryn's nostrils flared. The huntsmen cleared, giving Grey a direct view of her. She desperately wished she hadn't shaken off her blindfold.

"Elder," Grey said with chilling calmness, "get away from her."

Elder? Why was that name familiar?

The girl at Meiryn's side scrambled away, abandoning a small wooden bowl and a strip of cloth. It was with a sore twist of regret that Meiryn realized Elder had been trying to clean her wounds while the rest of the Guild slept.

Grey stalked toward her. Among the silent watchers, Meiryn spotted Lukas. She prayed he would see her, that he would step in and divert Grey's attention. But Lukas only scowled into the back of Grey's skull with a level of contempt that stemmed from some wound too deep for Meiryn to dissect.

She squirmed in place, tugging uselessly against her ropes and feeling her heart pound louder and louder as Grey drew near. His short swords reflected torchlight like beacons, and Meiryn fought the urge to grimace when the mixed scent of blood, leather, and steel filled her nose.

Grey crouched where Elder had been moments before. Meiryn found it impossible to hold eye contact for longer than a heartbeat. She examined his blades instead, taking note of the letter C engraved into each hilt.

How did a huntsman come to obtain such weapons, and what did that initial stand for?

Her questions scattered from her mind when Grey grazed a fingertip near the broken skin of her wound. "Did you kill Nona?"

Meiryn flinched. Her palms had gone clammy, and she was overcome by a humiliating stutter. "I— It wasn't me. I never... I'm not a killer."

Grey's expression did not change. Those eyes were as bright as sun-struck ice, yet deeper than the ocean and filled with more secrets than Meiryn would ever know. Sweat trickled down the back of her neck. When Grey suddenly stood, Meiryn jumped and leaned as far away as she could from the sword that faced her when he turned toward Faun.

"Why is she tied up?" he asked casually.

"She's a threat."

"As much threat as a mouse is to a cat." Grey scoffed. He clawed a hand through his black hair and rolled his neck, groaning when a few joints popped. "She's sunburned, dehydrated, and starved. But you have a good reason for keeping her alive, I'm sure."

Faun tapped a forefinger against her bicep. "If we let her go, she'll betray our location."

"She wouldn't make it half a mile on this leg," Grey said without missing a beat. "I'd be surprised if she makes it to the end of the week with both legs intact."

Meiryn fixed her eyes on Grey's weapons, but fear blotted out the shapes in front of her. Her body was shaking as if afflicted by a sudden chill. Her blood felt cold in her veins, and she only vaguely sensed when Grey looked down at her again.

"What were you doing in the forest?" he asked. His voice was patient and soft, but Meiryn did not let it lull her into comfort.

"My friend was taken by the Order," she managed. It had become a mantra these past couple days, a silently rehearsed speech reserved for the Wolf King's ears. She supposed that until she met with the Guild master, Grey would have to do. "They came for Nona, but they took Reina instead. I came here looking for help. I'm prepared to offer whatever I can in exchange. Anything you ask of me, I will do it."

Grey lifted one dark brow, gaze sharpening. "What good are you when you can't even stand on your own?"

A defiant part of Meiryn hardened, and her fingers curled

tightly behind her back. "Since I was dragged here, I haven't been allowed to stand. If I lose my leg, it's because no one has bothered to heal it."

Grey inclined his head ever so slightly. The blue of his irises was so pale it could have been silver, but a subtle warmth seemed to soften his gaze—just a fraction. Meiryn swore he was fighting back a faint grin. But he spoke with that imposing tone, loudly enough for his allies to hear. "You realize that if the Guild hadn't brought you here, you'd have been food for the wolves, yes? The huntsmen have done you a favor."

"Then let me repay it," Meiryn said. It was a ridiculous notion—repaying cruelty disguised as a favor with the promise of indefinite servitude—but begging for freedom had only earned derisive snickering, bargaining met with impartial shrugs. This was the last card in her hand. "Unbind me. Heal me, or let me tend to my wounds myself."

Grey leaned back, taking her in fully. He was silent for a long moment, and no one, not even Faun, interrupted his wordless evaluation. The huntsmen lingered, each seeming to hold their breath and wait for Grey to announce his judgment.

Meiryn studied him, too. Why would the huntsmen place so much weight on his opinion if he weren't some kind of leader to them? But if this man was the Wolf King, why would he risk his own safety to spy on the Order in Draconis? Why let Faun speak so brazenly to him? What king would tolerate that kind of undermining, especially in front of his other followers?

Perhaps a leader who saw his men as equals. One who respected them just as he commanded them.

Or maybe, Meiryn concluded when she searched beneath the stoniness of his stare, one who was just tired.

He unsheathed a knife from his belt and knelt at Meiryn's

side. Faun protested, then halted when Grey threw her a withering glare. Meiryn held her breath as he made quick work of unbinding her. A cool relief rushed to her wrists when the ropes fell away. She gave him a careful look as she brought her hands around to her front, rubbing the skin tentatively.

"Thank you," she mumbled.

Grey slid his knife back into place. He rose away from her, lifting his chin. "The Guild may yet have need of you, but do not mistake this freedom for acceptance. Regardless of your intentions, you were caught trespassing. You're a liability."

"Why free me if you think I can't be trusted?"

"Because if the Order is your enemy, then you're a potential ally to us." Grey nodded east, toward Draconis. "And because you said your friend was taken in Nona's place, yes? I have a theory—it's loose, but it's one that you might be able to confirm for me. Later, once you've settled in."

Confusion etched a frown on Meiryn's face, but Grey had already turned and left. Faun trailed after him, spewing indistinct protests that Grey merely ignored.

A slight figure shuffled into the edge of Meiryn's periphery, snagging her attention away from the other huntsmen. It was Elder, the young healer, waiting with her hands behind her back.

Elder met Meiryn's eyes briefly before looking down again. "I can take you to the healers if you want," she offered. "We can still save your leg."

Meiryn blinked. It hit her then. "You saw me in the woods. You alerted the huntsmen that I was trespassing."

There was no accusation or animosity in her voice, but Elder winced as if she had shouted. "I never wanted them to hurt you. I thought, once they saw you struggling, they might try to help, but Faun…"

"It's not your fault," Meiryn assured her. Elder was not the one who had strung Meiryn up in a tree, nor was it her hands that had dragged Meiryn back here. She thought she was doing good; Faun twisted those intentions to comply with her own thirst for revenge.

Meiryn glanced at her injury. Even without proper evaluation, she knew it was bad. Shame warmed her cheeks. "I'm sorry for lashing out earlier."

Elder managed a tentative smile. "You had a good reason to be scared. I should have announced myself." She fell quiet, then approached carefully, sinking down to Meiryn's level. She extended her right hand. "I'm Elder—in case you missed that."

Meiryn hesitated. Then, repeating the exchange she'd seen between Grey and Faun, she clasped Elder's forearm. Squeezed it once.

"I'm Meiryn."

———

Elder proved to be a proficient healer, young though she was. Her hands were light and careful, yet efficient and thorough. Despite the occasional spikes of pain as Elder washed her wound and sewed the cuts shut, Meiryn's breaths came easily and steadily.

The med tent was quiet. In the wake of Grey's return, Meiryn found herself in a suspended sort of peace—one that was comfortable enough that she stopped listening for signs of danger, yet fragile enough that she knew it could change at any moment. She lay on a makeshift cot—just a wooden board raised on some empty crates and covered by a thin white sheet—with her hands splayed out on her stomach. She watched shadows sway over the canvas roof while Elder worked by the light of a low-burning candle.

Meiryn caught a whiff of clean linen; she lifted her head from the cot to watch Elder wrap her leg carefully. The bandages were fashioned from a patchwork strip of spare cloths. Meiryn stared with furrowed brows.

Elder glanced at her sidelong. "These are clean, I promise."

Meiryn shook her head. "I'm not worried about that. There were huntsmen in West Glen," she recalled aloud. "Why rely on scraps when you have access to healers within the city?"

"Between all of us, we don't have much coin," Elder explained. She tugged the bandages tight, offering an apologetic look when Meiryn winced. "Sometimes, we'll send out our huntsmen to pose as sellswords, but that's not always reliable."

"No?" Meiryn would have thought mercenary work well-suited for huntsmen.

"The jobs that pay the best are usually posted by trappers. People who want to lure the Guild out of hiding," Elder added with a note of apprehension. She glanced about, as if one such trapper was lurking beyond the tent.

Meiryn let her head fall back again. It should have occurred to her earlier that, despite the rumors that painted an image of a ruthless and cutthroat Guild, the huntsmen would still have reason to avoid more densely populated areas. Their numbers were far fewer than she anticipated; sending out even a group of five would be a risk to the whole Guild.

And yet, Faun and Lukas had led an entire rescue mission for Nona. Surely they had to know that setting an Infernal loose in a woodland city would attract more unwanted attention than any mercenary job would. Why risk themselves like that? What, exactly, was Nona to them, that they'd throw her in front of the jaws of a fully matured dragon, only to scramble to snatch her out when things went south?

Meiryn's mind stilled at the sound of tiny pins clinking in a bowl. She watched Elder secure the bandages in place with expert care. Meiryn sighed and tapped her forefinger on the back of her opposite palm.

"I haven't pricked anyone in a full year," Elder said, somewhat stiffly. She drew her hands back into her lap and sat with a rigid spine. Her expression was one of slight indignation, as if she expected Meiryn to criticize her work, but Meiryn frowned and propped herself up on her elbows.

"I wasn't worried," she said earnestly. Elder's eyes narrowed, and Meiryn insisted, "You did a great job. You were more help to me than anyone else has been."

Elder looked like she was hiding a sheepish grin. She started to reply when someone ripped open the tent flap.

In marched a flustered, pink-faced woman who appeared to be in her late thirties. The instant she saw Meiryn and Elder, she huffed and planted her hands on her hips.

"What is this?" she demanded. "What do you think you're doing, wasting resources on a trespasser?" Flyaway hairs fell from a hastily wrapped knot of hair at the base of her skull. She was dressed in thin nightclothes, and if Meiryn had to guess, this woman had jumped out of bed mere moments ago.

Elder shrank back, dropping her head. "She was hurt—"

"Because of her own ignorance," the woman barked. "Our supplies are low enough without you expending them all on some girl who wandered into a trap."

Meiryn frowned. An old sense of protectiveness sharpened her tongue. "You're berating her for doing her job?"

The woman's face reddened. Her nostrils flared, like she couldn't believe that Meiryn had dared to speak. "Her job is to take care of huntsmen. *You* are not one of us."

Not that she wanted to be. Meiryn pushed herself upright. "I came here to offer whatever I can in exchange for the Guild's help. I can't hold up my end of the bargain if I'm injured."

"Then let this be your first task: starting tomorrow, you and Elder will both scour the woods to replenish the stores you indulged yourselves in so greedily."

Elder broke her silence. "But her leg—"

"You took well enough care of that tonight, didn't you?" the woman snapped. She glanced scornfully at the littering of supplies that Elder had run through. "If the girl is so eager to get to work, then we'd be remiss to stop her. And if you're really the healer you say you are, then she should be fine to walk by tomorrow, yes?"

Elder sagged. She mumbled a timid yet stubborn "Yes, Pyrrha."

"Good." Pyrrha gave another huff of breath and swiped the loose strands of hair back from her flushed face. "Now, clean this mess up. Your work starts early."

She spun on her heel and exited the tent, muttering in disgust—something about letting trespassers wander free.

Meiryn turned to Elder, who remained in a shrunken position until Pyrrha's heavy footsteps faded. She cleared her throat. "She's a pleasant woman."

She kept her tone light, trying to lift Elder's mood, but Elder braced her elbows on her knees and let her face fall against her palms. Voice muffled, Elder groaned, "She doesn't like anyone new. She only just got used to me as an apprentice. Now she'll hate me forever."

Instinct almost compelled Meiryn to sling an arm over Elder's shoulders, but she stifled the urge and clasped her hands in her lap. "You're a skilled healer, from what I've experienced. She'll forgive this."

"But now I'm…" Elder trailed off, and Meiryn couldn't help but interpret her silence as shame and regret.

"Stuck with me," Meiryn finished in a quiet voice.

The candle flame wavered, and it was another long moment before Elder peeked at Meiryn through her fingers. "It's not that I have anything against you. I just need Pyrrha to trust me."

"You're trying to become a full-fledged healer."

Elder nodded. "Pyrrha is our leader, kind of. She makes sure we know what we're doing before we operate on the huntsmen."

Meiryn gave her a lopsided grin. "Well, as your test subject, I can assure you that you know what you're doing."

"I know." A tentative smile drew the corners of Elder's mouth upward. She tucked her hair behind her ears and rested her chin on a fist. "I've been watching the healers since the moment the Guild brought me here."

"How did you come here?"

"Dragons."

That was all the explanation Elder needed to give. A feeling of kinship pulled at Meiryn's heartstrings. "Me, too. But the Guild never found me."

Meiryn had been displaced after a rogue Infernal reduced her village to blackened remains. She was just one among hundreds of children placed into an overfilled orphanage. She wondered how different things would be now if the huntsmen had lifted her from those ashes instead. Then she realized that she was grateful her path had led her to Reina.

Sympathy softened Elder's face. "I was lucky, I guess."

Meiryn gave her a strained smile. She could not yet determine if she agreed.

XII. REINA

Reina's body felt heavy. She couldn't pry herself from the ground without facing some aspect of death; even here, on the threshold of the open tomb, bugs crawled around her hands and knees, and she had the revolting mental image of worms slithering in and out of every orifice in her body.

It was Raiko's touch on her back—barely a graze of his fingertip—that brought her to her feet again. Her head felt light. She drew her collar over the lower half of her face and refrained from gripping Raiko's hand like a scared child.

"Come," he muttered.

Reina would rather have gotten lost in the tunnels at their back, but she followed him, mute, into the tomb.

It was worse here, where every turn exposed some new horror. Jaws hung slack, revealing rows of blackened teeth and lolling tongues. Tufts of hair tangled with thick cobwebs— some of which stretched from floor to ceiling. Flies swarmed each stack of corpses, and their incessant buzzing became white noise mingling with the snapping embers that jumped from the torches. On top of one of the pyramids was a more recently dead body; someone had drawn two Xs over the woman's eyes, and her lips were carved open in a permanent smile. Her left arm, hanging freely over the bodies beneath her, bore a single word: *DESERTER*.

"Rhysanthe," Korris murmured.

Reina turned, but Korris was addressing his captain. From the two swords that hung from his hips, he unfastened the one at his right. Aaron reached out slowly and took the proffered weapon—it was his fire sword, miraculously undamaged.

Aaron's throat bobbed before he asked hoarsely, "Where did you fall? Were you injured?"

"Hard to determine the distance," Korris answered in an equally hushed tone, "but it took me a couple hours to find the Crane twins. Fortunately, no one sustained anything worse than a few scratches and bruises. We've been wandering around, looking for the rest of you."

"And you found this tomb instead," Raiko said. His fists were white, his face a similar shade.

"This is no tomb," Iliana breathed. She sidled close to Evren, her expression deeply disturbed as she searched for some-place to set her gaze that wasn't touched by death. Finding nothing, she sighed and closed her eyes. "This is a pit that the Order scraped out of the earth to make us believe that they've reserved a place of honor for our bodies to rest after we've died."

Evren pulled his sister close into his side. She shuddered on an exhale and leaned her head against his shoulder.

Reina scanned the agents' faces. Each of them looked just as dismayed and shocked as Reina felt, but she knew the weight of this truth sank deeper for them than it ever would for her.

They promised their lives to the Silver Order. They took vows of allegiance and swore to protect Ver Signia and her people for as long as their hearts still beat. And as Fourth Division agents, this is what awaited them after death: an unmarked grave, a bed of bones and skin, a final resting place less dignified than Ver Signia's commoners.

Reina drew in a thin breath. "What exactly is the Fourth Division?"

"A conglomeration of agents who belong to no cadre," Evren said when no one else spoke up. "Usually, they're the acolytes who failed their training but who know too much to be freed from the Order's command. Fourth Division agents are prohibited from setting foot on the Nest. We are janitors within the compound; messengers who never wield a sword."

"Errand boys," Korris said in a clipped voice.

Reina frowned. "Surely not all of you failed your training." She had seen them fight and felt firsthand the brunt of their strength.

Evren shook his head. "In our case"—he motioned to himself and Iliana—"our names are too closely associated with dishonor and scandal. It never mattered how high we ranked in our cohorts. Our path was set in stone before we were even fitted for our acolyte uniforms."

"Then what's wrong with the rest of you?"

Tension stretched taut in the air. Korris merely gestured to his blind eye; Raiko adopted a look of reproach and resentment.

Aaron pinned Reina with a dark stare. "You've overstepped your bounds," he hissed. Even without summoning the flames from his sword, Reina could practically imagine the embers sparking off the blade. Aaron had never looked so enraged, but a stiff guard thickened his voice. "I've tolerated enough of your rambling. The next time you ask such a question, I'll carve that tongue right out of your head."

Reina made a face but thought it wise not to respond.

Aaron addressed his cadre. "Did any of you find a way out?"

Korris, Evren, and Iliana shook their heads in unison. Aaron's features hardened. He exhaled and scanned their surroundings. "We came from separate paths that led us all here. The only way forward must be through there."

He pointed his sword in the direction of yet another dark tunnel and started walking. Dreading the thought of wandering for several more hours until they happened across an exit yet desperate to escape the tomb, Reina filed after the cadre.

Korris and Raiko lit the path with their torches, and Aaron walked just ahead of them. The smell of decay eventually faded, and Reina let her shirt fall away from her face.

She never imagined that the crypts would stretch as far as they did. Every few meters, she smoothed her palm over the walls, as if feeling for some weak spot that might reveal a secret passageway.

No such luck.

After some time wandering, Aaron finally called for rest. He groaned stiffly when he slid to the ground, stretching his legs out in front of him. The rest of the cadre readily followed suit. Weak torchlight cast shadows that darkened the fatigue beneath their eyes.

"There has to be another exit somewhere, even if it lets out past Draconis," Aaron said.

"Why would they need to go that far, though?" Reina pressed. "These crypts were built to house the fallen agents of the Order, right? What would be the point in creating such a confusing system of tunnels? Wouldn't there be a map, or—"

"Athira, I don't know." Aaron sounded exasperated, too tired to demand that she keep her mouth shut. He placed his sword beside him and massaged the back of his neck with a slight grimace. Eyes closed halfway, he said, "Just rest for now. We'll continue after we've had some sleep."

But sleep, it seemed, evaded everyone, and after a few hopeless, restless hours, Aaron ordered them to carry onward.

It was impossible to tell how much time had passed. Exhausted, dehydrated, and starving, the cadre was covering less ground each hour. The light from Raiko and Korris's torches waned to pulsing embers; their feet scraped the ground; their spirits had dropped into despair.

Just when Reina sank into acceptance that this was their fate, a disembodied voice slithered into her ear. *"Find me."*

She swore and clapped her hands over her ears, jerking so violently that she crashed against the wall.

The agents whirled. Aaron approached with more urgency than he had shown since the dragon attack. "What happened?"

Reina panted. Her heart drummed against her rib cage, and it took every ounce of effort to muster a clear voice. "You didn't hear that?"

Aaron made a disgusted noise. "Dammit. Now you're going delirious."

"I'm not," she protested. "I heard a voice—here." She pressed her scarred palm against the tunnel and strained to hear that hissing whisper again.

The others looked at her like she was mad. Aaron had already dismissed her and was marching back to the front of the line. "Let's go."

"Aaron—" Reina jogged to catch up to him. "For once in your life, will you just listen to me?" She snagged the crook of his elbow, and he retaliated with a forceful shove.

Reina fell through the wall.

Raiko made a wild grab for her, shouting her name. Their fingertips just barely touched before she fell out of reach.

Darkness swallowed her as she tumbled down a steep incline. Stones clattered about, showering her like hail and knocking into her limbs. With a harsh grunt, she landed on her back. The impact left her winded. For a moment, she was blind. But when she turned her head toward the sound of the cadre's alarmed voices, she found the tiny glowing embers of the torches.

"Athira?" It was Raiko—calling like he was worried. Like he cared about what happened to her. He swore heavily when Reina did not respond.

"Get back, before you fall in, too." Aaron spat his words like venom. "If she's dead, then that's one less thing to worry about."

"She's your sister," Evren snapped.

"She is nothing to me."

Reina, halfway propped up on her elbows, froze. Anger burned away the hurt in her chest, and she shoved herself up to shout some equally hateful thing when her fingers grazed something smooth. She paused.

There, lying undisturbed amidst dust and dirt, was a small pendant attached to a thin leather cord. It was no larger than the size of a gold coin and shaped vaguely like an upside-down fishhook, but the outer curve split into three graceful arcs, like long wing bones. At the center was a three-ringed spiral, forming the impression of a dragon's barreled chest.

She slid the cord around her neck and dropped the pendant beneath her shirt. The instant it touched the skin over her heart, a rush of whispers, like wind howling through a tunnel, flooded her ears. A thousand voices overlapped one another.

Their words were indecipherable but paralyzed her all the same. It was as if she'd been plunged beneath the ice of a frozen lake.

"Athira!" Raiko shouted again. "Answer me, dammit."

Reina jumped and scrambled to her feet—too quickly. Her vision swam, and she knelt until her head stopped spinning. Breathily she called, "I'm fine."

Members of the cadre sighed in relief; Aaron was not one of them.

Raiko's voice sounded fuller now, as if he were leaning down into the cavern. "Can you see anything?"

"Is that a serious question?" Reina laughed humorlessly. Still, she scanned her surroundings.

It was eerily reminiscent of the space she'd wandered through in her dream, but this lacked the airiness of another realm. This was damp and cold, and as her eyes adjusted, her mouth fell open.

Stretching before her was a river illuminated by a faint, incandescent glow. Narrow-bodied cavefish swam aimlessly, unaware of the interloper that had fallen into their midst. A smattering of jagged stalactites reached down from the ceiling toward the water's rippling surface, and Reina peered farther into the distance. Her chest swelled.

Moonlight. An exit.

"Aaron," she called, fighting to keep her voice from wobbling in relief, "you need to come down here."

He snorted. "So we can all be trapped gods-know-where with you? Not a chance." He started to turn away, and Reina's patience shattered.

"Look at your men, Aaron. They are *dying,* and you would rather cling to your pride than consider the fact that there might be an exit down here. Listen." She splashed her hand through cool water to prove her point, and something groaned.

Reina froze. She shushed Aaron when he tried to speak, and as the echoes chased each other, she spotted movement to her left.

Like a butterfly breaking through its cocoon, one of the stalactites stretched open. A pair of gleaming red eyes blinked slowly. Rows of pointed white fangs revealed themselves through a wide yawn. A string of hot saliva dipped into the river, casting ripples over the water.

With a horrible sinking feeling, Reina peered again through the darkness.

Those weren't stalactites. None of them were.

They were cave dragons—a whole nest of them rising from their slumber.

Constricting her breath to shallow pants, Reina inched backward, feet sliding against the hill she had fallen down. Her palms were slick on the rocks.

"Athira?" It was Iliana this time, breaking the silence that would have kept Reina safe. "What is it? What are you seeing?"

She lost the courage to speak, but she didn't need to, because not a second after Iliana's last word, the dragon nearest Reina flared its wings and released a high-pitched, furious screech. The entire colony answered the cry. A swarm of leathery wings fluttered in unison. Hundreds of ruby eyes popped open, and the dragons erupted into flight.

The agents shouted in alarm. Reina ducked her head as a cave dragon swooped low, talons slicing through strands of her hair.

Through the noise, she heard Aaron arguing with his cadre. "Stay back!" he ordered. "You go down there, and you're dead."

Reina scrambled for cover. The colony was waking all at once. Their beating wings and snapping fangs were somehow more terrifying than the storm dragon that assaulted Draconis. She yelped when a thick rope of a tail smacked her face-first into the river.

"Raiko!" Aaron suddenly shouted.

Reina yanked her head up and spat water from her lips. Pebbles rained down, peppering the river and bouncing across her cheeks. Reina whirled.

Raiko was sliding down the hill, wielding nothing but a burned-out torch. He landed squarely behind her and, with a massive sweep of his arm, bludgeoned the skull of the nearest dragon. Bones cracked, and the dragon shrieked in agony, staggering away.

A set of unhinged jaws snapped too near for comfort. Reina flinched, but Raiko moved as swiftly as the wind. He delivered another blow to the next opponent. His strike was hard enough to fracture the torch, and he slammed the exposed splinters into the dragon's neck. Hot blood splattered against Reina's skin and dispersed in a thick cloud underwater. Panting, Raiko ripped away the broken piece of the torch and hurled it at the first thing that moved. He then dropped down, seized Reina by the arm, and hauled her out of the river.

"Stay by me," he commanded, his breath hot on her ear.

Reina opened her mouth, but the sound of boots skidding along the ground interrupted her. One by one, Iliana, Evren, and Korris landed around them. Reina stared, speechless.

They had defied Aaron's orders. To *defend* her.

"I hope you have a plan," Korris said to Raiko, metal whining as he unsheathed his blade. A look of delight brightened his eyes as he faced the oncoming horde.

Raiko shook his head once, ducking beneath the talons of an oncoming dragon. It soared over him and crashed into the wall. "Just hold them off until we find an exit."

"There," Reina directed, jutting a hand toward the silver rays of hope glistening at the end of the cave. "The river's flowing from outside."

"Through the dragon den," Evren said flatly, flipping his blades in his hands. "Of course."

Reina steeled her nerves as their enemies closed in. The noise was deafening, her clothes were glued against her like a second skin, and she jumped at every moving shadow. She stayed close to the agents as they battled along the river. Her hands were balled tightly, as if she could strike something down with her bare fists. She flinched away from what sounded like a miniature cannon firing, but it was just Iliana's whip-sword piercing through the heart of a dragon that hovered a meter away.

Iliana retracted her blade in time to spin out of another enemy's path. She seized the momentum and thrust her sword hilt-deep into the dragon's throat. A wave of water crashed over the shore as the beast toppled into the river.

Without missing a beat, Iliana tossed wet strands of hair away from her face and aimed her sword at the next dragon. Wherever she turned, Evren was there to face the opponent at her back. Nearby, Raiko took the tails of two dragonlings in each fist and hauled them toward Korris's sword. Blood sprayed. Their squeals of agony agitated the colony, but the agents faced the onslaught with violent and lethal counter-attacks.

Reina gaped. They were unfazed, unflinching—all of them.

The cadre moved with one mind, cutting through the den

like a star falling through black skies. Dragons crumpled at their feet and slipped, lifeless or wounded, beneath restless waters. Wings ripped like curtains; heads toppled from long necks. Once, an injured dragonling slithered up to Reina through the water, and in a moment of sheer panic, she kicked out hard enough to dislocate its jaw. It slunk away, wailing and tossing its head.

Blood roared through Reina's veins. Her hands twitched as she squinted toward the exit, trying to gauge the distance, when the sounds of clashing steel and hissing dragons dropped to a muffled drone.

You could end this fight now, a voice whispered in the sudden stillness. It was not the storm dragon; this was her own voice, but colder, eerier—like an embodiment of all her darkest temptations. *This power is yours. All you need to do is seize it.*

Reina grimaced and squeezed her eyes shut. That frenetic energy that throttled her in Draconis now writhed just beneath her skin. Her palms grew warmer, clammier. She had to keep them from shaking.

Give in to what calls you. Who here could stop you?

A deep growl shook the borders of her mind. She had the vague sensation of being jostled around.

"Rhysanthe!" Korris bellowed. His voice shattered her trance. Fear shot through her, but Korris was glaring beyond the fight. Reina followed his stare.

Aaron stood in the archway. Motionless. Watching.

Bastard.

"Move!" Raiko's frantic shout barely registered in her mind before he caged his arms around her and spun her out of harm's way. She rolled a few feet further, shoving herself up just as a dragon pounced.

Raiko grabbed a sharp stone off the ground and thrust his makeshift weapon over his head just as the cave dragon snapped its jaws. The jagged edges impaled the roof of its mouth. Blood geysered from the wounds, and the dragon reared its head in agony. Raiko lost his grip on the stone and flew backward, landing somewhere behind Reina with a breathless grunt. She barely had time to react before another dragon descended upon him. His pained cry split the air.

A blinding pillar of flame erupted from the archway. Reina winced as orange light from Aaron's sword spilled into the cavern. Her face slackened when she watched Raiko's body rise from the ground, hooked on a cave dragon's talons. Pain twisted his features tight, but he pounded his fists against its legs relentlessly.

In a voice that shook with all the fear in the world, Aaron cried, "Help him!"

Korris was facing a pair of dragons by himself; Iliana and Evren fought back-to-back, covering each other's blind spots. Evren feinted left but was caught by the dragon's sweeping tail. Iliana shouted in alarm as Evren fell. His daggers clattered right in front of Reina.

Without thinking, she snatched them up and turned on the dragon that had its claws hooked in Raiko's chest. She threw herself forward, and the dragon's back arched as the daggers sank all the way to the hilts. Raiko gasped as he hit the ground. Hands curling around her borrowed blades, Reina dragged them down, carving long, deep lines through soft, leathery skin. Blood spurted over her face and down her front, and she cried out as the dragon bucked her off its back.

Fire blazed when Aaron finally joined the battle. His shadow covered Raiko like a blanket, and he yelled wildly, slashing at anything that approached. The dragons recoiled from the searing heat. Their cries of rage and hunger turned to shrieks of fear.

Amidst the flurry of wings and blood, Reina found Raiko struggling to sit upright. He tore his ruined armor away, panting heavily, and his eyes met Reina's. His face was losing its warmth and color.

Reina crawled under Aaron's swinging blade and urged Raiko to lay flat. Still winded, she breathed, "You saved me."

Before he could respond, Korris shouted, "They'll lead us to an exit. Follow them!" He hacked through another dragon's thigh and flung blood across the wall as he pointed to their escape.

Reina caught blessed glimpses of moonlight. Clearer air beckoned her forward.

But the battle was not over. Aaron's blade sang in harmony with Korris's. Plumes of smoke billowed from the hilt of his sword, and embers jumped from white-hot steel each time his unwieldy attacks landed true. Blood sizzled on his blade. He brandished his flaming weapon against the beady eyes of every dragon that strayed too near. Shadows and light bounced erratically across the walls, and the dragons that once tried to tear him apart now scrambled to flee the sting of his sword.

Reina watched with an open mouth. If this was how hard Aaron fought, why in six hells would the Order drop him into the Fourth Division?

The question abandoned her when Aaron spun in her direction. "Get out of the way," he snarled. He dropped to one knee at Raiko's side and pushed an arm beneath his shoulder blades. Raiko's face whitened as Aaron helped him to his feet.

Reina forced herself forward. She tried not to dwell on the

sticky warmth that oozed against her skin when she slid an arm around Raiko's waist to keep him upright. Aaron's eyes flashed.

"You can thank me later," she spat before he could get a word in.

For once, Aaron said nothing.

Raiko mumbled breathily in Mal'dhi, his voice aimed toward Aaron. Reina couldn't translate, but Aaron barked out a rough command. "Save your breath. All that matters is getting you to safety."

Raiko only grunted, and Reina winced as his weight ground against her shoulder.

Korris and Iliana managed the last of the dragons, and Evren doubled back to retrieve his daggers. As he wiggled the blades loose from the dragon's motionless body, Evren glanced at Reina. Suspicion chased a fleeting, awestruck expression, but neither mentioned what she had done.

The dragon colony had cleared the tunnel. Their distant cries sent chills down Reina's spine, but the sound of Raiko's heavy breathing kept her grounded. She and Aaron hobbled unevenly as they balanced Raiko's weight between them. They fell behind the others, but Reina could see the moon's silver reflection now; could feel the cooler night air.

Just a little farther.

Reina and Aaron supported nearly all of Raiko's weight. His feet scraped along the ground, stumbling every half-step, and his head lolled against Reina's shoulder. She felt his sweat dampening his shirt. Even his back was drenched in a wet heat.

"Is it too soon to thank you?" he rasped with an audible, grim smile.

Reina blinked rapidly. "What—"

She yelped, and Aaron swore as Raiko's legs suddenly buckled. Aaron's sword clattered at his feet as he struggled to hold Raiko with both hands. Reina's arms were burning, and she could feel her own strength failing as quickly as Aaron's.

"Don't let him fall," Aaron urged. Had his voice just broken?

Reina shook her head and willed him to pull himself together. Now was not the time for desperation and worry. "I won't."

"Aaron?" Iliana had gone ahead with the others, but her call reverberated through the last leg of the tunnel. She sounded tired but still alert. "Where are you?"

"Back here," Aaron shouted. "Raiko's unconscious. I need —" He cut himself short, then blurted, "We can't carry him."

The sound of scuffling feet approached, and Iliana appeared again, Evren close to her side.

"Korris," Aaron gasped, glancing between the two. "Where—"

"He's scouting the area," Evren interrupted, already moving to take Reina's place. He bolstered Raiko's limp weight with only the slightest grimace. "We're not in Ver Signia."

Reina's ears pricked as Iliana pulled her back. "How do you know?"

"You'll know," was all Evren offered. He and Aaron carried Raiko by the shoulders and feet. Raiko's arm swung limply, and Reina swallowed a stone of guilt.

"What happened?" Iliana asked.

Reina grappled for words. In her mind's eye, she saw the dragon's claws lashing out for her. She felt its hot, wet breath. She heard Raiko screaming again, and all she could manage was a feeble "He pushed me out of the way."

Iliana nodded. "And then you saved him from that dragon."

"I didn't know what I was doing," Reina stammered. Her hands twitched at the helpless speculation that she could have done more. "He was in danger, and I just…"

It was an odd, somewhat awkward display of comfort when Iliana placed a light hand on Reina's shoulder. Her voice softened. "He's not dead yet, thanks to you. Now, come. Korris found our exit; we can assess our wounds properly when we're outside."

"The dragons—"

"Gone. Korris made sure of that."

Reina nodded tensely and followed Iliana on weak legs. Were it not for the whisper of fresh air that reached her nostrils, Reina would have submitted herself to another night beneath the earth. But when she saw vines hanging down from the mouth of the cave, her shoulders sagged with relief.

Clear water trickled from a wider bend in the river. Reina dipped her hands in, relishing the coolness that washed away the dragon blood. She planted her hands in the grass and tilted her head back. Stretching above them was a clear black canvas dotted with serene starlight, and in the distance, outlined by a thin silver sheen, were towering silhouettes of sky-scraping mountain peaks.

They had reached the Dragon's Spine, halfway between Ver Signia and Ashuma.

Dragon territory.

Reina dropped her head in her hands and trembled from sobs she barely held back.

A pair of heavy footsteps ambled close. "Rhysanthe," Korris murmured. When she didn't acknowledge him, he said, "Athira. Look at me. Are you alright?" He stooped at her side, his knee grazing hers.

She lifted her head. "Raiko," she said hoarsely. "He's hurt. He needs help right now, not me."

Korris stared at her with widened eyes. "You're covered in blood."

"Not mine," she managed. None of it was hers—all of it belonged to the dragon she slayed. It still rocked her, like she had murdered a person instead.

Korris nodded in understanding. "Your first kill is always your hardest."

Reina frowned. Before either of them could say anything more, Aaron called sharply, "Make room!"

Korris jumped back. He joined his companions as they slowly stretched Raiko out on his back and stripped away his ruined shirt. They crowded around him, speaking in hushed tones, and Reina stayed back, grateful she couldn't see the severity of his wounds. She wasn't sure she could stomach it after everything else that happened.

Iliana's voice cut through their anxious chatter. "We're too exposed here."

"He needs help *now*," Aaron insisted.

Iliana flicked her gaze toward Korris. "How much have you scouted?"

Korris only shook his head, and Evren piped up, "I'll help him clear the area. You just focus on helping him." He jerked his chin toward Raiko, whose face was a deathly shade of white beneath the full moon. "Is there anything you need us to look out for? Any herbs?"

Iliana murmured tensely, "I don't know what's out here. I'm just going to have to work with what I have for now. But what we all need is clean water. Food. See what you can find—

just make sure nothing else is waiting out there. And Evren," she added as he turned away, "be safe."

Evren's breath left him in a heavy exhale. The blue of his eyes seemed greyer now, dulled with exhaustion. "I will." Finally, he flicked his gaze toward Reina, then to the daggers in his hands, then back to her. His lips parted, but when Iliana shooed them away, he left promptly with Korris.

At Raiko's side, Aaron was teetering on the edge of panic. Deep lines of worry etched his brow. He chewed his lower lip, gaze roving over every gaping wound. He hadn't even glanced at Reina since making it out of the tunnel. His hands twitched at his sides, as if holding himself back from seizing Raiko by the shoulders and shaking him awake.

"You can save him, right?" he pressed.

Iliana gave him a firm look. "I will do everything I can, Aaron. You know that."

"I can't..." He paused, throat bobbing. Hoarsely, he whispered, "We need him."

Iliana already seemed to have blocked Aaron out of her mind. She worked with quiet fervor, hands ever restless. Reina leaned forward to offer her assistance, but Aaron shoved her back.

"Aaron—"

"Haven't you done enough already?" he interrupted, spit flying from his lips.

Wracked with guilt, Reina stammered, "I just wanted to help."

Aaron did not respond, just blocked her view of Raiko. And so Reina watched, mute, as Iliana worked and Aaron fussed. She saw the thin, quivering line of Aaron's mouth. Heard every sharp intake of breath, every shuddering exhale.

His anxiety was palpable, and when he reached out and brushed a damp lock of hair from Raiko's face, the realization struck like lightning.

Of course. *Of course.*

Suddenly, Aaron's abrasive behavior made so much more sense. He trusted Raiko to hold her captive—maybe even hoped that Raiko might learn to hate Reina just as much as Aaron did.

But Raiko had defied Aaron's expectations and wishes. He'd dragged Reina to the Order's base, thrown himself into danger for her sake. It drove Aaron mad, but the second Raiko was hurt, he forgot his anger. And now she knew it wasn't because he chose to disregard everything that brought them to this point, or even to ignore her out of some unspeakable hatred.

It was because he loved Raiko.

XIII. MEIRYN

AT THE BREAK OF DAWN, Pyrrha came marching into the med tent to shake Meiryn out of the first restful sleep she'd had in days.

"Get up," Pyrrha snapped. When Meiryn groaned and rolled away, Pyrrha clicked her tongue. "Are you as lazy as you are useless? I said get up. Elder's already awake—are you going to let a thirteen-year-old girl wander through these woods on her own?"

Elder was raised in these woods. She doesn't need my help.

Even so, Meiryn had made a deal with the huntsmen. If she wanted any chance of meeting with the Wolf King, she couldn't back out on her word at the first demand that was made of her.

A hiss of pain slipped through her teeth when she placed weight on her right leg. She could feel Pyrrha watching her with a critical eye as she slipped her ruined boot over Elder's carefully wrapped bandages.

Meiryn followed Pyrrha and beheld the camp for the first time in daylight.

Patchwork tents fashioned from burlap and canvas crowded

together in formless masses; barrels and crates of weapons, clothes, food, and other supplies were stockpiled and shoved away in a shady corner; between a few pairs of trees, hammocks swung precariously beneath the weight of waking huntsmen. Limited resources forced two to three huntsmen to share one tent, but a lucky few—notably Faun and Grey—enjoyed their own private spaces.

From a distance, one could assume that it was a village, but the two rugged wagons parked side by side at the furthest corner suggested that the Guild stayed ready to flee at a moment's notice.

As the huntsmen started their daily tasks, Meiryn scanned the milling crowd. She spotted Lukas just as he emerged from his shared tent, and she waved a hand in greeting. "Lukas!" she called.

He froze in his tracks. A few huntsmen heard her call and turned. Lukas blanched when he saw everyone staring at him, and he darted out of sight.

Meiryn's hand fell. She stared after him until Pyrrha shifted into sight. "Are you going to stand there all morning? Get moving!"

Pyrrha reminded Meiryn of the caretakers in the orphanage: brusque, impatient, curt.

Elder was waiting for them at the edge of camp. Resting on her shoulders were two satchels, but upon Meiryn's approach, she handed her one. "It's for the herbs we're gathering," she told her. She dropped her gaze. "How's the leg?"

Meiryn tested her weight on her right side. Her eye twitched in an involuntary grimace. "It's alright."

Elder gave her a sympathetic smile.

"There will be no aimless wandering today," Pyrrha

declared, arms crossed over her chest. "I don't want to see either of your faces until lunchtime, and by then, I expect those bags to be heaping full."

Meiryn said nothing, but Elder muttered, "Nothing will grow back if we pick that much."

Pyrrha pinned her beneath her signature glare. "I trust you to use common sense. The forest is bountiful. Take what we need, nothing more. But don't even think about skimping out on the water root. I know you know how quickly that stuff grows back."

Elder tilted her head back and groaned.

Pyrrha ignored her. "When you return, I'll have a new assignment for you."

Meiryn dreaded the notion of being on her feet all day, but she didn't have the liberty of protesting. She followed Elder, storing the image of Lukas turning away beneath a heap of other things she'd rather forget.

Shadows shrouded the forest. The path was invisible to Meiryn's eye, but Elder led the way with a certainty that implied she had walked this trail many times before. With her injury, it was a struggle for Meiryn to keep up. She was keenly aware of how many twigs snapped beneath her feet; how her body odor reeked amidst the crisp woodland air; how easily she could lose Elder if she so much as glanced away.

But the fear of being stalked by wild animals kept her in line with Elder, who seemed wholly unconcerned with their surroundings. Meiryn noted the brightness in her eyes, the way she stroked the plants that waved precariously into their path.

"We're nearly there," Elder said, tossing Meiryn a little encouraging smile.

Meiryn suppressed a groan. She thought *there* was *every-*

where. Her leg was beginning to trouble her, but a stubborn pride kept her from asking Elder to slow down. She scanned the shrubs around them, wincing when something sharp pricked her arm.

"These are just ferns," Elder said, grazing a leafy shape with her fingertip. "What we're looking for can't grow in such close quarters."

It made sense, but Meiryn lingered back when the treetops closed in. Rays of light were snuffed out by thick, hot shadows that trapped the summer heat. They had reached the everdark of the forest—the place in all the bards' tales where no light ever graced the earth.

Elder walked right in.

Meiryn blinked, feeling sweat roll down the side of her neck. She tightened her fist around the strap of her bag and called Elder's name just before she disappeared into the shade.

Elder stopped. She seemed not to have noticed Meiryn falling behind, and she retraced her steps, a curious look on her face. "Are you afraid?"

"I'm coming," Meiryn insisted. She shifted her weight on uneasy feet, feeling silly in the face of Elder's fearlessness. "I just..."

Elder looked over her shoulder, deliberating in silence, then faced Meiryn again. Not unkindly, she suggested, "Why don't you hang back, then? I can gather the nightshade and honey poppies myself."

Meiryn felt a pang of guilt. "We were supposed to do this job together."

And if Pyrrha finds out that we didn't, will the Guild consider that a failure? What will they do to me?

"You can get the water root," Elder said. She pointed in the opposite direction, where the light still broke through the tree-tops. "There's a stream about ten minutes that way that branches off the border river. You know how to harvest it, right?"

Meiryn just clutched her satchel tighter.

An eager smile graced Elder's lips She dove into an excited explanation. "Water root is easy to spot. It looks like that fluffy wild grass that grows on the plains—except it thrives in water." She swayed her arms to mimic the fluidity of the plant's body. "You can use the harvesting knife in your bag to dig up the streambed, or your hands, but just be careful not to cut any of the plant. It's useless if it's not completely intact."

Cut the plant from its bed. Don't harm the roots. It was simple enough in theory, but fifteen minutes later—Meiryn's limp slowed her down—she realized why Elder had dragged her feet when Pyrrha ordered water root.

The plant grew in thick, short bunches. The tops of each blade of grass barely breached the water's surface, and dozens of tiny freshwater fish had already made it their home.

Meiryn set her bag down and tugged her shoes off. She rolled her pants up to her knees, blinking against the light that glistened off the water's face. She dug the knife out from her bag and waded into the shallow waters.

A refreshing coolness flooded through her. Meiryn braced herself when the water seeped through the bandages, but it was a welcome respite from the summer heat. She stood there for a moment, eyes half-shut.

It was almost peaceful. Almost relaxing.

But the looming presence of the Guild within these woods kept her senses alert. At any moment, someone might find her here and decide to eliminate her before she could become the threat they believed her to be.

The thought alone was enough to snap her back to the task at hand. She bent at the waist, getting as close to the water root as she could, but as she started hacking away at the streambed, fish scrambling around her haphazard knife, she realized that there was no practical way to harvest the plant without dousing her entire self in the process.

Her work was just as Elder described: messy. The once-clear waters grew clouded as Meiryn slashed through dirt and sediments. Despite the refreshment of the stream, Meiryn was sweating just to unearth the entire root of the plant—which seemed absurdly long. She was soaking wet on her hands and knees, completely unaware of the approaching footsteps until a sneering voice called, "Having fun, princess?"

Meiryn whirled, flinching when a lock of wet hair slapped her cheek. Faun stood at the head of a small patrol. Behind her were two other huntsmen Meiryn didn't recognize, and lingering behind the three of them was Lukas. He refused to look at her.

Faun tilted her head, chin high. Shadows masked the top half of her face, and her teeth glinted like fangs when she threw Meiryn a cruel smile. "All that water can't wash the blood off your hands, you know."

Her fellow huntsmen glared at Meiryn. She saw it in their eyes: they thought her a murderer.

Meiryn pushed herself up into a kneeling position, knife dripping in her hand. "I never killed anyone," she said defiantly.

Faun barked a laugh. "So you're a trespasser *and* a liar. What else can you do?"

Meiryn didn't even blink. She had dealt with plenty of

bullies in the orphanage; Faun and her posse were no different. "I came to find the Guild. To seek the help of the Wolf King—not you."

The huntsmen muttered amongst themselves. A few of them rolled their eyes. Behind them, Lukas rubbed his arm and turned away.

Faun curled her lip. "And why in six hells do you think he would help you?"

"I thought the Hunters Guild was meant to help people," Meiryn pressed. She could feel her face growing hot now. "Or is that just a slogan you use to try and garner support for your little band of rogues?"

"This 'band of rogues' is the only reason the Order hasn't enlisted the entire kingdom into their deranged dragon campaign. We keep the people safe."

"Right," Meiryn scoffed, "and sending one of your own to set an Infernal loose was safe. I see how well that worked out for you."

Redness crept up Faun's throat, then burned brightly in her cheeks. She dropped her chin so that her anger shone beneath the glaring sun, then marched forward and swung her leg. A pile of carefully stacked water root tumbled into the stream.

Lukas spun, uttering Faun's name, but she jutted an arm out, fixing a loathsome glare on Meiryn.

"You are so entitled," Faun snarled. "You would rather grovel at the feet of your enemies and strike stupid bargains that you'll never fulfill instead of face the fact that you fucked up. *You're* the one who kept me from reaching Nona in time. *You're* the one who lost her own friend to the Order. *You're* the one who ran into my snare and injured herself. You just want to blame me for all your problems because you're scared, but you're equally at fault for everything that happened."

Meiryn ignored the water root that drifted around her. The stream rippled as she quaked on her knees. Her vision tunneled until all she saw was Faun's reddening face.

"I made a mistake," Meiryn admitted, hating herself even though she knew she spoke the truth. "But I'm doing everything I can to rectify the situation. What are you doing, other than taking your anger out on me? What more could you do that I haven't already suffered? The cadre that took Reina is the same one that killed Nona, but I don't see you chasing them down."

Faun curled a white fist around the leather strap of her quiver. "I'm not going to kill myself for revenge."

"Then maybe Nona didn't mean that much to you after all."

Silence. Stillness. The huntsmen held their breath. Lukas kept his face low and out of sight. And Faun...

No one had ever looked so terrifying yet so sad all at once.

Meiryn expected an unsettlingly calm threat. A quiet, hushed promise of a slow and painful death—anything would have been better than the dejected response Faun muttered.

"You have no idea what it is to lose the one person you loved, the one who..." Her throat bobbed, and no one, not even Meiryn, could find it in them to interrupt her. "Who gave you hope that this world could still be fixed. That *you* could be fixed."

Images of Reina, of her mother and father and brother, Silas, flashed in Meiryn's mind. She set her jaw and watched the water root float downstream. Against her better judgment, she muttered, "I do know."

"Then you also know why I can't risk my life now," Faun answered. "Why this is my fight to carry on, even when I would happily die tomorrow if it meant I got to see her face again."

"Faun," Lukas murmured. He reached out, but Faun pulled away. She stiffened her spine and readjusted her bow and quiver on her shoulders.

"Come on." She motioned to her scouts. "We've got a patrol to finish, and I'll be damned if we miss lunch again because we were too slow."

The huntsmen followed her obediently, but Lukas lingered behind. He finally met Meiryn's eye for longer than a heartbeat, and when he spoke, she felt a frail piece of her confidence chip away.

"You shouldn't have followed us." His words were hard, his voice impassive. "I'm sorry the Order took your friend, but there's nothing anyone here can do for you. She's gone."

The knife slipped from Meiryn's hand as Lukas trailed after his patrol.

———

At lunchtime, Meiryn sat far from the others. Elder, who retrieved Meiryn from the stream and guided her back to camp, had invited her to eat with the other healers, but Meiryn politely declined.

"I smell like fish, and I'm sopping wet," she offered as a feeble excuse. She gestured to her whole self, which was only just beginning to dry in the summer heat.

"No one will care about that," Elder dismissed. "Please, eat with me? You're the only healer who takes me seriously."

"I'm not a healer."

The answer was instinctive and thoughtless, but memories resurfaced of Meiryn's mother humming little tunes to herself while organizing her apothecary, of their neighbors in the village knocking on their doorstep and inquiring about a cure for their cough, of tending to Reina's recklessly earned wounds with a buried, intrinsic knowledge.

Elder pouted now, reminding Meiryn of Silas's expression when Meiryn was too busy to chase fireflies with him in the field.

Hope brimming, Elder said, "You could be, though, if you wanted to."

Meiryn scratched the back of her neck, ducking her head surreptitiously when a cluster of huntsmen hurried briskly by. "I'm here to help my friend. Just because I helped you out this morning doesn't mean I am one of you."

Elder's shoulders fell, and her sullen mood was almost enough to sway Meiryn into acquiescence. Still, she held her ground. Her presence alone was noted—and resented—by nearly all of the huntsmen. It was the kind of attention that painted a target on her back, and after her row with Faun, Meiryn was certain that the rest of the Guild would be frothing at the mouth, waiting for the next moment she slipped up just so they would have an excuse to kill her.

So Elder sulked off to eat with the senior healers, and Meiryn ate in solitude. She sat and watched the huntsmen. Listened to their conversations, witnessed the way they interacted with one another.

Those who ran the daytime patrols seemed to offer the more interesting gossip and reports. Most of the stories today, at least from what Meiryn could hear from this distance, were surprisingly mundane: traveling apothecaries were spotted trying to pluck entire bunches of pants and herbs from Guild territory; so-and-so sniped a buck from a hundred feet out; West Glen was slowly rebuilding after the fiasco from a few nights ago.

But it did not take long for someone from Faun's patrol to recount the spat that took place at the stream. Meiryn only realized they were talking about her when she caught, for the fourth time, several pairs of eyes watching her warily.

She sighed and took her rations into the med tent. As she replayed that awful conversation in her head, anger wrestling with shame in her gut, Meiryn picked at her stale bread and dried jerky. Both were tasteless and rough on her tongue, but it would hopefully be enough to fuel her for whatever job Pyrrha handed her next.

She had just finished her meal, and the huntsmen were stirring outside to disperse for their afternoon tasks, when light suddenly spilled into the tent.

Meiryn leaped to her feet when Grey strode in. He stopped when he saw her, and a frown tugged at his mouth. "Why are you all wet?"

"I was digging up water root," Meiryn said.

Grey nodded once, but his brows were furrowed, as if he had only been half-listening. He said, "I was looking for Pyrrha, but I'm glad I found you. There's something I wished to discuss with you."

Dread clenched her heart. Had he heard the rumors of her fight with Faun? "If this is about earlier—"

"It's about Nona, which means I'll be talking with Faun, too," he added with a pointed look. Meiryn picked at her arm. If Grey sensed her uneasiness, he paid it no mind. "After the events of West Glen and Draconis, our plan of action is altered.

Time, for now, is on our side, but we cannot let that sway us into a false sense of comfort." His tone implied confusion, but Meiryn was more bewildered with his rambling.

"I didn't kill anyone," she blurted before he could get another word in.

Grey's eyes flashed to her. "I never thought you did. But you were there. You're involved now."

"Involved in what?"

"We'll explain everything tonight."

"'We'?"

"Yes." Impatience sharpened his tongue. "You, me, and Faun—"

"I don't think that's a good idea," Meiryn interrupted. She could think of nothing she wanted less.

But Grey gave her a stern look. "And I don't think you're in a position to decline. You wanted us to help you, right? We don't offer our services for free."

Do you offer your services at all? she wondered. But, burying her apprehension, she acquiesced. "Fine. When do we set out?"

Grey was already halfway through the tent flap, responding before she'd even finished her question. "Whatever Pyrrha has you doing, make sure you're done before sundown. It'll be a long walk tonight, and we'll need to move quickly if we're to meet them on time."

"'Them'?"

No explanation, no pauses—he was gone. Meiryn lurched after him, only to slam into Pyrrha.

"Six hells," Pyrrha swore, recoiling as if she'd been burned. "I see now how you got caught in that snare—always walking headfirst without watching where you're going."

Meiryn blinked, catching the faintest glimpse of Grey, but Pyrrha blocked her path before she could follow him.

"You'll spend the afternoon sorting through what you gathered. Cleaning the leaves, ensuring that the plants are still usable." Pyrrha motioned to the two bags that Elder and Meiryn had dumped right outside the med tent. Both were bursting at the seams. "I suggest you get started. There is much work to be done."

XIV. REINA

Sleep came in nauseating waves. Reina tossed and turned against every rippling memory that swarmed her subconsciousness. She wilted at the sound of her father yelling at her from across the dinner table, burned with anger when Aaron sent her toppling into mud in front of a host of dignitaries. Memories from House Rhysanthe blurred into images of Meiryn reaching out to her through sheets of pouring rain, then bled into the dizzying sensation of seeing the storm dragon manifest outside the borders of childhood dreams.

When she awoke, she was still shuddering from the thundering bass of the dragon's voice. The gold pendant seared her skin with heat, as if it had just been pulled from a blacksmith's forge. Reina gasped and clutched her chest, nearly yanking the necklace clean off.

"Easy, or you'll waken every dragon within a mile radius."

Reina's eyes flew open, exposing her to spears of blinding daylight. She winced and shielded her face with a hand.

Iliana sat nearby, knees tucked close to her body. She grazed five lazy fingertips across the water. "I came to make sure you hadn't been snatched up by another cave dragon," she said, sounding unconcerned. "Everyone else has moved on; Aaron asked me to fetch you as soon as you were awake."

"'Moved on'?" Reina noticed that they were alone. Wind brushed her hair over the bridge of her nose, and she lengthened her neck, taking in their surroundings.

Thin stalks of bamboo and cattails swayed in a light breeze. Clouds smeared into formless white shapes across the sky, and straining to reach them were staggering karst mountains, all clothed in lush green foliage. Dragonflies danced down the length of the trickling river, birds flitted about with a call-and-response of staccato notes, and the wind carried leaves toward the south, deeper into the Dragon's Spine.

They might as well have stepped into another realm when they reached the end of the tunnel.

"You fell asleep quickly last night," Iliana said, tucking a lock of hair behind her ear. Her nails were lined with a dark red hue. "Korris and Evren found a village about fifteen minutes away from here."

Reina frowned. They dragged Raiko all that way?

Iliana misjudged Reina's expression, assuring her, "The village is abandoned. It looks like no one has even visited in years."

Reina had nothing to say. She assumed that if the cadre made camp, then it was safe enough by Aaron's standards.

"Anyway," Iliana continued, "you should clean up a bit before I take you back." She eyed Reina in a way that was eerily reminiscent of the expression she often earned from haughty, stuck-up noblemen and women.

Reina glanced down. Her cheeks flushed when she saw the smattering of blood on her arms and chest. She knelt at the riverside and doused her hands and face. She scrubbed her skin raw, trying not to think too much about last night's battle as she watched the blood drip off her chin and disperse into swirling pink clouds. The whole time, Iliana sat in uncomfortable silence. Reina wiped at her eyes and scrounged for something to talk about.

"That's an impressive sword," she tried meekly. "I've never seen anything like it."

"Evren designed it for me when we were drafted into the Silver Order."

Reina paused, water dripping through her cupped palms. "I thought the Order wasn't allowed to impose a draft. That's part of why they're favored over the Kingsguard, right?"

"Normally, yes. But Evren and I were"—Iliana scoffed bitterly—"a special case. Our cousin rejected the Order's invitation into the First Division, and we were drafted in his stead."

"Your cousin? What reason could he have to deny an offer like that?" Reina knew she was prying, but she couldn't help it. She retained only scraps of memory from when Aaron himself had applied to train with the acolytes of the Order.

The entire process was convoluted, and from what Reina could see, the Order was nepotistic: many of the renowned agents who dealt the killing blow to dragons on the Nest hailed from noble bloodlines. Acceptance into the Order was merely an expectation met; a direct invitation was perceived as the highest honor. To reject the Order altogether was unheard of.

And yet, here Iliana sat. She traced a bloodstained finger over the wing-shaped crossguard of her sword. "He was just another highborn who thought he could shirk all his responsibilities for selfish reasons." She pinned her stare on Reina now. "Kind of like you."

Reina ignored that.

"He turned his back on his house—no siblings left to take his place," Iliana continued. "Evren and I were his closest relatives, so we were forced to atone for his desertion."

Reina paused. A deep-buried memory edged into the foreground of her mind, but before she could turn mere speculation into a real inquiry, the grass behind her rustled.

She jumped back. Iliana drew her weapon and bounced her eyes across every moving shadow. Reina shuddered as the hairs on the back of her neck stood on end. She had no means of defense if trouble arose. She held her breath with Iliana—but there was nothing.

Iliana rose with her weapon unsheathed. "Let's go," she muttered. "We've loitered here long enough."

Reina couldn't have agreed more.

Pendulous vines and roots cascaded from the mountainsides. The river guided them through dappled patches of golden sunlight that warmed Reina's bare arms. Her skin tingled pleasantly at each whispering breeze, and for a moment, she lost herself in the fantasy of running away to a place like this. Here, buried amongst the craggy mountains, no one would find her. No one would even know where to start looking for her.

She would be free.

Evidence of human life emerged as suddenly as the river's path twisted and curved. Vines of ivy ensnared a leaning post that displayed a faded sign. Chipped paint hinted at a destination, and Reina's curiosity piqued when she spotted a small gatehouse half-buried in overgrown ferns and shrubs.

The building lacked a roof, and an entire wall lay blackened and broken. Birds flitted from a little nest stuffed between two planks of wood. Smoldering scars framed the entryway. Reina peered in, and her heart lurched.

Donned in charred remnants of lightweight armor and pierced through the ribs by a rusted blade was an empty husk of a skeleton. The earth had claimed the bones—tiny white flowers grew through the eye sockets, and the single ray of light that made it through the shattered window illuminated a brambled den that some little forest creature had made within the pelvic bones. Part of the skull was cracked and burned, and echoes of snapping embers filled Reina's mind as she remembered the way Ser Demerin had fallen so easily to fire in West Glen.

Reina pulled away, stomach knotting. Iliana hadn't stopped for her. Reina jogged to catch up and asked, "You're sure it's safe here?"

They were both thinking of the incident by the river. Iliana hesitated before nodding over her shoulder. "I trust my brother's assessment. If he said there's nothing out here, then we have nothing to fear."

They were stranded in the Dragon's Spine. They had everything to fear.

When they arrived at the village, Reina silently mused that *abandoned* had been far too gentle of a word.

This place was in complete ruins.

Similar to the outpost, the forest had come to reinstate its claim on the land. Many of the buildings looked like they were once homes, but whatever fire tore through here had shelled them out completely. Even now, ash drifted like snow in the dark and empty doorways. Scraps of tattered cloth hung from wooden lampposts that were snapped in half. What grew lush and green in the wake of fiery destruction could not mask the spine-chilling sensation that this place was haunted by the spirits of whoever died here.

The river boasted a wider girth where it skirted around the edge of the village. A broken wooden bridge—once bright red, now faded by time and weathering—led halfway across the restless waves, then leaned precariously into the current.

At the center of the village sat an empty fountain. Cracks in the foundation must have drained any water it once held. But that was not what ensnared Reina's attention.

Towering stone statues depicted a massive pair of wingless dragons entwined in an intimate embrace—or fierce battle. Their bodies were long and snakelike, bearing impressive manes that billowed in an imagined gust of wind. Each scale was carved with meticulous detail. Glimmering gemstones were embedded into the eye sockets—though the chips against the stone implied that someone had tried, and failed, to pry them out.

"*Kaeli rekks,*" Reina breathed, wholly entranced.

Rulers of the sky. These were dragons of old, ancestors of the winged beasts that ravaged Ver Signia's countrysides now. In the fables, these dragons were worshiped by ancient Ashuman civilizations. They had names, followers, and powers beyond human comprehension. They created Rhonestiel to be a world where humans and dragons could dwell in harmonious tandem. They were legends, sculptors, gods.

And then they had fallen.

Reina restrained herself from reaching for her pendant when Iliana stepped up beside her.

"Impressive, isn't it?" Iliana said. "Especially when you see what happened to the rest of this place."

Reina swallowed a knot in her throat. She couldn't explain

it, but there was a subtle sadness, a nagging discomfort sitting in the pit of her heart. "I wonder who lived here."

"Whoever they were," Iliana said, clearing her throat, "they're long gone. Just be grateful this place exists at all."

"This was someone's home."

"And now it's our shelter." Iliana sheathed her sword and crossed her arms. "Sentimentality has no leverage against survival. If we spared every ruin for the sake of honoring the dead, we'd soon be joining them."

Reina thought of Raiko again, throwing himself in harm's way for her sake, and curled her fingers into her palms. "Speaking of joining the dead—"

"There you are. I was wondering when you'd deign to join us." Evren strode toward them, accompanied by Korris. Both men looked weary but alert. They carried their weapons but had stripped and deposited their armor elsewhere.

Reina made a flat face. "You could have woken me."

"Your brother's priority was moving Raiko to a more secure location," Korris explained.

No surprise there.

Reading the silent question on Reina's face, he continued, "He's weak but alive, thanks to Iliana. His recovery won't be easy, considering we aren't equipped to deal with wounds that severe, but at the very least, he won't be dying on us in the middle of the night."

Reina loosened a tense breath. "Is Aaron still with him?"

"Yes," Evren answered. To Iliana, he said, "In fact, he sent us to fetch you."

Iliana groaned. "What else could he want? I've already done all I can."

Still, she followed Evren to the makeshift shelter. It was the only building unmarred by fire. Constructed from limestone, the structure sat atop an overhanging cliff that shadowed the rest of the village. Shallow steps built into the earth snaked a winding path up to the coin-shaped archway that led directly inside, and if Reina squinted, she could just barely make out the faint carvings of dragons chasing each other along the perimeter of the walls.

"We think it's a temple," Korris said, following her gaze. "It's the only thing that was left relatively untouched by whatever bandits scourged this place."

"'Bandits.'" She glanced about warily. "None of you are worried about anyone sneaking up on us in the night?"

"No." Not a trace of apprehension clipped his tone, nor did Reina detect a lie. He said, "Even if we do encounter something nefarious, we'll have the upper hand. It's always easier to defend a territory than it is to conquer it. Take last night, for example. We would have fared far better if we'd been the ones lurking in the darkness first. But those dragons..." He shook his head. "Well. No use in dwelling on what could have gone differently."

He seemed relatively unfazed by everything that the cadre had endured. Through the despair and stress that carried them to this point, Korris remained the most level-headed and composed of them all. He charged into battle without hesitation and fought with a fervor seen only in hardened warriors. In fact, Reina couldn't recall him being injured even once, despite being just as parched and famished as the rest of them.

"What?" Korris asked, mouth twitching at the way Reina was staring—or maybe he was disconcerted by the bloodstains on her shirt.

She took note of the scar running over his blind eye, the broadsword hanging at his hip, the way he approached combat like it was a dance. She blinked, picturing him on barren islands scarred by years of relentless warring. The pieces clicked into place.

"You were part of the First Division, weren't you?" Reina asked. "One of the dragon slayers."

He dropped his shoulders and gave her a look that told her she had overstepped some invisible boundary. But he sighed, and with a strained sort of admission, he said, "I failed my last mission three years ago. That's how I lost my eye; how I wound up in your brother's patchwork cadre."

A warm satisfaction soothed her prickling curiosity. "You must have felt right at home, then, when that storm dragon appeared."

"We saw no signs of such a creature when I was still on the Nest," Korris said, tracking her with his good eye as she paced idly around the centerpiece of the fountain. "Not even a whisper. What happened in Draconis was a freak incident. I don't know how anyone would slay a beast like that."

Reina deflated. Her fingertips grazed the webbed lines in her palms. "It must have been hiding all this time, then."

So why appear now?

"Whatever it's been doing," Korris said gruffly, "let's just hope that the Order has it under control. If the earth caved in over the catacombs, I can't imagine what the rest of the city must look like."

The thought had never even crossed Reina's mind. Her sole concern was finding out why the dragon appeared in her dreams and called to her in moments of abject fear—but she knew that her answers would not be found in the agents. They knew even less than she did, and confiding in any of them about what she experienced would only give them greater cause to deliver her to the Order's fractured doorstep. She was still their prisoner, after all; her remaining thread of autonomy lay in the secrets she kept.

Subconsciously, she felt for the pendant beneath her shirt. It thrummed with subdued energy, pulsing in time with her heartbeat.

"Find me, Rider."

She jumped, and Korris blinked in alarm. "What was that?" she demanded.

"I said, if you need anything, you can find me at the river." Korris eyed her like she was a trap waiting to spring loose. "We're parched and starving. I can spend the afternoon fishing and have dinner ready by sundown."

Reina raked a hand through her hair and nodded. "I suppose that means you want help, then." Part of her hoped he would say yes, if only to give her something to do besides speculate about the dragon's voice.

But Korris shook his head. "You're on your own. I am not your keeper."

Confusion rippled within her. "But Aaron—"

"Is clearly busy," Korris interrupted. "I'm not going to force you into my service, unless that's what you want."

Reina paused. "Would Aaron get angry with you if he learned that you let me roam free?"

"What would he do about that?" Korris chuckled dryly. "He's not exactly in the position to exile *me*. And it's not as if I can fall any further than the Fourth Division."

Reina chewed the inside of her cheek. She looked wistfully toward the temple, and Korris sighed. "Raiko will wake soon enough, but I wouldn't wait around to see him. Aaron is...quite particular, as I'm sure you well know."

Oh, she knew.

Deciding it was best to make the most of her time, Reina accompanied Korris to the river. He knelt among the cattails, a little way upstream from the broken bridge. Reina listened in earnest as he showed her how he rigged up a makeshift fishing line using nothing but spare wire—which, he said with no small amount of pride, he always kept on him for situations like this —and a simple throwing knife. He secured the handle to the first sturdy branch he picked up and waited for the fish to swim by; then, with deadly precision and accuracy, he speared them through.

He amassed a pile of three small trout before handing the spear to Reina, shaft first. "Your turn, little Rhysanthe."

She scowled at the pet name and adopted his stance, keeping her eyes trained on the rippling water. "Don't call me that."

Her first attempt was poor: she threw the spear too late and had to wade into the river to retrieve it before it floated too far downstream. On her second attempt, her boot slipped off the edge of the riverbank, creating a splash so loud and boisterous that it frightened the fish. By the third try, she was drenched head to toe, humiliated, and impatient.

"It's not easy," Korris said, watching with an amused grin. "Don't be ashamed if you come away empty-handed."

Reina threw him a stubborn glare. "I can do it."

She squared her stance and scanned the river for movement. Leaves, pebbles, and shadows flitted below the surface. Then, she spotted it: a larger fish—much larger than what Korris had caught. It was an easier target, slower than the trout, and it was hers to take.

She pointed the knife tip a few heartbeats ahead of the fish's path. Water rippled as its fins drew a thin wake in the current, and Reina hurled the spear.

The blade sank through its spine, and as a red cloud blossomed from the wound, Reina was thrown back into the previous night, when she had slayed the dragon with Evren's daggers. She felt the wave of hot blood choking her again; felt the dragon's body convulsing beneath her.

Reina lost her footing. She fell back and scrambled away from the river, gasping and sweating. Her hands trembled violently as black dots flashed at the corners of her vision. Raiko's scream echoed in her ears.

"Rhysanthe," Korris said. His voice was muffled until he knelt in front of her. He had discarded the spear, along with her catch, and his brows were drawn tight with concern. "Breathe, Athira. You're safe."

She blinked rapidly. She dug her fingers into damp earth to ground herself, but there was an anxious buzzing in her veins. Something longed to be freed, to be *out* of her body.

She splayed a palm over her chest and forced her lungs to fill with air, then released it all slowly. Korris instructed her to take two more breaths like this; Reina obeyed. She breathed until her world stopped spinning and her hands stopped shaking.

Korris leveled her with a stare. "Are you alright? What happened?"

Reina was grappling for an explanation when, a few yards away, someone cleared their throat. She whirled at the sound, and words failed her altogether when she saw Aaron.

Dark bags hung low beneath his eyes. His hair was unkempt and oily; he hadn't even bothered to wash away the gore of last night's fight. He was unarmed, which surprised Reina most, but he still walked with that rigid, straight-backed pride.

"I'd ask the same," he said, "but frankly, I don't quite care to know." He shifted a dull look from Korris to Reina. "Get up, and wipe that look off your face."

"Where are we going?" Reina managed to ask.

Aaron gestured for her to follow. "Raiko is awake now. He's asking for you."

Reina stared. She didn't move a single muscle.

"He's weak," Aaron continued in a hollow voice, "but he insisted upon seeing you."

"Why?"

"Gods only know."

Reina glanced furtively at Korris, finding him looking just as perplexed as she felt. He gave her a subtle nod of encouragement, but it did nothing to assuage her rising apprehension.

"Athira," Aaron called, now several paces away, "I won't tell you again."

She jolted to her feet and followed him, if only to put the awkwardness of her incident behind her.

Wet ropes of hair flung water droplets everywhere as she walked, and she ascended the stone staircase with extra caution, feeling her boots slip on every step. Aaron said nothing when they stood before the gaping archway, but Reina could just tell that he longed to barge inside.

A muscle in his jaw twitched when he moved aside for her. "Don't keep him waiting, now."

"You're not coming?"

Aaron rolled his eyes. "I told you, he asked for you."

"*Only* me?"

"Trust me, I'm just as surprised as you are." Despite his militant stance, there was a certain pain in his voice that Reina could not ignore. She saw the way he stole another glance into the temple.

"Now, keep your voice low," he ordered. "And make sure he lays flat so he doesn't break open his wounds again."

"I'll be gentle," Reina promised lightly.

But Aaron was as serious as death. "I mean it, Athira. You made a habit of ruining everything that I...that was important to me, when we were younger. I will not allow you to do the same now."

She shook her head in confusion. "What—"

"You're wasting time." Aaron slapped a hand between her shoulder blades. He shoved her inside, and Reina spun, barely catching her brother's eyes glistening before he turned and bounded down the hill, taking the steps two at a time.

XV. MEIRYN

The afternoon trickled by. Sorting each herb into its respective inventory felt somewhat convoluted, though that might have been because Elder explained the organization process in such a way that Meiryn wondered if she was making it all up just to fill the silence and busy their hands.

Regardless, the work provided a welcome distraction from Grey's approach earlier, and the shade of this oak tree offered a respite from the sweltering summer heat.

Meiryn hadn't even cleaned half of the water root when the sun began to set. The pads of her fingers were wrinkled like prunes. Her spine and neck ached. She arched her back, twisted from side to side, and spotted Faun stalking in from a distance. At her side was Grey, and both looked like they were gearing up for war.

Elder followed Meiryn's gaze. She lifted her hand in greeting. "Hi."

Faun just nodded, stopping several feet away. Grey walked a little farther and offered Elder a faint but warm smile. "How was everything today, Elder?"

"Better than usual," she chirped. "I think foraging is my least favorite task, but it's always more fun with new friends."

Meiryn pretended not to hear Faun's stifled snort.

"It's safer, too," Grey said with a mindful tilt of the head. "I'm sorry to ruin the fun, but I'm going to need to borrow your"—he chuckled breathily—"new friend. Is that alright?"

Elder's shoulders dropped, but she nodded. "If you must."

Grey grinned—an expression that looked wholly foreign on his face, and one that did not match the depth of his voice. "Don't worry, we'll return her in one piece."

If he was trying to be humorous, he was failing spectacularly.

Meiryn bade Elder a good night and stood to face Grey and Faun. They had equipped their weapons, and Meiryn looked down at her own outfit: old and tattered, sun-dried and stiff after splashing around in the stream, and, perhaps most grievously, weaponless.

She glanced at the harvesting knife at her feet. Gestured to it awkwardly. "Should I take this?"

"That won't be necessary," Grey said, his tone hard again. His hand fell to one of his swords. "This is just a precaution. As long as we stick to the path, we'll be safe, but there are always trespassers to be wary of."

Meiryn glanced at Faun, anticipating another biting remark, but Faun was uncharacteristically quiet. Maybe it was because Grey was standing between them.

Maybe he's the one I've come all this way for.

The thought nagged at Meiryn, but she silenced it as Grey led them into the forest, the falling sun blazing against their backs.

Night fell before they reached their destination—which neither Grey nor Faun had yet disclosed to Meiryn. The treetops obstructed the moon's glow, keeping the path hidden. Meiryn's only guides were the two huntsmen, but neither was too concerned with slowing their pace to accommodate for her injury.

She kept up as best she could, but after spending much of the morning on her feet, that dull, slow-burning ache had returned to her right leg. Sweat beaded at her brow and dampened her neck. Every heavy-footed step earned another teeth-grinding frown from Grey, and when Meiryn snapped two twigs in a row, Faun whirled back to face her.

"Are you trying to alert every animal to our presence?" she hissed.

Meiryn halted, panting slightly. "I'm sorry," she tried. "It's my leg."

Faun groaned impatiently. "Why did we bring her along again?"

"Quiet, both of you," Grey ordered. He flicked his gaze upward, catching the black shadow of a crow. "We're almost there. Keep up."

Meiryn swallowed her protest and pushed through the pain. Night-tales of the southern woods filled her head. Every living thing could be watching them as they trekked through darkness. She strained her ears for the low growl of a wolf, or the scuttling of little hares, but the loudest disturbance was her own footsteps. She might as well have been a beacon for whatever lurked in the trees. And the scent of her fear and trepidation had to be stinking up the place. Once, she squealed in disgust when her arm tore through the thin strings of a spider's web. A black crow, perched on a low-hanging branch, *caw-cawed* and tilted its head at her, as if mocking her incompetence.

Several more minutes passed, and still they walked. Meiryn was beginning to wonder if there was no destination in mind—if this was, in fact, a test of strength and endurance. A test to see if she could persevere through the most trying of pains. But then, why was Faun here? Just to see if Meiryn would break beneath the disparaging word of someone who hated her?

Meiryn was just about to question Grey's motive when he emitted a low, three-toned whistle. Faun halted, and Meiryn froze a few paces behind her.

A chittering noise replied from somewhere nearby, followed by a brittle *caw-caw*. Grey whistled once more, and the crow flitted into the dark.

The trees rustled. Meiryn's head spun, and her heart hammered. She shuffled closer to Faun, though she might as well have thrown herself into a raging fire to evade a bed of thorns. Meiryn stifled a gasp when the darkness moved.

From the shadows emerged a broad figure, which split into two distinct human shapes—one male, one female, both lithe and graceful as they cleared a path through the low-hanging branches. The haziness of Meiryn's night vision blurred the newcomers' faces, but the woman's accent was distinctly Ashuman when she greeted Grey.

"It is bold of you to summon us here, after all that has happened." Stoic, the woman clasped Grey's forearm like he was an old friend. Her head turned an inch, and she offered a slight dip of her chin in Faun's direction. *"N'benem, amia."*

Faun echoed her words in a low murmur. "I'm sorry we had to meet under these circumstances."

Meiryn stared. It took her only a moment to realize. "You're Nona's family, aren't you?"

The woman lifted her head in Meiryn's direction. Her voice was guarded. "She was our sister. Who are you?"

Faun interjected, "She was there during Nona's final moments. She witnessed the moment when..." Her throat bobbed, and her voice became hoarse. "When Nona died."

The man hissed, "She stood by and watched it happen?"

Meiryn flinched, and to her relief, Grey stepped in. "Meiryn played no role in Nona's death."

"Then why is she here?" the woman demanded.

"Because the Order took her friend in Nona's place." Grey held a hand up to keep the woman from storming up to Meiryn, but he did not touch her. "Nyrōna, listen. There is a reason I called you here. I saw things in Draconis. Things that can't be explained in a letter or trusted in the wrong hands."

Nyrōna turned her head with terrifying slowness. "But you are content to send a crow to tell me that my sister is dead?" Anger shook her voice, but there was also a deep sadness ebbing against the rage. It was a crashing wave of emotions, the kind of sadness that could not be justified by words.

Grey blinked twice, but he held his ground. "If I knew I could find you in the Spine, I would have come to you."

The Dragon's Spine? Meiryn thought that those mountains were uninhabitable, not just for their steep slopes and hidden dragon dens, but also because of the many wars that had ravaged the land in a desperate squabble for ownership. Even now, years after Ver Signia and Ashuma declared the Spine neutral territory—a bridge between rival nations—some said that the river winding between the many peaks still ran red.

"And instead, you asked *us* to risk our lives crossing into enemy territory," the man at Nyrōna's side said gruffly. He crossed his arms and glared. "You know Elysia is at risk here."

Who? Meiryn held a tense breath.

"I promise, Temaerys, this is worth your time." Grey looked between the four people he'd summoned to this place. A sliver of moonlight struck his eye, and Meiryn caught the faintest hint of uncertainty. She took a cautious step forward.

"What does Reina have to do with any of this?" she asked.

"That cadre mistook her for Nona, right?" Grey answered. Behind him, Nyrōna and Temaerys shared a quick glance, intrigue rippling between them. "Presumably, she's Ashuman."

"How is that relevant?"

"Because there's an ancient Ashuman bloodline that descends from a smaller race of people called Drāga. I think your friend might be one of them."

Meiryn blinked, and Nyrōna gasped. Her eyes glittered with hope, but Temaerys's brow furrowed. "How could you possibly make that assumption?"

"What I saw in Draconis will explain everything." He looked sullenly between Nyrōna and Temaerys. "I wanted to speak with Nona about this. I can only hope that you'll hear me out now, and know that I'm only speaking the truth."

Grey relayed his story with as much directness as a courier. It was the most Meiryn had ever heard him speak in one turn, but the more he talked, the less she wished she had heard. Chills whispered down her spine. Her hands tightened into clammy fists while she listened in disbelieving silence.

Grey had been in Draconis to observe the dragon campaign. Somehow, he'd sneaked around the Order's base and spied on them from the shores. Sailing in from the barren archipelago that the dragons called home were massive cargo ships, but aboard each deck were live dragonlings that writhed against their bindings. Great steel muzzles clamped their mouths shut, and their parents and elders lay dead beside them. Once the ships docked, dragon tamers dragged off the young while smiths and armorers harvested the bodies of the others.

"Gods," Temaerys said in a voice wavering between fury and numbness. He glanced over his shoulder, then said to his sister, "I told you we should have left Elysia behind. It is not safe here for her."

Meiryn narrowed her eyes. Was Elysia a *dragon*?

Nyrōna raised a hand to silence Temaerys. She hadn't looked away from Grey. "What else did you see?"

"The Order is taming the dragonlings—"

"To turn them against the rest of their clans on the Nest," Faun finished. Her eyes were wide, brows stitched close. "That would take ages. Generations, even. Why would the Order go through the trouble when they're already so close to driving the dragons to extinction?"

"It doesn't matter why, because something happened not long after those ships docked. Something that'll set them back even further."

He continued his story, telling them how, in a matter of minutes, the weather had taken a sudden dark turn. Stormy seas were not uncommon off the eastern coastline, but Grey swore that the clouds above the water had come alive. That they breathed and rippled like muscles beneath skin. He told them about the black sky that stretched over Draconis; about the crackling gold lightning that tore open the clouds; about the dragon that brought the storm on its back.

"It was...pure chaos." Grey stared at the ground with a glazed look in his eye that told Meiryn that no number of words could ever describe the horror he had witnessed. "Infernals and Hiberns ravaged that city. They broke the chains from their young, led them back across the water."

"What about the one that brought the storm?" Nyrōna asked, leaning forward. "What became of it?"

Meiryn was more concerned with the people, but she couldn't deny that Grey's story sparked a grim sort of fascination in her.

"There was a moment," Grey said, his voice falling beneath the chirping chorus of crickets and cicadas, "when the storm dragon's power...reflected."

"'Reflected'?" Temaerys echoed. Doubt narrowed his eyes. "How do you mean?"

Grey shook his head and rubbed the back of his neck. "Lightning just—exploded. A spear of it shot through the rain, and then it doubled back toward the dragon. The whole city shook from the blast."

Faun shifted her weight between both feet. She passed a hand over her face, looking deeply troubled.

Nyrōna lifted a hand to her mouth. "Only a Drāga could wield such power."

"Drāga." Meiryn tested the weight of the word on her tongue, finding it lopsided and clumsy. "What are Drāga?"

No one answered her. Temaerys fixed a hard stare on Grey. "Are you certain this is what happened? Did you actually *see* the person who did this?"

"I couldn't make this up," Grey said, not defensively. He huffed a laugh. "Ver Signian artificers might be clever, but we've never had to defend ourselves against a creature like this. No weapon or shield could have deflected that lightning."

"Hang on." Meiryn threw herself into the circle of allies. "Go back. What are Drāga?"

Nyrōna snapped her head in Meiryn's direction. A prideful gleam sharpened her eyes. "They are people who share a special bond with dragons. They can hear their voices, share their powers. Their very souls are intertwined with the dragons that your people slaughter like pigs."

Meiryn's brows shot upward. She glanced at Grey and Faun, searching for some hint of a smirk or the light of a joke twinkling in their eyes, but both huntsmen were straight-faced.

Faun leveled her gaze on Meiryn. It was the first time she'd addressed Meiryn without condescension. "Nona was Drāga. You and your friend saw her that night in the arena, didn't you? You saw the way she directed that Infernal's flame."

Meiryn hadn't been watching much of the fight at all, and she certainly hadn't seen anything resembling the impossible image Faun conjured up now. "What I saw was a girl throwing herself in danger. You don't seriously think—"

"She was Drāga," Faun interrupted, louder this time. Her voice wobbled. "She told me that she heard the dragon crying out to her, that she felt its power like it was her own. And I believed her. I saw what she could do. She could have changed everything if she hadn't died."

"She never should have left," Temaerys ground out.

Nyrōna hissed, "She never would have unlocked her powers."

"At least she would still be with us." Pain and anger, still bleeding in their rawness, leaked into his words.

Grey lifted a hand, silencing the argument before it could derail the conversation.

Meiryn took advantage of the pause and said, "I still don't see what any of this has to do with Reina."

"No one else could have shot that dragon's lightning back," Nyrōna said exasperatedly, as if it were obvious. "You say the cadre took your friend instead of my sister, yes? If they planned to execute her at their headquarters, she would have been there at the time of the storm dragon's awakening."

"Grey didn't actually *see* who did that, though," Meiryn pressed. "It's too coincidental to be linked to Reina."

Nyrōna clicked her tongue. "There are no coincidences—only that which was fated by the Ancient Ones. If what Grey says is true, then your missing friend may very well be the most powerful Drāga this world has ever known."

Meiryn laughed. She couldn't help it.

The others stared, and Nyrōna adopted a forcibly placid tone. "Have I amused you?"

"It's ridiculous," Meiryn managed. "Everything you've said —it's nonsense. You're talking about *magic*. Reina doesn't share some mystical bond with a dragon. She's...normal. Besides, what about other Ashumans? Are you telling me that the entire southern empire is populated with these—these Drāga?"

"The Drāga scattered after the war that erased them from history," Temaerys said curtly. "Any number of them could still exist, but with *your* people hunting down every last dragon, we may never know how many of them could have realized their true potential as riders."

Meiryn sidled away from him. "Dragons are dangerous. They're the ones doing the killing."

"I wonder why," he retorted. Rage emanated from his stiff

stance. "Your kind treat them like monsters, so it is monsters they must become, if they wish to survive."

Her *kind*? Meiryn had nothing more to say to him. She turned to Grey. "You really think Reina is the one you saw in Draconis?"

"I didn't see anyone," he clarified. "But the pieces fit too well for it all to be a coincidence. Nona was imprisoned, yet your friend wound up in the Order's clutches. Someone shot that dragon out of the sky and calmed the storm. I highly doubt it was anyone from the Order."

"Does Nona's death mean nothing to you?" Faun blurted. All eyes settled on her. She met them with fire in her gaze. "She's *dead*, and you're here talking about some other girl who *might* possess the powers you think she does. This is just another impossible mission."

For once, Meiryn agreed.

Nyrōna lowered her face. "None of us have forgotten Nona. She spoke fondly of you, *amia*, but remember that she was our sister before she was your lover." Fierce possessiveness brittled her words.

Faun shut her mouth, but a look of hurt flashed across her face. "What we have...*had* was rare, but I didn't love her any less than you do."

"Then it should be easy to understand that this task was of the utmost importance to her," Nyrōna said, only a touch gentler. Her slender hand fell upon Faun's shoulder. "If this girl is indeed Drāga, then we must find her and unite her with her dragon. We must protect them both at all costs."

She spoke in the hypothetical sense, but Meiryn saw the look on her face: the subdued hope straining against the urge to embark on this next mission at once.

Compelled by a surge of protectiveness, Meiryn said, "You can't do that. Reina is *my* friend. *I'm* going to save her from the Order."

"If the Order discovers her powers, she will have much more to fear than losing her life," Nyrōna snapped.

"What—"

"Do you have any idea of the horrors your ancestors inflicted upon mine?"

Meiryn paused, annoyance clawing at her pursed lips. Of course she didn't—how could she? She'd only just heard the name of the Drāga tonight.

Nyrōna approached with her fists clenched tightly at her sides. Only when she drew close did Meiryn see the twin spears crossed behind her back. The pointed blades glinted in a fractured patch of moonlight before Nyrōna stepped forward into darkness, and Meiryn felt the tiniest flicker of fear that Nyrōna would simply run her through.

Instead, she said in a voice that shuddered with untapped anger, "While *rhakshas* like you fell asleep to the night-tales of fantasy and happily-ever-afters, I was taught that my demise was woven into the very seams of this world by the ones you call kings and heroes—simply for the blood that runs through my veins. Ver Signians tore open the Drāga—*our* ancestors—while they still lived." She gestured between herself and her brother, eyes flooded with fury. "They drained their blood into vials, fashioned their bones into weapons, carved their beating hearts right from their chests—all to see what made Drāga so powerful. Ver Signia wanted that power for themselves, you see. Why were their own people denied the gifts of the dragons? Why were they so *ordinary*?"

Nyrōna breathed deeply, like she was fighting to keep her

voice at a lower volume. "The war incited a genocide that eradicated the Drāga. Dragons and riders severed their bonds to protect their own. But even now, centuries later, the precious few descendants are being hounded by bounty hunters who wish to profit off the blood of legends. Ver Signia remains a threat, and Ashuma renounced her kin long ago. So if a little power sways in our direction, believe me when I say that we will claim it."

Power. War. Bloodshed. Revenge.

Meiryn saw a desire for all these things shimmering in Nyrōna's eyes, along with a vision of what such a world would look like: dragons would ravage the skies; villages, towns, entire cities would collapse beneath the rule of these Drāga; the northern kingdom and its enemies in the southern empire would kneel to the very beasts that were so tenuously contained on the Nest.

A chill chased down her spine. "You can't wrap Reina up in this plan," she whispered. "I won't let you."

"You cannot stop it," Nyrōna said. "If our theory is correct and this girl is Drāga, then her connection with that dragon would make her the First Rider of the Storm. She could reshape the world."

"*If* we are discussing the same person," Faun blurted, "then it's very likely that she is still in the hands of the Order. Who's to say that they won't sway her to their cause once they tame that dragon? She could become a weapon for the king."

"Which is precisely why we must act now," Nyrōna said.

Faun jabbed a finger angrily in an indeterminate direction. "You're placing too much stock in this girl. She can't replace what I...what *we* lost. She might not even be enough to change the world. It's broken beyond repair."

Sadness cooled the temper in Nyrōna's glare. "Is that truly

how you feel? Not two minutes ago, you said that Nona could have changed everything."

"Because she was *Nona.*" Faun's voice trembled. "She was wild and brave and strong. She knew who she was, and she could have conquered kingdoms if she wanted to. This girl you want to chase after..." She squared her shoulders and breathed slowly. "If she is anything like Meiryn, then I assure you, she is *not* who you are looking for."

Indignation stabbed at Meiryn, and she lifted her chin. "Reina isn't helpless. She was in the wrong place at the wrong time."

"Or," Nyrōna insisted, "she was exactly where she needed to be. What are any of us against the will of fate?"

Meiryn and Faun turned on her at the exact same time. Faun seethed, "You think it was *fate* for Nona to die that night?"

Temaerys glowered threateningly, but Nyrōna held him back with a hand. "What I think is irrelevant. What I know is that Nona found the Infernal who whispered in her ear and danced with her in dreams. You only knew her for a short time. I knew her when all she wanted was to find this dragon, to free it from its cage. If she were here now, she would be urging us to find this other girl, to finish what she started, and to restore the Drāga."

"You'd be painting a target on their backs," Faun protested.

"History has already forgotten us," Nyrōna said. "Our name was smudged off the scrolls, burned out of every library. It would be the highest dishonor to spend our days in hiding just to preserve our own lives."

What she proposed would incite a war. She would use

Reina as a pawn to revive some fallen empire that no one remembered. It was ludicrous—too large for Meiryn's brain to process.

Grey spoke for the first time in several minutes. "I brought you all here to tell you what happened before rumors started to seep into every corner of the continent. What you choose to do now is up to you, but you would do well to remember who your allies are."

Nyrōna and Faun waged a silent battle, their faces hard as rock. Grey's expression revealed nothing, and Meiryn dared not even glance in Temaerys's direction, lest she find yet another opposing stance on what was already an absurd proposition. At the very least, she knew that she was wholly against the idea of entertaining this war.

It was Temaerys who broke the impasse. Arms crossed, jaw set, he regarded Grey with a look somewhere between anger, hurt, and disappointment. "Any alliance we might have had was severed when your people let Nona die."

Nyrōna and Faun rounded on him. "Temi," Nyrōna whispered, "we *need* them."

"We only needed Nona," he said. He jerked his chin at Grey and cast dark glances at Faun and Meiryn. "This Hunters Guild provided a clearer path to her Infernal than anyone else could have given us, which I will not soon forget. But neither can I forgive how reckless you were with her life." He tore his gaze away from Grey and addressed Faun, who—to Meiryn's utter horror—appeared moments away from crying. "She called you *dha'katsi*. Did you not swear to protect her while she scoured this kingdom in search of her counterpart?"

Faun's mouth opened, closed, then opened again—but

words seemed to fail her. One hand closed tight around her bowstring. She wouldn't look up.

Temaerys shouldered his way past Grey and Nyrōna, only coming to a stop when he towered over Faun. "She was my sister. I trusted her to you, and under your watch, she died."

"*Temaerys*," Nyrōna spat, reaching for her brother. "Hold your tongue. If there is another Drāga out there, then we need the Guild's help in finding her."

He recoiled and shook his head. "Our people are dead. The time of the riders has passed. You and I are the last of the Drāga, sister. This alliance is nothing to us now."

Nyrōna looked aghast. She pried him away from Faun and spoke in rapid Mal'dhi, eyes glittering with tears she held back. Temaerys replied in that same stony voice. Nyrōna's next words broke on a sob, and Meiryn had the uncomfortable sensation of being an unwelcome witness to a vulnerable conversation.

She looked at Faun: the archer's head was bowed, her shoulders stiff and her breaths forced. Temaerys's words had wilted her, reduced her from a proud and brazen woman to a trembling, heartbroken girl.

It almost made Meiryn sympathize with her.

Grey's face was an impenetrable wall, but when he cleared his throat and interrupted Nyrōna's pleading, he sounded like he was fighting to keep himself calm. "This alliance was about more than reviving the Drāga. It was about balancing the scales. Placing the people in power rather than subjecting them to the bidding of a king who refuses to rise from his glass chair."

Meiryn's ears pricked at that. She knew the Hunters Guild was a rebellious faction, but it had never occurred to her that their ultimate goal was usurpation. Theirs was an impossible task—one that, if achieved, would throw the kingdom into utter chaos. She could hardly claim that the way things were now was fair, but was true equality worth the civil war it would bring about? What good was a war for justice if no one remained to rise from the ashes?

Grey continued, "We won't get anywhere if we split our forces now. The Silver Order is weakened after the attack in Draconis. Like Nyrōna said, this is the perfect moment to strike, and—"

"Just like a Ver Signian," Temaerys interrupted, his words dripping with venom. "You are obsessed with power, thoughtless to the ones you might throw in harm's way to obtain it."

Grey's voice turned to steel. "I cared about Nona, too. Her death affects us all."

"So in her memory, we must persist," Nyrōna insisted.

Temaerys scowled. Faun heaved a sigh, swearing under her breath. The threads of Grey's feeble alliance were snapping, and Meiryn could only stand back and watch.

"If we are wrong about the girl," Grey said, looking at each person he had summoned, "then we've lost nothing but time, and we have enough of it now that we can take that risk. But if we're right, then the price of sitting back and doing nothing will be our lives."

How easily he spoke about Reina like she was a pawn— another piece in this mess of a puzzle they were trying to glue together.

"Our lives are already lost," Temaerys muttered. He dropped his shoulders and let his chin graze his chest. "Our hope for change died with Nona. There is nothing for me here. I will wait with Elysia. And Nyrōna," he added as he turned, "do not linger. There is nothing here for you, either."

Nyrōna called after him as he stormed back the way he'd come, but he ignored her. The darkness folded around him.

A moment later, the rattling growl of a dragon split the quiet.

Meiryn threw a bewildered look at Nyrōna, who touched two fingers to the base of her throat and murmured incomprehensibly. The treetops rustled in response. Without warning, a dragon shot into the air.

Meiryn staggered back, mouth falling open at the blackened silhouette that flew southward: a massive dragon, bearing the weight of one rider. Her heart shuddered, and her mind folded in on itself.

Impossible. Dragon riders were a thing of fiction.

Right?

Nyrōna dragged a hand through her long, dark hair. "I will make him see reason, Grey. Your efforts will not be wasted."

He did not acknowledge her whispered assurance. He looked like he was buried in some internal conflict—silent. Unmoving. His brow was furrowed, and a muscle in his jaw twitched. When he turned back to the others, Meiryn only found a heavy fatigue weighing beneath his eyes.

"We should head back," he said to Faun and Meiryn. He started to say something to Faun, but she jerked away.

"I'll find my own way," she said, barely audible.

No one stopped her.

To Nyrōna, Grey dipped his head in farewell. Shame flashed across his face before his expression became neutral once more. "I'm sorry I couldn't do more for you, or for Nona."

Nyrōna thinned her lips. Dropped her gaze. "And I, as well. I will urge Temi to think on what was said tonight. He is hurting, as we all are, but he will see reason."

Grey waved a dismissive hand. "I know firsthand that forced cooperation never works. If he is adamant, then nothing can be done."

Nyrōna set her jaw. Her parting words sent a cool ripple through Meiryn's nerves. "If I do not try, then nothing *will* be done."

XVI. REINA

THE SCENT of bitter herbs and steaming tea flooded Reina's nostrils, clouded by a haze of incense that had long since gone stale. Piercing through it like a blade was the metallic odor of blood.

Pools of daylight spilled in through the glassless windows; thinner veins of light scribbled along the floor from fractures in the ceiling. Reina stood in the archway while her vision adjusted, but Iliana graced the room with six candles, each stumpy and tinged with the scent of embers and smoke. Their weak flames illuminated murals of dragons—wingless and winged alike. The paint was chipped and faded, but Reina could still make out each pair of wild eyes that glowed with powers beyond comprehension.

She searched for the dragon that invaded her dream, but none of the paintings depicted a black-scaled beast that fought with the power of the storm. Her chest warmed as the pendant hummed silently.

"Athira."

She jumped at Iliana's voice. At the center of the space,

beneath slivers of light, Iliana knelt at Raiko's side. He was barely conscious, but when his gaze slid through the darkness and found Reina's, he managed a thin smile. "*Dha'katsi.*"

Reina couldn't translate the greeting, but she did not miss the way Iliana's brows shot up. Reina lingered by the entrance. "What did he say?"

"He said—"

"I said, 'Welcome.'" Raiko waved a limp hand, beckoning her forth. Iliana only cocked her head as Reina approached on careful feet. Raiko turned to Iliana. "You may go."

Much to Reina's surprise, Iliana rose to her feet. She stopped Reina a few steps away from Raiko and lowered her voice, though her words still echoed. "Ensure that he rests. He insists on sitting up, but I won't have anything to wrap his wounds again if he starts bleeding. And make sure he drinks that tea."

"You mean the dirt you sprinkled into a pot of boiling water?" Raiko commented.

Iliana scoffed. Without turning, she said, "It'll ease the pain. Drink it or be miserable for the next few days. It's your choice."

She brushed past Reina and retreated down the grassy steps, leaving her alone with Raiko.

Reina kept her distance. She felt incredibly awkward standing here, and when she saw the makeshift bandages covering Raiko's torso, a deep sense of guilt clawed at her. Looking anywhere but at his face, Reina asked, "How are you feeling?"

"Like *skorhui.*"

Like shit. That much, she could translate. Reina smirked. "Well, at least you haven't lost your sense of humor."

"No, just a couple liters of blood. All will be well, though."

Reina pressed her lips together, and Raiko looked her up and down. The sarcastic edge in his expression softened to light concern. "Have I made you uncomfortable, my lady?"

"No. And don't call me that." As if to prove that she was nothing like those snotty, conceited highborn ladies, Reina closed the rest of the space between them and plopped gracelessly at his side. She leaned back on her hands, tilting her head skyward while ignoring the sensation of Raiko staring at her.

"Korris was teaching me to fish," she said after a while. "It went poorly."

"So you gave up and decided to visit me instead?"

Reina grunted. "You called me here. I assumed you had something to say."

"I did, although I admit I did not think you would still be around."

Reina snapped her head toward him. "Why wouldn't I be?"

He furrowed his brow. "Have you *not* thought of running off the first chance you got?"

She'd toyed with the idea, yes. She figured that as long as Raiko remained injured and prone, Aaron wouldn't notice her sneak away. But there was the concern of being followed by the rest of his cadre. She had no idea where she was—only that if she went north, she'd eventually end up back in Ver Signia. A southward path would lead her into unfamiliar land where she knew only scraps of the language.

"Leaving now is suicide," she determined aloud. "We don't know where those cave dragons went, or if they'll come back to their nest. I've never had any formal weapons training, and it's not like any of you are going to teach me. Besides, even if I did manage to make it to Ashuma, I wouldn't know where to go."

Raiko looked puzzled. "Why would you want to go to Ashuma?"

"It's freer than Ver Signia. The people are treated more fairly under the empress's rule."

"That," Raiko said with deliberate slowness, "must be the most ignorant thing I have ever heard you say."

Reina paused. She didn't know why his words stung so deeply—only that there was nothing that could comfortably fill the silence.

"My mother didn't speak of home often," she finally said, "but when she did, she only ever spoke of it with longing and fondness."

She remembered days from her early childhood, memories framed in a hazy golden glow. She would accompany the Lady Rhysanthe on walks through the family's gardens, still young enough to perch comfortably on her mother's hip. An orchard of magnolias had been planted in one small corner of the field as a wedding gift—an homage to the lady's Ashuman heritage. This was her favorite spot to wander, to reminisce on the life she had before being swept into an arranged marriage with her Ver Signian husband, and Reina still carried with her the stories that her mother imparted. Stories of the mountains whose many faces were brushed clean each morning by a southward wind; of her friends back home, who ran away screaming each time she chased them with handfuls of crickets; of nights so quiet and peaceful that cities like Verilonne felt worlds away.

"She loved Ashuma," Reina said. "I bet she still does, even if it isn't everything she remembers."

Her fond reminiscence clashed with Raiko's disdain. "She should consider herself lucky, then, to hold such memories of an unbroken country."

"You're referring to the war." Reina drew upon cobwebbed recollections of her history lessons. "That war ended in a truce. The Accords were established to keep both countries safe."

Raiko snorted. "Is that what they taught you?"

The savagery of his rage took Reina aback. A few wordless seconds passed before she tripped over her feeble attempt to mitigate his anger. "That's what happened. It's just history."

"From the victor's perspective," Raiko retorted. He looked her over once, eyes sharp as steel and lips curled, as if disgusted by her ignorance. "The Accords calmed those who protested for a ceasefire, but Ver Signia felt like their enemies needed to be reprimanded like children, to be put in their place. They made this proposal to our empress: in exchange for our contribution to their dragon campaign, they would spread Ver Signian knowledge and technologies across Ashuma. They would ensure that no dragon from the Nest touched Ashuman soil, and in turn, Ashuma would house Ver Signian citizens displaced by those rogue dragons."

Reina knew all this, but she still didn't understand why it had to be spun so villainously. The fighting had ended. Ver Signian and Ashuman families alike no longer worried about losing their sons and daughters to mindless bloodshed. And the debts of war were forgiven when both countries channeled their strength and manpower into fighting the dragon campaign.

"What exactly is wrong with the Accords?"

"Ver Signia deceived my country," Raiko seethed. His face reddened as he propped himself up on his elbows, threatening to tear open his wound again. Reina tried to calm him, but she'd stirred up a storm of repressed rage. He spat, "I hate Ver Signia. I am certain your king tells every tutor in the kingdom to speak of this war as some noble, tragic victory, but those

Accords you defend so adamantly allowed foreigners across our borders. Ashuma's people were thrown out of their homes to make way for these refugees whose king refused to shelter them from the violence he incited. We could either stay and fight and die, or live and watch our homes turn into Ver Signian settlements.

"The Order sent in recruiting officers who wove promises of wealth and security for our families, and the minute we fell for their lies, they occupied our villages, outlawed our language, our culture, our way of life. They criminalized and demonized us in our own home... Athira, *how do you not see?*"

Reina did not move a muscle, nor did she dare to speak, lest she offend him further. She searched Raiko's face for any sliver of a lie, any indication that all of this was just some cruel attempt to divert her from her dreams of escaping Ver Signia.

But the tears swimming in Raiko's eyes were real. The agony in his voice was real when he whispered, "My home is gone, and so is your mother's. Six years have passed since I left my family, and I have not heard from them once. For all I know, they are wandering the countryside of Ashuma, homeless and starving, while I am here, fighting for the very people who do not want me here anyway."

Reina drew in a trembling gasp when a tear splattered against the back of her palm. She wiped it quickly, but Raiko had seen. His silence now was unnerving.

But what was there to say? She thought she'd been clever and sly, slipping beyond the reaches of House Rhysanthe. It was the first step in a grand escape. She thought she'd find an empire of open lands untouched by dragon's breath, more opportunities than she'd ever had before. She thought she'd find freedom.

Now...

"There's nothing waiting for me, either." She blinked hard. "Ver Signia will always look at me and think *malduna*, but I've never set foot in Ashuma. I don't know the language; I don't know its people or its way of life."

"There is not much left for you to learn," Raiko said with a scowl. "Your king made sure of that when he sent tutors to purge us out of our own history books."

"He is *not* my king."

"You are Ver Signian by birth and by blood." Raiko gave her a sympathetic look when she glared. "But you are right. This kingdom will never accept you, and you would still be a stranger to Ashuma, regardless of the blood that runs through your veins."

Was that all this world had to offer? Two countries constantly on the brink of war, its people never knowing a day of peace?

There had to be more than this accursed continent, more beyond the black clouds that sat over the storming eastern sea. No sailor had ever returned from their attempt to breach the Veil, but surely the whole of Rhonestiel could not be reduced to this single mass of broken and scarred land. Surely she belonged *somewhere*.

And yet, Reina found no comfort in the thought of Ver Signia or Ashuma.

It was dimmer in the temple now. Only four of the candles remained lit. Beneath cracks of daylight, Raiko's eyes lost their battle-hardened edge, and suddenly, he was no longer the agent trying to chain her to the Order he so deeply hated. Nor was he Aaron's stoic and loyal second-in-command. He was just... a man.

Past the sorrow the two of them shared, there was something softer. Tentative, almost, as if neither wanted to name it. But Reina felt it tugging at her heart: a silent extension of compassion. Perhaps even something like friendship, because while both suffered from wounds the other would never truly understand, at the very least, they now knew that they were not alone. They both clung to dreams that may well never be fulfilled.

Raiko's voice became quieter. "I did not mean to upset you, *dha*—Athira."

She drew her brows close. Sniffed once. "What does that mean? *Dha'katsi.*" The Mal'dhi sounded clumsy and far less fluid on her own tongue, but a tiny smile quivered upon Raiko's lips.

"Nothing you should concern yourself with. I did not call you here just to shout at you. Please, accept my apologies." Reina shook her head, but Raiko was already moving on to other matters. "I brought you here because I never properly thanked you for what you did."

She stiffened. "You don't need to—"

"Thank you," he interrupted gently. "You had no obligation to save me, yet you did so without hesitation. Customs dictate that I owe you a life debt, as does Aaron."

"Aaron?" Reina couldn't hold back her surprise. "But I—"

"Your brother and I are bound by a blood oath." He opened his right hand, revealing a long, thin scar that ran across his palm. "The kindness you extended to me also graces your brother—which means that we *both* owe you favors."

Reina sucked in a breath. Years ago, the thought of Aaron being indebted to her might have excited her, but now, all she could do was shake her head. Memories of Raiko cascading down into the darkness flashed through her mind, and she forced herself to hold his gaze. "You saved me first, remember? You defied direct orders from your captain."

"Because they were, to be frank, shit."

At that, Reina couldn't hold back a weak laugh. The sound loosened the tension between them, and for a second, Raiko's smile was the brightest thing in the room.

"Even if I still considered you our prisoner, which I do not," he added with a pointed look, "there would be no honor in sitting back when I was trained for more."

Were acolytes not trained to follow orders?

Reina shifted uncomfortably. "Aaron would have been happy to let me die."

"I do not think that is true," Raiko said, voice steady, "but even if it were, I would not have allowed that to happen."

"Then you would be robbing him of his one wish in life," Reina spat. "I'm almost certain that the only reason I've made it this far is because Aaron couldn't outright strangle me in front of our caretakers and servants. He took every opportunity he had to make my life miserable, to make sure I knew that I was the biggest thorn in his side. He would have celebrated my death last night, but instead, he's fussing over your wounds today. It must be killing him."

The thought incited a bitter sort of smugness. She hoped that her survival—her defiance against Aaron's best efforts to see her fall—tormented him. She hoped he looked at her and pictured her death as vividly as she pictured his failure. She hoped she stood in the foreground of all his worst nightmares. She hoped—

"Do you really want all that?"

Reina stopped. It was only then that she realized her

thoughts had been verbal, that she'd let all her rage spill like blood into clear waters.

Her face flushed. Her hands curled into fists that she kept close. "I don't... I want—"

"You want to be seen," Raiko said. He looked at her clearly, and he spoke without judgment. "You want him to see you for all that you are instead of all that you were supposed to be. Right?"

Reina clenched her jaw. Hardened her gaze. "Do not presume to know what I want. You don't even know me."

"I know that you ran from home at sixteen years old. Your abandonment is the reason Aaron was prohibited from joining the First and Second Divisions."

That was news to Reina. Still... "What of it?"

Raiko continued, unwavering, "I know that you were betrothed to a man twice your age, which compelled you to leave in the first place. When you refused his hand, your older brother Alexander was forced to take some other nobleman's daughter as his wife. I know that the wedding was awful, and that the marriage has nearly torn your two houses apart from the inside. I know that you never looked back when you ran. You never once stopped to check the damage in your wake. You left your family to pick up the pieces of all that you broke while you chased after some unattainable fantasy. Have I got it all?"

Reina sat there, still as stone. She knew none of that, so how could Raiko, unless Aaron had told him? But why would Aaron confide all the family's worst secrets to a colleague, an outsider?

Because he loves Raiko, an inner voice reminded her. *He loves Raiko, and he hates you, and he would do or say anything to ensure that Raiko hates you, too.*

Well. He accomplished one thing: Reina despised herself.

Alexander—kind, softhearted, sensitive Alexander—deserved so much more than the life he lived now. Marriage for Ver Signian nobles was, before all else, a business arrangement, one with which Lord Rhysanthe seemed perfectly content to burden his daughter. Anything to get her out of his sight forever.

If Reina had known...if she'd anticipated what might have happened to Alexander once she left, she never would have gone.

Wouldn't you have, though? that slithering voice hissed. *You know everything now, and yet here you sit, content to leave your house, your family, in smoldering ruins.*

She silenced the voice with a shake of her head. "There is so much more that you don't know. So much more that would tear down this glorified image that you have of my brother."

"Enlighten me. Tell me how you could justify turning your back on your family."

Reina bristled, and her face reddened. Why should she have to justify anything to him? Just because he missed his own family did not mean she was obligated—or even able—to feel similarly about her own.

But fine. If he wanted to know her reasons, what loss was it to her to divulge her buried pains?

"I had a horse, once. Gifted to me by Alexander for my tenth birthday. I rode it through the fields every day, ignoring my tutors and shirking my lessons. Aaron must have grown tired of hearing Father shout at me, because one morning, when I sneaked out of my room for another ride, the stable hand told me that Aaron had taken the horse to the auctioneers not half an hour earlier."

"And you have held a grudge all these years?" Raiko laughed like she'd told him that Aaron had merely pushed her into a mud puddle when they were toddlers. "You were lucky just to afford a horse."

"I'm speaking now," Reina said in a dangerously quiet tone. Raiko stubbornly shut his mouth. "I doubt Aaron would have told you about the time Father ordered a physician to come and shatter both of my legs so I would finally sit through my tutors' lessons."

She reveled in the way Raiko's unfazed expression shifted to stifled horror. "From dawn to dusk, it was the same: history, economics, war, high society. Did Aaron tell you that those lessons ran twelve hours each day? Or that one night, he drugged my dinner so that I'd stop crying from the pain in my legs? I didn't wake for days. My heart slowed so severely that Alexander and the healers feared I was dead, but that didn't seem to bother either of my parents—or Aaron, for that matter. As long as he had his peace and quiet, what did it matter that he could have killed me?"

Raiko winced as he sat upright, an insufferable kind of sympathy tightening his features. "Athira, stop."

She would not. "Did Aaron tell you about the friend I had, the one he then took away from me?" Reina asked coldly. A knot formed in her throat. She had not spoken of this in years. Had not even allowed herself to think of it.

The memory bled like an open wound now.

"I befriended the second son from House Corvere. We met at a winter fete his family hosted one year and quickly bonded over our distaste for high society. The opulence and masquerading disgusted us both. Our two houses never quite got along, but he and I exchanged letters with his crows. We forged a close friendship over the years." Hurt—raw and aching still, after all these years—breached the walls she had built to lock it away. "I thought we were careful. I thought no one saw me sending his crow back, but one night…"

Her voice failed, and in that instant, she fell into a stifled memory, like a dream that haunted her through the years. Torches burned in brass braziers. The sound of her hurried footsteps echoed down the long corridor of the gatehouse—halted by a steady *drip, drip, drip* of blood on the ground.

"Aaron found us out," she whispered. "He shot the crow. Exposed my crimes to our parents. I never heard from Greysen again."

This was the first time she had spoken his name since leaving the noble ring. It cut deep, like a knife dripping poison.

"What happened to him?"

Reina shrugged. "My father acted as if House Corvere had never existed in the first place, but I knew that even he didn't have the power to wipe them off the map, no matter how much he might have wanted to. I did everything I could to find out if Greysen was okay, if he had faced any retribution for my carelessness—but I heard nothing. Father soon sold my hand to the highest bidding lord in need of an heir, and I occupied myself with plans of escape. I never found Greysen or heard his name again, so I assume he was killed for what we did."

"He was killed for harboring a friendship?" Raiko sounded incredulous, but it was nothing new to Reina.

"We were the youngest children of assassins and military geniuses, the last in line for anything, which meant we could do whatever we wanted—in theory, anyway. We were the biggest liability. What if we were plotting to overthrow our houses? Upend the way of life in high society?"

"Were you?"

"Don't be ridiculous." Reina laughed humorlessly. "We

might have been miserable, but we were just children living for the hope of escaping to a better life."

Raiko blinked slowly. "And is this it? Is this the life you wanted?"

"No." The answer came so easily, so *readily*. Reina paused, weighing the past four years of her life against the dreams she once had.

She left Verilonne to be free of Ver Signian nobility, but the world beyond the walls of her gilded estate was nothing like the rippling hills she envisioned. No one congratulated her on her miraculous escape; no one knew who she was or cared to ask her name. She was a *malduna*, and she had laid down the shield of nobility that kept people from saying it to her face. She was a beggar haunting the corner tavern in every little town she crawled to. She'd abandoned fine silk clothing in favor of torn patchwork pants and boots that were always too wide for her feet. She learned to stomach the fatty, tasteless meat scraps she found because turning away any amount of food was subjecting herself to starvation.

She might have broken free of the golden cage, but by no means had she found freedom.

"I'm still looking for what 'better' means for me," she said. Her eyes traced along the slithering bodies of the painted dragons, then toward the vines of ivy creeping in through the hollowed window. "I don't know if I'll find that in Ashuma or Ver Signia, or somewhere no one else knows. But I can feel it—like a thread pulling on me."

"A pull?" Raiko drew his brows together.

"Yes. It's soft, but nagging. I think it might have been there my whole life, but I've only recently become aware of it." She was spewing her thoughts without restraint now, hardly mindful of what she was saying before she spoke. "I felt it when I left home. I felt it as Draconis was falling, and I feel it now. I don't know where it's leading me, but the only time it goes still is when I'm asleep."

The dragons in her periphery seemed to turn their gazes upon her all at once, and Reina looked desperately to Raiko.

"I feel like I'm always...reaching. Like there's something that's always just beyond me, but no matter how hard I try to chase it, I only grow farther away from it. But it *feels* like it's inside me." She placed a palm over her heart for emphasis. "Like it's been with me my whole life and if I could just get away from everything, it'll finally reveal itself. I don't know what it is or what it might look like, but I *know* I'll recognize it when it comes to me."

Reina paused on an inhale, prepared to say more until she saw Raiko's face.

His mouth was pressed thin. Sympathy pulled his dark brows low over his eyes, and Reina felt the back of her neck warm with embarrassment. He did not understand how she felt —only that she was grappling with some insatiable thing for which she lacked a real name, and that this hole in her being was what kept her running across the continent, searching for the missing piece.

"I've taken up enough of your time," she whispered. "I'm sure you didn't care to hear me complain about my own problems." Indeed, some small sense of shame curdled her insides now that she had revealed so much of herself to him.

"But I did not mind it."

Reina made no comment. She kept her face hidden in shadow as she pushed herself up. Her limbs felt stiff. The guilt surrounding Raiko's condition had subsided, but in its place came a certain *lack*. A hollow weight that reminded her of just how lost she really felt.

She murmured a quiet farewell and made to leave. Just when she reached the archway, Raiko called her name. She turned.

"Tell Aaron that I am well," Raiko instructed. "Tell him that he need not worry so much."

If only Aaron would believe her. But Reina nodded and promised that she would pass on the message. She turned her back and squinted against the glare of broad daylight.

Aaron was waiting a few steps down. Had he been standing there the entire time? At the first sound of Reina's footsteps, he was at the threshold of the temple, his eyes wide and alert despite the fatigued shadows hanging beneath them.

"What did he want?" he demanded. "I heard shouting—is he okay?" He started to shove past Reina before she could even respond, but she grasped her brother's arm and yanked him back. The look on his face could have curdled blood.

"Raiko is fine," she assured him. "He merely wished to thank me for saving his life."

Aaron scoffed. "Saving his life? You're the reason he nearly died." He wrenched his arm free and marched inside, Raiko's name already tumbling from his lips.

Reina dropped her shoulders, and with each descending stair, she stacked her mental walls high again. She heard the men's muffled voices floating out from the window on the side of the building, heard Aaron spit her name like it was venom, and some small part of her curled tightly within herself.

Waiting at the bottom of the flight, almost like an attendant from her family's mansion, was Korris. He gave her a warm smile that she felt obligated to return.

"The twins are down by the river now," he said. "Evren's keeping watch while Iliana harvests some of the herbs—I don't remember which, though. If you want something to keep you busy, I'm sure she'd appreciate the help."

Reina was not so keen to return to the river after her incident with the fish. She scratched the back of her head. "I thought I'd explore the ruins, actually. Familiarize myself with our surroundings."

Mostly, she wanted to be alone. If Korris sensed an ulterior motive, though, he was merciful enough not to comment on it. "That's fine. Just stay where we can find you if anything goes awry."

Reina stroked her fingers along the scars of her palm. "Gods forbid that should happen."

XVII. MEIRYN

MEIRYN BRACED herself as Elder unwrapped the bandage with deliberate slowness. Fresh cloth was hard to come by, so it was only now, three days after Elder initially bandaged Meiryn's wound, that they were getting a chance to inspect it.

Elder's hands were careful and focused, but she chewed her lip or blinked rapidly every time Pyrrha, who loomed behind her like a shadow, grunted or sighed or made any movement at all.

"You're not going to change the outcome by moving at a snail's pace," Pyrrha said, watching Elder peel another layer of cloth back. "Either she's better or she's not."

"It *feels* better," Meiryn offered.

Elder cast her a grateful look, then swallowed and removed the last layer of cloth, discarding it in a small wooden bin, and Meiryn couldn't suppress the sharp intake of breath.

She hadn't had the chance to take a proper look at her wound before Elder tended to it a few nights ago. While Elder worked to remove the bandage, Meiryn had braced herself for mangled, bloody skin. The past couple days of hiking in the woods had robbed her of the rest she would have preferred to give her leg, and it would not surprise her if she had contracted an infection.

But her fears melted; the wound was healing. The skin was still red and tender around the stitches, but as far as Meiryn could tell, everything was normal.

Pyrrha leaned over Elder's shoulder and evaluated the handiwork herself, scrutinizing every stitch like a jeweler appraising a precious stone. After a moment, she leaned back and glanced at Elder, who had been watching her with bated breath.

"Hm," Pyrrha said. She nodded toward the exit. "There's a pile of fresh cloth out in the supplies chest. You'll have to sew the pieces together yourself."

She left without another word, and Meiryn frowned. "I thought you did a great job with it," she said, feeling sorry for Elder.

But Elder was beaming. Her eyes glittered like stars, and she shook her head, nearly tripping over herself as she jumped to her feet. "She's pleased. Pyrrha only comments if I've done something wrong—but this time, she said *nothing*!" She squealed in delight, dancing in place. "Oh! I'm going to get your new bandages. Don't go anywhere."

Meiryn could hardly do so, considering the state of her leg.

Elder exited the tent, humming a cheery tune to herself, and Meiryn leaned forward, tracing a fingertip over her wound. The scars were violent and grotesque, like cracks in a mirror. They would probably welt her skin forever, but Meiryn wasn't perturbed. In fact, she felt a glimmer of pride when she pictured the skin fully healed. It was a mark of her survival, a display of all she had overcome to get here.

Reina won't believe me, she thought, the tiniest grin tugging on her lips. *But if she meets Faun, she won't be able to question it.*

The thought had barely crossed her mind when an arm of light reached into the med tent. Meiryn squinted and shielded her eyes with a hand. Elder couldn't be back so soon—

But it was Faun who peered inside. "Is...this a bad time?"

Meiryn straightened at the waist. She hadn't seen or spoken with Faun since Grey led them out into the forest two nights ago. They had each returned to their respective duties, and Meiryn was content to keep her distance after everyone left on more than tense terms.

So the fact that Faun had sought Meiryn out herself, and was now asking for *her* permission to enter, felt entirely out of character.

Meiryn was still gawking when Faun seemed to interpret her silence as an invitation. She strode in, that long red tail of hair swinging against her back, and took a seat on the cot beside Meiryn's. She sat with her legs pressed together, knees intentionally turned away so as not to intrude on Meiryn's space.

Meiryn cocked her head. "Did you need something?"

No response.

When Faun continued squirming, Meiryn studied her face. An almost otherworldly glow of green eyes sat above a pointed white nose and sharp cheeks dusted with a smattering of freckles.

Meiryn dropped her good leg over the edge of her cot. She leaned into Faun's line of sight, and with delicate enunciation, she repeated herself. "Did you need something?"

Faun blinked twice. Her gaze focused on the space between Meiryn's brows. "I need your help."

Meiryn snorted—she couldn't help it. She hid her smirk

behind a hand and twisted away, pretending like the affronted flush in Faun's cheeks didn't plant a tiny seed of satisfaction.

It was too ironic, after everything that had transpired between them—the threats, the cold shoulders whenever their paths crossed, the outright maiming, all of it. Meiryn would have thought Faun was joking if she didn't look so serious now.

"The other night gave me a lot to think about," Faun explained, still unable to look at Meiryn straight, "so these past couple days, that's all I've been doing. Thinking."

Meiryn stared. "Is that..." She shook her head and gave a one-sided shrug. "Difficult for you?"

Faun's mouth twitched, but the faintest creases above her cheekbones suggested the strain of a hidden smile. She readjusted in her seat so that she had plenty of space to lean back. Her gaze flicked to the angry red lines running down Meiryn's leg.

"You know, that trap was the best I've ever made," Faun said casually. "I got an entire coil of steel wire from the night market in exchange for some lizard skin that Nona dressed up to look like dragon hide."

Meiryn said nothing. If Faun was just reminiscing for the sake of garnering pity, she'd come to the wrong place.

"Nona was...cleverer than any of us." A sad sort of smile played on Faun's lips. "She was quick on her feet, adapted easily to stressful situations. Losing her like that wasn't just a blow to the Guild. It was an insult to everything she was."

"You think I don't feel the same way about Reina?"

"I know you do," Faun said, nodding. She combed her fingers through her hair and looked Meiryn up and down. "You love her, just like I loved Nona."

The tips of Meiryn's ears warmed. She did love Reina, but never had she allowed herself to think that their bond could transcend friendship or sisterhood. Reina never paused to consider such matters. Why, then, should Meiryn?

Still, she ducked her head against Faun's accusation, letting her hair fall around her like a curtain. "It's not like that. She's looked out for me all these years, and it's my job to repay the favor."

"It's not, though. You could have just given up that night, but here you are, still trying to do whatever you can to help her. What is that, if not love?"

Meiryn blinked hard. She met Faun's hard stare, unwilling to let Faun just waltz into the confines of her heart and dig into every weak spot. "What's your point, then? To remind me that I have no idea what I'm doing? That I'm helpless on my own? I *know* I am."

"I came to ask for your help in seeking out that cadre that took your friend."

Why would you ask me? *Why not someone else you don't despise?*

Meiryn swallowed a knot in her throat. "The Order is untouchable. You were in West Glen. You saw what they did to that city just to capture a girl."

"I also know that they took the wrong one without even questioning it," Faun pointed out. "And if what Grey said is true, then they're struggling just like the rest of us now. They're not so infallible."

"So, what?" Meiryn scoffed, tossing her hair over her shoulder. "You think the two of us are going to storm into Draconis, get Reina out, and just leave?"

Faun stretched her arms. A mischievous grin tugged at one side of her mouth. "Come on, princess. Haven't you been around enough huntsmen by now to learn that we have our own ways of getting what we want?"

Meiryn's fingers scraped the edge of her cot. She reexamined the crimson scars lacing around her leg, then heaved a sigh. "I'm not going anywhere until I meet the Wolf King. I came all this way for him—"

"And you found us instead," Faun interrupted. Her voice was clipped, impatient. She hadn't blinked in the last minute. "You need help. That's why you came all this way, isn't it? I can't imagine you were enthused by Nyrōna's plan."

It was true: secretly, Meiryn had been grappling with ways to rescue Reina before Nyrōna made it to Draconis. The trek would be long and arduous. Meiryn hardly knew these woods beyond where Elder took her, and even if she did make it to the city on her own, it could take days to find Reina—even more to smuggle her out of the Order's grasp.

Still, Meiryn wasn't sure if she liked the idea of storming the city with Faun at her side, either. She had already come so far; it would be just her luck if she decided to side with Faun and leave the camp just before the Wolf King returned.

Before she could interject, Faun started speaking again—too quickly for Meiryn to get in another word.

"All I want is to avenge Nona, and all you want is to rescue your friend. Don't you see? Our objectives are aligned. I'll make sure you don't walk into any more snares, and you'll help me find that cadre. Maybe we can get the Guild on our side, too. If we work together, we can both get what we want."

If we work together...

Meiryn lowered her voice. "Why in six hells would I want to work with you?"

Faun faltered. She looked genuinely taken aback. "I—"

"You strung me ten feet up into a tree, ridiculed me every chance you got, and now you're asking for my help?" It was absurd. Audacious beyond reason.

Faun blinked twice, her mouth opening and closing as she struggled for words. Meiryn raised an expectant brow, nails digging against the side of her cot, and Faun managed, "I thought you would want to help. I thought rescuing your friend was important to you."

"It's all that matters to me."

"Then you have to realize that you can't do it on your own," Faun reasoned. "You think you can just walk right into Draconis and pull your friend from the depths of their cells? Let me tell you something, princess: when the Order decides that someone is worth detaining, they *never* let them go. It doesn't matter the crime they committed. Those monsters either torture their prisoners to death, or they turn them into another one of their mindless dogs."

Her voice was quivering, a red flush creeping into her cheeks. "Everyone here has lost someone to the Order, yet you have the gall to act as if you alone are a victim of their cruelty. I'm sorry if things haven't exactly gone your way, but acting like a brat when I try to help you is a shit way to change things for the better."

Just then, Elder came bouncing back into the tent. Meiryn turned her back before the girl could catch a glimpse of her face.

"Oh," Elder said, surprise lifting her tone. "Hi, Faun. I didn't realize you'd sneaked in. Did you need something?"

"I was just leaving," Faun ground out with strained pleasantry. She pushed herself to her feet and brushed past Meiryn without looking at her. She bade Elder a curt farewell, and only when her footsteps faded did Meiryn breathe out again.

She was shaking in her seat. Her pulse was elevated, and she could barely see past the black spots of rage edging into the corners of her vision.

Elder slid into the seat Faun had vacated. "How's your leg feeling?" she asked casually, placing a fresh roll of bandages at her side.

"Fine." Meiryn's response came sharper than she intended, and in her periphery, she saw Elder stiffen. In an attempt to soothe the tension, Meiryn sighed and ran a hand through her hair. She lifted her face. "I'm feeling great, Elder. You did a good job."

Elder smiled, but Meiryn knew she wasn't convinced. Still, she did not pry, and Meiryn did not divulge anything.

———

At dinner that evening, Meiryn stayed close to the healers' tent —not because of any pain in her leg, but because she knew Faun would be near the campfire. Elder was gracious enough to retrieve a plate of food for her without questioning why she couldn't get up and do it herself, and the two sat side by side in the fading light. Shadows of the tents around them stretched like the distant peaks of the Dragon's Spine. Meiryn ate in thoughtful silence, all the while sensing that Elder was growing more and more restless.

Finally, after Elder's fifth comment on how good the roasted rabbit was, Meiryn said, "You weren't interrupting anything important today. When Faun came to visit me, that is."

Elder's ears went pink. She licked her fingertips and gnawed the last bits of meat off the bone, then tossed the scraps into the darkness behind her. "You looked angry," she said carefully, wiping her hands on her pants. "Is everything okay?"

"Yeah." Dwelling on it would only worsen her mood, and she'd only just begun to shake off her indignation. "It's nothing you need to worry about." She thought it would put Elder's mind at ease, but Elder just looked sullen. Meiryn frowned. "Are *you* okay?"

"Everyone always acts like I'm too young to understand anything," Elder muttered. A strand of hair fell over her brow, but she didn't brush it away. "It took me almost two years to convince Pyrrha that I was capable enough to be her apprentice. Nearly all the huntsmen still exclude me from their conversations."

Meiryn's ears pricked. "'Nearly'? There are some who trust you?"

"Just one." When she didn't elaborate, Meiryn leaned close. Elder suppressed a sheepish grin and said in a quieter voice, "It's Grey."

"Grey?" Meiryn couldn't help her surprised outburst. From her observations, Meiryn had surmised that Grey was the most elusive and, frankly, abrasive of the huntsmen. She couldn't tell whether it spoke more about Elder or Grey himself that he trusted her with select secrets.

Elder nodded. She picked at the grass with a bored expression, but Meiryn clung to every word. "He's like an older brother to me. We're closer than you'd think, though it may not seem like it. He trusts me more than the others, which kind of makes up for Pyrrha not wanting to promote me to a full-fledged healer, I guess. But it also means that the huntsmen treat me differently. Sometimes I can't tell if they're being genuinely nice or just trying to get me to say things I shouldn't."

Meiryn caught half of her words. What did Grey know that he withheld from the rest of the Guild, and what did he stand to gain from keeping his silence? How many of those secrets had he shared with Elder?

Elder shook her hair back from her face and said, "He's been gone the last few days. I don't know where." At Meiryn's alarmed look, Elder explained calmly, "His work keeps him away. It's because of him that the Guild has more allies beyond the woods. So when he leaves like this, I'm not usually worried."

Interesting.

"How long is he typically gone?" Meiryn asked with a nonchalant air.

"Sometimes days. Sometimes weeks."

Long enough that Meiryn could sneak into his tent and pry for more information on the Drāga. Perhaps she might even learn more about the Guild itself—the dreaded Wolf King, any alliances, schemes for the future.

The gears were already whirring in her head when Elder stood and stretched her arms high. "Anyway," she said around a wide yawn, "what Grey does is his business. If he chooses to tell us what he's been up to, that's his choice. I learned early on not to press him for information; I think that's why he likes me better than the others."

Meiryn nodded absentmindedly. She wasn't so much concerned with getting Grey to like her as she was with finding out what she had gotten herself into by seeking out the huntsmen. These rogues and spies survived for this long in a losing battle because they kept their secrets close; they clung to shadows that ran deeper than blood.

And if Meiryn wanted to learn any number of those secrets, if she had any hope of finding her way back to Reina, she would have to envelop herself in that same darkness.

XVIII. REINA

While Raiko recovered, the cadre idled and tried to make themselves useful. Days dragged through mind-numbing patrol: Evren and Korris joked once that they were trampling a new dirt path around the perimeter of the village, and Iliana could only join them if she wasn't being called away to tend to Raiko's wounds—which was often.

Nights became restless for Reina. She'd begun lying awake for hours, trying to sleep yet fleeing from it the moment she started to fall. The storm dragon was a frequent solicitor in her dreams, but each time he emerged from black clouds, he was weaker, bleeding from his legs, his torso, his mouth. Reina had started to *feel* the pain from his wounds as if they were her own.

So she refused to sleep.

Tonight, Korris was on guard duty, but over the past few days, Reina had learned that he had a poor habit of drifting to sleep not half an hour into his watch. She lay awake now, blinking into the darkness, waiting for the telltale rumble of his snore.

At the first sign, Reina pried herself off the ground. With

Raiko tucked safely away in the temple and Aaron hunched over just outside, the rest of the cadre slept on makeshift pallets beneath the cover of patchy roofs. The grass beneath her rustled, and she winced, glancing in Iliana and Evren's direction.

The two were curled on their sides, facing each other. Both slept with their weapons in hand, and the steady rise and fall of their chests was identical. They weren't particularly light sleepers, but nevertheless, Reina made sure her feet fell without a sound.

She took a wide berth around Korris and wandered down to the river. Kneeling at its edge, she dipped her hands in, hoping the water might soothe the faint tingling sensation rippling from her lightning scars—or at least cleanse her mind.

But when she stared into the current, someone else's face blinked back at her.

The dragon: eyes bleeding black ink; fangs dripping blood; limbs and wings chained in iron.

The pendant against her chest suddenly flared. Reina yanked it out of her shirt, hissing at the heat in her palm. A ray of moonlight struck the golden arc, and a low groan resonated deep in her skull.

"Find me."

She pressed her hands against her ears, panting unevenly. Why could she not shake him from her mind?

She might have wept from helplessness if she hadn't caught a rustle of movement across the water—exactly where she'd spotted it several days before. She held her breath. Held her ground.

A face, half-concealed behind a cluster of brambles, stared at her through the darkness. Hope glittered in the eyes of the woman beneath the thin hood. She was Ashuman, though she seemed just as curious about Reina as Reina was terrified of her.

A hand reached out from the darkness, as if to beckon her forward.

Reina bolted.

She didn't know if her watcher followed; she didn't dare to look back.

In her haste to return to the safety of camp, she woke Korris. He blinked wildly, brandishing his sword. Reina dropped the pendant beneath her shirt and threw her hands up just as he focused on her. He lowered his weapon and hissed, "Don't sneak up on me like that, Rhysanthe. Gods."

"I wasn't sneaking," Reina retorted. "You fell asleep again."

If it were daytime, Korris's embarrassment might have been more visible. But he sheathed his sword and asked, "What are you doing up, then? Trying to take my job?"

There was a teasing dig in his tone, but Reina was in no mood for humor. She retreated to her pallet with an incoherent, murmured response, keeping one eye on the forest as she stretched out on the ground.

No one but Reina knew of the watcher. Part of her hoped it had been a trick of the mind, but it was naive—and arrogant, she felt—to think that just because the cadre had found shelter here, they were safe from whatever lay hidden in the mountains.

She stayed far from the river the next morning, but killing time in the ruins proved a depressing endeavor. Most of the homes lacked bookshelves, which ruled out the hope of finding journals or diaries that might have been left behind. It shouldn't have surprised her, yet she was frustrated when her exploration left her empty-handed. Bandits and scavengers would have looted anything of value. Drawers were left half-open; cupboard doors hung precariously from their hinges; even the curtains had been harvested for scrap cloth.

What remained untouched by human greed were thin canvases decorated with family portraits. Though many paintings were ruined beyond repair, a small few were mostly unharmed. Reina knelt before one such portrait and traced a fingertip over the figures in the painting.

The artist's hand was light, yet deft and masterful in capturing the bright faces of their smiling subjects: a family of five, including two parents who hovered behind a neat row of three daughters. The youngest couldn't have been older than five years; the middle sister wore a fiendish smirk that Reina could mirror with ease; the eldest donned a serene, wise expression. Quick brushstrokes outlined her thin brows, and those narrow, almond-shaped eyes captured a slyness that often settled upon Aaron's face.

These were real people. Families.

Reina frowned. She'd spent a lifetime wishing away the very things that were so cruelly torn from the people who once lived here. The estate that bordered her childhood was nearly as impenetrable as the king's castle. House Rhysanthe was wealthy enough to employ its own guards, who would defend the estate with their lives. Fire could tear through the streets of Verilonne, and the gold and white face of the mansion would stare down at the ashes, resolute and unmarred. And despite the resentment that Reina harbored for her family, she couldn't ignore the glaring fact that they were, at the very least, alive.

But if that was all her family amounted to—a cluster of strangers who shared a surname and once lived together—then had she really lost anything at all?

Reina dropped the portrait. Thoughts like these would only trap her within an echo chamber of her own fears.

As she started to leave, a spear of light pierced her eye. She grimaced and pinpointed the source: a small golden trinket half-buried beneath the rubble. Reina crouched and brushed away the debris, and her heart stopped.

The gold finish was fading and the edges of the pin were chipped, but the shape was unmistakably identical to the pendant Reina wore now. A dragon caught in mid-flight, the minimal outline of its wing stretching onward in a graceful arc.

Entranced, Reina traced her thumb over the spiraling impression of the dragon's chest, feeling a strange tug of familiarity. She'd seen this before—and not just in the tunnels. Before then, too. It was the briefest flash of memory, but it was there, anchoring her to a lifetime of things she tried to forget.

Those memories were swept away in a gust of wind that slammed every cupboard door shut and rocked the house on its unsteady frame. Reina jumped at the sound of Evren's warning call, dropping the trinket.

She rushed outside, but Korris and Evren had ducked low into the nearest shadows, weapons drawn and eyes trained upward. Standing in the hollowed archway of the temple was Aaron; just behind him, Reina barely made out Iliana's slight frame. And behind her—

Raiko was standing, healed and strong again.

He barely caught Reina's eye before Korris hissed and motioned for her to find cover. Reina glanced up just as a fully matured Infernal soared dangerously low over the cadre's makeshift camp.

"Shit—"

Heart hammering, Reina fell back into the house, slapping

a hand over her mouth and praying that the dragon hadn't seen her. She held her breath and watched the Infernal circle the village. Eyes like stones of amber glittered within deep sockets of brown, scaly leather. From here, Reina could almost smell its fiery breath. Her hands went clammy. She pressed herself closer to the wall.

The dragon perched atop a cluster of trees and craned its neck down toward the village. Its nostrils flared, and the blood in Reina's veins ran cold when it unhinged its jaws and scented the air.

Moving as slowly as she could, Reina fisted a handful of ash and smeared it across her neck and face. Dust settled in her lungs. Her eyes watered as she suppressed a cough.

The Infernal peered through the canopy. Its ridged tail waved in lazy motions, but its gaze was as sharp as a hunter's arrowhead. Was it searching for prey? Scouting for intruders?

Just when Reina thought the Infernal might descend to the forest floor and find the cadre hiding, it threw its head back and screeched.

Every hair on her body stood on end. Reina curled tight with her hands pressed against her ears, but she felt the pendant against her chest thrumming with that restless energy again, pulsing like someone else's heartbeat.

Like it was answering the Infernal's call.

She squeezed her eyes shut and ignored the noise until she felt the air shift. The sound of beating wings—then all was quiet again.

An unknown amount of time passed before a hand shook her shoulder. Reina gasped and blinked against glaring light.

"Athira," Raiko said. He was crouched at her side. The

color and warmth had returned to his face, and his voice sounded much stronger now. "It is safe now."

She glanced behind him to where Aaron loomed in the doorway. Poking out from their hiding places, Evren and Korris chattered nervously about the dragon. Iliana had raced down the temple steps to meet her brother, and Reina vaguely heard her mention something about tracking the dragon's flight before she finally dragged her gaze back to Aaron.

"At least you didn't draw its attention," he muttered, looking her over.

Reina dropped her hands. "Where did it come from?" She'd only ever known Infernals to come from the archipelago, but that was miles away.

"There are nests scattered throughout the Spine," Aaron answered in a tone that implied it should have been obvious. His arms were crossed, feet planted shoulder-width apart. "Just be grateful your stench didn't give us away."

Reina made a face but chose not to respond. Addressing Raiko, she said, "I see you're feeling better."

Raiko gave her a lopsided smile, straightening at the waist. "I was in good hands. You, however, look like you have seen better days."

She forgot she'd dirtied herself. A hot wave of embarrassment flushed her cheeks. "Does this mean you're well enough to travel again?"

"Why? Had enough chance encounters with the *kaeli rekks*?" he teased with a slight lift of his brow.

Reina huffed and shook her head. "You have no idea."

Raiko grinned.

Aaron, witnessing every second of this interaction, flexed

his arm and cleared his throat, but he earned only a slightly annoyed glance from Raiko.

Reina loosened the tension in her body, forgetting that she'd dropped the golden trinket nearby. When she pushed herself to her feet, Raiko spotted it before she could step over it. He went rigid, and his eyes widened.

"Impossible."

"Oh, no—"

He'd already plucked it off the ground. Aaron marched forward, and the Rhysanthe siblings watched as Raiko traced the dragon pendant with a trembling finger.

"What is that?" Aaron asked, shooting an accusatory glare in Reina's direction.

But Raiko replied in a shocked whisper, "I thought they were just legends. Characters from my favorite night-tale."

"Who?" Aaron and Reina asked at the same time. Their gazes met with equal aggravation.

"*Reksari*—dragon riders," Raiko clarified for Reina. "They called themselves Drāga, equals to the rulers of the sky. In the stories, they were warriors whose powers matched those of the dragons we fear today. They ruled an ancient dynasty in tandem with the *kaeli rekks* of old."

Whose powers matched those of the dragons we fear today...

Reina was barely breathing, but Aaron snorted. "This is nothing. Not even the looters found any value in it."

But Raiko was utterly transfixed, turning the trinket over in his hand. "Perhaps. Still—it has been a long time since the Drāga crossed my path, in stories or otherwise. And we are so far from Ashuma."

"This used to be Ashuman territory, right?" Reina pointed out. She recalled the family portrait she'd found, the Ashuman faces smiling back at her. "Before the Spine became neutral land, this village belonged to the Ashuman Empire. Maybe these people passed the stories on to their children, too."

Some part of her wanted to believe that this was what happened—if only because that meant there were others out there who knew what this symbol represented. The warriors Raiko spoke of sounded terribly familiar to everything Reina was experiencing in her dreams.

And the more she dwelled on it, the more she feared that *she* had caused the explosion in Draconis. That *she* had wielded the storm dragon's magic.

Her heart trembled nervously, and she clasped a fist around her own concealed Drāga pendant.

Raiko sighed. "Even if that is true, those children are long gone, as are the *reksari*."

"Who were just folklore to begin with," Aaron added.

"Yes. Of course." Raiko cast a crestfallen look around the crumbling home, and it struck Reina then that this was his first time seeing the village. He hadn't yet explored the ruins that gave the cadre shelter from the elements. She recalled how emotional he'd gotten, telling her all of the deception that Ashuma suffered from Ver Signia, and it almost compelled her to reach out and comfort him.

But Raiko closed his hand around the gold trinket, then pocketed it. He blinked twice, erasing his wistfulness. "We should join the others, yes?"

"You go ahead," Aaron said. His gaze slid to Reina. "I want a word with this one."

Raiko looked warily between them, but he nodded and left without another word.

Arms folded, Aaron blocked Reina's path to the exit.

"If you're here to blame me for what happened, save your breath," Reina said before he could get a word in.

His face was stone. "What are you talking about?"

"The cave dragons," Reina elaborated. "Raiko jumped in to save me. He was hurt because of it. I know you must hate me, now that you both owe me a favor. I know you still want me dead." She dropped her stare, searching for Aaron's sword, but he was unarmed.

"I never planned to kill you," he said.

But neither would he prevent her death. He just wouldn't bloody his own hands—not when a dragon or even their father was just as capable.

"So," Reina breathed, "you plan to turn me back in, then. I'm surprised we haven't been ambushed by any of our attendants. Did your letter get lost?"

A muscle in Aaron's jaw twitched. "Enough." He sounded so weary, he couldn't even combat her snark.

Reina almost pitied him. Almost.

"What, then?" she prodded. "You don't have anything to say to me, you just want me to stay as far away from Raiko as possible, because I'm nothing but bad luck and I'd only get him hurt again?"

She wanted to hear him say it. Wanted that angry admission of his hatred.

But Aaron gave the tiniest incline of his head. "I was going to thank you for saving him."

Reina stared. Even though Raiko was healed, even though he was upright and walking around, weariness and worry dulled the coal-black of Aaron's eyes. His shoulders sagged, his back curved. But there—Reina could have sworn she saw it: a glimpse of gratitude on his face.

Aaron sniffed and looked away. When he spoke again, his voice was stronger, but forcibly so. "Iliana said that if the puncture wounds had gone any deeper, Raiko would have..." He trailed off and shuddered. *Shuddered.* "You saved him, so thank you. That's all. Just—thank you."

She felt wretched. Despicable.

"Aaron—"

He spun on his heel and left, stirring ash into the air.

That evening, the cadre enjoyed a meal of roasted trout that Evren and Korris fished from the river. It was the first time they had all shared a moment together without someone being tied up or bleeding out somewhere, and their spirits were noticeably lighter. They sat around a tiny fire constructed in one of the hollow houses, letting the pillar of smoke filter through the trees.

Reina watched the thin grey clouds reach for the distant stars. "Aren't you worried someone might find us here?"

"Who?" Evren asked around a mouthful of food. "Korris and I scoured this place. We're the only ones out here."

The watcher from the river surfaced in her mind's eye, but she bit her tongue. They were safe; nothing had happened. Iliana looked more at ease now that she was relieved of her healing duties, Evren merely looked happy to have his sister at his side again, and Korris updated Raiko on everything that happened while he was recovering—which, to be fair, was not much.

Sitting at the edge of the circle was Aaron, leaning back on one hand and observing his cadre. Fondness warmed his gaze, and for once, the hard lines of his permanent scowl softened into the more delicate curve of a smile.

He resembled their mother in that moment, wholly unlike himself yet more at ease than Reina had ever seen. Why risk saying anything that would revert him to his unbearable, authoritative state?

Dinner ended when the fire burned out. Korris stamped out the flickering embers and offered to take the first watch. He then pointed at Raiko. "You're up next, though. You've had it easy these past few days."

"Yes," Raiko deadpanned, "it was all too easy fighting for my life every night."

Iliana snorted, and Aaron made some disgruntled comment that no one understood.

"Why don't I take first watch?" Reina piped up. Five heads turned in her direction. "I haven't had a night watch yet. The rest of you deserve a break."

Suspicion wiped the laxity from Aaron's face, but Korris said, "I'll entertain that offer, little Rhysanthe. Thank you."

Reina graced him with a generous smile. She pretended not to notice Aaron's dagger-eyed glare as she addressed Evren. "I'll need a weapon in case there's trouble."

Evren glanced at Aaron, who shook his head, then turned back to Reina and offered her the daggers hilt-first. "You handled yourself alright the other night, and these woods are safe enough. But in case something does happen, I trust you'll remember where to point these."

"Of course." She examined the blades, furrowing her brow at the engraved *C* on the hilts. Hadn't she seen this somewhere before?

The memory dashed beyond reach when Aaron shoved

himself to his feet. He said not a single word, but his anger was palpable as he stalked into the shadows.

It must have been tearing him up inside, watching his agents defy his orders for *Reina's* sake.

A cruel part of her delighted in the moment. Was it not deserved after all Aaron had put her through in West Glen? Why should she give a damn about what he felt?

Reina blocked him from her mind while the others briefed her on how to keep watch through the night. Mostly, they advised her on how best to stay awake. She heeded their words like it was an inside joke they all shared. It only hit her when the cadre scattered to their separate pallets that their lives were in her hands. Any danger that approached in the darkness was her responsibility to handle.

The first hour crawled by. Reina paced in a wide circle, hands fisted tightly around Evren's daggers. Boredom became her greatest enemy, not fatigue, for she had learned to stave off tiredness these past few nights.

At the second hour, Reina double-checked that the cadre was fast asleep before diverting from the trail and making a straight line for the river. She hadn't come this close to the riverbank since the other night, but something called to her now. It was that same pull she felt in Draconis. She stopped by the water's edge and stared across to the other side.

Darkness and ferns. Treetops glistening silver beneath the moon. Fish shimmering within a restless river.

Nothing.

Reina sighed and rolled her neck. She passed the dagger from her right hand to her left so that both blades were clutched awkwardly in one fist. With her free hand, she tugged on the leather cord around her neck until her pendant surfaced.

Raiko's fascination with the insignia perplexed her. She'd never heard of the Drāga until today, yet something about the name filled her with a sense of yearning—like the truth of what happened to her in Draconis might lie with these warriors of legend.

As she pondered, her senses dulled. She lost herself in her thoughts and stopped listening for the snapping of twigs, stopped watching for movement in the shadows. She only wondered who these Drāga were and whether they might be the missing piece to her puzzle.

When a shadow flitted over the river and blotted out the starlight, Reina barely flinched. Her head was down, her gaze locked on her mysterious dragon pendant when a pair of footsteps landed softly in the grass.

Reina had barely tossed her second dagger back into her right hand when something rushed toward her. One warm hand smothered a cloth over her mouth and nose; another cradled her weight as she fell unconscious.

XIX. MEIRYN

IT SEEMED that rejecting Faun's proposed alliance had inspired a foul sort of hatred in her, and as a result, Meiryn faced even worse ostracism from the Guild. The taunting and jeering might as well have been mockingbird calls. Navigating the campsite was a gamble of whether Meiryn would be barreled over by a huntsman who deliberately veered into her path. Even the herbs she gathered sometimes were found in tattered ruins, for which Meiryn was blamed.

She refused to stoop to their level. Despite their hostility, she found solace in Elder's company and instruction. She learned to distinguish fishtail ferns—restorative plants growing in the more humid regions of the forest—from snake tongue, an invasive species of poisonous ferns that thrived in drier, sunnier areas. Water root, which she worked with nearly every day, required immense care and attention to maximize its healing benefits. Nightshade berries could be brewed into a sweet-scented potion that would stop an enemy's heart in a minute.

Other plants, like the honey poppy, sun rose, and dragonling nettle, filed themselves away in Meiryn's mind—each accompanied by distinguishing characteristics that she'd committed to memory during her long hours of work. It helped that Elder, in that quietly insightful way of hers, took Meiryn on as many excursions as she could to help her get away from the strain of being around the others.

"You know, you don't have to save me from anyone," Meiryn said one morning. She worried that avoiding the huntsmen seemed only to deepen their mistrust.

Elder tilted her head to the side and drummed her fingers on the empty bag hanging at her hip. "We have work to do. Pyrrha left you in my hands, so I'm just training you to become a full-fledged healer. Nothing more."

Her words were innocent, but her insistence implied a more pointed motive.

Another day of work passed. Meiryn and Elder were nearly back at camp after foraging beneath the shaded forest, chattering about whether they thought the huntsmen would have successfully snared that stag someone saw the other day, when Meiryn halted.

"Dammit," she swore. Her bag was suspiciously light.

Elder came to the same realization. "We forgot the propagations."

Meiryn nodded, already backtracking into the forest. Elder started after her, but Meiryn waved her away. "I'll be fine. Here, take these and store them away. I won't be long."

She handed off her bundled herbs. Her bag hung from her shoulder, empty save for a few glass jars. She bade Elder farewell and retreated toward the stream.

This early in the evening, the sun was still hot. She walked in the shadier path, trampling foliage if she needed to, until she reached her destination.

The water was lukewarm, and she took care not to accidentally trap the tiny fish in her jars. Once both were full and the lids were fastened, Meiryn set her things aside and cupped her hands. She let the water pool in her palms, then splashed her face and washed away the sweat.

It would be a mercy to linger here until nightfall. The work she accomplished with Elder kept her fears for Reina's safety at bay, but she'd grown too comfortable here. Even Elder's kindness could not desaturate the huntsmen's cruelty or Faun's rage.

Time was surpassing Meiryn. She was no closer to saving Reina than she was to enlisting the Guild's aid.

The glass jars clinked together as Meiryn shouldered her bag, but just before she rose to her feet, a crow's call sounded nearby. She flinched a second later when the black bird swooped low enough to sweep a few strands of her hair out of place.

A crow...

Meiryn stayed low to the ground, holding her breath to listen for sounds above the trickling stream. It was a moment before anything happened, but then—

Two voices in the distance. Arguing.

"—had no choice. The Spine grows more restless every day. Just the other day, an entire colony of cave dragons erupted from their nest."

Meiryn froze.

That was Temaerys. But what was he doing this far north of the Spine? Her surprise only heightened when Grey responded, sounding agitated.

"Send my crow if you can. I can't help you if you're caught by our enemies, and without Nona, the Guild has lost faith in helping to restore the Drāga empire. If any of the huntsmen saw you out here, they'd be suspicious."

Temaerys snorted. "Your huntsmen are lazy and arrogant if they think 'their forest' is so easily guarded by repeating the same patrols. Anyone with eyes could walk their path and trace it back to camp."

"For your sake, I won't take that as a threat." Meiryn heard Grey take a deep breath and release it slowly. "You're here now. What was so important that you crossed enemy lines?"

"The cadre of interest. We found them."

Meiryn abandoned her things at the stream and crawled toward the sound of their voices. She pressed herself against the earth, peering through the underbrush to see the men.

"You've already moved forward?" Grey demanded. "I thought I told you—"

"They are not in your fortress city," Temaerys interrupted calmly. "Nyrōna spotted them within the Spine. We do not know where they came from or how they got there, but they have taken refuge in the ruins of an abandoned village. They are injured, and it is all I can do to keep Nyrōna from rushing up to capture the girl."

So Reina was still with the cadre. They hadn't killed her—yet. But what were they doing out in the Dragon's Spine while Draconis sat broken and crippled?

Grey frowned. "How can you be so sure she's the one you're looking for?"

"When Nyrōna found the cadre, she spent days spying on them. She said she saw the girl by the river, wearing the signet of the Drāga around her neck."

"It could be a coincidence."

"Nyrōna is adamant. She says she can sense the girl's power straining against her own doubt."

This was absurd. Just false hope born from numerous coincidences. Humans weren't powerful—at least, not in the way Temaerys implied.

These Drāga were figures of imagination. Nothing more.

Grey muttered indistinctly. Temaerys answered in a matching tone, and Meiryn held her breath, just barely catching the last part of Grey's warning.

"...but those cadres are dangerous. My cousins were drafted in my stead when I left the noble ring. The Order turned an inventor and an alchemist into dragon-slaying machines. They train those acolytes to forget who they once were."

The rest of his speech fell beneath the blaring repetition of his earlier words in Meiryn's head: *When I left the noble ring.*

Did that mean... No, it couldn't. Grey was a huntsman—distant and colder than the others, but still trusted. He could not have come from nobility.

Could he?

Temaerys scoffed, slicing through the knotted threads of Meiryn's speculations. "We are not part of your network of rogues. We make our own decisions."

"It's not about freedom of choice," Grey insisted. "It's about preserving lives. Haven't you lost enough already?"

When Temaerys replied, he sounded dangerously calm. "I might ask the same of you, Corvere."

The earth scuffed beneath Grey's boots as he surged forward, his face close to Temaerys, who didn't flinch a centimeter. In a low whisper laced with stifled fear, Grey said, "Don't ever say that name again."

Meiryn committed it to memory. *Corvere.*

Temaerys chuckled. "I have not forgotten what became of your so-called Wolf King. Even now, stories of his death ripple through your allies, severing their loyalty to your huntsmen and sending them scurrying back home. You should be grateful to have any allies left at all."

Sweat trickled down the back of Meiryn's neck. She wasn't moving. Hardly breathing. The trees themselves seemed to defy the breeze that rustled their branches, but the ground beneath her felt like it was trying to shake her off its back.

"Nyrōna grows more restless every day," Temaerys continued when Grey remained silent. "I had to trust that she would not do anything reckless in my absence. I implore the same trust from you when I say that you must turn your forces against the Order. Unchain the dragon."

Grey grunted. "I thought you'd given up hope of restoring the Drāga. Why should I throw my men into danger now?"

"Hope is lost," Temaerys said plainly, "but Nyrōna helped me see that this is what Nona would have wanted. If I could not be there when my sister breathed her last, then I will do what I can to honor her greatest wish now."

"Even if this girl is not what you think?"

"Even so."

Meiryn shook her head vehemently. Her throat ached to release her fury, a scream that would rattle the forest. She clawed her nails into the dirt and heard the blood roaring in her ears.

Grey and Temaerys had the audacity to end their conversation with murmured farewells.

Meiryn stayed flat on her stomach long after both men's footsteps receded. She did not know how much time passed, but when she finally rose again, it was past sundown.

By now, Elder would be searching for her, but Meiryn

couldn't let herself be found here. Not when she was still reeling from what she'd learned.

Grey was of noble blood.

Reina lay stranded in a cadre's captivity, a walking target for Nyrōna.

The Wolf King was dead.

Meiryn was on her own.

She barely processed the feeling of grass peeling away from her cheeks. A hole gaped in her chest, and when she managed to push herself onto all fours, it took her a moment to regain her bearings.

She blinked at the dark sky. Beyond the treetops, she could just make out a few winking stars. She thought of Reina. How many nights had passed since they'd been separated? Time blurred; Elder's friendship had lulled Meiryn into a false sense of comfort.

Her mission was to rescue Reina. That was all she had ever hoped to achieve by throwing herself at the Guild's mercy. But if the Wolf King was a mere memory, then who was left that could help her?

An image of Faun—sheepish and somewhat embarrassed as she proposed some far-fetched scheme—flashed in Meiryn's mind.

No. Meiryn shook her head. Faun was out of the question. Never mind that she had come to Meiryn already; never mind that their goals were aligned. Faun had proven that she was not a friend or an ally.

And yet...she remained the only person who might be able to get Meiryn where she needed to go. If Temaerys spoke true, and the cadre really had found their way into the Dragon's Spine, then it didn't matter what Grey wanted to do about the rest of the Order, or Draconis. Meiryn only needed to find the cadre.

And the only person who still cared enough to find them was Faun.

Meiryn dragged herself upright. She'd never dreaded returning to camp more than she did tonight.

"Where were you?" Elder cried when Meiryn finally slipped into the healers' tent. She abandoned her dinner, crashing into Meiryn with a tight embrace around her waist. "I was getting worried. I was about to send for help—"

"I'm alright," Meiryn interrupted gently. She glanced at the extra plate of food beside Elder's, feeling a twinge of guilt. She rubbed Elder's back, then held her at arm's length. "I can't eat with you tonight, though. There's something I need to do."

"Oh." Elder's shoulders fell. "Is everything okay?"

"Yes." The lie came too easily for comfort. "Enjoy your dinner before it grows cold. I'll be back soon enough."

Meiryn exited the tent, making a straight line for the blazing bonfire. Huntsmen chatted mildly amongst themselves, sharing another meal of roasted game. Sitting close to the fire, Meiryn found Faun surrounded by her friends. Among them was Lukas, who hadn't spoken a word to Meiryn since that day at the stream.

Meiryn inhaled deeply, letting her breath seep out between her lips, and approached the huntsmen. A warmth that had nothing to do with the fire washed over her face when Faun and her posse regarded Meiryn with identical glares.

"I need to speak with you," Meiryn said, keeping her eyes trained on Faun.

Faun's brows shot up, and she dropped her dinner scraps on

a plate of tree bark. "Whatever for, princess? Do you need me to read you a night-tale so you can sleep soundly?"

Her friends snickered—all except Lukas, who refused to lift his gaze past Meiryn's shoulders.

Meiryn steeled her nerves. "It's about Nona."

No one smiled or joked. In her periphery, Meiryn saw Lukas shuffling uncomfortably in his seat. Faun's face had gone slack, and her grip on her plate tensed. "Are you here to apologize?"

Meiryn bit her tongue. She refused to apologize for something she did not do. It was not her sword that stopped Nona's heart. It was not her arrow that strayed too wide of Nona's killer.

So, she said, "I was surprised by your visit the other day. You left before I had the chance to think about what you said."

She reveled in the way Faun shrank under her friends' stares. Judging by their bemused expressions, they had no idea that Faun sought Meiryn out a few days ago. As far as they were concerned, their ringleader was above groveling.

"Well." Faun combed a hand through that tail of red hair. "If you have something to share, then enlighten us."

Fine. If that's how you want it.

Meiryn cleared her throat and gave her a plain look. "That alliance you proposed—I've reconsidered."

One of Faun's friends choked on their drink. Lukas halted mid-bite, eyes widening, and Faun rose to her feet, discarding her dinner scraps into the fire. Embers cracked and jumped from the pit.

"Follow me," Faun sighed, leaving her friends without a parting remark. She wore a placid mask, but as she marched off, Meiryn saw the whiteness of her fists.

Lukas blinked twice as Meiryn passed, opening his mouth like he wanted to say something, but Meiryn ignored him.

The low chatter of the huntsmen pelted their backs like stones. Meiryn distracted herself from their restless murmurs by watching the way that long red tail of hair lashed back and forth as Faun led her to a more private area. She watched the way Faun walked: chest out and chin up, her steps sure and deliberate. Meiryn subconsciously had begun to mimic Faun's strides when they finally reached the edge of camp, where they were alone.

Faun whirled. "You have my attention. Don't lose it again." Her tongue was sharp, but something like admiration chased the brimming anger.

Meiryn met her fire with an unshakable resolve. "You were right. About the alliance, I mean. What we want is too closely aligned not to figure this out together."

"You're parroting my words now?" Faun scoffed. She narrowed her eyes. "Were you robbed of any original thought when you fell from that tree?"

Meiryn ignored the jab and leaned close. "The cadre you're after is no longer in Draconis."

At that, Faun's arms dropped. She searched the darkness, as if expecting an eavesdropper to pop out at any moment. In a savage hiss, she demanded, "How could you possibly know that?"

Meiryn dove into an explanation. She relayed everything she had overheard, choosing to omit the detail of Grey's origins. She spoke so fervently at times that her words stumbled over one another. All the while, she watched Faun's expression meld from shock into disbelief, then finally into anger.

"So Nyrōna is already throwing herself at another Drāga," Faun spat. "Nona has only been gone for a few weeks."

Reina had been imprisoned for just as long, but Meiryn thought it wise not to point that out. Faun was muttering to herself—words Meiryn could barely understand—while pacing in antsy circles. Meiryn was growing dizzy just from watching her.

"You see now why I came to you?" she pressed, hoping it might snap Faun out of her mumbling.

Faun just shot a brief glare her way. "You could have been a little more subtle, if I'm being honest."

"How—"

"Anyway," Faun rambled, "we need a plan of action." Her brow was creased in thought, as if she had been waiting for this moment. As if she had anticipated, somehow, that Meiryn would come back to her. Meiryn didn't know whether she liked that or not. "Nyrōna is already two steps ahead of us. If she gets your friend—"

"*Reina.*"

"—then that cadre will scamper back to the Order with their tails in between their legs, and we'll have lost them for good."

Meiryn agreed wholeheartedly, which was why she insisted, "We should talk to Grey. See if he can get Temaerys to convince Nyrōna to hold off."

Faun barked a malicious laugh. "If Grey hasn't told us any of this himself, it's for a reason. He probably thinks I'd try and sneak away from the Guild to find that cadre on my own."

"Would you?"

"Of course."

Meiryn threw her hands up in a helpless gesture. "Well, if Grey won't trust us, then we're on our own."

Faun halted and side-eyed her. Cautiously, she asked, "What about the Wolf King?"

Meiryn glowered. "You can drop the pretense. I know he's dead."

A mix of bitterness and relief dashed across Faun's face. She nodded once. "Good. As long as you're not still chasing night-tales in the woods."

"Why not tell me upfront?" Meiryn asked, unable to hold it in. "Why let me make a fool of myself in front of the entire Guild?"

"If we told you right away that there was no Wolf King, you'd have left to find help elsewhere. We couldn't risk you spilling our whereabouts to the first stranger you met."

"And it's less of a risk to integrate me into your numbers and *then* run away?"

Faun jerked her chin at Meiryn's leg. "You're not running anywhere with that limp. And besides, the Guild has been watching you all this time. Even if you tried to desert us now, we've learned enough about you to stop you before you could even set foot beyond these tents."

She stated it so plainly, as if her words were meant to reassure Meiryn that no one was actually going to hunt her down now, but Meiryn's privacy had never felt more violated. She hugged her arms close to her chest, paranoid that she was being watched at this very moment.

"What's your plan, then?" she asked, glancing toward the woods. "Are you just going to take off on your own?"

"No." Faun said it like she had to really think about it. She gave Meiryn a pointed look. "You wanted this alliance, too, didn't you? *We're* going to take off on our own."

Meiryn choked on her breath, and a slow grin spread Faun's lips wide. Were it not for the huntsmen still gathered around the campfire, Meiryn might have spewed her dissent loud enough to scatter the birds from the treetops. She regained her composure with a trained breath.

"Wouldn't that be considered desertion?" she asked. "Grey would never—"

"Grey is just a spy. He's not the Wolf King or Guild master," Faun interrupted. A hard edge crept into her voice. "No one is. We can't break the rules if there are none to break."

"That's a dangerous philosophy to live by." And it was eerily reminiscent of how Reina might handle the situation.

"What was ever accomplished by playing it safe?" Faun's eyes glittered in the night. She extended her forearm and held Meiryn's gaze. "So, what's your move, princess? Are you with me or not?"

She arched a rust-colored brow over one eye. Around the dark moons of her pupils were tiny sapphire flecks, brightening the deeper green tones. Something about it drew Meiryn in; the lucrative deal of an alliance, yes, but also the faintest push of a challenge. A test of strength and willpower. And Meiryn was tired of waiting for someone else to save her.

Emboldened by the thrill of finally *doing* something for herself, Meiryn reached forward and wrapped her hand around Faun's forearm. Her skin tingled as Faun mirrored the gesture.

"I'm with you."

XX. REINA

Someone was humming a lullaby that Reina remembered from the vaguest memories of her early childhood, when her mother still loved her. She murmured wordlessly, nuzzling against a soft pillow that smelled of jasmine.

A gentle but callused hand stroked her hair back from her face. An unfamiliar voice spoke words that Reina could not translate, and she pried open her eyes, training blurry and unfocused vision on a face looming above her.

"Greetings, *amia*," an Ashuman woman murmured. She said something else, but her words were in Mal'dhi.

Reina's tongue sat uselessly in her mouth. Every muscle in her body felt heavy and numb. Her eyelids dragged shut, then slid open again in a slow blink. She couldn't even pull herself away when the woman reached out and cupped her face.

"Ver Signian," the woman realized aloud, brows creasing ever so slightly. Her gaze flitted back and forth as she studied Reina's features, but that look of awestruck wonder never strayed far. "So far from home. Do you even know who you are?"

Reina could only manage a panicked grunt. She willed movement into her limbs, but whatever poison coursed through her veins kept her paralyzed on this bed. Her breaths quickened, though her heartbeat was sluggish and her chest barely rose an inch.

The woman smiled again. For one vulnerable moment, Reina wanted to trust those soft brown eyes. She wanted to be lulled into docility by that warm voice.

But then she remembered the cadre. How long had it been since she was captured? Did they even know she was gone?

Why would they care? a little voice asked. *Aaron was content to let you die. You think he'd come looking for you now, when you were the one who got yourself into this mess?*

Reina curled her hands into fists. "Who are you?" she tried to ask, but what came out was an incomprehensible groan. She went rigid when the woman hooked her forefinger around the leather cord on Reina's neck. She lifted the dragon pendant between them and smiled.

"Drāga," the woman whispered.

Reina inhaled sharply. The urge to divulge every detail of what happened in Draconis clashed against the instinct to keep her secrets close. The fog in her brain cleared when the woman spoke in a hushed tone.

"You met your counterpart," the woman stated, as if she already knew. As if she had already *seen*. "The dragon who calls to you will never leave you. Across time and space, your souls are bound by an unbreakable thread. His memories will become your own, and with practice, you will become a conduit of his power. The catalyst for change."

Reina shook her head. "No," she uttered. It was all she could manage. "No. No. No."

The woman ignored her protests. "This is what you were destined for. Are you not visited in dreams by this dragon who marked you?" She took Reina's wrist and opened her hand, revealing the webbed scars at the center of her palm. Reina pulled, but the woman's grip was too strong. "His is the voice that speaks to you when you feel scared or lonely or helpless. His is the power you will wield to restore all that was lost."

Whatever had been lost, Reina had no part in it, and she had no intention of submitting herself to some predestined fate.

She searched the room, noting every possible exit. Behind the woman was a wooden door that likely led into another room, but on one wall was an open window, covered only by a thin curtain.

That was her escape.

Reina could feel the effects of the poison wearing off. She felt her strength rolling back to her like the tides creeping further up the shoreline. Her thoughts became clearer, her vision sharper. She found her voice again, raspy though it was.

"What if I refuse?" She glared at the woman, who blinked in shock, as if the very idea of refusing this fate was blasphemy. Reina reveled in her dumbfounded expression. "Why would I do anything for you, when you poisoned me just to talk nonsense?"

"This is not just for me," the woman breathed, one hand covering her heart. "This is for the forgotten dynasty—*our* ancestors. This is for all of us who have fallen to Ver Signia's greed for power. For my sister, Nona, for—"

"What?" Reina's blood ran cold. She lifted her head from the pillow. "What did you just say?"

The woman opened her mouth, but a shrill cry erupted from just outside the window. "*Athira!*"

It was Raiko. A second later, Aaron's voice boomed another command.

Reina's heart jumped. The cadre had found her.

The woman whirled, and Reina threw herself from the bed. She grunted as she hit the ground on all fours. The world rocked beneath her, but she spun out of reach when her captor dove to grab her again.

Plumes of fire shot through the window, thin and sputtering but still hot enough to singe the curtains. The woman swore in Mal'dhi and reached for her weapons—two spears, the blades of which gleamed like moonlight on the river. She glanced outside, then ducked beneath the window just as Iliana's whip-sword shot into the room, ripping the curtains.

"Aaron!" Reina shouted hoarsely. "Aaron, I'm here!"

At the same time, the Ashuman woman pressed two fingers against the hollow of her throat. Her eyes glazed over. "Elysia," she breathed.

The earth trembled, and the snarl of a dragon answered the whispered summons. Orange light flashed into the room. One second, the woman was crouched on the opposite wall; the next, she was leaping through the window, weapons spinning.

Reina staggered upright. She tore the curtains from where they hung and clutched the frame of the window, willing strength into her legs. Her heart dropped.

It was the Infernal that had peered into the village ruins. At its side, battling the cadre, was Reina's captor, whose strikes were as deadly as the dragon's flame. Reina stared with an open mouth. This woman was fighting *with* the Infernal. As she deflected the cadre's attempts to wound the beast, the dragon kept her safe. Flames laced around her arms and coiled around her spears—but they never burned her.

Just like Nona.

Reina jumped when Raiko shouted her name again. He was running for her, ducking beneath the dragon's swooping wing, but the woman blocked his path with the shaft of her weapon. His eyes flashed, and the two engaged in a wrestling match for the spear.

In the time it took for Reina to clamber over the windowsill, Raiko seized possession of the woman's spear. He spun it on her, forcing her to jump back. She lunged forward with her other hand, lightly slicing Raiko's arm.

Raiko bared his teeth in a pained grimace, but he fought to kill, each blow coming harder than the next.

Reina pulled herself to her feet when Iliana slithered past the dragon's defenses. Her white braid was singed black at the ends, but she darted for Reina without looking back. She was a small target—too small for the dragon to reach while Korris and Aaron kept it preoccupied. The woman whirled, making a wild grab for Iliana.

Evren hurled his dagger, and the blade pierced through the woman's arm. She screamed and dropped her spear. Raiko slammed his shoulder against her chest, and she fell in a bleeding, gasping heap. Flames white-hot with anger spewed from the Infernal's mouth, drawing beads of sweat over Reina's brow.

Iliana dropped into a crouch, yanking Reina down with her. "Are you alright?" she demanded over the sound of the fighting. "Can you run?"

Reina nodded numbly, though she had just barely recovered her strength. Iliana ushered her to her feet, but when Reina caught sight of Raiko, poised to kill the Ashuman woman, she jolted forward.

"Stop!"

Raiko snapped his head in her direction. Korris delivered a hard kick to the Infernal's jaw, cracking bone. The dragon staggered, smoke billowing from its nostrils, and Aaron raised his sword.

"I said *stop*!" Reina screamed.

Aaron plunged his blade through the dragon's throat. Blood splattered his sword, and on the ground, Reina's captor wailed in agony. The Infernal coughed up gore and embers, legs buckling. Evren leaped back as the beast toppled, gave a rasping groan—then lay still.

All was quiet.

The woman choked out words in Mal'dhi that only Raiko seemed to understand. He spat out some retort, but she didn't seem to care. Her attention was locked on the fallen dragon.

"Elysia," she wept, stretching out her uninjured hand. "Elysia, *mi'amiya*." Tears bled into crimson on her cheeks. She turned only when Raiko pressed the spearhead against her chest. There was no fear in her eyes—only pain and rage. She spoke to Raiko again, and Reina caught the faintest glimpse of remorse on his face before Aaron stepped up, sword dripping red.

"Give me one reason why I shouldn't kill you now," he demanded, thrusting the tip of his blade between the woman's brows.

"Aaron," Reina tried.

He ignored her. "Who are you? How long have you been watching us? Are there more of you?"

The woman uttered a chilling sound: something between a heartbroken sob and a vicious laugh. "How arrogant can you be, to think you were alone in these woods?" Reina froze when her captor jerked her chin at her. "This one noticed. She saw more than any of you ever did."

Aaron slid his gaze to Reina. If looks could kill, she'd be buried six feet beneath the earth already. But he blinked, turning his attention back to the woman under his sword. "Answer me: are there more of you?"

Salt streamed from the woman's eyes, which trailed mournfully to the fallen Infernal. "There could be, if Ver Signians like you did not slaughter every dragon you laid eyes on."

More of them. *Drāga.*

Reina swallowed hard. She pulled against Iliana's grip and stepped forward. When Raiko tried to ward her away, Reina ordered him back with a single glance.

The woman watched her approach. Her brows softened, and grief-stricken tears gathered against her lower lids. "You are so much like her."

Like Nona, she meant. Reina could see the resemblance now that her mind and body were no longer plagued by poison: this woman shared Nona's eyes, her earthen brown hair that shimmered in firelight, her high-set cheekbones.

Shoving away an unexpected swell of emotion, Reina whispered, "Who are you?"

It was not a name she wanted. It was an answer to the question that had been nagging at her since that black storm dragon ravaged Draconis. Since she wandered those long-forgotten tunnels and heard the dragon pendant whispering to her. Since Raiko mentioned the legend of dragon-riding warriors.

Who are we?

The woman locked her gaze with Reina's. Despite the pain clearly riddling her body, she kept her words steady.

"I will impart all that I know," she promised, "but you

would have to leave everything that is familiar to you. This blood that runs through your veins, the voice that calls out to you in dreams—none of it is a mistake, *amia*."

"You are not her friend," Raiko barked. "You poisoned her. Kidnapped her."

"I never intended to harm her," the woman snapped. "I only ever wanted to show her who she is."

"She already knows who she is."

All heads turned to Aaron.

His eyes were cold as steel, yet every inch of him seemed to be burning. His knuckles were white around the hilt of his blade. If Reina focused through the dark, she could see him trembling with the anger he suppressed.

"She is Athira of House Rhysanthe," Aaron whispered, "the daughter of a lord and lady, and she is my family. If you dare to even look at her again, I will set the rage of House Rhysanthe upon these woods and smoke you out until I run my blade through your heart."

The woman's expression darkened. "If only you knew the power locked inside of her, you would see how empty your threats truly are. She is so much more than some nobleman's daughter. She is Drāga, the hope for our future. She is one of the last *reksari*."

Raiko blinked twice, his grip on the spear faltering. Reina ducked her head, but not before Raiko found her watching him.

He looked at her like she was some otherworldly, ethereal thing. Reverence mingled with awe until Reina felt like she was no longer herself, no longer a girl of fractured origins—but a legend. An impossibility come to life right before him.

She turned to her captor. "Whatever you have to say, you can say in front of all of them."

The woman thinned her lips. "These are secrets meant only for your ears, *amia*. Stay with me. I will address every question you have."

She didn't say: *Or turn away, and never learn the truth.* Never silence the call, never be free of the dragon who haunted her.

Reina stared at a blank space on the ground. She might as well have been standing on the edge of a chasm. If she stepped forward, she would tumble into dark waters and drown beneath waves that would strip away every part of who she was, then spit her out into some version of herself that was wholly unrecognizable. If she stepped back, nothing would change. She would always be some nobleman's wayward daughter, the thorn in her brother's side, the girl who ran.

Running left her tired, fatigued—but it was all she knew. She lived for the rush of it all, the thrill of never knowing what came next.

This woman spoke of power. Of secrets waiting to be unlocked. But she also looked at Reina like she was a ghost resurrected, like she was the embodiment of every lost hope. She even said it—*she is the hope for our future.*

Whose future? Certainly not Reina's. She had never been allowed to think of the future as something that belonged to her. It was always a part of someone else's plan. And this "we" that the woman spoke of referred to people Reina did not know, had no ties to. How could she be indebted to someone she knew nothing about?

Reina lifted her chin. "You threatened my life. Put my allies in danger. Why would I ever choose to come with you?"

She watched the woman's face fall. The color drained from her skin, making the blood on her arm seem ten shades darker. "You...you must. You are Drāga."

"No, I'm not." Again, when Reina glanced at Raiko, she found that awestruck gaze.

Don't look at me that way.

Something like panic seized the woman's voice, and her words tumbled out clumsily. "You have a gift. A power that, if unlocked, would change the course of history. You can reshape this world, you *must*—"

"Power means nothing to me if I am bound by someone else's will." Reina was born into a position of power. She watched how her father hungered for it, how his greed bled into Aaron and deepened the divide between the whole family. She knew how power could warp a person's mind, and she refused to become susceptible to something so fragile.

The woman's breath left her in a weak gasp. It seemed that the pain of Evren's dagger in her arm had finally caught up to her. She groaned, cradling her arm against her chest. Raiko had stepped away and lowered his stolen spear, but Aaron had not moved an inch. His eyes were still storming; his chest still rose and fell rapidly. It was impossible to tell whether the brunt of his rage was directed at Reina or this woman who had spirited her away while the rest of them slept.

Either way, Reina wanted to be far from him when he finally erupted.

"What are we doing?" Korris prompted, glancing between his fellow agents. "It's your call, Rhysanthe." Reina looked at Aaron, but quickly realized that Korris had been addressing her. Aaron, too, awaited her instruction, as did Evren and Iliana. Raiko hadn't torn his gaze from her this whole time.

Their next steps were hers to lead.

Reina hardened her voice so that it became cold and detached like her mother's. "Leave her."

"Alive?" Aaron barked.

Reina dipped her chin. "She could have killed me, but she chose not to. Nothing changes that."

A collective dissent tainted the air. At her behest, four of the agents sheathed their weapons. Aaron did not move.

Reina spoke his name. It was a warning and a plea all at once. He blinked with forced slowness. Lowered his blade an inch, so that the tip of the sword grazed the woman's nose.

"You truly are the weakest in our family." The disappointment in his voice shook Reina harder than she expected. Aaron sheathed his sword, lips curling in disgust. He reached down, grabbed the handle of Evren's dagger, and yanked it out.

The woman screamed, clutching her arm as blood spewed between her fingers. She panted hard, leaning against the dead Infernal for support, and dropped her head in defeat.

Aaron tossed the soiled dagger at Evren's feet. With a snap of his fingers, his agents stood in rigid form.

"We're moving out," he said. He cast an unimpressed glance over the dragon's unmoving form and the woman who wept at its side. "Someone tie her up—and make sure she doesn't follow. I do not extend mercy twice."

———

The walk back to the village was tense and silent. No one dared to speak, fearing that Aaron would finally unleash all the anger he contained behind a mask of stoicism. He walked with his shoulders back, chin up, and spine straight. Reina could not see his face from where she dragged at the back of the line, but she imagined that if she could, his expression would haunt her for years to come.

It was not love, she knew, that compelled Aaron to find and save her tonight. It was a sense of duty and obligation to House Rhysanthe, to hold the family's name to the highest standard in every situation.

And by sparing the life of her captor, Reina had sullied their family's pride again.

That old, familiar shame sank deep until Reina was several yards behind the rest of the cadre. She reached the village after the others had dispersed for the night and found Aaron waiting for her. His hands were loose at his sides, and he waved one in the direction of the river.

"Walk with me."

Reina obeyed. She retraced the steps that led her into danger, knowing that Aaron must have been cursing himself for trusting her with the night watch. He stopped at the edge of the water and sighed deeply. His head fell back so that his eyes reflected starlight, and for a long moment, Reina wondered if he was going to speak at all.

Then, like a knife slipping through skin, he said, "You are the worst thing that's ever happened to me."

Reina stared at her feet.

Searching the black sky, Aaron continued, "You have always been my darkest shadow. Is your one goal in life to destroy everything that I've built?"

When Reina remained silent, Aaron straightened his neck and turned to face her. He repeated himself with a voice like death.

Reina couldn't meet his gaze for longer than a second. "That was never my intention."

"Then what?"

Gods—he sounded so defeated. So tired.

"Why, Athira? Why can you not follow a single order given to you? Why must you insist on carving a path for yourself, even if it means breaking down the very walls that were meant to keep you safe?"

She didn't know how to respond. Her rebellion was not some part she played just to make a scene or to get under her brother's skin. She rejected noble society because it would have left her in subjugation. As long as she lived behind the walls of that estate, she was never safe.

"I'm sorry," she offered.

"I don't want your apology. I want an answer."

Reina sucked in a breath, pressing her nails against her scarred palms. Her words knotted in her throat, but she forced them out one by one in a voice unrecognizable to her own ears. "That life was never mine. You know that."

"I know that you rejected every good thing that was ever offered to you—and for what? So you could run around the kingdom bearing a false name and wreaking havoc wherever you went? Where's the honor in a life like that?"

"Why do you care what I do with my life?"

"Because you are a Rhysanthe," Aaron snarled. "Because you are my flesh and blood, and because everything you do is reflected onto me."

Reina snorted. "Don't be ridiculous. If we didn't share the same parents, no one would believe that we were related."

"No Ver Signian house is as disreputable or as broken as ours," Aaron said. "Alexander hasn't spoken a word to me since you left. Mother spends most of her time drowning herself in wine. Father has only grown more impatient and abrasive now that our name is the butt of every inside joke among the nobility. People know that you ran, and they haven't let us forget the shame of letting you slip through our fingers.

"It did not matter that I joined the Silver Order. Once my trainers realized I was a Rhysanthe, they dismissed me. Branded me a deserter when I was barely an acolyte. Do you know how hard I worked just to become a full-fledged agent? I trained harder than anyone in my cohort. I wanted it more than any of them, and I watched our superiors take these half-baked excuses for warriors onto the Nest just to let them die by dragon fire. No one in the First or Second Divisions wanted me in their cadre, nor would I be respected as a mentor in the Third. I was already the second son of a disgraced nobleman, half a *malduna* by birth, and because of your scandal, I became a pariah. I spent years of my life training to join the Silver Order, just for them to turn me into a glorified errand boy. I am a disgrace to our family because of you."

Reina blinked hard. This was nothing she hadn't already guessed, but hearing it was somehow worse than merely believing it to be true.

"What do you want from me, then?" she rasped. She lifted her gaze and found Aaron's face tinted red in the shadows of the night. "How can I erase a lifetime of ruin?"

"You cannot."

Reina dropped her shoulders. Here she stood, poised to flounder under every impossible demand he made of her, and he had finally raised the white flag. Was it fear of his rage or guilt for her crimes that moved her to tears?

"Aaron," she said slowly, "I'm sorry. Truly."

He clasped his hands behind his back and straightened his spine. "Don't be sorry. Be better. Be the person I know you can be." He blinked hard, as if he could see past the veil that concealed her true nature. "You ran away from home at sixteen, and yet you remain as stubborn and hotheaded as ever. You wouldn't have made it this far if you weren't strong, yet you squander that strength every day. Whatever you're looking for, you won't find it in Ashuma."

She knew. Raiko had squashed that hope already.

Aaron continued, "Life makes no promises. It doesn't care about your dreams or who you want to be. Who you are is already determined, but what that amounts to is up to you. You were born into power—*real* power—simply by being a Rhysanthe. You have more freedoms as a highborn than any commoner in Ver Signia. You could do so much with your life if you would just stop running."

How wrong he was. If he knew what it was like—being sold into marriage like mere chattel—he would never again accuse her of petulance. If he even tried to understand all she had suffered—at his hand, no less—he would never try to train her into submission.

But he would never understand, would never listen, and that hurt worse than anything else he had said to her tonight.

"I don't want any of that," she said. "You think you can lure me back with promises of comfort and wealth, but it's just like you said: life promises me nothing."

"Athira." It was like the mere sound of her name gave him a headache. "You're not just turning your back on comfort and wealth. You're abandoning your family."

"Blood is all that binds us," she whispered. "That, and a name that I discarded years ago. Real family is more than that."

"And what would you know of 'real' family?"

Reina paused. An image of Meiryn flickered in her mind: vague and distorted after all this time away from her. Reina's shame only doubled as she realized she'd not spared a single thought for Meiryn since their separation until tonight.

"I only know that whatever this is"—she gestured between herself and Aaron—"it is *not* family."

His expression became unreadable.

Reina softened her voice, searching the face that mirrored her own. "You saved me tonight because I'm a Rhysanthe, not because you actually cared about my safety. Letting that woman take me, even if it meant letting me die, would have brought you peace. Right?"

Aaron said nothing, but his eyes twitched—almost too quickly to catch.

But Reina saw. She laughed airily and shook her head. "You think you've done us both a favor, but you only proved my point: you are bound by obligations that I have long since forgotten. I have abandoned nothing, Aaron, because we were never truly a family. Not in that house."

She stepped back and waited for him to say something. Anything. She waited for what felt like ages, but the sky was shifting from black to grey as dawn edged up against the horizon—and he had yet to speak a single word.

Maybe she had finally broken him. Maybe he would finally see that nothing he did or said could restrain her, change her mind, turn her into another version of him.

When the stars began to fade into a lighter sky, Aaron cleared his throat. He reached back and scratched the base of his skull, eyes downcast.

"I saved you," he whispered, "because you are my sister. Because to me, you are still family."

Reina crossed her arms. "And what, exactly, does that mean to you?"

He stared into the river, watching the fish strain against the current. A thick guard hardened his voice as he summoned previous words to make up for his lack of a true answer: "You are my flesh and blood. A Rhysanthe by birth. That makes us family, whether you accept it or not."

"Family could be more than just a name," she urged quietly.

"But it isn't," Aaron snapped. The faintest hint of regret broke through his armor. "Not for us, anyway."

"Don't you think it could be?"

"No." He inhaled, rolling his neck and shoulders to ease the building tension. "No, I think you and I are...irreversible. We can't ever be more than what we are now, so just—forget it, Athira."

The sound of her name shattering at his feet twisted her heart, but she only bowed her head as he trudged back toward the village, motioning for her to follow.

XXI. MEIRYN

HALF OF MEIRYN'S thoughts remained focused on her healer's studies; the other half lingered in that darkness with Faun, where they stitched together the haphazard threads of an alliance.

Neither woman saw much of the other during the days, which meant that their evenings were spent on the outskirts of camp squabbling about the best course of action to take. Dinners with Elder became scarce, and Meiryn found herself caught in heated debates with someone who had despised her just a week ago. It was a constant push and pull of opinions, ideas shot down no sooner than they'd left the speaker's lips.

It carried on for days.

The only good thing to come of this new alliance was that the huntsmen finally stopped treating Meiryn like an outsider. Most still ignored her, but at least the torment and ridicule had ceased. Faun's influence seemed to run deeper than Meiryn had realized. Without a Guild master, the huntsmen conformed to the natural hierarchy that was popularity. And in spite of all the work she had done to prove her trustworthiness, Meiryn was widely unpopular.

"It's not exactly your fault," Faun told her around a mouthful of food one night. "The Guild survives on the lies we tell. At any moment, our truths could slip into the ears of couriers all over the kingdom, and every one of our weak points would be exposed."

"You mean, if people learned that the Wolf King died years ago?" Meiryn asked.

Faun stilled. She eyed Meiryn sidelong and tossed her dinner scraps behind her. "Yes," she said slowly, "but there are far worse secrets than that."

Like Grey's noble origins.

"Don't be offended if no one trusts you with everything just yet," Faun continued. "You've only been here a few weeks, after all. Spend a little more time with us, and you'll learn more than enough to satisfy any questions you may have."

How she wished that were true. From the day she set foot in this camp, Meiryn's list of questions had only grown.

Meiryn shook strands of pale hair away from her face and rested her chin on her fists. She watched the sky turn hazy shades of pink and orange, then fade to lavender and indigo as the night grew darker. The sun was slipping beneath the horizon earlier these days. Summer was coming to an end, and with it came an invisible, looming presence.

She couldn't explain it. It was simply a feeling: the same subtle, nagging anxiety she felt all those summers ago when she was still a child; the inexplicable fear that ensnared her in the days leading up to the rogue dragon attack. Her intuition had warned her of an oncoming danger. She ignored it then, and it had left her homeless and alone.

Now, even with the storm dragon allegedly in chains, it was all Meiryn could do to rein in every horrible fear.

"Hey." Faun nudged her. "Were you listening?"

Meiryn gave her an absent look.

Faun sighed and nodded toward the glow of the campfire. "We should find out what Grey is up to. I heard earlier today that he was packing his things again."

So soon? Meiryn frowned. "He spends all of two days here before he's gone again. How do you trust that he's not running off, selling the Guild's secrets everywhere he goes?"

"You haven't seen any noblemen or agents storm into camp, have you?"

"No, but—"

"When the Wolf King died, Grey was the one who kept us all from losing our heads," Faun told her. "He was still a recent recruit, too. If nothing else proves his loyalty to you, let that assuage your fears. That being said, I doubt he would share his whereabouts if we asked."

Elder might know. But I'd have to pry it out of her, and that's time we don't have.

Meiryn rubbed her temples. "So what are you thinking?"

They had already spent days deliberating their next move. For all she knew, circumstances regarding Nyrōna and the cadre had changed.

"I proposed this idea the other night," Faun said, "but you didn't seem too keen about it."

"What?"

Faun smirked at Meiryn's deadpan tone. "I want to follow him. If he leads us into the Spine, then we'll know the cadre is still there, and we can follow him right to their little hideout.

We won't have to worry about dealing with the rest of the Order, either."

"And if he's going elsewhere?"

"Then at the very least we'll see what our dear spymaster is up to."

Meiryn chewed her lip. "I don't know. It seems like the risk outweighs any potential benefit."

"You'd rather sit here another day waiting for something to happen?"

No, but she couldn't lie to herself: she felt safe with the Guild. Despite the way the huntsmen silenced their conversation or turned their backs when she approached, she knew she had at least earned their protection.

"I just don't want to throw ourselves into unnecessary danger just because we're getting restless," she finally said, looking at Faun solemnly. "We made a pact. We're allies, and that means that we defend each other, keep each other safe. If you run headfirst into fire, then I am obligated to make sure that you don't burn."

"Oh." Faun's brows stitched together. Her face flushed, and her next words fell in a hushed whisper. "You...would endanger yourself for my sake?"

If you insist on endangering yourself.

"Yes."

Gratitude—the first genuine display of it—warmed Faun's expression. She dropped her gaze and murmured, "Here I was, thinking nothing could surprise me."

"You thought I would just let you figure things out on your own?"

"That's how it usually goes," Faun said. "Before Nona came

along, if I wanted something done, I was on my own. Lukas offered his assistance, but I tried not to rely on him for anything. He's brave, but he prefers to do things 'by the book.'"

Meiryn stiffened at his name. "He certainly knows how to make himself scarce," she said, constraining as much bitterness as she could.

Faun chuckled. "True. But he had his reasons. You were a trespasser who followed him. I'm sure it just reminded him of the other trespasser he let into the Guild."

"The *other* one?"

"Yeah," Faun said grimly. "He...well, it's not my place to tell that story. Just know that we still haven't fully recovered from what that trespasser did. A lot of people still blame Lukas for what happened. I think he feels guilty, too, most of the time."

Meiryn looked at her hands in her lap. "Someone could have told me."

"Would that have stopped you from trying to enlist his help?"

Probably not. If she had known that Lukas was just worried about the past repeating itself, she would have done everything in her power to show him that he was wrong. She might have pestered him until he finally snapped and drove her off for good.

Instead, he made it obvious that he wanted nothing to do with her.

"Don't take it personally, princess," Faun said. "If he wants to help you, he'll come to you."

"I don't need him anymore," Meiryn answered readily. At Faun's inquisitive stare, Meiryn elaborated, "I have you."

She had watched Faun from afar. She saw the way Faun

threw herself into her work, and she had spent enough hours in debates to see that Faun was wholly dedicated to reaching this common goal.

What had Lukas proven, other than his fear of tarnishing his reputation?

Faun leaned back and stretched her neck. A faint smile played on her lips, one that barely reached her eyes. "That you do," she murmured. "But don't discredit yourself so soon. You went through six hells just to find the Guild, but you still got here on your own."

"I got here because I walked into your trap."

"And now you know what to look out for when you're wandering the forest," Faun said, as if she had done her a great favor. She yawned without covering her mouth. "Anyway. It's getting late. We should prepare ourselves for whatever lies ahead. Pack anything you think you'll need. We don't know how long we'll be gone."

Or if we'll come back.

Deep down, Meiryn knew that this was their only option. Their individual desires were tangentially related to wherever Grey was headed—the Spine, Draconis, or elsewhere—and if they let him slip away, so too would they be abandoning hope.

Treetops rustled; leaves drifted to the forest floor. Meiryn looked up. The silhouette of a crow flashed overhead, nearly invisible against the darkening sky. She tracked its flight until it disappeared and blended with the shadows looming in the east.

Later, after bidding Faun a warmer farewell than they'd shared in all this time, Meiryn dreamed of the night she met Reina. Back then, Meiryn was an eighteen-year-old waitress in a tavern spending over half her monthly wages on a dingy loft above the dining hall; Reina was a haggard beggar on the streets, skin and bones held together by pure spite.

They spoke not a word to one another after Meiryn spotted her lying out in the rain, but Meiryn was the one who took pity on Reina—or, as she called her before she knew her by name, the Scavenger.

What started as sporadic tendencies dependent on whether Meiryn thought she could get away with it grew into routine expectations—even if it meant sneaking down from the attic in the middle of the night. She left dinner scraps out on the back step, and each morning, she would retrieve the empty dish and scrub it clean before anyone else had awoken. She never saw the Scavenger, only knew that she was still around.

This carried on for a month, until one evening, Meiryn was caught.

Her employer struck her harder than any of the chastising nurses who raised her in the orphanage. She'd never forgotten the way her ears rang after that first hit. Sweat trickled down her neck as he raised his hand again—

And out sprang the Scavenger. She was still thin, just a wisp of a girl, but after a month of living off a regular supply of leftovers, she had regained an alarming amount of strength. She fought like those reckless men who gambled their lives in the dragon fighting pits. Her dirt-caked nails dug long, gashing wounds down the man's face. When he spat and thrashed and called her a bitch, the Scavenger's eyes lit up with some kind of primal fury, and she plunged her teeth into the crook of his elbow.

Meiryn never forgot the screaming, the bloodshed, the breathlessness of fleeing that decrepit little village with the Scavenger's hand clasped tightly in her own.

But she forgot the name of the man who paid her less than half of what she deserved after a year's worth of work. She forgot her loneliness when the Scavenger introduced herself as "Reina." And she forgot the years that passed between the families she learned to love.

The parents who raised her nearly to adolescence and the brother who chased her with crickets in his little hands lived within frozen portraits in the back of her mind. Their village by the sea shone with the light of a sun poised just over the horizon. Meiryn tucked those images away, holding them as closely as the king held his crown.

Reina was the light that speared through the rain clouds. She reminded Meiryn that existence was not—*could not* be reduced to survival. By Reina's side, Meiryn relearned the sound of her own laughter. She stopped waking halfway through the night, drenched in sweat from a nightmare that chased her through the years. And though they traveled from town to city, tossing ideas through the dark of escaping to Ashuma, Meiryn never looked for home beyond the shape of Reina's figure.

Upon waking, Meiryn half-expected to find Reina nearby, already watching the sunrise. But the med tent was empty. She was alone.

Her dream left her with a hollowness in her chest. A blaring call to find Reina again.

Meiryn propped herself up on her elbows. She yawned widely as the birds outside chirped to one another. Early morning light, pale and delicate, reached her when a breeze blew the tent flaps inward. An autumnal crispness bit at the softer edges of the warm air.

Meiryn shuddered as the blanket fell away from her shoulders. She rose to find a serene campsite before her. It was still early after dawn, and many of the huntsmen had yet to rise from their sleep. Meiryn ambled to Faun's tent, but when she called for her, there was no response.

She frowned. Was Faun on an early morning patrol? She hadn't mentioned anything about it earlier.

"Faun?" Meiryn tried again. It took a great deal of self-talk to muster enough courage to peer inside.

Her mouth went dry.

The tent was empty—entirely cleared out. The only evidence that Faun had lived there at all was the faint imprint of a bedroll flattening a patch of grass. Her bow was gone, as were her quivers of arrows, any clothes she might have had, everything.

All that remained was a single note scrawled in a hurried hand.

Sorry, princess. I can't let anyone else burn for my sake.

Meiryn read the note twice, three times, four. Her heart thundered in her chest, louder and louder with each beat. She flipped the note over, held it to the light—tried anything to make sure she wasn't missing some hidden clue.

But the truth glared her right in the face: Faun had left her. Set out sometime in the middle of the night while...

While Grey left in quiet solitude.

Meiryn gasped. She crumpled the note in her hand and ran with a staggering gait to Elder's tent. Without warning, she barged in and demanded, "Where is he? Where has he gone?"

Elder yelped, bolting upright. In one fist, she clutched a tattered animal made of cloth that vaguely resembled a wolf. She wiped at a line of drool with the back of her hand.

"Who?" she mumbled. "What happened?"

Meiryn dropped to a crouch, ignoring the ache in her right leg. She leaned close to Elder—close enough that Elder flinched back.

"*Grey*," Meiryn said, stressing the single syllable of his name like it held all the weight of the world. "Where did he go?"

The faintest crease appeared between Elder's brows, and she shook her head. "I don't know."

Liar.

"Please, Elder," Meiryn implored. She clasped the girl's shoulder in a light grip. "I need to know where he's gone. Faun went after him."

Elder blanched. "What do you mean? Why would she do that? I thought you two were friends."

"Allies," Meiryn corrected, "but she's gone now, and I need to find her. I can only do that if you tell me where Grey went first. This is very important to me, Elder, so I need you to be honest. Where did Grey go?"

She searched Elder's face. Those brown eyes that twinkled when she laughed now glistened as she held back tears. Elder shuddered with each exhale and clawed her fingers into the heart of her stuffed wolf.

"I can't tell you," she whispered.

It took everything in Meiryn not to shake her or burst into a swearing fit. She dropped her chin to her chest and forced herself to breathe. When she lifted her face again, Elder looked like she was fighting the urge to cry.

"Elder," Meiryn said, "I know you're close with Grey, and I don't want to do anything to compromise the bond you two share. I promise you that if this wasn't a matter of life or death, I wouldn't be asking you now."

"Grey wouldn't hurt anyone. He's loyal to the huntsmen."

He's highborn, Meiryn refrained from saying. *He's the lost son of some self-important nobleman.*

She just nodded in agreement. Best to stay on Elder's side as long as it took to coax Grey's destination from her tongue. "I know. But wherever he's going is dangerous. If Faun follows him, she could get hurt. She could die."

Elder wilted. "I promised him I would never tell anyone his secrets. We made a pact."

"Faun and I made a pact, too," Meiryn told her gently. "We promised to protect one another, and that's all I'm trying to do now. Help me, Elder. You won't regret it."

Finally, *finally*, Elder dropped her guard. Her shoulders sagged with defeat, and her eyelids lowered. "Draconis," she whispered. "He's going back to Draconis."

That could only mean that Nyrōna and Temaerys were closing in. The cadre had already slipped beyond their reach.

Meiryn loosened a tense breath. She hugged Elder tight, but her friend did not return the gesture. Meiryn held her at arm's length and tilted her chin up.

"*Thank you.*" Relief chased the gratitude that bloomed in her chest. "You've done a good thing. I am in your debt." She rose to her feet, but she barely made it two steps outside when Elder's little hand clasped around her wrist.

"Wait," Elder blurted, her voice breaking. Meiryn froze. Elder wore an expression of guilt so wretched that it chipped away a piece of Meiryn's heart. Drawing in a thin breath of air, Elder said, "Don't go after them. Please. I don't want you to get hurt again."

A flashback to the night they met threatened to shatter Meiryn's resolve. It would be easy to back down now and keep

Elder's trust. She could just let Faun walk unknowingly into danger. It was Faun's choice to leave, after all, and for whatever reason, she hadn't even bothered to tell Meiryn. Was all that talk of working together just a way for Faun to channel her anger into a real plot to avenge Nona?

Meiryn should have felt used. She should have felt angry and hurt.

But, for some inexplicable reason, she didn't.

"I have to go," Meiryn said. "Don't tell anyone where I've gone. I'll come back, I promise."

"Meiryn—"

She wrenched herself free and hurried back to the med tent. Other huntsmen were slowly waking to face the day, but Meiryn pushed them out of her mind.

Adrenaline coursed through her veins. Ensuring that Pyrrha was nowhere nearby, Meiryn stuffed her bag to the seams with herbs and supplies. Water root, fishtail fern, bandage rolls, a harvesting knife, a flask for water. She fastened a traveling cloak around her shoulders and flipped the hood over her head, then rose on quick feet and marched eastward into the forest.

She was on her own again, but the night-tales that once frightened her might as well have been arrowheads blunting against iron shields. The shadows were a thick veil that kept her invisible as she left the Guild behind. The rustling of wings in the treetops and animals scampering through the underbrush covered the sound of her limp.

From the eastern sky came a tiny pinprick of light. Like a beacon leading her home, it stretched through the forest and pierced the space over Meiryn's heart.

She clung to a mental image of Reina: eyes crinkling as she smiled, bright laughter carrying on the wind, black hair outlined by a bronze glow. Meiryn imagined their reunion—a clash of arms and tears and words of relief, promises to never let the other out of sight again.

Meiryn tightened the grip on her knife. Her cloak billowed behind her as she willed speed and strength into her legs.

Draconis awaited.

XXII. REINA

Leaves trickled into the river, casting little ripples that danced and reflected onto the surrounding trees. Fish wove freely between river rocks until further downstream, by the broken bridge, Korris made himself useful by spearing them onto the Ashuman woman's stolen weapon. He'd already amassed a gleaming stack of trout for their journey. Iliana was harvesting anything that might be useful for healing; Evren trailed behind her as a chaperone and pack mule.

At the edge of the village, where Aaron could keep an eye on Reina and his cadre, he discussed with Raiko which path home would be best. They didn't agree: Aaron wanted to cut a straight path back to Ver Signia, which would save time but force the cadre onto uneven terrain where they might stumble across another dragon den, while Raiko suggested they follow the course of the river, sacrificing time for the sake of maintaining access to resources provided by the river and the surrounding forest. They passed a drawing stick between them, tracing lines in the dirt, their argument turning to little more than a drone in Reina's mind.

She hadn't slept a wink all night—not because of her talk with Aaron, but because she feared that the storm dragon would come to her again, crying out for her to find and save him. For all she knew, it was mere delusion. Fear-induced hallucinations.

And yet, she remembered how her captor had cried out when Aaron slayed the Infernal; how the dragon's death seemed an agony worse than heartbreak. She remembered how the woman fought at its side and was never burned by its flame. And she remembered the words spoken to her in that little hut.

"The dragon who calls to you will never leave you. Across time and space, your souls are bound by an unbreakable bond."

Could it all be true, then? The legend of the Drāga, the power shared between human and dragonkind?

Reina traced the scars on her palms and battled the nagging sensation that she'd just slammed the door on the answers she craved. Returning with the cadre had not only solidified her alliance with them, but also left her estranged from the only person who might have been able to tell her what was happening to her.

She replayed that day in Draconis, watching in slow motion the energy colliding between herself and the storm dragon. Watching the earth cave in. Watching a brilliant light consume her world.

That couldn't have been *her* doing, could it?

"Certainly not alone."

The dragon's voice jolted her so violently that Reina jerked forward, as if escaping a speaker who was standing just over her shoulder. She tumbled into the river, sputtering and coughing. Her feet scrambled to find purchase on the slick rocks, and someone shouted her name.

She was still blinking water from her eyes when Raiko dragged her back onshore. Aaron stood a few yards back, arms folded tightly; Korris had paused his fishing to ogle.

"I don't need your help," Reina spat when Raiko offered her a hand up.

He gave her space while she composed herself, though she could feel his stare weighing heavier by the moment. Cautiously, after she'd wrung her hair out, he asked, "What happened?"

Reina tore off her boots and drained the water. Humiliation burned hot in the tips of her ears. "I'm fine."

"You just threw yourself into the river."

"It's none of your concern," she insisted. With exaggerated, savage movements, Reina shoved both shoes back on—water be damned—and marched away.

Raiko's worry gave way to annoyance, and he called after her, "Of course not. You wandered off during your watch last night, got yourself captured, and now you throw yourself into a river—because that is the sign of a perfectly sane person. My mistake, *my lady.*"

Something in Reina snapped. She stormed up to him, catching his wrist and spinning him around. She didn't care that Aaron watched. Didn't care that his hand had slowly fallen to his sword.

"Don't belittle me, Raiko. You understand far less than you know."

Raiko leaned in, a half-smile teasing his lips. "Then, by all means, enlighten me."

A blush crept into her cheeks as she realized how close they were standing. All at once, her rage withered. She smoothed out her clothes and tucked her hair behind her ears, but under her breath, she muttered, "You have no idea what it's like, hearing a dragon speak to you every night."

Raiko's smile dropped. "A dragon?"

Reina nodded, then cast a furtive glance in Aaron's direction; Raiko took the cue and gestured to Aaron wordlessly. The displeasure on Aaron's face was unmistakable, even from this distance, but he gave a curt nod and granted Reina and Raiko a few minutes of privacy. Further downstream, Korris resumed his fishing.

"He won't leave me." Reina exhaled. She raked her hands through her hair, as if she could pierce through her skull and extricate the dragon herself. "I hear him in my sleep, and I hear him when I'm alone. Ever since Draconis—"

"Wait," Raiko interrupted, leaning close, "are you talking about the storm dragon? You believe you are hearing its voice?"

"His," she corrected, "but yes. I *know* I am. And I keep thinking about what that woman said to me last night, about the Drāga—"

"Mere fantasy. The Drāga from the stories were immortal warriors who shared a blood bond with the dragons they tamed. No human like that has ever existed."

But even Reina could hear the hesitation in his voice, as if those words were rehearsed, not believed. She leveled him with a stare and reached for the necklace beneath her shirt. Raiko's eyes went wide when he recognized the pendant as identical to the one he'd picked up yesterday. He traced the delicate spiral with a tentative fingertip.

"Where..."

"The tunnels," she explained. She glanced toward the village when the trees rustled, but it was only a couple of birds taking flight. Still, Aaron would likely come to pull Raiko back any moment now. "When I fell through the wall, I found this on the ground. I picked it up on a whim, but now I'm almost certain I was supposed to find it."

As soon as the words left her mouth, she realized how ridiculous they sounded. But what spurred her even more was the fear of never knowing what all this meant.

"What are your intentions?" Raiko asked, keeping his voice lower than the burbling of the river. He stood mere inches away. The village, the river, the mountains faded behind the warmth of his face. "Aaron plans to return to Draconis, but he will not allow you to go near that creature, especially if you believe you are Drāga."

"I don't know what I believe," Reina ground out, wishing it didn't sound as ludicrous as it felt. "I only know what I'm experiencing. And it's just as I told you: everything changed after Draconis. He's calling me to find him—the dragon, I mean. I have to know what's happening."

Because no one, not even a madwoman who *might* have been wielding an Infernal's flame, could provide the answers Reina sought.

Raiko's touch strayed from the pendant in Reina's hand. His fingertip grazed her palm, dangerously close to her lightning scars hidden just beneath the pendant, and she withdrew her hand, concealing the necklace again.

"Aaron can get me to Draconis," Reina said, "but I'll need help if I'm to get away after that."

A troubled expression creased Raiko's brow. He rubbed the back of his neck, wincing as the movement strained his stitches, and looked over Reina once.

"Do you think the woman spoke true?" he murmured. "That you are a descendant of a legendary bloodline?"

Reina hugged her arms around herself. A deliberative moment passed before she said, "I think all legends come from some version of truth. Whether the Drāga were real or not is what I hope to find out."

"And if they were real?" Raiko pressed. "What will you do then, Athira, if you discover you wield the power of a dragon?"

A sure answer to his question eluded her. Such power was undeniably lucrative: she would never again have to feel so small or helpless against anyone—but would that not turn heads? Cast whispering ripples across the entire continent? There wouldn't be a soul in all Rhonestiel who wouldn't know what she could do, the things she could unleash upon the world.

That kind of power was feared, and what was feared was almost always destroyed.

"Well," she said finally, "I suppose I'll figure that out when the time comes—*if* it comes," she added with a pointed look.

Raiko shifted his weight. "You wish for my help."

"You haven't denied me."

Despite himself, Raiko grinned. He ducked his head, but the smile lingered in his voice when he said, "Very well. I will do what I can."

Reina's chest collapsed with relief. She might have thrown her arms around him if Aaron hadn't appeared in her periphery. Her demeanor shifted the instant he approached.

"Raiko," he ordered, "if you're done here, you and I have unfinished business."

Much to Aaron's—and Reina's—dismay, Raiko waved a flippant hand. He drawled, "We shall take your path, if it pleases you most, Captain. After all, this is your cadre. I am merely at your command."

With a dramatic bow that left Aaron gawking and flustered, Raiko dismissed himself.

Reina shuffled her feet. She half-anticipated Aaron to demand she spill every detail of her conversation with Raiko, but when he turned back to her, he asked, "What happened earlier, when you fell?"

The casual air in his voice set off warning bells in Reina's head.

"I didn't rest well," she said with a shrug. "I suppose all this waiting around put me to sleep, and I slipped in."

Aaron pursed his lips. He didn't quite believe her—that much was apparent—but he simply nodded. "We have a long journey ahead of us. You need to look after yourself if we're to make any ground at all."

"Over the mountains and through the dragon dens?" Reina gestured skyward. "If I didn't know any better, I'd think you were trying to attract trouble."

Aaron rolled his eyes. He marched back toward the village; Reina stayed hot on his heels. She noted that the rest of the cadre had gathered in the yard—that their stares followed her and Aaron—but she gave them no acknowledgment.

"I overheard you talking with Raiko," she said as he shoved into one of the abandoned homes. The door had been broken down long ago. Aaron stomped over it while Reina painstakingly stepped around haphazard stacks of splintered wooden planks. She blinked as her vision adjusted to the shade. "You should listen to him. Even if the river path is longer, it's safer. We'll lose more time than we can afford by encountering a dragon unprepared than we will by taking advantage of what this land offers."

"Which is what, exactly?" Aaron asked without looking

back. He knelt in the tiny kitchen, just shy of a patch of sunlight that fell through a hole in the ceiling, and Reina leaned against the half-standing wall.

"Food. Water. Shelter."

"To whom?" He started rummaging through cupboards, ducking his head into shadows and emerging increasingly dirty.

Reina cocked her head. "Sorry?"

Aaron slammed the cupboard door hard enough to detach it from its hinges. He scoffed and moved to the next room, where a family might have spent their evenings together. In one corner sat a small firepit. Aaron hastened toward it. He poked and prodded through the ash, clattered through kindling tools, and smeared soot over his fingers until he found what he was searching for: a thin vial of liquid, barely half-full but apparently sufficient for his needs.

Reina watched as he unsheathed his sword and got to work dismantling the hilt. The pommel screwed off, revealing an inconspicuous chamber that Aaron fervently began to clean.

"To whom," he started, again without looking at her, "do you think the land offers all those great things you listed? Food, water, shelter, the like."

She'd been so preoccupied watching him perform maintenance on his sword that she'd almost forgotten she was still waiting on a response to her question.

Uncertain, Reina tried, "Travelers—"

"Wrong." A black cloud puffed from the mouth of the hilt chamber and settled on the skin around Aaron's eyes. He paid it no mind, save for a single light cough, then reached for the vial.

The entire hilt was a fuel chamber, Reina realized as he emptied the contents of the vial into it. His sword, balanced on its tip, glittered in the needles of light and illuminated every tiny dust particle that drifted about the room.

Watching his blade consume every last drop of oil, Aaron continued, "This mountain range is habitable land. It was a home once"—he gestured at the ruins around them—"but no longer. But as we saw last night, some few still linger. Considering the rising tensions between Ashuma and Ver Signia, we cannot risk exposing ourselves to any spies or bandits who may be lurking within that shelter you wish to camp beneath."

"So you would rather endanger your cadre to a dragon than human spies?"

"A dragon," Aaron sighed, as if this conversation were boring him, "cannot report to an enemy scout."

"No, but it can kill your men in an instant."

"Then I suppose we'll do our best not to encounter any such beast." He reassembled his sword and shouldered past her, eyes flashing like stones of coal still hot with fire.

Reina spun on her heel and called after his receding figure, "You're taking a risk on the others' behalf. On *my* behalf. What happened to 'you're still family'?"

Aaron bristled, but he said nothing.

Trotting around an overturned end table, Reina speared her words toward him. "What good does it do to put everyone in danger like this? Your men trust you, Aaron."

Again, he said nothing. His insistence upon silence loosened Reina's tongue even further, and she threw herself in his path, blocking his exit.

"You saw what awaits you in those tombs. The Order couldn't care less about you, or any of your men. How is it fair to risk their safety when they won't be honored in death anyway?"

Steel whined as Aaron sheathed his sword. Nostrils flaring, he replied, "I am their captain. Where I lead, they follow. Fairness is not a concern."

"It should be if you love Raiko at all."

Before her words even registered in her head, Aaron slammed her back against the wall—one hand squeezing around her throat, the other pinning her in place. She choked as he leaned close enough for her to see every dirt-filled pore on his face.

"If you ever say that again," he seethed, "I will kill you."

In an instant of sheer terror, Reina gripped Aaron's wrist. A bolt of frenzied energy shot through her hands, and Aaron cried out, falling over charred wood that crumbled under his weight.

Kicking himself further away, Aaron cradled his wrist close to his chest. "You..." he breathed, glancing between their hands. "What did you just do?"

"Never threaten me again," Reina panted through clenched teeth. She had slipped to the floor. Dirt clung to her damp clothes. Trembling against the borders of her mind was a distant rolling thunder. She clawed her fingers into the ruined floorboards, letting the pain keep her grounded. "Do you hear me? That was the last time, Aaron, that you will ever lay a hand on me."

It was shock more than fear that widened Aaron's eyes. He nodded mutely, and he'd just managed to stagger upright when Raiko burst inside, followed closely by the rest of the cadre.

Evren, Iliana, and Korris had drawn their weapons. Raiko wielded a stone in his fist, but his hand lowered when he took in the scene: Aaron, one hand closed around his hilt, towering over Reina, whose back was still pressed against the wall.

For a stunned moment, no one spoke.

Then, voice hard with alarm, Raiko breathed, "What is this?" He only tore his gaze from Reina to pin an accusatory glare on Aaron. "Did you hurt her?"

Aaron fumed scarlet. "Why—"

Raiko moved toward Reina to help her stand, but Aaron jutted an arm out.

"Do *not* touch her," he ordered. It was fear, not anger, that yanked those words from his throat; that kept his palm splayed flat against Raiko's heart; that urged his gaze toward Reina, as if she might pounce if he lowered his guard.

But Raiko had never looked more furious.

Reina slid her back up the wall and stood on wary feet. "It's alright," she said to no one in particular. She looked anywhere but at the agents' faces: the dusty and weathered floor, the vaguely familiar letters engraved on Evren's daggers, the ruined mattress on the bed in the next room over.

"Athira," Iliana said. She let her sword graze the floor, but her grip remained tight, poised in case Aaron made a move to actually harm her. "What happened?"

She shook her head. "Nothing—I fell. We're fine. We need to leave."

Doubt drew Iliana's brows together, but Evren hushed her when she tried to inquire further. Korris, ever the peacekeeper, sheathed his sword with a shriek of steel and said, a touch too loudly, "I agree. We're losing daylight. Captain?"

Aaron hadn't taken his eyes off Reina, but at Korris's prompt, he looked at each of his agents. His hand fell from Raiko's chest. Reina pretended not to see it trembling at his side.

"We'll follow the river," Aaron decided aloud.

Raiko and Reina shared a brief look of surprise—which Aaron duly ignored as he shouldered toward the exit.

He paused in the doorway, where the sun could only reach half of his face. His brows creased, and he turned back to face his cadre.

"Stay vigilant in the coming days," he warned. "We don't know what dangers lie within these mountains."

He pinned his stare on Reina, and she dug her nails deeper into her palms. The power she'd wielded earlier still burned at her fingertips.

"Find me," the dragon's cold voice hissed, *"and learn what such power can do."*

In the stifling summer air, Reina shivered. She hugged her arms tight around herself and nodded in response to Aaron's warning. Lifting her chin and steeling her voice, she said, "Lead the way, Captain."

Lead me to the dragon. Let me end this.

Distant thunder rippled through the dark sea of her thoughts.

"This," the dragon foreboded, *"is only the beginning."*

Reina clenched her fists until they were pale as moons.

Act III

All That Burns

XXIII. MEIRYN

MEIRYN MADE it two full days on her own before realizing that she was being tracked. She heard it when she awoke before dawn: a *snap* of a twig.

Someone was watching her.

She scrambled to her feet, planting them several inches apart to stay balanced—mimicking the huntsmen she'd observed in training. Her palms were clammy, and she struggled to keep a tight grip on her knife. She held her breath, flinching at the tiniest movements, still shaking from her mind the remnants of her dream—in which Reina was at her side again, but her eyes were not her own; instead, they burned like golden suns—when the leaves to her left rustled.

Meiryn gripped her weapon with two hands. Why couldn't she stop shaking? Her heart beat faster and faster. Surely even the birds could hear it.

"I can hear you," she called as bravely as she could muster. She narrowed her gaze when the leaves stilled.

Surely not.

Sternness sharpened her tone as she said, "Elder, if you're hiding, you need to come out now."

The sound of footsteps, then—

"*Lukas*?" Meiryn's mouth fell open when he pulled back a low-hanging branch and emerged before her. His bronze sword was strapped to his back, and he wore a grim expression. Despite the disappointment that drew his mouth into a frown, his eyes softened with mild relief.

"I was hoping I'd find you soon," he told her by way of greeting. No mention of how or why he'd followed her. "You shouldn't be out here on your own."

Meiryn was still reeling from his sudden appearance. She grappled for words. "I was looking for Faun. She—"

"Left." He nodded. "We know."

We—as in the Hunters Guild.

"What are you doing here?"

When Lukas didn't respond, Meiryn's eyes drifted from his face to his sword, then back to the guilt seeping into his gaze.

She exhaled sharply. "Did the Guild send you?"

His prolonged silence was her answer. Sunlight crept over the forest and cast a sinister glow across his face, but he hadn't moved a muscle.

Meiryn lifted a defiant chin. "So what now? I'm not going back until I find Faun, and the longer you keep me here, the—"

"The Guild didn't send me to bring you back."

Meiryn blinked several times, processing, too slowly, what he meant. When it finally sank in, all she could muster was a breathless, shaky, "Oh. I see." She pictured the next few moments as a series of stepping stones wobbling precariously in the middle of a roaring river. She could either try to run, though she'd not make it far with her limp, or she could reason with him, try to sway him to help her instead of carrying out his orders.

Her heart trembled in her chest. Sweat collected at the back of her neck. Lukas hadn't moved toward her, nor had he drawn his sword. Yet.

"You wouldn't kill me," she whispered.

"I barely know you."

"But you know Faun well enough." He winced; Meiryn let it embolden her. "If she found my body here, she would never forgive you."

Lukas looked like he was being torn in two. "I don't want to do this, but I am bound by promises I made to the Guild. You wouldn't understand."

Annoyance swallowed her fear. "Do you do everything you're told without question?" She couldn't help but wonder if the distance he kept from her at camp was of his own volition or someone else's dictation.

"I do what I'm told because it keeps others safe."

"So you believe I'm dangerous."

"No—"

"Then why are you here?" Meiryn discarded the stiff formalities. "You had every chance to help me before, but you did nothing. Don't punish me now for turning to someone else. I have no intention of betraying the Guild or any of the huntsmen. Faun is supposed to help me find Reina, but she can't do that if she throws herself in danger just to exact her revenge on Nona's killer."

Hurt softened his rougher edges. "Why wouldn't she tell me where she's going?"

Meiryn only shrugged, evading the more extensive truth. Until she had confirmation of Lukas's support—or at least assurance that he wouldn't drive his sword through her spine the minute she turned her back—she would reveal nothing more than what he'd already pieced together for himself. Fortunately for her, it amounted to the barest bones of her scheme. Lukas had no idea that following Faun to Draconis would also lead them to Grey.

"I'm going after her," she told him. "You can't stop me."

Lukas clawed a hand through his hair and held it there in those chestnut waves. "I don't want to hurt you, Meiryn. Please, believe me. But this is my chance to... If I don't kill you, the huntsmen will think I've betrayed the Guild. They'll think I'm smuggling trespassers into our territory."

Meiryn said nothing. If it was absolution he was looking for, he'd not find it in her.

"Faun is my friend," he continued. "She's been with the Guild for a long time, but even she's starting to test their patience. You wouldn't believe the number of times I had to cover for her while she and Nona sneaked off to gods-knew-where. And now, Nona is dead, and unexplained forces are endangering everyone. People are scared. They've lost their trust in her."

"And I deserve to die because of that?" Meiryn demanded.

Lukas wouldn't meet her eye.

Coward, Meiryn raged silently. She wanted to shout, to run, to never look back. It was a strange new feeling, this defiance against death. Before, she would have dissolved into a weeping, pleading mess.

Now, she only wanted to be released.

"Lukas," she said, her voice steady. Her heart still pounded and her blood still burned, but she held her head high. Commanded him to look at her.

With slow reluctance, he obeyed.

"I'm not going to fight you." She motioned to her leg. "I can't. But killing me to appease the Guild won't solve anything, either. Faun will still be out there on her own. Whatever past guilt you carry will only be replaced by the guilt of killing me now. All I want is to reach Faun."

Shame collided with some fiercer emotion and tightened Lukas's features. He set his jaw and dropped his hand. "You were right."

Meiryn blinked. "I—what?"

"I should have helped you in the beginning. I wanted to," he insisted, "but my hands were tied. The huntsmen were watching my every move, waiting for me to slip up. I knew I couldn't do anything for you—not without the Guild becoming more suspicious of us both. So I had to think of something else. Something that would get them off my trail."

"I don't understand."

Lukas gave an exasperated sigh. "Why do you think the huntsmen left you half-dead at the stake instead of killing you outright? Do you think Elder would have come to help you if someone hadn't encouraged her first? Do you think Pyrrha would have let you even breathe in her presence if I hadn't told her to make you useful as a healer's apprentice?"

Like daylight creeping over a dark horizon, it finally made sense why the huntsmen were so oddly merciful. The hands that brought her scraps of food and water during those first couple days in the Guild; the confusion and fear that dragged her through those long hours under the sun; even the cot she was allowed to sleep on—all of it was his doing.

She should have been grateful—should have been thanking him—but...

I didn't ask to become one of you. You abandoned me when I needed you most.

"None of that matters if you kill me now," she reminded him, jerking her chin toward his sword.

"I know."

"So what are you going to do?" She crossed her arms and glared. For whatever reason, she wasn't afraid of him. He could overpower her, kill her, drag her body back to the Guild—but she didn't believe he would, even after bringing himself all the way out here. She could see the underlying sadness in his face. He regretted following her; dreaded carrying out his orders.

After a long pause, he unsheathed his sword.

Meiryn's mouth went dry. She took a step back, but he extended his other hand. Holding her gaze, he said, "Give me your cloak."

She stared. Moved not a single inch.

Doing what he asked would require her to put away her own feeble weapon—not that it would help her much against his blade. She weighed her options: she could take her chances and run, or she could do as he said and risk dying here.

Either way, her odds against him were small.

"I'm not going to hurt you," he promised.

Meiryn scoffed. "Forgive me if I don't believe you."

He inclined his head. "You have my word: I will never turn my blade against you."

"You gave the Guild your word, too. Am I supposed to believe that you've had such a sudden change of heart?"

"Weren't you listening?" he said, exasperated. "I wanted to help you from the start. You can either let me do that or turn me away. The choice is yours, but from what I understand, you're against the clock. You want to help Faun, and so do I. We can figure out what to do about the Guild later. Let me make this right."

Nothing had been *right* since Reina was taken from her. Meiryn clutched her knife. "How can I trust you?"

Lukas chewed the inside of his cheek. He glanced between his sword and his open palm. Then, before Meiryn could stop him, he drew the blade across his skin. He grimaced as a line of blood blossomed from the wound, but again, he reached toward her.

"Your cloak. Please."

Silently, and with her knife still equipped, Meiryn unfastened her cloak, balled it tight, then tossed it to him.

He caught it with his bloody hand. Streaks of red stained the cloth. Meiryn watched as he took his sword and tore holes through the bloodstains. He made quick work of ruining the fabric, and when he was done, he discarded it carelessly at her feet.

Meiryn met his eye, perplexed.

He offered her a tentative half-smile as he sheathed his weapon. "You could chop off a bit of that hair for dramatic effect if you think it would be more convincing," he suggested.

The joke fell flat. Meiryn scanned the forest behind him, her guard still raised. "They'll be expecting you," she said. "If you don't return to camp, they'll come looking, and they'll find a bloody cloak with a missing body."

"They don't need to find you. We just need to buy enough time to reach Faun. Then maybe the two of you can tell me what's really going on," he added pointedly.

He flexed his fist, flashing the faintest wince, then strode past her, putting a safe distance between them. When Meiryn only stared, he paused and looked back. Sunlight outlined his silhouette in rippling shades of bronze and amber as he tilted his head eastward. "Are you coming or not?"

Meiryn studied him. He wanted to help—that much was obvious. But whether she could count on him to remain true to his word was still an unwieldy gamble. She'd grown past her childish habit of throwing herself at the first person who extended a shred of kindness. Her time with the Guild, even those hours spent with Elder, had taught her that regardless of any promises made, she could only truly rely on herself.

Lukas had told her that he wanted to help her all along, but his fear, much like her own in some ways, had kept him from doing that. If he only found his courage when the eyes and ears of the Guild were closed, what might happen if the huntsmen found him abandoning their orders?

But turning him away would leave no question: the huntsmen would track her down and kill her slowly, even though she'd committed no crimes.

Meiryn blinked, seeing Lukas in a newer light. He was a liability, a tenuous ally. But still, she couldn't deny that he presented an opportunity she'd be foolish to refuse.

And so, Meiryn lifted her knife to the ends of her hair, severed an inch or two, and let the scraps drift down to the ribboned cloak at her feet. A careful smile graced Lukas's lips, and Meiryn ducked her head to hide the warmth creeping into her cheeks. The two of them continued onward, oblivious to the rustling leaves behind them.

XXIV. REINA

IT WAS RAINING HARD. Murky waters sloshed over bowing cattails and softened the earth. Mountaintops pierced the black and grey clouds, and at every streak of lightning, Reina half-expected to see the dragon peering down from the sky again.

But he had been silent. Her mind was clear, her thoughts uninterrupted.

They put the Dragon's Spine behind them in a matter of days, taking minimal breaks to rest. The first night they crossed into Ver Signian soil, Reina sensed a collective wave of relief wash over the cadre—especially Aaron. He stopped scanning the skies every few seconds, as if being back in Ver Signia automatically guaranteed that they would never face another dragon again. Instead, his attention was set on the woods. The path they took through the Spine led them directly into Guild territory, and the short-lived ease hardened into agitation.

"Stay alert," Aaron told his agents, keeping his voice below the hush of distant crickets. "Don't speak unless it's necessary, and do not wander off." With his last command, he turned a pointed eye to Reina, but she had no intention of disobeying. This region was nearly impossible to navigate.

Reina had more to fear than encountering one of Ver Signia's notorious outcasts. Her urgency to get to Draconis now seemed like a childish impulse. A choice made because it was convenient, because Aaron was also trying to get back to the Silver Order.

If he knew the true reason she came so willingly, he would leave her stranded and ensure she would never again set foot in Draconis.

Hiking through the swelling landscape of the southern woods offered no more respite than Aaron's preferred silence. The trees suffocated the air and snuffed out the light; the agents tensed at every fluttering noise; no one dared to break too far away from the group—not even when Korris pointed out a stag prancing through distant shadows.

Their bellies were empty, their tongues dry. Reina was no stranger to this discomfort, and neither, it seemed, was the cadre. Aaron only allowed them to scour the area for food and freshwater sources when the trees cleared enough to let in the sunlight. By then it was nearly sundown. Raiko started to steer Reina away from the group, but Aaron halted him.

"I want her with Iliana," he said, tilting his head toward Iliana, who stopped in her tracks.

"We've been through these woods before," she protested. "If trouble arises, we'll be fine."

"If trouble arises," Aaron pushed back, "we need every pair to have at least one weapon. You're taking Athira. Raiko, you're with me."

And so the cadre split: Aaron and Raiko went in search of water; Evren and Korris set up snares with Korris's spare wire;

and Reina and Iliana left in search of forageable herbs and berries. Reina trailed a few paces behind Iliana, feeling awkward —it was clear that Iliana would have preferred her brother's company, but she was gracious enough not to make Reina feel too unwelcome.

She directed Reina to a lush part of the forest. Pools of dimming daylight shone on bushes rife with berries. Reina started to pluck a few, but Iliana slapped her hand away.

"Nightshade," she said, like Reina would know what that meant. She assessed Reina's face, sighed, then explained, "Those berries will kill you in an instant."

Reina dropped her hands and let Iliana guide her. They made idle chatter while harvesting edible mushrooms, plucking elusive red apples from tree limbs that were too high to reach, and staying vigilant for signs of the Hunters Guild.

Straightening her back after hunching over the earth for a stretch of minutes, Reina asked, "What do you think we'll find in Draconis?"

Iliana's expression darkened at the sudden turn in conversation. "I don't know," she said, somewhat distantly. She cradled her foraged goods in one arm and stepped over an unearthed tree root. A knowing look glinted in her eyes before she knelt a few feet away, pawing through the dirt. "Are you expecting to find something more than a ruined city?"

Reina held her tongue. She didn't like how Iliana so deftly turned the narrative back on her.

But fine. She would play this game. "I think we should be cautious. I know Aaron is trying to be noble by returning to the Order, but we don't know what's happened since we've been gone."

Iliana buried her head beneath a shrub. Leaves rustled as she shook the branches, and a few berries tumbled loose. Voice partially muffled, she replied, "We know enough."

Reina waited for her to say more.

Nothing.

"Care to elaborate?" Reina prompted.

Iliana straightened at the waist, strands of hair sticking out like twigs of a bird's nest. She cast a *you're-so-oblivious* sort of look in Reina's direction. "The woman in the mountains said you are one of the last *reksari*. Dragon riders. I don't know what might lead her to that conclusion, but I think you do. If you're hiding something that might help us, I suggest you tell us now, before we get to Draconis and find out for ourselves."

Reina's internal walls stacked themselves high. When had she become a target of Iliana's scrutiny? Did the others harbor similar suspicions?

For the past few days, as the cadre drew nearer and nearer to Draconis, Reina felt this inexplicable pull, an irresistible urge to travel eastward. It was the same sense of foreboding she felt when they left the village, except this time, she could hardly hold herself back from sprinting ahead of everyone and seeing for herself what awaited within those towering fortress walls. The sensation was incessant, and it fought against every rational thought in her head. It left her breathless when her pace was steady and even; agitated and antsy though she rested well in the evenings. It was so impossible to ignore that she nearly spilled the whole truth right then and there.

But she kept her silence. Cradled her secrets close. If she confided in Iliana, word would eventually make it to Evren, who would share it with Korris, who would undoubtedly report to Aaron that Reina had been lying all along.

So no—Reina had no intention of telling Iliana anything.

"I know just as much as you do," Reina said, hand on her hip. "I'd never even heard of the Drāga until that woman dragged me to her little hut. She was probably just insane and needed someone to talk to."

Nothing she said was a lie. At least, not entirely. Her understanding of this connection she shared with the storm dragon amounted to mere scraps, flashes from her dreams and unsolicited whispers in her ear at inopportune moments. Even when her captor guessed that Reina had seen the dragon in her dreams, heard his voice, felt his breath, Reina was still left to wonder about this power to which she alluded.

Iliana wasn't convinced. Or if she was, her face was arranged the wrong way. "She called out to that Infernal when Aaron killed it," she recalled aloud. "It was like a part of her died, too."

"Your point?"

"What if she wasn't just a madwoman?" She shrugged as if she hadn't just landed both feet squarely on Reina's deepest fear. "Ver Signia knows so little of our southern neighbors. Who's to say they're *not* hiding some impossible feat of magic?"

Reina swallowed hard. Her fingers twitched, and she felt the hairs on the back of her neck rising. "Then that still doesn't explain why she took *me*. I don't know anything."

Liar, the voice in her head chuckled.

Sniffing, Reina broke her stare and turned. "If you think this is enough to keep us from starving during the night, then we should head back to the others."

She knew Iliana had more questions, more theories, more suspicions, yet Reina would allow none of them to be spoken. Iliana must have sensed this because she pushed herself to her feet and wiped the dirt from her hands.

"Very well," she said, making no effort to mask her disappointment. "I suppose it has grown dark."

She cradled all her foraged items in two slender arms. Reina, whose hands were far less full, started forward to offer her assistance, but Iliana threw her a warding glare. Reina watched from a distance, only somewhat amused when an apple fell from Iliana's pile.

Iliana snorted and shook her head. She crouched, scooped the apple back into her arms, and rose right into the path of an oncoming arrow. She howled in agony. The food she carried spilled around her feet as she clutched her right shoulder.

Nearby ferns shook, and Reina just barely caught a glimpse of a wild red mane.

The archer from West Glen.

Reina dove toward Iliana, pulling them both to the ground. Another arrow flew inches over their heads.

Iliana groaned and held her arm against her chest. "My sword," she choked out, tears glistening like ice on her lashes. Her voice roughened. "Get my sword."

Reina yanked the whip-sword from Iliana's scabbard. She could hear the trees rustling and strained to feel the ground trembling beneath the archer's feet. For a moment, all was quiet. Then—

"*Murderer!*" the archer screeched. She pounced from the underbrush. Her bow was strung over her shoulders alongside a quiver of handcrafted arrows, and she lifted a dull hunting knife over Iliana's chest.

Iliana rolled away from death's strike. She bit down on her lip as the arrow shifted in her shoulder, but she did not lower her guard. The archer seemed locked on Iliana. Reina surged forward with a shout, and the archer rounded on her.

Pain sliced low across Reina's stomach. Sword high, she'd left herself open. She staggered, and the wind *whooshed* from her gut as the archer kicked her away like she was a pest.

Reina fell in a daze. The whip-sword fell uselessly from her grasp—beyond Iliana's reach. Distantly, she heard Iliana call her name.

Adrenaline coursed through her veins, and in response, she felt her power roiling inside her. It surged upward before she reined it back in, nearly doubling over from the punishing wave of nausea that came from restraining it.

The other two women were squabbling in the dirt, but Reina hardly made sense of their venomous screams. She could only focus on holding back this restless, writhing energy.

"How long have you been following us?" Iliana hissed, dodging a wild swing of the archer's knife. Pain seemed not to touch her now. She was fearless against the archer's threats, unflinching against her blows.

Reina rolled onto her stomach. She swore she saw thin golden light wreathed around her wrists—just for a heartbeat. Fear gripped her, and she covered her ears, as if that would silence the resounding roar in her skull.

Control. She *must* control it.

The archer's voice nearly split her concentration. "I've wanted your head from the moment you took her from me." She wiped blood from a split lip and charged again, forcing Iliana back onto uneven terrain.

A feverish heat now ravaged Reina. She could hear the blades clashing, but the sound was muffled and slow, as if every one of her breaths equaled ten of theirs. Only after the buzzing in her veins subsided could Reina muster enough strength to stagger onto her hands and knees. She reached for the hilt of

Iliana's whip-sword. Her index finger grazed a trigger, and when she applied pressure, the sword recoiled with enough force to send her reeling.

The archer shrieked as the sharp-tongued blade struck close to her spine. Reina yanked her arm back, and the whip retracted like a fishing line. Blood sprayed from the archer's wound and splattered Reina's face. She blinked furiously. Her opponent whirled.

"*Bitch.*"

The archer lunged with her knife extended. Reina threw herself out of the way, rolling to maintain her momentum, and came up into a half-crouch. One hand cradled her stomach; the other held Iliana's sword. Her finger curled around the trigger.

"Who are you?" Reina demanded. Her voice sounded foreign to her own ears: authoritative like Aaron, angry like her father.

The archer flipped her blade in her hand, aiming the point toward Reina's chest. Her eyes glittered like emeralds. "No one of importance to you. Step aside, Ashuman. My fight is not with you."

Reina bristled. She lifted her chin and positioned herself between Iliana and the archer. "You attacked my companion. That makes you my enemy."

The archer bared her teeth in a savage snarl. "Have it your way."

Iliana shouted in warning as the archer pounced. She tackled Reina in a mess of arms and fists and blades that sliced dangerously close to arteries and tendons. With humiliating ease, the archer pinned Reina on her back. Metal flashed, and Reina jerked her head to the side just as the knife punctured the earth. The bridge of her nose stung. Blood tickled her skin as it trailed down the side of her face.

Unable to free her sword arm from beneath the archer's boot, Reina brought her knee up hard. The archer wheezed, and Reina threw her off with a frantic shove, praying to every impassive god that her enemy didn't feel the jolt of power that jumped from her hands.

Iliana had recovered from her shock. She called to Reina, open palm extended for the sword. Reina reached back just as the archer swept out with a leg and smacked the weapon from her grasp.

Reina spun, unarmed and reeling from the blow. She held her arm against her chest, feeling bursts of wild, untamed energy spike through her body. No sooner did she blink than the archer nocked another arrow in her bowstring.

Time slowed.

Reina stared down the thin shaft of an arrow. Blood rushed through her ears. The roar of the storm dragon echoed in her skull, demanding that she unleash their power.

Their power. A magic that they shared.

Shuddering, wispy fractals of light expelled from her hands—

And Aaron's blazing fire sword blocked the arrow's path with a high-pitched *clang*.

Flames spat from the impact. The arrowhead blunted, and Aaron snapped the shaft in half with a heavy-footed stomp.

Time resumed its passing. The cadre rushed into battle, and the dragon's voice faded, along with the light that lit up the battlefield for mere seconds.

Evren gave the archer no time to recover from her dismay. He lunged like a viper, tackling her away from Iliana. The archer grunted as Evren wrestled her in the dirt. Evren had a good amount of strength on her, but she was quick and agile. She dodged his heavy blows and struck in the open spaces he left, slowly chipping away at his defenses. With only a small exertion of energy, she slithered free of his grasp—only to slam face-first into Korris.

He grabbed her collar and lifted her from the ground as if she were made of air. She kicked uselessly before he threw her yards away, where she landed against the roots of a tree with a sickening *whack*. Reina saw her reach for her bow before Raiko barreled forward, shouting for one of Evren's blades.

Steel flashed as Evren hurled a dagger toward Raiko's open hand. The archer took her shot. In one fluid motion, Raiko caught Evren's dagger, spun away from the oncoming arrow, and used the momentum to fling his weapon toward the archer.

Her eyes bulged. She ducked and raised her hands in instinctive defense, and the blade severed her bow clean in half, lodging deep in the tree trunk above her head.

Korris cornered her with his sword. Raiko, after a stiff nod from Korris, circled back to Reina and dropped into a crouch at her side.

"Easy," he panted. He brushed hairs away from her face. One hand lowered to cover her stomach. "You are wounded."

Reina strained to sit upright, but a searing pain tore through her stomach. A slick warmth seeped through her clothes, and she groaned before she could stop herself. Her shirt was stained a deeper black than she remembered. With trembling fingers, she touched the dark spot. Her skin came away red.

Shit. *Shit, shit, shit.*

Panic burrowed into her heart. She clutched at Raiko's

wrist, if only to anchor herself to something tangible. *I'm not ready to die, don't let me die—*

She could feel her strength waning. Every breath shuddered in her lungs, and formless black shapes edged into her field of vision. Was her heart beating slower already?

She drew in a desperate gasp. "Raiko—"

"Lie still," he ordered. He pressed a bloodstained hand against her cheek, and a shadow flitted over them.

Aaron. He kept his gaze straight but addressed Raiko. "Keep her safe. This one is mine."

"No," Reina croaked. But her voice was little more than a cracked sob.

She strained her neck and watched Korris make way for Aaron. Her brother's face was unreadable, his eyes burning like charcoal. He dragged his sword through the dirt alongside his feet. Tendrils of smoke curled from the sword point, and blades of grass turned to smoldering black fingers. Tiny fires sparked in his wake.

The archer grunted, trying desperately to make a last stand. She managed to wrestle Evren's dagger free from the tree trunk just as Aaron approached, but when she turned toward him, he disarmed her with as little effort as one might expend to swat away a fly. The tip of his blade met her heart.

The archer bared her teeth in a defiant snarl.

"The Guild will find you," she promised. Leaves and twigs were stuck in her hair, and her lip gleamed red. "They find every trespasser."

"Oh, I'm not concerned about the Guild." Aaron's voice was like smoke. Thin. Deadly. "I'm interested in the fool who tried to kill my sister."

The archer's face dropped. Reina's head spun. She propped

herself on her elbows, ignoring whatever Raiko murmured into her ear, but the pain from her wound had spread to her chest. Her vision blurred, then tunneled so that all she could see was Aaron. Something hot trailed down her cheeks.

Don't let me die don't let me die don't let me die—

The feeling of weightlessness loosened the tension in her body. Her head fell back, but she didn't feel it hit the ground. The forest faded, unveiling a million tiny stars scattered throughout the darkness. Rain, gentle and light, soothed the burn in her stomach and eased her pain. She sensed the dragon before his eyes opened above her.

"Come," he whispered. He blinked slowly and swept his wing over her like a blanket, but there was nothing comforting in his stare. *"Know my pain, as I now know yours."*

Lightning flickered between galaxies and constellations. Reina reached for the stars as if they might save her from the pull of death, from the dragon's cold grasp.

One by one, they blinked into oblivion.

XXV. MEIRYN

Meiryn and Lukas trekked eastward. He spoke little; Meiryn spoke less. She let him trail ahead where she could keep an eye on him. His presence was not exactly unwelcome, but neither was it solicited. It was good, she supposed, to have another keen pair of eyes and ears to catch whatever slipped past Meiryn's defenses. Lukas also proved himself useful in spotting Faun's trail, which had been wholly invisible to Meiryn until now.

An indentation in a patch of grass indicated that Faun may have rested for some time. A loose thread hung from a gnarled branch that Meiryn would have walked straight past if Lukas hadn't pointed it out. He even halted to draw Meiryn's attention to a single red hair, gleaming in a ray of light.

With no small amount of shame, Meiryn realized that she would have been hopeless without his company.

It was now the third sunset since she had left the Guild, and while Lukas's tracking skills were undeniable, they had yet to actually cross paths with Faun. Hope waned with each passing hour.

"How far do you think she could have gotten?" Meiryn asked.

Lukas drew his collar over his face, wiping away a sheen of sweat. Jokingly, he said, "She could make it to Draconis in two days if she really wanted to."

Meiryn frowned.

Lukas read her expression and softened his tone. "She's cunning, but she's not inhuman. No one could cover that much ground unless they acquired a horse."

"There are stables in West Glen."

Lukas shook his head. "She can't afford a detour like that. None of us can."

Meiryn eyed him carefully. "So what do you consider this, then?" She gestured between them as they walked, not missing the slight flush in his cheeks. "You said the Guild sent you to kill me, but you haven't told me *why* you chose to help me instead. What do you get out of defying the huntsmen?"

He worked his jaw, silent for a few minutes. Only when the sun's last light faded did he say, "I'm just trying to make sure no one else gets hurt."

"'No one else'? Who's in danger—"

"No one," Lukas replied, exasperated. He grimaced at the sharpness in his voice but didn't lower his guard. "Not yet, at least. There's a lot you don't know, and if you did...you'd understand why the Guild ordered me to kill you in the first place."

Meiryn placed a few more cautious inches between them. Her limp was bothering her now, and in the darkness, it was even more difficult to ensure both feet walked a steady path. "That's hardly comforting."

"Let it be enough to just know that I have no intention of

harming you," Lukas said. "I've never lied to you, Meiryn. It's like I said before: I wanted to help you from the start. Your intentions were pure, and you didn't deserve to be treated like a criminal just because you were in the wrong place at the wrong time. Helping you now is a way for me to make amends and to ensure that Faun doesn't get herself into trouble."

"And what comes after that?" Meiryn pressed. "After we find Faun, assuming she isn't already in Draconis, what's your plan? Will you drag us both back to the Guild to be tried as traitors?"

"No." He seemed offended that she'd even suggest it.

"What if the huntsmen come after us? Will you hand me over then?"

"*No.*"

"Then what do you intend to—"

He dove for her. One hand clamped over her mouth; the other locked her in an iron grip. Meiryn thrashed against him, a scream building in her chest when Lukas brought them crashing down beneath a stony overhang clothed in ivy and lichen. She reared her head back, baring her teeth to bite his hand, when a man's voice rang out.

"Did you hear that?"

Meiryn froze. She'd heard that voice before. Lukas released her only when she reached up and pinched the back of his hand, and she twisted around to peer out from where they hid.

Her heart dropped.

Huntsmen—an entire group of them, led by Rook, a man Meiryn recognized but had never spoken to.

One of the huntsmen in his party sniffed twice. "I smell smoke."

"It's coming from over there!"

Meiryn followed the outstretched arm to a distant point in the forest. No sooner did she find the firelight piercing through the shadows than a chorus of shouting erupted from a distant fight.

The huntsmen bristled and drew their weapons. "You think they're ours?" one man asked.

Rook's mountainous silhouette leered toward the fire. He muttered under his breath and snapped his fingers, and someone shoved a smaller figure into view.

Elder. She looked frightened and guilty for even being there, and she flinched when Rook seized her by the arm and dragged her close.

"You said we'd find them if we went east," he barked, "so east we went. There's no trace of that trespasser or her traitor friends."

At her side, Lukas swore under his breath. The crackling of fire had grown louder, and Meiryn wasn't sure where to pin her eyes: on the jumping shadows in the distance, or on Elder, who was pale and wide-eyed.

"I don't know where they'd be," Elder insisted. "All I know is that Meiryn went after Faun."

"And where was that archer going?" Rook was growing impatient. The smoke had drifted over them. Some of his followers were coughing, but he seemed not to notice or care.

"*I don't know.*" Elder's voice broke, and at the same time, a pained cry shuddered through the trees and sent birds fluttering skyward.

Faun.

The huntsmen heard her, too. Every voice dropped; every head whipped toward the cry.

Meiryn would have leaped out from her hiding place if

Lukas hadn't clenched a fist in her shirt and held her back. His expression was tense, conflicted. With Meiryn unarmed and Lukas alone against several other huntsmen, they stood no chance of confronting Rook directly. But neither could Meiryn stomach the thought of Elder or Faun being hurt worse than they already were.

The smoke was thickening, and the sound of jumping embers and cracking wood had nearly overtaken the restless chattering of the huntsmen. Rook insisted that they continue their pursuit of Meiryn and "those traitor bastards." His men urged that the fire was a more pressing concern. If the whole forest burned, one huntsman insisted, it would leave the rest of the Guild vulnerable and exposed. They'd be forced to move again.

Again? Meiryn cast an inquisitive look toward Lukas, who merely shook his head.

Meiryn nearly choked trying to suppress a coughing fit. Her eyes began burning, and she could tell that Lukas, too, was growing more uncomfortable by the second.

Finally, one of the huntsmen seemed to talk some sense into Rook. He acquiesced, but only because Elder squeaked, "The longer you argue, the worse things will get."

Rook growled. He looked affronted that Elder had even dared to speak without first being addressed. "Alright. We'll take care of the fire, then move out. Gods know we've wasted enough time already."

He kept his thick hand locked around Elder's arm, dragging her in tow as he and his band of huntsmen raced toward the growing flames. Only when the last silhouette dipped out of view did Meiryn and Lukas emerge.

Fire ravaged the woods. Meiryn stood paralyzed, remembering all too well the flames that robbed her of her family, her home. Her breath caught in her throat, and sweat dampened her skin.

"Lukas," she said, shifting her weight, "do you hear that?"

Not the sputtering embers or sizzling ferns. The silence. The lack of Faun's voice.

It had already dawned on Lukas. He drifted toward the fiery glow, worry and horror contorting his features, but he made it all of three steps before halting.

Meiryn glanced at the sword in his fist, then back to his face. She spoke his name first, fighting the urge to push him forward. "Faun needs us. Elder, too. We can't stay here."

"And you think we're of any help to them if we follow them into fire?" Lukas pointed the tip of his sword toward the orange light spilling through the trees. "For all we know, they're already dead."

Meiryn couldn't afford to think like that. She surged forward and yanked his sword out of his hand. She teetered from the sudden added weight but managed to stay upright. Though they were still covered by shadows, Meiryn could just make out the firelight reflecting in Lukas's pupils. She saw her own silhouette, backed by distant flames with a sword in her left fist, and lifted her chin.

"If you don't go after them," she seethed, "I will."

He gaped.

Meiryn stared hard, daring him to argue, but an eruption of battle cries stole her attention. She whirled and scanned the smoke-screened forest. It was impossible to make sense of anything, but she could still hear people shouting, spitting, cursing at one another.

Meiryn broke into a run. Her right leg protested with every

bounding footstep, but she clenched the hilt of Lukas's sword tighter to block out the pain.

Lukas caught up to her easily. They'd breached the front line of the fire now. Nothing was discernible amidst the smoke. Meiryn staggered on a flaring injury, and she yelped when Lukas suddenly caged an arm around her waist and spun her out of the path of a falling branch.

He hissed as sparks singed his arm. Meiryn stumbled back, waving the bronze sword haphazardly, and Lukas held a hand out.

"You're off balance as it is," he said, nodding to her leg. "And you don't know how to use that."

"Not yet."

Still, she relinquished the blade and followed Lukas. He led them in a wide arc around the worst of the flames. Meiryn shielded her eyes from the glare, discerning several shadows flitting between flaming trees.

Where the smoke thinned a little, Lukas found cover amidst a bushel of ferns. His eyes were fixed on a battle raging within the wall of fire, but Meiryn scanned their surroundings.

No sign of Elder or Faun.

Rook's massive frame loomed prominently in the fire. He slashed at darting shapes that evaded every strike. His huntsmen clashed against other armed fighters, and Lukas suddenly swore.

"Agents."

Fear like ice spiked inside Meiryn's chest. She leaned closer, then nearly screamed when a pillar of flame burst from the middle of the battle. Huntsmen shouted in alarm, and Meiryn realized, with no small amount of shock, that one of the agents was wielding the flames on his sword.

Lukas was engrossed, his expression grim. "They have to get

out of there," he said, tracking the huntsmen with wide eyes. Though the agents were outnumbered, they were far more skilled, far more powerful than the huntsmen they fought. They were *fast*—too fast for Meiryn to even see their faces or anticipate their next move.

Her hope crumbled. Then, at the edge of the battleground, she spotted Elder peering out from behind a tree. The firelight washed the color from her face. Tears glistened on her cheeks, streaking through soot and dirt.

Meiryn started forward. Lukas hissed her name, and she had barely risen from her place when a cold, shaking hand clamped around her waist and yanked her back hard enough to pull her off her feet.

She toppled backward over a grimacing, wounded Faun. She was without her bow, though her quiver of arrows still hung from her back. Meiryn scrambled to all fours. Dread sank deep when she spotted a dark stain spreading across Faun's shirt, but she was given no time to question her.

"Do *not* engage," Faun gasped. She shuddered and clutched her wound, brows drawing tight as she dropped her chin to her chest.

Meiryn started to reply, but Lukas interjected, "We can talk later. Right now, we need to run. Can you?" he added, glancing at Faun. He didn't even seem fazed to see her.

Faun just gave a thumbs-up, then wiped the back of her hand beneath her nose.

"But Elder—" Meiryn twisted her neck, trying to find her again, but where her friend had once been hiding, there was only empty space. Smoke clouded Meiryn's lungs, and she choked on her protest when Faun and Lukas dragged her to her feet and shoved her toward refuge.

The fighters were dissipating now. Rook ordered his allies to keep pursuing the agents, but the one with the fire sword cast a long, blazing line into the earth, creating an impenetrable wall between the huntsmen and his own cadre.

The world rocked as Meiryn staggered after Faun and Lukas. She was still searching for Elder even after they cleared the path of the flame and threw themselves into a cooler, darker clearing.

Faun crashed on trembling limbs. Her arrows spilled around her, and when her head touched the ground, she burst into loud, hiccupping sobs that wracked Meiryn's heart with pity.

Lukas reached Faun first. He sheathed his sword, took her by the shoulders, and started shouting. "What in six hells were you thinking? Why would you try to fight an entire cadre on your own? You against six agents—you're damn lucky to be alive right now. Never mind that *we're* the ones who found you. What would you have done if Rook had gotten to you first?"

Faun ignored him. Through her tears, she mustered, "I had her. She was right there, Lukas."

Meiryn went rigid. "The agent who killed Nona?"

Faun nodded, but Lukas spoke before she could get a word in. "I couldn't care less about some vendetta you have against the Order. You *cannot* throw yourself into danger like that, do you understand me? I've lost enough; I won't lose you, too." He crushed Faun against him, pressing one hand tight against her back and cradling her head with the other.

Meiryn sat back, feeling as if the air had been stolen from her chest. She averted her gaze as Faun sputtered out a hoarse apology and returned Lukas's embrace.

If Faun had encountered the cadre they were looking for all

this time, that meant she had to have seen Reina, right? The question burned on the tip of her tongue, hot and bitter as smoke, but Meiryn couldn't bring herself to ask. Not when Faun was in such a frazzled, wounded state.

So instead, Meiryn cleared her throat and announced, "I need to inspect Faun's wound. We can't go any further if she's injured."

Lukas slowly peeled himself back. The front of his shirt had been stained by Faun's blood, but she pushed away his worrying hand when he tried to steady her wobbling frame.

"I'm fine," she croaked.

She was not. Even in this darkness, Meiryn could tell that Faun was paler than usual. Whatever injury she had sustained was dire enough that the healing process might cost them another couple days of travel—time they could not afford to lose.

As if sensing Meiryn's restlessness, Faun breathed deeply and forced strength into her voice. "I won't apologize for leaving you behind. I knew this was a dangerous choice. I just didn't want you to get hurt."

"Like you were?" Meiryn challenged, feeling the suppressed hurt and resentment resurfacing.

Faun chuckled wryly. "I admit, I was brash, but so were you, taking off after me. And you roped Lukas into it, too." She wore a strained smile, but her eyes went sharp as daggers. "Do what you want, princess, but don't you ever drag my friends into danger again."

Meiryn and Lukas exchanged a glance.

Faun narrowed her eyes. Even in her weakened state, she was no less perceptive. "Are you going to tell me what's going on," she began with a slow, warning tone, "or am I going to have to threaten you, too?"

Lukas cleared his throat. "Sit back," he ordered, nodding at Faun's wound. "Don't interrupt; let Meiryn help you, and I'll explain everything."

XXVI. REINA

THE SOUND of war drums beat in time with the heavy footfalls that carried her. Reina jostled around in someone's arms, sweat beading at her brow, blood pooling from her stomach. People were shouting, calling to one another; their cries bled into the resounding echoes of blaring war horns.

Smoke and the smell of burning oak wafted into her nose. She thought of Aaron's sword but heard an entire army raising a battle cry. Her reality blurred into dizzying images from someone else's memories.

Fleets of dragons crossed the sky like falling stars. Atop their backs were armored riders, each bearing the signet of the Drāga upon their chestplates. The riders wielded dragon bone weapons—swords, spears, bows—all indestructible and unmarred by the fire and ice their dragons spewed upon the enemy. Rogues and spies broke through enemy lines on the backs of smaller silver shapes: dragons of the wind, who could turn an archer's arrow upon his own ally with a mere flick of the tail.

Reina flinched away from flaming balls of stone that flew

from towering trebuchets. The impact upon the earth shook her as if she herself had been struck. Hundreds of warriors fell beneath waves of enemy attacks. A river that once ran as clear as cloudless skies now churned with blood and ruins of endless fighting.

This was the war that killed the Drāga. This was the war that no one remembered.

It was the storm dragon's eyes through which she witnessed the slaughter; his senses that heightened her own. Every trail of smoke drew tears into her eyes. The pounding drums rattled the teeth inside her skull as if she were the one marching through the valley of the Dragon's Spine. To the east lay an open sea, unobstructed by storms, not a single cloud in sight.

The dragons fled across those uncharted waters when too many of their riders began to fall to Ver Signian blades. Reina watched them go. Pitted against smoke-screened skies, the dragons' silhouettes were like massive arrows aimed toward sea. They abandoned their riders, just as the Drāga abandoned their motherland.

Green and silver banners were erected across every stretch of land that Ver Signia claimed as its own. Drāga villages were emptied, pillaged; those who stubbornly remained were captured, mutilated and dissected, their corpses dumped into the sea.

Rhonestiel was a changed world. The fearsome warriors who once danced with dragons now cowered from humans who lacked even a kernel of magic. Ashuma closed its borders to refugees. Ver Signia scoured the Spine to eradicate the Drāga and their wild dragons that terrorized northern territories.

In a last-ditch effort to survive, the Dragon Lord took the

four major clans—Wind, Fire, Ice, and Storm—and fled Skystead, the birthplace of all dragons.

Trapped within another body, another mind, Reina flew on black wings that tired quickly. This body was too young to be traveling such great distances. She hardly remembered what the Dragon's Spine looked like before the war; hardly remembered the gruff, rippling laughter of her kin before their voices roared only in defiance and despair. A great, heavy sadness weighed in her chest. None of her kind, the Clan of the Storm, lived to see the dragons leave Skystead. None knew the chaos brewing in her heart, the rage that would build for centuries to come.

She would never take a rider. Never be ensnared with a saddle or mounted like a common steed. The power she carried was hers alone, and she would never sully the name of the Tempests by forging a bond with another human who would squander their gifts just as every other Drāga had done.

This was her vow. Her promise to dragonkind.

Through the wall of anger came a single thread of memories from a stranger's distant future. It was raining over a grand house that held many grand halls and grand rooms. Inside one of these rooms, there sat a young human girl, marveling at Ashuman storybooks containing illustrations of a legendary dragon kingdom. A woman cradled the girl in her lap, tracing her finger along faded words as she read aloud the story of the *kaeli rekks*, before they migrated to the scattered islands off the eastern coast. The little girl stared in awe at a watercolor painting of a dragon's eyes: like pools of molten gold, they gleamed with power and rage and beauty.

"I want to meet one someday," the little girl said decidedly.

Her mother clicked her tongue and shut the book.

"Humans have driven the dragons from their homes. There are none left who would greet you so kindly."

The rain pitter-pattered against the window. Lightning flashed, glaring against the softer halos of candlelight. Wind threatened to tear vines of ivy from the ivory banisters.

Unafraid, the girl shook her head, her little braids smacking against her mother's chest. "I won't fight it. I'll be good. You'll see. I'm going to meet one, and it will love me just like you do."

"Yes." The mother smiled sadly and smoothed her daughter's hair back. "I suppose we'll see."

Thunder rocked the house, reducing the memories to mere echoes in time.

———

When Reina woke again, her head was spinning and throbbing. She'd not been this dehydrated since Meiryn found her starved and dying behind some run-down little tavern.

Daylight was the first thing to greet her. She grimaced and raised a hand to block the glow, but the movement took a monumental effort. Her muscles felt atrophied, as if instead of healing her, Iliana had sapped every drop of strength she had left. Reina groaned, her breath rattling in her chest, and a shadow fell over her. A face blocked the sun.

Raiko. He blinked, lips erring into a tentative smile teetering on hope. His gasp fell upon her cheek like a ghost's touch. "Athira?"

She felt him take her wrist and squeeze it gently. She was too weak to move, and her throat ached when she asked, "Where are we?"

He shook his head in a dismissive *don't-worry-about-it* way.

His hand moved as if to graze her cheek, but he held himself back, lifting his head to address someone else. "She is awake. Bring some water. Now."

Reina took all of one breath before a flurry of footsteps rustled through a bed of leaves. She blinked, and the cadre popped into view like blades of grass poking through the winter's last snowfall. A waterskin was shoved against her lips, and she drank until it ran dry. When she felt a dull stab of pain against her belly, she dropped a hand to the tail of her shirt and lifted it.

Like edges of a serrated knife, the stitches traced a long line across her lower abdomen. The skin was still red and sensitive to the touch. Reina flicked her gaze toward Iliana. "You did this?"

"Of course." Iliana nodded. Her smile was pretty. She reached up and clasped her own shoulder, where the archer had shot her. "You saved my life first. That woman would have killed me if you hadn't been there."

"I recognized her from West Glen," Reina said. Her mind was dragging itself back together, as were her memories. "She was trying to save that Ashuman girl—Nona. The one who set that Infernal loose."

The cadre fell into an uncomfortable silence. No one had discussed the reason for Reina's capture since the fall of Draconis, and it was clear that bringing it up now was a humiliating reminder that they had indeed taken the wrong woman.

Reina blinked slowly, still addressing Iliana. "The archer called you a murderer."

Iliana grimaced. She traced a line in her open palm with her thumb. "There was an Ashuman huntress who found me in the alleyways...before I met back up with the cadre. It was her or me."

So Nona was dead. Killed on Iliana's sword. Reina remembered the woman in the mountains, wracked with agony when her dragon died. She had already lost Nona, then, too. What more would she be willing to sacrifice for the sake of restoring the Drāga?

Evren rubbed his sister's shoulder comfortingly. A protective edge hardened his voice. "You had no choice. What's done is done, and I am grateful that you still live."

Iliana said nothing.

"How are you feeling, Rhysanthe?" Korris asked, ushering the conversation away from less pleasant matters. He motioned to Reina's wound. "You lost a lot of blood. It's taken you a couple days to come back to us."

"'A couple *days*?'"

It should not have surprised her. The visions she swam through in her unconscious state had dragged her through another lifetime. They were so vivid that her own body felt foreign and weaker than normal. Gone was the magic coursing through her veins, ebbing and flowing with every breath; it was reduced to a faint tickling sensation deep inside her chest. And if no one spoke of it now, Reina could only hope that meant they hadn't seen the bit of power she'd let slip in those final moments of the battle.

"We feared you would not wake again," Raiko murmured. "We thought the archer's knife might have been laced with poison, but Iliana found no traces of it. Once we were sure that you were stable, we kept moving. We are nearing the city now, where you can rest properly."

It was only when he spoke that Reina realized it was his hand pressing between her shoulder blades, keeping her upright. Reina glanced at him, all too aware of how the warmth from his palm soothed the ache in her back. She told herself it was fatigue that allowed her to lean back into his touch.

The thought of rest was enticing, but, noting that only four of the agents were present, she asked, "Where's Aaron?"

She hadn't expected the question to elicit such dramatic responses. Raiko went rigid; Iliana and Evren shared a quick, worried glance; Korris fell into a mild coughing fit.

Reina lifted her brows. She repeated herself with precise enunciation. "Where's Aaron?"

Evren spoke up when no one else seemed brave enough. "Your brother is alive. The archer most likely lives as well. We aren't sure."

"What?" A ripple of panic shot through Reina. She started to prop herself up on her elbows, then halted with a pained grimace. She shook away Raiko's worrying touch. "What do you mean you aren't sure?"

"Our escape was not as easy as it should have been," Evren said. "We were ambushed by huntsmen. We got away, but just barely."

Reina loosened a tense breath. "What happened?"

Iliana opened her mouth to speak, but Aaron's voice came first: "It's nothing you need to worry about. What matters is that we escaped in one piece."

Reina craned her neck until Aaron's face came into view. She blinked hard.

An unfamiliar cloak—likely looted off one of the defeated huntsmen—barely concealed the hilt of his sword, and gone was that arrogant swagger that straightened his spine. His hair was unkempt and stuck out at every angle, as if he were constantly raking his hand through it. Shadows cradled his eyes, and when he approached, Reina's nose wrinkled at the lingering smell of smoke.

"What did you do?" she asked, glancing at his weapon.

The quickest flash of guilt crossed his face, but he crouched and said casually, "Again, nothing you need to worry about. How are you feeling?"

"Fine." She was wary of this uncharacteristic display of concern. The way Aaron looked at her now was free of contempt or scrutiny. He seemed genuinely worried for her. "You?"

Aaron nodded once. "Fine."

An awkward silence hung between them, made even more awkward by the cadre's looming presence. Reina read her brother's face like a book: he wanted to speak with her. Alone.

What could she possibly have done to anger him this time?

Korris was the first to excuse himself. Evren followed suit, and only after another slew of grateful remarks toward Reina did Iliana trail after the others. Raiko was the last to go, though he seemed highly reluctant to leave Reina's side.

"Are you well enough to stand?" he asked when Reina pulled herself up.

She swayed on her feet but nodded once her head stopped feeling so light. "I'll be alright. Aaron is here if anything happens."

Raiko gave her a look that implied that was exactly what worried him, but he said nothing, opting instead to give the Rhysanthe siblings the privacy they both needed and so deeply dreaded.

In the wake of his departure, neither Reina nor Aaron quite knew what to say. They stood several feet apart and refused to meet each other's stares. Reina scratched tenderly around the scarred skin beneath her shirt.

Finally, Aaron broke the silence. "You have nothing to fear from me. I don't wish to harm you, and even if I did, your new friends would surely stop me." His obvious bitterness provoked Reina's annoyance.

"I don't know if I'm allowed to call them friends," Reina said. That, and she wasn't entirely sure what they were to her. They'd moved past the hostilities and coolness that writhed between enemies, but it seemed too presumptuous to claim them as friends.

"Well," Aaron said dryly, "Raiko seems to have taken quite a liking to you."

Heat flushed through Reina's cheeks. Hastily she started, "I never meant—"

"Stop." Aaron huffed a soft laugh. Light lost its luster in the dark pools of his eyes. "I saw it that night in the tunnels, when he was the first to fight off those cave dragons. And that ridiculous pet name he uses for you when he thinks I can't hear. *Dha'katsi*." He drew out the vowels, contorting the word into mockery rather than endearment.

Reina frowned and asked, "What does that mean?"

Aaron pursed his lips. "There is no direct translation into Vers. It's more of a feeling than a name. It's a strong emotion— one usually shared between two who share a deep affection for one another. But Raiko..." Something like pain flashed over Aaron's face, but it was gone when he blinked. His brow lowered over his eyes the same way that their father's did when he was lost in thought. "Well, he cares deeply, and he was never forced to be subtle about what he felt. Or didn't feel," he added more hesitantly.

Reina breached the invisible line. "Does he know how you feel?"

Aaron just opened his right hand, revealing a long white scar—one that matched the one Raiko had shown Reina in the temple. "Raiko told you that we took a blood oath when I formed this cadre," he answered stiffly. "He is my second, my shadow. There is no closer connection between two agents of the Order. I trust him with my life and my men."

"Aaron."

He bristled at the unspoken demand for the rawer, forbidden truth. At first, it was anger etched into his face. Then, for a heartbeat, his eyes held all the sadness of the world. He swallowed hard, and Reina knew that he would never bring himself to admit the depth of the pain he buried. Not to her, not to anyone. He would silence these emotions for as long as he lived because that was his duty as the captain of his cadre. Raiko was his agent to command, not a man whom he could love, and there was no other path for them.

Some odd tug of sympathy almost compelled Reina to offer her brother a shred of comfort, but it was too strange for them. They were never close, and to extend that kindness now felt out of place, even if it originated from genuine concern.

"Well," she said to sever the silence, "thank you for saving me. And for whatever else you did when those huntsmen showed up."

"It is nothing to be proud of. But you're welcome."

Reina tilted her head. "You saved me. You saved your cadre. What isn't there to be proud of?"

"Plenty." He scratched the back of his skull, further mussing his hair. He cleared his throat and reached into the folds of his uniform. "This, however, might absolve me of any… hard feelings."

He pulled out a folded piece of parchment and held it out for Reina to take. She stared like it was a flask of poison. "What's this?"

"Just read it."

Cautiously, Reina took it and opened it. Weeks of travel had weathered the parchment with sweat, rain, and even a few spots of dried blood. She scanned the first two lines of the wrinkled page before her breath hitched.

Dumbstruck, she whispered, "This is the letter you wrote to our parents." A knot formed in the base of her throat, and she met Aaron's gaze with disbelief. "I thought you already sent this to them."

Aaron blinked slowly. He stared at the letter with a glazed, faraway look. "I fully intended to notify the lord and lady of your capture when we returned to Draconis. But that dragon—well, to put it bluntly, things went to shit before I could employ a courier."

Reina gaped. After a moment, her mouth split into a wavering smile that Aaron began to mirror before he quickly ducked his head, hiding his expression.

Leaves flurried at Reina's feet when she threw her arms around her brother, ignoring the biting feel of her stitches straining. Aaron stiffened in her embrace, but she hugged him tight, blinking hard against burning tears. When he pushed her away—gently, she noted—he was smiling. A true smile: no hint of cruelty, no sardonic smirk. It warmed his features. Softened the rigidity of his posture.

"I was angry," he started. "When we found you that night in West Glen, I hated the mere sight of you. I saw your face, and all those memories came back to me. All those years at home. I wanted you gone, no matter what it took. But then, everything changed, and I watched you integrate yourself into my cadre. You saved Raiko's life. You just saved Iliana's, and I…"

He lowered his voice, as if there were eavesdroppers of which to be wary. "I must have burned acres of the forest because of that archer. I saw what she did to you, and I—I don't know. Something in me snapped. I couldn't watch you fall so easily after all we've been through. And besides, Raiko would never forgive me."

Reina searched his face. She hardly believed what she was hearing.

Aaron wasn't finished. "All this time, I've been grasping for reasons to shun you, to hate you. But when that archer nearly killed you, I hated her more. I hated her for daring to hurt someone under my watch. I hated myself for letting you remain unarmed. I hated everyone else for not protecting you."

"You can't protect me," Reina interjected. She traced the scars on her palms, thinking back to the woman in the mountains. "No matter where we go, danger always seems to find me."

"That's hardly any fault of your own."

Reina stood there, at a loss for words. She'd grown up with a brother who blamed her for everything—even things that were out of her control. Who was this man standing before her now, offering reconciliation like common currency?

She was still staring when he reached for the letter. She relinquished it, reluctantly, and tensed when he drew his sword. But he made no move to harm her. He clicked the button on his hilt, drawing a low flame over the blade.

Reina gasped as he held the parchment over the fire. She

watched with a strained sort of fascination as the letter curled and shriveled into black ash.

"When this is over," she began cautiously, "I don't plan on staying with you. You know that, don't you?"

Aaron paused for a moment before replying. He watched the ashes drift away on a cool breeze, then extinguished the flames and sheathed his blade.

"I know I can't control you." He turned his gaze eastward, blinking against the wind. "But I also know that 'this'—whatever started when that storm dragon touched Ver Signia—will not be over anytime soon. We are, all of us, entangled in something far greater than we know."

Reina followed his stare to where grey clouds crawled over the distant sky. The storm dragon's eyes glistened in her mind, and she drew her hands to her chest, feeling a warmth pulsing from the pendant beneath her shirt.

XXVII. MEIRYN

While Meiryn worked on Faun's wound, Lukas talked. He repeated to Faun information that Meiryn already knew—that the huntsmen had already decided they were all traitors and deserters; that Lukas had been sent to kill Meiryn and drag Faun back for questioning.

"I'm no traitor," Faun said indignantly. "Everything I've ever done has been for the Guild. And Meiryn's hardly a threat to anyone."

Meiryn was unsure whether to feel reassured or affronted by that statement.

"You might be one of the few who actually believes that," Lukas replied. "The Guild cares about its people, Faun, but you know how dangerous it is to confront the Order on your own. At least, I hope you do now."

Faun scowled and opened her mouth to retort, but when Meiryn tightened the bandages around her torso, Faun bit down hard on her tongue. Strained, Faun said, "I'll take that risk if I know it's the right thing to do."

"But it means nothing if you die in vain." Lukas crossed his arms and glared at her. "You think we can afford to lose any more of our huntsmen? You're one of the best. We need you."

"We need Grey, too," Faun shot back, "but you don't see anyone else chasing after him when he leaves."

Meiryn's shoulders fell. *No use in hiding that anymore.*

"That's why you left?" Lukas's brows shot to his hairline, and he glanced between Meiryn and Faun.

"I thought he would lead me to the cadre," Faun huffed in annoyance. "I was wrong, alright? Why don't you save some of that anger for Grey? No one ever questions him."

Lukas laughed humorlessly. "Believe me, I have plenty of questions."

As did Meiryn. But Faun said that Grey's loyalty was true, and even Elder had revealed he could be trusted.

Even so, Grey wore his secrets like armor. What did he have to gain by keeping so much—like his noble heritage—hidden from his allies?

"Maybe you can ask him when you see him," Lukas spat.

Meiryn blinked, realizing after a panicked moment that he was responding to something Faun had said when Meiryn wasn't paying attention.

Faun propped herself up against the tree and pushed away Meiryn's hands. She seemed not to notice or care that she was still bleeding. "I won't get a chance if you decide to play hero and drag me back to the Guild, will I?"

Lukas looked only somewhat offended. "I'm trying to stay true to my word."

"As am I."

Meiryn would have been wise to keep her mouth shut. This was a feud that stretched across years between Faun and Lukas, and her opinion felt mostly unwarranted.

Still, something nagged at her. She asked Lukas, "Are you still going to try and take us back, then? Even if they want us dead?"

A conflicted look crossed his face. He seemed to shrink under her unwavering stare. "I will do my best to make sure no one harms you."

Faun scoffed and rolled her eyes. "What makes you think the Guild would listen to a word you say? They want blood, Lukas. If they feel they've been betrayed, they won't care about any explanation. They'll kill her on sight if they see her again."

Maybe it was the stress of the night or the strain of traveling, but Meiryn couldn't find it in herself to feel afraid. She only wanted to find Reina and be free of the Guild's tangled secrets and rumors. That was all she had ever wanted.

"What we need," Faun continued, "is to keep moving. That cadre has already left the Spine, so either Grey wasn't looking for them at all, or he's somewhere else entirely. I need to find him, and then maybe he can—"

"He's going to Draconis," a timid voice interrupted.

Meiryn whirled. From the shrubs and ferns, Elder emerged. She looked like a doe staring back at three starving wolves, but Meiryn jumped to her feet and swept her into a bone-crushing hug.

"You're safe," Meiryn breathed, sending silent prayers of thanks up to the blackened sky. "Gods, I thought..." She trailed off and held Elder at arm's length, taking her in.

Elder's face was streaked with soot, and grey flecks of ash sat atop her head like snow. Her eyes were still wide and afraid, but she hadn't pulled away from Meiryn's embrace. Her voice wobbled when she said, "I thought you were angry with me."

"No," Meiryn insisted, kneeling to her level. "I'm sorry for how I spoke to you before. I was scared for Faun's sake, and I shouldn't have shouted at you."

Elder took a shuddering breath before breaking down into a weeping fit. She threw her arms around Meiryn's neck and cried on her shoulder, bumbling over endless apologies.

Meiryn shook her head and hugged her tight. "You've nothing to be sorry for."

"I—I told them where you'd gone," Elder choked out. She rubbed her fists against her eyes and sobbed. "I thought they would help you, but instead I put you in danger."

"Did they follow you here?" Lukas asked, scanning the darkness. "How'd you get away?"

Meiryn glared over her shoulder at him, but Elder sniffed and replied, "The fire. They scattered after the trees started burning. I think they forgot about me."

"You'd better hope so," Faun snapped. "If you've led them right to us—"

"Enough," Meiryn barked. She smoothed Elder's hair down and held her close, as if she could shield her from Faun and Lukas's abrasive remarks. "We're safe. That's all that matters now."

Elder cried, her head weighing heavier against Meiryn's shoulder. "Rook knows where Grey is going. He knows Grey wants to free the dragon."

The adults went rigid. Meiryn cast an alarmed look at Faun, who merely gaped, arms slack at her sides. Lukas wasn't speaking; Meiryn could hardly catch the sound of his breathing over Elder's hiccupping cries.

"How would he do that?" Meiryn asked.

Elder wiped tears from her face. "He wouldn't tell me."

"I think I know how," Faun said. "The Drāga prisoner—the

one he thinks may have reflected the lightning back against the dragon the first time."

Lukas blinked twice. "Come again?"

Meiryn ignored him and asked Faun, "You truly believe that *humans* are capable of that?"

Faun nodded solemnly. "I knew what Nona could do. It doesn't surprise me at all that there are other Drāga out there."

"But this dragon is the first that we've ever seen of its kind," Meiryn fought. "If Drāga are real, and *if* they possess these powers, then the odds of one of them finding their way to the dragon at the right moment would have been small."

"Small, but not impossible." Lukas scratched his jaw. "If it's another Drāga that Grey is after, then that changes things."

Meiryn stared in alarm. "You know about them, then? These Drāga?"

"Of course." He still looked unenthused by the idea of turning his back on the Guild, but the mention of another Drāga seemed to pique his interest. "You were in West Glen, weren't you? Didn't you see what Nona did?"

Meiryn exhaled heavily, rubbing her temples to ward away an oncoming headache. "You're telling me that Grey intends to risk an entire city for the mere hope of turning the tables against the Order?"

Faun glanced between Meiryn and Elder. "Based on what the two of you have told me, I think it's safe to say that that's exactly what he plans to do."

Silence fell between the four of them, save for Elder's occasional sniffle as she composed herself. Meiryn was still reeling from it all while everyone else seemed to just accept it.

Assuming that every impossible thing they spoke of was true, and assuming that Grey achieved his goal of setting the storm dragon free, it would change the course of the world. It would mean that magic was real, that some tiny minority of humans could wield it, and that they were that much more powerful with their dragon counterparts.

It was too big to imagine. Too incredulous an idea to entertain.

But all else aside, what Meiryn wanted had not changed. "I came all this way to find Reina. I don't care about the dragon or about the wrath of the Guild. I was never really one of you, anyway."

Elder tugged on her sleeve. "You can be, if you want. You still have a lot to learn about healing, and I could teach you everything I know."

Meiryn pressed her lips together. Elder had done much for Meiryn's sake, and her friendship was invaluable—but Meiryn could not imagine that her future with Reina lay within the ranks of the Guild.

"Well," Faun said, quelling the raw emotions, "I think it's clear that our path takes us east. We should get moving as quickly as we can. We've lost enough time as it is."

She started to push herself to her feet, but she winced in pain and fell back. Meiryn reached for her, only to be pushed away again.

"I'm fine," Faun panted. "It's not even a deep cut, I just lost some blood."

"You need rest," Lukas said sternly. "We all do, actually. We have a long walk ahead of us."

Meiryn side-eyed him and lifted her chin. "So you intend to accompany us to Draconis?"

He scratched the back of his head. He looked like he wanted to put up another fight, propose some alternate perspective that might convince them to return to the Guild, but when they stared, unblinking, he gave a defeated sigh and dropped his shoulders. "There's no point in trying to sway your minds, is there?"

"There never was," Faun answered brazenly. "You can come with us and help us find Grey—"

"And Reina."

"—or turn back with your tail between your legs. I'm sure the Guild will be happy to see you empty-handed."

Meiryn suppressed a grin as she watched Lukas's face, recognizing in the tiny shifts of his features the mental hoops he jumped through just to find a reason to follow Faun and ensure she stayed out of more trouble. And Meiryn knew, even before he spoke, that he would come to some justification—even if it was nothing more than a desire to keep a friend safe. It was how things went between Meiryn and Reina; Faun and Lukas were no different.

Finally, Lukas acquiesced. "Alright. But the moment things go to shit, we're out—regardless of whether you've found your target or not. Understand?"

Faun nodded with the enthusiasm of someone who would completely disregard his conditions.

Elder piped up, "I'm coming with you."

"Absolutely not." Faun dropped her smile. She jabbed an accusatory finger in Elder's direction. "You sold us out, remember?"

Meiryn stood protectively in front of Elder. "She wouldn't have had to if you hadn't first run off on your own and prompted me to chase after you. She said she thought the Guild would help us. It's not her fault that they were angry instead."

"It's okay," Elder said, stepping out from behind Meiryn. "I know I made a mistake. I panicked. I didn't want anyone to get hurt."

Faun scoffed and looked away.

"I still want to help," Elder pressed. "Please, believe me."

"I don't think you intended any harm," Lukas assured her, "but where we're going is dangerous. You'd be safer with the huntsmen."

Meiryn cocked a brow and gestured over her shoulder. "You saw how Rook treated her, didn't you? You can't seriously think that sending her back on her own is the best choice."

"Rook will have taken his followers to Draconis," Lukas said dismissively. "She'll be in no danger from him if she turns back now."

"*She* is right here," Elder whined. "And I can make my own choices. I want to come with you. I want to help."

Pride swelled in Meiryn's chest, and she couldn't help her smug grin when Faun and Lukas exchanged dull looks. She knew they wouldn't send Elder away if she was that insistent upon joining them.

And so it was settled: the four of them packed their things and distanced themselves further from the battle they'd escaped. The crackling of fire had long since died down, but the smoke still drifted on an idle, creeping wind. They walked until Faun's panting was louder than her footsteps—only then did she allow Elder to help her.

Lukas, the only one of them properly armed against potential threats, kept vigilant watch while Meiryn helped Elder tend to Faun.

"You took a lot of supplies," Elder noted, rummaging through Meiryn's bag.

Meiryn winced. "I didn't mean to steal. I just needed to be prepared for anything."

Elder gave her a tiny smile. "I know. I'm not mad."

And there it was—silent and warm, though neither had expected nor asked for it: forgiveness.

Meiryn and Elder worked silently while Faun seemed content to lay flat and stew in her own thoughts. She hadn't sustained any fatal injuries, but the bleeding, coupled with the stress of the moment, had weakened her. The healers patched up the wound with plenty of supplies to spare, and not long after they had finished, Faun drifted into a quiet slumber.

Meiryn breathed deeply for the first time all night. Her hands were still clean, though Elder's fingertips were tinted dark. There wasn't a stream anywhere nearby, so Meiryn reached for her flask of water.

But Elder pulled away. "Don't waste it on me," she murmured. "We'll need that to cover the rest of the journey."

"I could find another stream."

But Elder shook her head. "The nearest body of water is half a day's walk from here. We're at the mercy of the elements now."

Meiryn tried not to feel too apprehensive. She'd managed to ration out her water up to this point, but that was when she was traveling alone. In the last day, she'd gained three party members —one of whom was injured; another was a child. There was no need to point out how the odds had shifted against their favor.

"We should get some rest," Meiryn whispered. She didn't want to think about what lay ahead of them until it was staring them in the face. Sitting on anxious thoughts would only cause her to question herself, and Meiryn was too tired to ruminate on whether she made the right choices.

She packed away her things and stretched out on her back. The stars were half-hidden behind the thinnest veil of wandering smoke, but at least they'd evaded the fire.

Her eyelids were drooping when the grass beside her rustled. Meiryn blinked twice, heart jumping, but it was only Elder.

"Can I sleep next to you?" Elder asked quietly. Exhaustion aged her by a couple years. The sight of her standing there in the darkness reminded Meiryn, with no small amount of heartache, of the little brother she'd lost. If he had survived the rogue dragon all those years ago, he'd be around Elder's age.

So it was with practiced ease that Meiryn welcomed Elder to nestle in close for the night. They had no blankets; Meiryn had given up her cloak to feign her own death. Elder lay facing Meiryn, and her large brown eyes reflected the faded starlight of the night sky.

"Do you think we'll find Grey in time?" Elder whispered.

Meiryn nodded. "He can take care of himself. He'll be okay."

But Elder only looked more concerned. "He's always alone. Sometimes I think it makes him sad, but he won't ask anyone for help."

Interesting. "How did you two become so close, then?"

Elder emitted a wordless murmur, brow creasing in thought. She rolled onto her back. Her chest rose and fell with each slow breath.

"When Grey first came to the Guild, he suffered terrible nightmares. Sometimes I'd wake to hear him crying out in his sleep. It happened more often than not, and the huntsmen were growing tired of it.

"So one night, I bundled together some eldervine and tried

to string it up inside his tent." At Meiryn's bemused expression, Elder offered a quick explanation. "Eldervine is a very rare plant found only in the everdark of the forest. It's where I got my name. My mother told me that in ancient times, the witchfolk believed that passing under a bundle of eldervine could help people sleep easier and have good dreams."

"You believe those stories?" Meiryn asked.

"Maybe." Elder shrugged somewhat sheepishly. "No one else was helping Grey, and Pyrrha wasn't training me yet, so I just did what I thought might help.

"Grey caught me, of course. He saw me trying to reach the ceiling of his tent, but he wasn't angry like I thought he'd be. He told me that I should save the vine for myself in case I ever had bad dreams, too, but I wasn't the one waking half the Guild every night. I asked him to help me string it up inside his tent. If nothing happened, then there was no harm done anyway."

"It's hard to imagine Grey accepting help from anyone," Meiryn thought aloud.

"I know, right?" Elder propped herself up on her elbows and faced Meiryn again. A curtain of hair fell over her face, and she shoved it back impatiently. "I think he was just humoring me because I was young, but you know what? It *worked*. I didn't hear a peep from his tent until he rose the next morning." She beamed with pride and laid flat again. "After that, Grey never questioned me. He was the first to suggest to Pyrrha that I be properly trained to heal people. If I had any opinion to offer on the work he was doing with the huntsmen, he took me seriously. So many of the huntsmen ignored me because I was a child, but Grey was never like that. He knew I could help people if I was given the chance."

"So, now, you want to help him," Meiryn murmured. She

turned onto her side, tucking her arm beneath her head. Elder nodded, and Meiryn chewed the inside of her cheek. Softening her voice, she said, "Grey left on his own for a reason. Are you afraid of what we might face in Draconis?"

Elder's smile faded, but after a moment, she shook her head. "I was afraid of Rook when he dragged me out here, but I'm not afraid of you, or Lukas or Faun, and especially not Grey. I know that whatever we face, I'll be safe with you."

A heavy exhale escaped through Meiryn's nose. She inched closer to Elder and reached up with a careful hand, tucking locks of Elder's hair behind her ears.

"You're very brave, then," she told her.

"You're the brave one," Elder countered gently. "You persevered all this time, even when the huntsmen hated you. Seeing you care for Reina so much... You're inspiring, Meiryn. We'll find your friend. I know we will, and we'll keep her safe from anyone else who might try to hurt her, too."

Meiryn's chest ached. "I wish I had your confidence."

"No." Elder yawned, eyelids fluttering. "It's not confidence. It's hope. Don't lose it, Meiryn. It's what made you strong enough to keep going."

Meiryn circled her arm around Elder to pull her close. Elder was warm, her head light as she rested it on Meiryn's chest. The trees sighed in the cool, eastward wind. It didn't take long for Elder to drift to sleep, and when her breathing finally evened out, Meiryn pressed a tiny kiss to her forehead and let her own eyes fall shut.

XXVIII. REINA

Storm clouds churned over Draconis. It took Reina several minutes to realize what was wrong with the city's crippled silhouette, but when it hit her, she stopped dead in her tracks.

Morturrim was missing. At its full height, the towering prison protruded from behind the walls like a thorn. But now, it was nowhere to be found.

What other ruins lay within the city?

About half a mile out, a steady rainfall dampened the road. The cadre looted enough cloaks for only four of them, which left Reina and Evren—neither of whom accepted the cloaks offered to them by Raiko and Iliana respectively—to brave the rain. Wind from the eastern sea cooled their skin and shoved them into a tight huddle: heads down, arms crossed over shuddering chests.

Reina walked on the outside of the group, squinting against the rain. Her feet sank into the muddy road. Every step left her legs burning, and her breath was becoming shallower and shallower. Though she silenced her misery, she couldn't hide her dragging pace. Even Raiko, who had been content to travel at the back of the group with her, was beginning to trail ahead. He turned when she finally fell about a yard behind.

"Hurry now," he called. He waved his hand to spark some urgency in her step. "The faster we move, the faster we will be out of this rain." He leaned close when she narrowed the distance between them. "Are you feeling alright?"

How to tell him that shelter alone could not soothe her ailments? That it was not the rain that slowed her, but the burden of shouldering someone else's pain?

Reina struggled to breathe evenly. She'd expended more energy than it should have taken to catch up. She pressed a hand to her pounding heart. "It's this weather," she dismissed with an unconvincing laugh. "Just dragging me down, I think."

Raiko grunted wordlessly. "Are you worried about the dragon?"

"No." The answer was sharper than she meant, and it caught Aaron's attention.

"Come on, you two," he commanded. "Unless you'd rather spend a night out here with these people." He glanced around them and drew his cloak tighter around his shoulders with one hand, clutching the hilt of his sword with the other.

Reina blinked at the lumpy forms lining the road that led to the gatehouse. With her head down, she hadn't even looked at how the road transformed into a broad path between little shelters. Tents. Hundreds of them were strewn about the field with seemingly no particular system of organization. Water pooled atop canvas roofs. Families grimaced as rain dripped into bowls half-filled with cold and tasteless porridge. Children ran underfoot, splashing mud in games of tag. Parents tried to soothe wailing infants whose cries pierced the air—and Reina's ears—

like daggers. Torches had been staked into the ground, rendered obsolete in this weather. Reina peered up at a wooden post they passed. Someone had nailed a sign at the top that read, in messy lettering:

WE FALL OR WE MARCH

Evren scrunched up his nose and glanced at the others. "What in six hells does that mean?"

"It means they're angry." Reina knew the call of a riot when she saw one. These people were drowning in their discomfort. "It's a rallying call."

She scanned the field. A few city guards patrolled the encampment to keep order, but they, too, appeared as sullen as the citizens who had been displaced. Not a single city official walked among them. The councilmen who occupied the governing seats of Draconis were likely cozied up in their homes—that is, if the storm dragon hadn't blasted them to bits.

Aaron strode up to the closest person at hand and asked, "What are you all doing out here? It's dangerous outside the city."

The man snorted. "Get off me," he barked, shrugging Aaron off with a disgusted look.

Aaron's nostrils flared, but Iliana surged forward. "Please, sir," she said in a more amicable tone, "we just want to know what happened."

The man's expression softened, but only a little. He glared toward the gatehouse. "Don't we all? Damned Order told us nothing before they threw us all out with naught but a tent and a few blankets for our families. Told us to ration our food or go hunting in the gods-damned forest ourselves. As if there aren't huntsmen waiting to feast on our corpses already."

No one knew what to say to that. Revealing that they themselves were agents of the Order would condemn them to whatever wrath was brewing in this field. Iliana stepped back as the man left, tracing a wide berth around Raiko and Reina.

She caught the faintest whisper—"*Malduna.*"

Raiko must have caught it too, for he looked at Aaron and cocked a brow. "Are you glad to be back, Captain?"

Aaron said nothing and set off at a brisk pace toward the gatehouse.

Upon approach, a pair of city guards blocked their path with crossed halberds. The taller of the two said, in a rather bored voice, "No passage for civilians. Please return to your tent—"

Aaron yanked his hood down. "We're agents of the Silver Order, you idiot."

The shorter guard blinked. He looked startled—less at the insult and more at the fact that someone had dared to speak back. He took Aaron in, then the rest of them. His eyes narrowed. "If you're truly agents of the Order, what are you doing out here? Where are your weapons?" He jerked his chin toward Raiko and Reina, who both shuffled out of view.

Aaron puffed his chest out. "I am Aaron Rhysanthe, First Captain of the Fourth Division—"

"Fourth Division?" the first guard repeated with a cruel laugh. "I thought we were about to sink into deep shit. But you're just the commander's dogs."

Reina shrank back. She lacked the energy to witness the brunt of Aaron's rage, but before he could get another word in, a disbelieving voice gasped, "Rhysanthe? Gods—where in six hells have you been?"

Reina went rigid, but the speaker bounded over to Aaron, shoving right past the guards. All at once, the cadre snapped to attention: backs straight, eyes low, heads dipped as a woman—short, middle-aged, and soaked by the rain—approached. Her uniform matched the ones the cadre hid beneath their cloaks, but crimson streaks intertwined with her emblem of silver flames, as if stained with blood. Pinned over her right breast was a row of tiny medallions.

"Commander Quill," Aaron managed. His voice was hardly more than a surprised squeak, but he cleared his throat and saluted his commanding officer with a stiff nod. "I am relieved that you—"

"Enough of that," Quill interrupted. She grabbed Aaron by the shoulder and dragged him past the guards without acknowledging either of them.

The rest of the cadre followed only after Evren pushed Korris ahead of him. Iliana trailed behind, pinning her stare on the back of Commander Quill's head, but Reina hesitated.

Wind howled from within the city, echoing through the tunnel like a haunted groan. She half-expected the storm dragon to whisper in her ear again, but it was Raiko who spoke.

"The commander is not a patient woman," he warned, prodding her forward with a light hand between her shoulders. "Keep going, *dha'katsi*. We will rest soon."

Reina's ears pricked at the affectionate term, but she said nothing.

Her brother and the commander conversed in hushed tones that bounced off the curved walls of the tunnel. It was a list of things that happened, things that needed to be done, and things that could not be done—all of which turned to meaningless mush inside Reina's head.

The Order's forces were halved in the assault. Contact with the First and Second Divisions had been severed when the shipyard sank into the chasm—taking every cargo ship heaping with dragon carcasses with it. Third Division mentors were busy keeping their acolytes from deserting, which left the scarce few agents of the Fourth Division to assume the role of damage control. Did that include assuaging the angry people outside the city? No, that was the job of the city guards, poor bastards. Harbored within Draconis were the agents prepared to defend the city should the people actually revolt. Why impose a mass exodus? Because the citizens would riot if they knew the Order had captured—but not yet killed—the storm dragon.

Before she could stop herself, Reina blurted, "What are you doing with him?"

Commander Quill halted mid-sentence. She blinked at Reina, as if seeing her for the first time. Reina had the sickening feeling of being dissected alive.

"And who are you?" Quill asked, sounding only mildly perturbed at the interruption.

Reina balked, but Raiko stepped forward and said, "An acolyte. We found her outside Draconis, trying to flee back home."

No one blinked at the quickness of his lie.

Opening her mouth had been a mistake; now, the commander's attention was fixed on her, and all Reina could do was lower her gaze in feigned respect.

Quill's eyes were pools of amber eclipsed by black pupils that contracted as she studied Reina with uncomfortable scrutiny. Only then did Reina realize what was at risk: Quill could discern the similarities between Reina and Aaron. She'd know that Raiko was lying; that something larger had happened to land Reina in her brother's company; that there had to be some greater reason to bring her here instead of shipping her back home.

But when the commander approached, Reina found no such revelation on her face, only a cold command for obedience.

"The punishment for desertion is death, girl." Quill scanned Reina up and down. The corner of her thin mouth twitched. "Still, that's more merciful than any fate you could have suffered in your country."

"I was born here," Reina said instinctively.

Aaron darted forward and seized Reina's scruff. "Apologies, Commander," he said, shoving Reina into a deep bow. "She will not speak out of turn again, I assure you."

Reina lifted her head. She couldn't help herself. "Are you the one who left all those people out there? Why risk a rebellion instead of telling them the truth?"

"Silence—"

Quill held up a hand, cutting Aaron off. She crouched so she could face Reina. "Which version of the truth should I have fed them?" she asked. "The one in which a dragon lies prone on their doorsteps, poised to awaken at any moment? Perhaps the one in which their city, their jobs, their lives will never be the same again? Or should I have told them that the Nest now lies unguarded and unmonitored, and that we have no way of knowing when the next assault might come?"

"You're supposed to keep the people safe," Reina stated plainly. "The storm dragon has been at your mercy all this time, but you've kept it alive. What are you doing with...it?"

The agents in Reina's periphery flinched, but the

commander smiled. Cocked her head. "Such noble concerns," she said. "You think I should have just killed the beast, then?"

No. Reina set her jaw. "I think you're holding back."

She's hiding something, the voice in her head crooned giddily. *The dragon frightens her—see it in her eyes? She fears his awakening.*

Reina nodded toward the city at the end of the tunnel. "You're losing control, and it's because of that dragon, isn't it?"

Quill's eyes flashed—the faintest glint of anger, the tiniest shred of emotion. She stood abruptly, motioning for Aaron to release her. He obeyed, but with enough force that told Reina he'd much rather have bashed her head into the wall.

Reina straightened at the waist and adjusted her clothes. The pendant beneath her shirt felt warm against her heart, but the rest of her body was overcome with an unpleasant chill. She shuddered involuntarily, a motion that the commander seemed to interpret as submissive fear.

"Speak out of turn again," Quill said placidly, "and I'll have your tongue delivered to me on a silver platter."

And judging by the look on Aaron's face, he would jump at the chance to be the one to deliver it to her.

Reina, wisely, said nothing.

As they neared the end of the tunnel, she braced herself for fallen buildings, fractured roads, and a handful of civilians—stranded, begging for help—but when the cadre gazed out over the ruins, Reina felt the color drain from her face.

The eastern walls were gone. Where Morturrim once scraped the sky, there was nothing but empty space. The chains holding up the prison lay somewhere within that mound of rubble that no one had yet bothered to clear away. Thick spires of ice had outlasted the summer heat and speared through shades of black and grey as a reminder of the assault. Toward the coastline, Reina could just make out the crater in the earth. Ribbons of seawater spilled over the edge, and her gut twisted as she recalled how helpless it felt to plunge into nothingness.

But the echoes of terror and rage seemed another lifetime ago, for Draconis now sat in eerie silence. Even here, on the outskirts of the city, windows were dark. The suspension bridges flapped uselessly against stone edifices, preventing access to the upper levels of the city. It was like the storm dragon had wiped out the entire population in a single burst of lightning.

"Take it in," Commander Quill said in a foreboding voice. "Imprint it into your mind: this was your home; these were your people who gave their lives to push the beasts back to the archipelago."

"What about the civilians stranded outside the city? Are they not our people, too? Commander," Reina added hastily after Aaron turned a slow, murderous glare on her.

The commander sighed deeply, never once looking away from the wreckage. "You saw the signs as you approached. They are angry. That makes them a threat to *my* people. Agents. I won't endanger good men for the sake of appeasing a few unhappy laborers."

"They're starving and cold."

An abrupt sound, like someone choking on their food, erupted from the commander. Reina realized quickly that she was laughing. Quill faced her, wearing an incredulous expression.

"You think I care whether they're starving and cold?" she asked. "They are alive. Their families are together *because* of the choice I made. If I had allowed all those people to remain in their little hovels, I would be subjecting them to the brunt of whatever rage lies within this beast."

Reina clenched her fists.

Quill continued, "Those people might hate me for the rest of their lives. Others may grow to see how I acted in their best interest. It falls beneath my concern, because there will always be another issue, another debate, another battle to fight. No matter which side I choose, someone will hate me."

Reina dropped her gaze. She searched for fault in Quill's philosophy, but a counterargument eluded her. She knew Quill was right. No one could deny the obvious danger that lay before them.

"There is no solace in adoration," Reina murmured, mostly to herself, "because power is an isolating burden."

Deep in her core, a quiet, thrumming energy pulsed.

"Commander," Iliana piped up tenuously, "where are we needed? Is the hospital still standing?"

Quill rolled her neck and started marching. The cadre followed suit. "The hospital fell through the earth, along with most of our compound. We've vacated some of the nearby homes to use as makeshift hospitals and barracks."

"And the survivors?"

The commander gave a one-shouldered shrug. "Surviving."

The agents exchanged uneasy looks; Reina was the only one whose gaze was still turned toward the east. She could hear the ocean hissing all the way from here as it spilled into the chasm. Could feel the wind growing colder as they neared the coast. And when a forceful breeze shoved her hair back from her neck, she heard the storm dragon calling to her again. Her breath hitched, and she froze.

"Keep up," Raiko barked. He doubled back to retrieve her,

but his grip remained light on her wrist. The concern in his touch was as fleeting as the bolt of lightning that sliced through the swirling clouds.

Reina let him drag her along, ignoring the churning sky. Ignoring the cavernous groan of thunder.

———

Commander Quill led them in a roundabout path through the city, exposing them to the wreckage left behind by the assault. Massive spikes of ice speared through broken windows; blood stained the walls and streets; carrion birds circled over motionless bodies; a few buildings—forges, Reina recognized—were blown to pebbles.

"Infernals," Aaron said needlessly, stepping over a pile of charred wood. "How would they have known to hit the forges?"

"Dragons are creatures of rage and ruin," Quill answered, her stride never faltering, "but do not mistake that for mindlessness. They are more intelligent and organized than any beast known to man."

Reina's stomach clenched, and she shuddered from a wave of nausea. She walked with her head down—mostly to keep the steady rainfall out of her eyes, but also because she sensed that Raiko was growing increasingly worried.

Each passing minute found Reina lagging further behind. Strength abandoned her around every street corner. Her feet were aching like she'd spent days running without rest, and each breath sent tongues of flame through her body. A sheen of sweat beaded her forehead. She couldn't keep pace with the others, despite every effort to stifle her ailments.

When she teetered around a corner for the third time, a broad hand closed around her bicep, and Raiko tugged her back. "I cannot watch you struggle like this. Do not strain yourself just because of the commander."

Reina shook her head, pushing against him weakly. "I don't need to rest."

In truth, she was terrified. Terrified that if she set her head down, if she lowered her guard, she would jump back into the storm dragon's memory—or, worse, his consciousness. He was here somewhere, and he was close. That was the only explanation for her afflictions: whatever torment he endured was becoming *her* pain, *her* burden to carry.

She dug the heels of her palms against her forehead, as if that might root her in her own body for a little while longer. What started as a pinprick of discomfort in her skull on the outskirts of Draconis had grown into a raging headache. It would kill her if she found no relief.

Raiko took her wrist. "What is this?"

Her eyes snapped open as Raiko's thumb smoothed over the webbed scars on her palm. She flinched away from him so abruptly that she staggered into the middle of the street, stomping through ankle-deep puddles. The others whirled around.

"Ath—Acolyte," Aaron snapped. Impatience—and maybe a flicker of worry—sharpened his voice. "What's the issue?"

"Nothing," Reina panted. She balled her hands into fists and hurried to rejoin the group, but Korris caught a glimpse of her face. He blinked, alarmed, and stopped her with a hand on her shoulder when she tried to barrel past him.

"You're paler than a ghost." He spun her toward Iliana. "Are you certain that archer's knife wasn't poisoned?"

"An archer?" Quill inquired. The intrigue in her voice was mild, but laced with enough venom that Reina knew they were treading thin ice. One wrong word, and their lies would come undone.

"We faced trouble on our way back," Aaron explained hastily.

"Back from where?" Quill arched a brow. "Surely it couldn't have required *all* of you to chase down one deserter?"

Aaron's hurried excuses slurred to a drone in Reina's ears. Her vision jumped, and for a heartbeat, she felt the weight of six chains bearing her down; heard the muffled chatter of Ver Signian draconologists discussing her condition; exhausted herself trying to grasp a power just beyond her reach—

Slender, callused hands clasped her face, and Reina nearly vomited as she slammed back into her own body.

"Six hells," Iliana swore. Her nose hovered inches away. She turned Reina's face toward Aaron, who looked grateful for the diversion. "She needs help."

"How badly?"

"She might be dying, Captain." Iliana's tone brooked no room for argument.

Aaron went rigid. Reina wondered if he'd have displayed any amount of concern if Quill had not been interrogating him. He squared his shoulders and lifted his chin, donning a cold stare.

"Leave her, then." Reina watched his throat bob. His eyes went dark as ink. "We can't waste time or resources on a deserter."

"Aaron," Raiko argued.

Quill stepped forward, contempt curling her lip, but Reina sputtered, "He's right."

All eyes turned to her. She'd caught on to Aaron's reason for his quick dismissal: their ruse was up. Quill's suspicion alone would damn them all if Reina stayed with them, but she also had bigger problems—problems that could not be faced in front of this many witnesses. It took every effort to ground herself as the rain trailed down her neck and plastered her hair to her cheeks.

"I did this to myself," she gasped, clutching her wound. "I have only myself to blame." Aaron took a step forward, as if to extend *comfort*, but Reina shrank against the nearest wall. She gestured toward the darkened threshold of a building whose door was missing from its hinges. "I'll take shelter there. Reconvene when…if I recover."

"You have no supplies," Iliana argued.

"And we cannot trust you on your own," Raiko added. He gave Reina a pointed look and cleared his throat. "The acolyte was my responsibility. I will stay with her; the rest of you must continue forward."

No. No, he couldn't. He would see—

Aaron squeezed the hilt of his sword. "Splitting our numbers is unwise. An angry mob awaits beyond the city, and we don't know how much longer our men can contain the storm dragon. If anything goes wrong, neither of you are equipped to defend yourselves."

"Then do your job," Reina ground out, "and make sure nothing goes wrong."

Indignation carved a frown into Aaron's face. He looked to Commander Quill for guidance, but she only shrugged.

"Assess and deliberate, Captain," she said, her voice muffled beneath the battering rainfall. "The hospitals lie northward. I will lead you toward the chasm, where your help is needed. The choice is yours, but you have no time to waste."

Aaron tilted his head back just as a flash of lightning lit up the city. Reina suppressed a groan. The clouds were circling over the east, the sky growing ever darker. It could have been midday for all they knew. Winds as cold and sharp as winter's breath howled through the streets, and the rain cut like knives. If it weren't for Iliana's hand bracing her weight, Reina might have staggered to her knees.

"Captain," Reina mustered, wiping cold moisture from her brow, "you can't stay here." And neither could she allow them to be anywhere near her when this incessant power finally broke free.

She watched Aaron glance between her and Raiko. Pieces were falling into place in his head, but she hadn't the faintest clue as to what the full picture looked like. Was he trying to devise some way in which they could all make it through this without Quill unveiling their lies? Perhaps it was the prospect of leaving her alone with Raiko that tormented him.

Finally, he fixed a hard stare on Raiko and closed the distance between them. "Keep her in your sight at all times," Aaron ordered.

Iliana's mouth dropped. "Captain—"

He silenced her with a wave of his hand.

Dutifully, hesitantly, Iliana released her hold on Reina's arm. Korris and Evren shifted on uneasy feet. The only person who seemed entirely unfazed by this turn of events was Quill: she watched from afar, her face betraying nothing.

"Watch over the acolyte until she is well enough to travel again," Aaron continued. "Wait out the rain if you must." He unfastened the belt that kept his sword strapped to his waist and passed it to Raiko, who merely stared like it was a venomous snake.

When Raiko remained frozen, Aaron reached out, closed a careful grip around Raiko's wrist, and pressed the hilt into his hand.

"I'm trusting you." Aaron searched Raiko's face, some raw emotion seeping through the commanding mask. In a lower, gentler tone, he said, "Be safe."

Raiko swallowed thickly. He grasped the fire sword and secured the belt around his waist after Aaron let his hand fall away. "You as well."

Aaron then turned to Reina. Where she expected to find anger or annoyance, she found only a desperate plea. His words were mere breaths in a cold wind. "Stay out of trouble."

She blinked once, and he turned away.

"We're ready, Commander," he said, holding his chin up. The rest of his cadre, sans Raiko, fell into step behind him.

Reina nearly protested—nearly ordered Raiko to follow them—but he prodded her gently, forcing the words back down her throat.

"Come," he muttered. "We must get you out of this rain."

He took her hand and led her the opposite way. The smell of oil and grease mixed with the pungency of sewage and waste, and beneath it all lay the sharpness of blood. Reina grimaced. The stench was doing nothing to help her sickness, which had only worsened in the time they spent debating whether to split the party.

She tried to ignore it, to seize control every time the thread tying her to the storm dragon yanked taut. But the pulses were coming faster now, and without fail, her vision jumped sporadically: one moment, Raiko led her past shelled-out storefronts;

the next, she was clawing uselessly at an iron collar fastened around her neck.

Each time she found herself trapped within the mind of another, the storm dragon would snarl and gnash his teeth—a sensation that only echoed in her head—and shove her back into her own body. The force of it defied the gravitational pull that kept them orbiting one another like two stars burning brighter and hotter, seconds away from eruption.

She craved the collision just as much as she dreaded it.

Reina clung to the slippery feel of Raiko's hand around hers, the glimmering image of Meiryn's smile, the scornful glare of her brother. Things that should have grounded her now faded like a dream she couldn't recall. Rain pierced her to the bone, and she felt that cursed, invisible thread coil around her neck, then *pull*.

A violent spasm sent Reina toppling into Raiko, who swore when golden spectral light burst from her fingertips.

No—

Reina recoiled, grunting when her spine collided with brick. Pain lanced through her whole body. She pulled her knees to her chest and wedged her hands between them. Every inhale threatened to throw her back to the dragon; every exhale offered a short-lived respite.

"Athira." Raiko knelt before her, his palm sliding against her cheek. She turned away, but he held her fast. Water jumped from his lashes as he blinked. He was smiling. Awe and admiration emanated from that soft brown gaze. "She spoke true. You are legendary."

Her chest rose and fell feverishly. It took every drop of strength she possessed to focus on his face, to not let herself be spirited away again.

"You can't be here," she gasped. She curled her fists until they were white, but the lightning sparked anyway. Tears scorched her cheeks. "Go, Raiko."

He clasped her hands in his. Brought them to his lips. His words were warm against her skin. "I am not afraid of you. What you fear, I shall fight."

"Raiko—"

In a few swift motions, he tore off his cloak and fastened it around her. The sodden cloth did little to warm her, but he pulled the hood over her head to shield her eyes from the rain. Then, before she could muster another protest, he lifted her from the ground and took off at a sprint.

Reina's head bounced against his shoulder as he raced down the street. She sought comfort in the darkness behind closed eyes, but the agony only bled deeper.

The dragon, a voice whispered to her. *Find the dragon. Free him, and you will free yourself.*

But she could hardly lift her head—how was she to find him when the wind itself was strong enough to send her to her knees? Her senses left her. She barely registered the sound of Raiko pounding his fist on a door before he resorted to kicking it open. The rain ceased as he lumbered inside, and Reina shuddered as he stretched her out on a flat surface.

"Where..." The word stretched over a breathless groan. Reina pried her eyes open, seeing nothing but a dark ceiling made of wooden planks. "Where are you?"

In the back of her skull, the dragon's voice came to her, clearer than it ever had been in the mountains. *"Come to me."*

"Where?"

Raiko loomed over her, but his voice was distant and muffled, as if she'd been plunged underwater. "Here, *dha'katsi.* I am with you." He cradled her face, and intense worry creased his brows. "I will find Iliana, and I will bring her to you."

"Find me," the dragon growled in her ear.

Raiko's eyes flashed gold, pupils growing narrow and sharp.

Reina gasped shallowly, grasping the pendant beneath her shirt. Her fingers twitched with weak discharges of lightning, and though her body felt slow, her heart raced.

"You're so close," she rasped. "Where are you?"

A soft hand grazed her cheekbone. She saw the dragon hovering over her, but it was Raiko who spoke gently. "Here, Athira. You are safe with me."

Outside, pale golden light streaked through the clouds. Raiko did not notice. He wrapped the cloak tightly around her shoulders. He whispered something in her ear, something she could not understand, and pressed a parting kiss to her forehead.

There was nothing left to keep her grounded.

Reina descended into hysteria. Memories swarmed her, and she was a child again, flailing in the arms of house servants who restrained her while her mother relinquished her to their care. She didn't know why; didn't know what she'd done wrong. Fresh tears blurred her view of Lady Rhysanthe's receding figure.

"Don't leave me," she cried.

Her mother stopped. Looked over her shoulder. The dragon's voice slithered from her tongue. *"I am here. Come find me."*

The memory cracked like glass, and Reina collapsed, back in her own body.

One moment, she was on the ground; the next, she'd managed to stand. It was silent in this abandoned house. Dark.

Cold. She was alone, but not: the wind rattled the door in its frame, and the rain slapped against the window, reminding her of the dragon that awaited her.

Reina did not process the next moments fluidly. She watched in snapshots as her knuckles went white around the door handle. The rain pounded against her eardrums, and then she was outside. In an instant, she was soaked through. Her head tilted skyward. She stared, unblinking, into the storm.

I'm coming to find you. Her thoughts swirled with the clouds. *I'm coming to end this.*

Veins of lightning threaded the sky. Thunder bellowed its rage, and like a moth drawn blindly to flame, Reina followed the sound of its call.

XXIX. MEIRYN

ACCOUNTING for one rest stop per day and several hours of sleep each night—not to mention the one time that Faun reopened her wound by exerting herself too far, thus setting them back an hour—the rest of the journey took a couple days on foot. Over the course of those two days, the huntsmen watched clear skies turn grey and stormy, and as they approached the edge of the forest, they found themselves battered by steady rainfall. But Meiryn was far less concerned with the weather than she was with what lay before them.

"What are all these people doing out here?" Faun wondered aloud. She held her arms out for balance, each step lilting as mud squelched around her feet.

Tents were scattered across the outer field of Draconis. People wrapped in blankets and cloaks swarmed the front gates, waving wooden stakes, pitchforks, crude weapons. The shouting alone drowned out the battering rain. A cluster of fearful mothers at the back reined in their children to watch from a safe distance.

Meiryn stood on tiptoe, straining her neck to see over the

masses, but to no avail. Their numbers were large, their anger palpable.

Something was wrong. Not just with the rage in the air, but with the entire scene. When she envisioned Draconis, she thought they would find a wounded city welcoming in relief efforts. She had braced herself for the aftermath of destruction, but this was far worse than anything she anticipated.

"They've barricaded the gates," Lukas said. Standing taller than any of them, he had a clearer view of what was happening. His expression soured. "These people were cast out from the city. They're demanding to be let back in."

Elder was jumping every other step just to catch a glimpse of the chaos. She was out of breath by the time they neared the first line of tents. With a frustrated groan, she asked, "How are we supposed to find Grey?"

No sooner did the words leave her mouth than a boy around her age slammed into her from behind. She yelped, tumbling forward, and the boy cast her a dirty look over his shoulder. "Do something useful or get out of the way!" he yelled. He wielded a small, blunted knife in his hand and joined a man whom Meiryn presumed to be his father. Together they joined the faceless crowd.

Meiryn steadied Elder on her feet. "Are you alright? Here, stay by me."

"I'm fine." Elder rubbed her shoulder and frowned. "But what's his problem?"

"I think they might have an answer," Faun said. Meiryn followed her glare to where a single line of city guards, each wielding a sword and shield, blocked the path to the gatehouse. No one listened to their booming commands. Anger and impatience fueled the riot. Rocks hurtled through the air, clattering against the guards' shields and helmets—sometimes striking an eye.

"This is bad." Lukas pressed close behind Meiryn and Faun, the former of whom kept her hands locked on Elder's shoulders. With Lukas towering behind them all like a shield, they were protected from anyone who came barreling from behind. "Where are all the agents? Why is no one *doing anything*?"

"I think we have a bigger problem," Elder said, her voice rising. She pointed across the way, where Meiryn just barely spotted Rook and his followers.

They were missing a handful of their men, and they wore expressions of alarm similar to those of Meiryn and her allies. But when the crowd parted and gave Rook a clear view of the four of them standing together, his shock turned to bloodlust. He drew his sword and shouted words that Meiryn did not wait to hear.

Dragging Faun and Elder with her, Meiryn bolted. Lukas was close behind, and with Rook practically screaming after them, they were riling up the crowd. People who were already protesting and spitting curses at the guards mistook the huntsmen's outraged cries as rallying calls. The entire mass surged forward, pressing ever closer to the guards' spears. Rain and hail pummeled the stampede, and the wind threatened to topple any straggler off their feet.

Meiryn squeezed Elder's arm, lest she lose her to the storming riot. Her ears were ringing, her heart was pounding, and her blood ran cold when she realized just how close they had gotten to the guards in their desperation to escape Rook's followers. Faun's words were inaudible, though she stood right beside Meiryn. Elder's arm shot out just as lightning flashed, bright as a summer sun.

"Grey!" she shrieked.

Thunder bellowed in the wake of her call, but somehow, Grey had heard. Meiryn peered through the darkened haze. She lifted one hand to shove mops of wet hair out of her face.

There, near the front of the masses, stood Grey. He looked like he was trying to keep the protesters back from the guards' pointed spears, but at Elder's voice, he spun around. His hood billowed and dropped. Shock and horror widened his eyes, pale as ghosts. His lips formed words that were lost when someone behind them screamed.

Meiryn whirled. People fell to Rook's sword. His huntsmen cleared a path for him, unfazed by the carnage they left in their wake.

Elder wanted only to reach Grey. He lifted his hands and called for her to stop, but she either did not hear or did not listen.

"Wait—" Meiryn choked on rainwater, trying to keep herself upright. She lost sight of Faun and Lukas, and instead, she watched the guards grow anxious. They shouted for backup that never came. They shuffled in place, and their weapons trembled in their hands.

Elbows jabbed at Meiryn's face and knees knocked against her, threatening to send her sprawling underfoot. Hands clawed at her back, yanked on her hair as people pressed in tighter. She shouted for them to back away, but her voice was just one among hundreds.

Someone slammed into her back. Meiryn grunted, using Elder as a counterweight, but Elder lost her balance and stumbled through the front line of the protesters.

One of the guards jumped and thrust his spear forward.

Blood sprayed from Elder's neck. She staggered, then

careened into Grey, whose hands turned dark the second she fell.

Thunder drowned out Meiryn's horrified wail. The witnesses stood. They watched Elder choke and thrash while Grey cradled her close. They watched the guard who dealt the killing blow turn white.

And then they charged.

Meiryn's legs gave out when the people breached the invisible barrier. The stampede could have rocked the earth. People tramped over one another, racing like starved animals toward the gatehouse. Bodies splashed to the ground. Voices screamed for justice, for blood, for the fall of the Order.

Fingers clawed into Meiryn's arm and hauled her to her feet. Mud dripped from one side of her face. She gasped in pain, and her heart stopped when Rook grinned, revealing two rows of yellowing teeth. "Here you are."

She didn't care. She craned her neck, looking for Elder.

Steel glinted beneath lightning when Rook lifted his weapon—

Then his mouth stretched into a silent scream. His grip slackened, and he twisted his head around, facing Lukas. A bronze sword tip protruded from the center of Rook's chest. Rain plastered Lukas's hair to his forehead, but Meiryn could still see his eyes.

Dark. Furious.

Rook let out a horrible groan as Lukas yanked his blade out.

Meiryn shoved herself away. She spun and scrambled on all fours to where Grey still held Elder. One hand supported her limp body; the other was pressed against the tear in her neck, as if he alone could stop the bleeding.

It was pointless. She was dead.

Meiryn was shaking violently. She clawed her fingers into the earth, bile rising in her throat.

She's alive. She's alive. She's alive.

If she repeated it, Meiryn told herself, then surely it would be true. Time itself would fold backward, and Elder would be standing again. Her skin wouldn't be gleaming crimson. Her face wouldn't be so pale.

Lukas was at her side again, urging her to stand. Meiryn lashed her arm out, but he caught her and shouted into her ear, "Faun's gone ahead!"

He pointed his blood- and rain-soaked sword toward the gatehouse. The path was clear. The guards lay dead in an emptying field while the rioters stormed the barricades. "We have to stop her and get out of here."

Faun would never turn back. Not now that the barriers were breached.

"Wait," Meiryn gasped.

At the sound of her voice, Grey lifted his face. His lips were parted, shaking. *Help me,* his eyes seemed to say. Meiryn reached again for Elder, as if she could stitch the hole in her neck shut if given the chance, but Lukas grabbed her outstretched hand.

Meiryn screamed. Lukas flinched at the rawness of the sound, but urgency chased the remorse off his face.

"There's nothing you can do," he said. He gripped her tight, just like she had held Elder mere moments ago. Meiryn barely felt herself move. Barely discerned human from shadow, fire from lightning.

"Keep moving." Lukas dragged her along, panting as he raced after the rioters.

In the distance, Meiryn could hear glass breaking, doors

splintering. The noise echoed through the tunnel and scattered her thoughts, leaving her with nothing but Lukas's command.

Keep moving.

Elder lay dead behind her.

Keep moving.

Who else would she lose if she carried on?

Keep. Moving.

She'd have rather sunk through the earth and burned in all six hells. It was what she deserved after bringing Elder into so much danger.

The storm was worse inside the city. Hail struck hard and sharp enough to bruise and draw blood. With each sporadic lightning strike, Meiryn pieced together the broken shards of Draconis.

Banners were ripped from their poles. Loose debris sent people toppling into the walls, each other, the ground. The smell of salt permeated the air, and Meiryn squinted until she could just barely make out the crumbled ruins of the eastern shore. Squatting like a straw hut against a hurricane was the Order's base—nearly consumed by a vortex of wind that pulsed and throbbed like a pair of gasping lungs.

Through the chaos came a single thought: *Reina.*

There was no reason to believe that Reina was anywhere near the center of the storm. No reason to even consider that she was here. Meiryn saw now how naive—how utterly, painfully foolish it was to think that anyone could have survived the storm dragon's rage.

Have I lost them both today?

She was numb to the rain. Numb to the hail that beat against her arms and legs. Lukas was shouting again, but she made no sense of his words; only wanted him to stop being so loud. Everything was loud. It was too much, yet a grim curiosity beckoned her all the same.

Meiryn watched an ethereal glow emanate from within the swirling wind. She lifted a hand, pointing toward it. A warning perched on her tongue—

The sky lit up with a violent flash of gold. Thunder roared like an angry beast, and the earth itself shuddered in terror.

Lukas dropped to a crouch and pulled Meiryn with him. He slung an arm around her shoulders as a black shape, darker than the storm yet ten times as deadly, surged skyward.

The dragon, the one that brought the storm—it was still alive. It was *here*, in the dying heart of Draconis.

The guards had failed to keep the people at bay, and now every soul in the city knew the secret brewing within: the Order had failed them, too.

Lukas rose on cautious feet. Rain tore through the cloud of dust that blew over them. People scrambled like mice into the nearest buildings and barricaded the doorways. A faint distress horn resounded over the torrent before an inhuman screech drowned it all out.

The black dragon soared low over the rooftops. It teetered and rocked mid-flight, as if afflicted by some injury, but the wind bowed to its will. Lightning pulsed in its veins, flashed within its chest, and sparked across the sky.

Lukas swore heavily. He was fixated on a point down the street, and Meiryn followed his stare.

Faun was still on her feet. She dodged huddles of scared people and sped around a corner, quick as a fox. She was heading east, toward whatever remained of the Order.

"We can't let her go alone," Lukas urged. He closed his

hand around Meiryn's and pulled her along. "Stay with me. Do exactly as I say."

It was her own choice, not his dictation, that compelled her to follow him. That, and the words resonating in her skull: *Keep moving.*

Behind her lay a calm field. Safety. Elder.

No—Elder was dead. Gone. It came back like a knife twisting in Meiryn's gut.

Grey had her. Grey was still out there, and the dragon was loose—set free by someone else. But who?

Meiryn's thoughts raced as wildly as the wind changed directions. Down one street, she and Lukas were boosted by heaving gales at their backs; down another, they pushed against invisible hands that threatened to pin them to the ground and drown them beneath the rain. Obstructing their path was evidence of the first assault: fractured cobblestone streets, bridges that once stretched between the upper levels, now scorched and warped beyond repair, and massive spires of ice, still cold to the touch, protruding from shattered windows.

They turned another corner and knelt for a brief respite.

"Six hells," Lukas panted, dropping Meiryn's hand to rake his hair back from his face. He readjusted his baldric and drummed nervous fingertips on the leather strap. "There's no use getting anywhere until that dragon clears out. Where are the agents? Why hasn't anyone captured that thing yet?"

Meiryn stopped listening halfway through because there, through the sheets of pouring rain, a slim figure chased the path of the dragon. Head tilted skyward, cloak billowing behind her, the figure had not yet spotted Meiryn.

But Meiryn recognized that gait. She could recognize that cloaked silhouette anywhere. Her heart swelled with emotion.

She shoved herself onto quaking legs, deaf to Lukas's orders and consumed by her own dismay.

Hope—brittle and wretched and desperate—lifted Meiryn's cupped hands to her mouth and drew a wild scream from her chest.

"*Reina!*"

The figure skidded along the cobblestone street and slammed to a sudden stop. Reina dropped her head. She stared straight at Meiryn. Lightning flashed, illuminating a warm flush in her cheeks. Her eyes reflected the gleam like golden suns.

Meiryn took a rigid step toward her—

Reina spun and fled.

XXX. REINA

ONE HOUR EARLIER

Rain trailed down Reina's face like cold tears. The taste of stale water dripped into her open mouth, and her lungs burned with each frantic breath.

Skidding along wet cobblestones, Reina stumbled through the streets of Draconis like a wayward arrow. Her feet led her path; her mind could barely make sense of anything now.

She watched herself from outside her body: a slight, sickly figure staggering aimlessly through abandoned alleyways and around confusing corners. Anyone witnessing this must have thought she was deranged. But the streets were empty; not a soul remained to accompany her on this path that grew darker with every step she took.

She was a puppet, moved by an invisible string and the disembodied voice in her head: *"Find me."*

The call had grown louder, clearer as she lurched onward. It was a primal force tethered to her core and wrapped around her very soul. Her legs knocked against one another—as if protesting, resisting—and every breath felt like it might be her last. But she knew, somehow, that the relief from this pain she carried could be obtained only by finding the dragon and setting him free like he demanded.

Did you not vow never to be controlled by another? the crueler voice hissed. It was her fear, a shadow curling in the corner of her heart. *You were untamable. Do you yield so easily when pain grows hard?*

She spoke into the storm. "I don't yield."

A thin chuckle resonated between her ears.

She wiped rain and sweat from her brow. Moisture gathered on her lashes, and she blinked her vision clear. The hairs on her body stood rigid. Her heart wanted to soar, wanted to break free of her rib cage.

But the rush of water flooded her ears. Beneath the current, voices: dozens, then hundreds. She had followed the flashing, blinking images she saw through the dragon's eyes; followed them all the way to the Order's base.

She walked along the walls to avoid detection, but these agents were so blind. So arrogant. They walked in oblivious pairs, complaining about the weather and exchanging degrading jokes about the people camped out on the field. They did not see her slinking through the shadows, though her weakened state made her an easy target.

Her veins buzzed. The energy lashing within her was thrilling and new, yet familiar all the same.

She folded herself into the darkness as a group of agents passed dangerously close. None of them wore the face of anyone she recognized. When they slipped out of earshot, she peered around the corner. Her heart leaped.

She found the grave of Morturrim. What was once Ver

Signia's most formidable prison was now little more than a pile of black stones and rubble.

Lying prone atop a bed of obsidian bricks was the storm dragon. His eyes were shut; his chest rose and fell shallowly. Long tubes protruded from his shoulders and flank, leeching his blood and collecting it in glass tanks. The six chains that kept Morturrim upright had been refashioned into leashes: one for each of the dragon's four legs, one to muzzle him, and one that pinned the base of his wings together at a painful angle.

No one stood nearby to guard him. Why waste the men, when these iron chains kept him comatose?

Reina rubbed a sore spot between her shoulder blades. Her heartbeat felt slow, but her breaths were rapid and labored. She started forward, blood roaring in her ears. The hill grew taller as she drew closer. The dragon felt so far away, but she swore she could feel him breathing; swore she could feel the rain warming her skin and filling her with steady strength.

She started the precarious ascent. She paid no mind to the bruised and death-grey limbs that poked out from beneath the rubble. Rags of hair spilled through the cracks like dark rivers. The bricks were slick beneath her hands and feet, and she gasped when a loose rock slipped out from under her and clattered against the ground, drawing attention from somewhere nearby. Someone raised an alarm, and a huddle of agents rushed for her.

She scrambled up the side of the hill, grabbing at whatever she could to pull herself upward. *Closer,* she urged herself. The clouds were spiraling. A black eye formed at the center of the squall, right over the sleeping dragon, and the current swept an arrow off course. It struck where her hand had been a mere heartbeat ago.

She bounded from foothold to foothold, fingers scraping against rough edges. *Faster.*

As she neared the dragon, she saw him panting. His limbs were twitching, claws grasping open air, his wings straining against the iron. The storm pulsed with each ragged gasp.

Reina crested the hill on all fours. The horde below her blurred out of focus. A wall of grey wind and gold sparks shielded her from their arrows and spears. The rain drenched only their enemies on the ground. It was silent in the eye of the storm. Rays of daylight filtered through the clouds, allowing Reina to finally see the storm dragon in the flesh. He looked just as he appeared in her visions. Her skin felt warm again, her strength just within reach.

Kneeling, she lifted a trembling hand to the dragon's muzzle. His breath grazed against her palm, and as if in reply, lightning danced around her scars.

"I found you," she whispered. Her hand closed around a thick chain, and she spoke the name that was fed to her in dreams. The name that would finally awaken him. "I'm here, Aelythius."

His eyes snapped open.

There was a violent *whooshing* sound, like air being vacuumed into a pair of massive lungs. All at once, the clouds retracted, then burst over the whole city with a tenebrous bellow of thunder.

Jagged webs of lightning fractured the sky. Hail flogged the streets and shattered glass. Rain fell in thick waves, swept in all directions by the vortex of wind.

Aelythius peeled his lips back in a feral snarl, rattling his muzzle. He tried to claw at the iron, but the leash around his foreleg held him fast.

Reina stood, transfixed by her own ephemerality reflected in his gleaming, ageless eyes. Below, the agents were shouting—some retreating, others still trying to climb the ruins of Morturrim—but Aelythius met Reina's gaze. His pupils narrowed in focus. He was the storm itself, and she had awakened his rage.

She gave him space as he heaved himself to all fours, lifting his head high upon that long neck. A strained groan slipped between pointed fangs, and with a brutal *snap*, the chain around his wings clattered against the bed of obsidian, plucking a couple of siphons out with it. His chest swelled with his first full breath in weeks. Bricks clattered down the hill as Aelythius stomped his paws, and agents fell away as lightning coiled along the length of the iron chains.

It was his breath that exhaled through Reina's lungs; his power that coursed through her veins; his words that shook her thoughts from her head.

"I've waited a long time for you, Rider."

———

Reina could hardly make sense of what happened after she awakened Aelythius. One second, she stood before him in a moment frozen in time: peace balanced on a fragile string that hung over absolute havoc. The next, that string snapped, and her world lit up in gold.

Like waking from a dream where she was free-falling, she slammed back into her body. She peeled herself off a rain-soaked street. Her ears were ringing, and dozens of feet slapped through puddles around her. She lifted her head just in time to watch Aelythius break his chains and take flight.

The glass tanks that contained his blood were broken, spilling crimson through cobblestone grout. The Order abandoned its reconstruction efforts. Every force was aimed toward restraining their specimen. Wiry steel nets shot through the air, but Aelythius was a swift-moving target in a storm of his own creation.

Reina scrambled upright. Not a single agent in the swarm paid her a second glance.

Heart thundering in her chest, she watched the clouds writhing in the wake of the dragon. She knew, somehow, that whatever output of power Aelythius discharged would also draw from her own well of unlocked magic. Why else would her entire body feel so alive now, so *free*?

Aelythius soared listlessly. At first, Reina thought it was the wind that rocked his course; then she remembered—his wings had been locked into place for weeks. The chains had inflicted more damage than either of them realized. He let loose a warning screech just before he collided with a stone wall. Bricks crumbled at the impact. He flapped his wings furiously to right himself, but the movement strained his injury. A hundred bolts of lightning spewed from his jaws as he roared in pain.

Reina clamped her teeth down on her tongue, but she couldn't contain the sparks that jumped from her fingers. Panic seized her: what if someone saw? What if they drew the connection between her and Aelythius? What if she was the one whose blood they would collect next?

She sprinted as far from the Order as she could, shoving blindly through throngs of people—

People? Did the defenses at the gatehouse fall?

Her concern scattered when Aelythius took flight again. Reina ran beneath him and tried to access that place in her mind where his voice was clearest. *I'm here,* she shouted against an unbreakable wall. It was like pounding her fists against the great ivory gates of her parents' estate. *I'm here—I found you. What do you want?*

Nothing. Where was he? She threw her head back and stared wide-eyed into the storm, searching the black skies for his figure—

"*Reina!*"

Her blood froze. Before she could stop herself, she turned toward the call. She blinked, seeing—but not quite believing—a face growing more hopeful by the second. Aelythius's golden light revealed Meiryn at the end of the street, standing beside another man and cupping her hands around her mouth. Rain trickled between her brows.

Meiryn stepped forward, reaching out her hand.

Reina sped in the opposite direction.

Why was Meiryn here, of all damned places? The city was falling into the earth, the Silver Order occupied every district that hadn't been wrecked, and now this dragon threatened to finish what he started and smother it all again. This was the last place in all Rhonestiel that Meiryn should have been wandering.

A sudden realization cut a deeper fear into Reina's heart: Meiryn was *here*; so was Aaron and every other member of his cadre. Both parties would be looking for Reina, but if any of them found her, they would discover the secrets she was keeping. Aaron would learn that she freed the dragon; that she had felt his lightning crackling at her fingertips; that she carried his magic inside her. He would see that she posed just as great a threat as the dragon himself. And Meiryn would learn that Reina had been lying from the very start. She'd learn of the past that Reina tried so desperately to hide, and she would hate her for it.

Athira or Reina—it mattered not what she called herself now. Every part of her was damned.

Nothing was undone yet, she reminded herself strictly. None of those agents had seized her—they were probably too intent on restraining Aelythius to even think about her. Aaron and the others were likely occupied with the same objective. And Meiryn...she had never heard the name "Athira Rhysanthe," and Reina vowed that she never would.

Nothing was undone. She had not fallen yet.

"Rider," the dragon bellowed.

Reina screamed and slapped her hands over her ears. A gust of wind shoved her against a wall, where she vaguely processed pain in her shoulder before Aelythius spoke again. *"You meddle with forces beyond your comprehension. This city will fall because of your ignorance."*

No—it wasn't her fault. "You wanted me to find you," she panted into her knees. The image reflected in a pool beneath her feet was that of a scared little girl. "I—I did what you asked."

From behind the terrified face that stared back at her from the water, Aelythius rose like a flower unfurling its petals. His horned head lifted above the rough edges of a broken roof. Eyes like burning suns pinned her with an unwavering glare.

"Only you could awaken me," he spat. *"You, whose soul was twined with mine from the accursed moment of your birth. Fate led you to me, but you were never worthy of wielding such power."*

What? No, she wasn't destined for anything. Never wanted to—

"I shall lay waste to this pathetic stronghold, and you will watch. And then, when your allies lay dead at your feet, I will

devour you and reclaim what is mine." He gave a mighty beat of his wings and rocketed upward into the storm. Lightning wreathed his head like a crown, and before Reina could try and follow him, a pair of slender white hands gripped her shoulders.

"Athira!" Iliana dragged her back to her feet. "Six hells—we've been looking everywhere for you. Raiko said you needed help, and Aaron—"

"Where did he go?" Reina demanded, still searching the sky.

Iliana pointed toward the compound. "He's with Korris and Evren. Commander Quill—"

Reina tuned her out. Iliana did not understand what was happening, and it was that ignorance that would kill her if she stayed here.

Energy swelled within Reina, lighting her veins on fire and sending her vision spinning. Whips of lightning struck the towering buildings. Aelythius circled the city, flying faster, urging the winds to hasten in his wake. Debris and sand from the sunken shores rose into the funnel—among them were fragments of dragon-trapping devices, glinting metal swords, shredded remnants of banners bearing the Silver Order's emblem.

He was going to slaughter them all.

Reina grabbed Iliana's wrist and yanked her toward the outer districts of Draconis. Fragments of countless plans collided in her mind, each shattering against a mounting wall of fear and helplessness.

They bled into a thick stream of civilians. Voices clamored over one another, some crying out in pain as the horde trampled them. The mass surged and throbbed like muscles convulsing beneath skin, and Iliana suddenly swore.

Reina looked where she pointed: a scattered few of the people caught in the crowd were armed. They slashed at city guards and agents alike.

Huntsmen. Their numbers were few, but they rallied the citizens with their war cries and brandished their weapons like conductors of a frenetic symphony, directing their rage toward anyone wearing the crest of the Order. They must have helped the rioters gain entry through the gatehouse.

But why were the huntsmen here? What else could they be doing, other than...

"Shit," Reina panted, leaping back as someone fell away from the crowd. The huntsmen had seen the Order's weakness, and they had come to ensure they never again rose to power.

As Reina uttered Aaron's name, Iliana's lips formed the shape of Evren's. The two of them shared a tiny moment of mutual terror for their kin when a roar of thunder shook the air.

Reina jolted. She grabbed Iliana's hand to ground herself and ran. She searched for the gatehouse, but the fighting in the streets blocked every path.

Iliana suddenly pulled against her. She shouted a warning that Reina didn't register until a knife hurtled toward her head.

Reina twisted at the last second, feeling the blade nick her ear. She snatched the knife off the ground and whirled just as the redheaded archer lunged for Iliana.

Their attacks blurred behind a thick curtain of rain. Fists flew into ribs; nails clawed deep into wet faces. Iliana kicked hard against the archer's stomach, sending her reeling and wheezing. She yanked her whip-sword from its scabbard and pointed it at the archer.

Blades shot forth like crossbow bolts, wayward in the violent wind. The archer threw a crate in their path and scrambled for cover as the wood splintered in every direction. She landed hard, her pained cry drowning beneath a roll of thunder.

Iliana was already moving, feet sliding over slippery ground. She teetered toward the archer. Her braid waved like a white flag, and her eyes flashed like ice as she raised her sword for the kill.

As if spat out from the storm, someone tackled Iliana from the shadows.

Not just someone. It was a man, the same figure Reina had seen standing beside Meiryn. She had caught just a glimpse of his face, but she recognized that bronze sword he unsheathed.

The archer cradled her side. A pained grimace pulled her lips back and bared two rows of gleaming white teeth to the rain. Her hands shook against a reopened wound that ran with fresh blood.

Reina shrank behind cover and watched with bated breath. Iliana had squirmed free of the swordsman's grasp. She was a small target, too swift for the wide, frantic grabs he made for her. White hailstones threatened to trip her, but she danced around her opponent like a viper, a teasing grin tugging at one corner of her mouth. This was a game for her. She was toying with him, just as she toyed with all her enemies.

Her whip-sword lashed toward his heart. He dodged right, but Iliana anticipated his evasion. Slipping over wet stones, the man fell straight into her kick, grunting loudly when her heel slammed against his shoulder. His sword clattered to the ground, and Iliana drove her knee against his stomach. She pulled the trigger on her hilt. The swordsman cried out as the blades retracted behind his back and cut deep into his side.

"Lukas!"

Meiryn. She watched from the alley, leaning heavily against the wall. She hadn't seen Reina yet; her gaze was fixed, horrified, on Iliana as she reared her arm to land the killing blow—

Reina jumped out from her hiding spot. Lightning cracked above her head as she screamed, "*Stop!*"

Iliana froze mid-strike, blinking in confusion. And then her eyes went wide. A terrible gasp sputtered from her throat, and Reina slapped a hand over her mouth as blood sprayed from Iliana's spine.

The archer knelt behind her, smiling as water trailed down her face. She yanked her hand back. Clutched in a crimson fist was a small silver knife.

Iliana whimpered. Looked down at the small hole in her chest. Her sword slipped from her hand, and she crumpled like a ragdoll, turned toward Reina. Blood trickled from trembling lips and kissed a puddle of rainwater that cupped her cheek.

Reina watched that blue light in her eyes fade to grey right as Evren darted from the far end of the street. Korris tumbled behind him, and both stopped short. The color drained from Evren's face when he found his sister lying motionless and pale. Waves of thunder drowned out his voice when he shouted her name. His gaze slid to the archer, then to Lukas, and finally to Reina. His face went slack. His brow lowered.

No. *No.*

They'd heard the fighting. They knew what she had done.

Behind Evren, Korris drew his weapon. His good eye darted between the huntsmen, but when he found Reina standing, unharmed by either of them, his blade turned toward her.

Reina bolted.

Guilt crashed through her in waves. Adrenaline was the only thing keeping her upright, but even that was not enough to thaw the freezing realization of what just happened.

Iliana was dead—and it was *Reina's* fault.

She choked back a sob, swallowing rainwater.

Let Evren's blades clash against the archer's. Let the archer die beneath Korris's brute strength. Let Korris believe he'd only seen a mirage of Reina. Let them all wonder where she disappeared to, because no amount of explaining or pleading could absolve her now.

Above the carnage, the sky rippled like water. Lightning shattered the darkness, and Aelythius's guttural voice seeped like smoke into the deepest chambers of her mind.

"I see you, little storm thief. I can feel you everywhere." Violent tremors seized her hands as gold sparks littered her path. *"I see you, and I am coming."*

She forced her legs to move. If she stopped or looked back, then she was dead. If the dragon didn't kill her first, Evren would.

It's what you deserve after what you've done.

She bit her tongue against the guilt. She had to get out before the torrent enveloped the entire city. Darkness pressed inward, save for the fragmented seconds when lightning lit up the earth.

Draconis shuddered. Toward the coastline, the sea and the rain flooded the crater in the earth. Waves of saltwater polluted by debris and corpses sloshed upon the streets. The broken remains of Morturrim were swept away, as if the tower had never stood in the first place. Draconis was drowning.

A hand fell upon Reina's shoulder, and she screamed.

"Athira," Raiko panted. She started to shove herself away, but he hugged her close. His heart beat like a fist against her chest. "I thought you...never mind. Are you hurt?" He held her at arm's length, cupping her face as he looked her over.

Reina tried to speak, but Aelythius broke into her mind, his voice louder than anything around them.

"You seek comfort from the most fleeting things," he sneered. *"Remember my promise, girl. What you cherish will fall at my will."*

Reina sobbed. "No, please—"

Raiko thumbed tears away from her eyes. "Your brother has been searching for you, but the Guild is here. We must find shelter until this storm blows over."

"I can't—"

But he was already pulling her along. The earth trembled as the ocean slowly devoured the rest of Draconis. They ran parallel to the destruction, and Reina couldn't help but marvel at how easily these buildings, which had withstood decades of weather and stray dragons, yielded to one storm.

But it was the power of the last Tempest. She remembered his name from her dreams. Remembered the powers he adopted from the wind dragon who sheltered him on the Nest.

How had anyone managed to massacre an entire clan of these monsters?

Aelythius's cruel laugh sounded between her ears. She could practically see his macabre grin. *"A monster, am I, for exacting revenge upon the ones who killed my people? What, then, does that make you?"*

Reina blocked out his prying accusations. He may have witnessed her crime, but that was all he saw. She felt his anger flare. Sensed another berating remark—but she flung up a wall between them.

If she could keep him at bay, she might still escape undetected.

No sooner did the thought crossed her mind than lightning

flashed behind her. Reina yelped as bolts struck the ground. Chunks of rock exploded at their heels and butchered the smooth path ahead.

Raiko wheeled sideways, jerking Reina with him. He caged her against a wall—one hand cupping the back of her head, the other clamped around her shoulder. His entire body was her shield.

Reina clapped her hands over her ears when Aelythius shattered her mental ward.

"You think you can keep yourself from me?" he demanded. *"I am a part of you. For however long you have left in your wretched life, we are bound, you and I."*

Tears merged with rain and saltwater on her face. She could hear the floods nearing, felt them sweeping around her feet. Raiko was shouting, urging her to *move*, but she had stopped listening.

Aelythius hovered just below the eye of the storm, bathed in an ethereal glow that he wove into jagged spears of raw power. His eyes locked onto Reina's. Lightning that he summoned surged through her body—restless, untamed, constricting, and freeing all at once.

His voice filled her mind, echoed through the air, resonated across the hungry waves of the Abyss. *"I am Aelythius of the Storm, the last Tempest of Rhonestiel, the Heart of Chaos."*

"Stop it," Reina pleaded. Her hands fisted at her sides, but she felt his power engulfing her, inundating her will to resist.

"We may be the last of our kind, little storm thief," he growled, *"but we are not the same. Your ancestors squandered their gifts. They did nothing when my people were slaughtered like pigs, and I vowed never to take a rider. Yet here you are, chasing your own shadows with* my *power in your blood."*

"I never asked for—"

"Athira, we must *go*." Raiko shook her, his voice breaking on her name. Fear shrank his pupils. He pulled again, but she was an unmovable force. He did not see the way her palms opened against her will. He did not see the dragon looming behind him like a harbinger of death.

Aelythius narrowed his gaze on Reina. *"May the Titans take you."*

NO—

A spear of pure electricity shot toward them. Raiko gaped as Reina lifted her hands to shield herself.

The invisible string in her chest went taut. Sunlight beamed from the veins in her arms. She held the storm in her hands.

You will not touch me.

She released a hellish roar. Light that burned, light that shocked, light that *lived* surged through her and gored Raiko's chest, colliding with Aelythius's attack.

XXXI. MEIRYN

THE HEAVENS themselves opened and swallowed the storm, the dragon, the chaos. There was a bone-rattling *boom*, and the resounding shock wave sent broken scraps of the city flying in every direction.

Meiryn lost her bearings. She didn't know where Lukas was, though he was the one who had dragged her away from those agents. And Faun...

She could only pray she had somehow survived.

In the distance, near the site of the explosion, came a deafening crash, like a hundred massive bones snapping all at once. The ground trembled. Buildings bowed toward the ocean when a hollow groan and a rush of water bellowed over the rising screams of survivors. Meiryn mustered the strength to lift her head.

Gone was the shoreline. The chasm on the edge of Draconis had doubled in size, and any evidence of the Order's existence was consumed in a massive pit. Where a great, towering fortress once stood, there was only an open wound, mirrored by a scar in the sky. Grey and black clouds were crippled by the blast, and when the storm dragon's dissipating cry echoed through the air, Meiryn plummeted into a memory locked deep within her mind.

Her village lay in smoldering ruins. She cowered beneath planks of wood, Silas's little body motionless and bloody behind her. People were screaming for help, for their loved ones, for the mercy of the gods to grace them once again.

No one was coming to save them. No one was coming to lift her from where she lay.

Blinking away the memory, Meiryn took in a ragged breath and curled her fingers against whatever shelter had kept her safe. The taste of copper and salt sat on her lips. Her arms were heavy and her ears were ringing, but soon that gave way to a wailing city.

Survivors sped as far away from the chasm as they could. Some knelt beside piles of rubble, desperately clawing through bricks; others lay half-buried, and thin streams of blood leaked from between chunks of stone.

"Lukas," Meiryn rasped. She pushed herself to all fours and blinked against the rain. Faces blurred past—agents, civilians, all of them strangers.

Fear strangled her voice. "*Faun! Lukas!*"

Her cry joined those of the masses.

Something warm trickled down the side of her head. She touched her fingertips to her temple, whimpering at the sting, and brought her hand to eye level. Blood stained her skin. Blood roared in her ears. Blood wafted in her nose.

Motion to the east turned her gaze, where a black figure rocked and swayed like a bird with a broken wing. Tiny whips of lightning crackled and fizzed around its hazy shape, and it disappeared over the churning waves of the Abyss.

The dragon was gone, and, in its absence, the storm grew weaker. But Draconis lay dying beneath the weeping sky.

Meiryn staggered to her feet. She winced at the slightest amount of weight she placed on her right leg. When her head stopped spinning, she searched for any sign of her allies. Lukas had been with her at the time of the explosion; Faun trailed somewhere behind; and Reina...

Reina had run from her. *Why did she run?*

Meiryn hobbled forward. If there was any chance of finding her friends, it would not be here, where the buildings caved in and the rain bled through to her bones. Reina was *alive.* Somewhere in this gods-forsaken city, she was alive and scared—just as scared as Meiryn was, but that was okay because Meiryn would find her. She would, and when she did, they would leave this place and never look back.

She made it halfway down the street when a pair of footsteps bounded close. A hand landed on her shoulder, and Meiryn whirled, heart jumping.

A young man about her age steadied her with a grip like blunted daggers. His face was paler than a sheet, but his eyes burned like coal. He was unarmed, clothed in black, and covered by a cloak that clung to him like a second skin.

"Raiko," he panted. He repeated the name, louder this time. "*Raiko*. He's Ashuman, he's my—where is he? Have you seen him?"

Meiryn struggled to speak. She could only shake her head, and his grip tightened. A panicked sob built in her chest. "I don't know," she choked out.

The man shouted at her, spit flying from his lips. "He left me. He went after her!"

"Who?"

"*Athira*. My sister." He said it like Meiryn should have known whom he was talking about. "Raiko went after her—he's *gone*, and I can't find them!"

"You're hurting me!"

Meiryn shoved him hard, but his fingers pressed further into her arms. He was bleeding from a wound in his head, spewing nonsense about his sister, the dragon, the Order. He was mad. He had to be. Driven insane by the horrors that befell the city. He would break her arms before he found whoever he was looking for, and Meiryn was too weak to push him away—

"*Hey*!" Lukas's voice cut through the other man's chatter. Meiryn could have melted in relief.

The madman threw her to the ground. Pain lanced through her elbow and shuddered along the length of her arm. The man bolted before Lukas could catch him, darting down a path with few obstructions. Meiryn watched him race toward the sunken earth.

"Wait!" she called.

He did not. He ran until he disappeared from view.

Meiryn flinched when Lukas crouched beside her. Before he could get a word in, she blurted, "Have you seen Reina? Or Faun? Anyone—"

Lukas winced, and it was only then that Meiryn noticed one of his hands, pressed against his side, was streaked red.

"I don't know where anyone is," he ground out. "It's a miracle I found you."

Then that meant... No, it couldn't. Meiryn breathed shallowly, biting back the rising panic. *Someone* had to be alive.

"Grey," she managed. "He was still outside the city. He was with Elder, and she—she's—"

Lukas hushed her and stared out over the warped silhouettes looming in the distance. He lingered for a heartbeat too long on the chasm, and with forced steadiness, he told her, "We'll find our allies. They're here."

Meiryn shook her head. Tears burned her cheeks. "You don't know that. We don't know anything."

It felt like the end of the world. Like the gods had finally come to unleash their wrath upon their sinful, remorseless creation. In an instant, half the city sank beneath ocean waves, taking countless lives with it. But the death began out on the field. It began when Meiryn stumbled into Elder, who died on that guard's spear.

And her blood would forever stain Meiryn's conscience.

She ground out a hateful curse, dropping her head into her hands. She could barely take in a full breath, much less ward away the guilt that wracked her.

She's dead because of me. Dead like Nona. Dead like so many others.

"Meiryn." Lukas softened his tone, trying to soothe her, but she barely heard him. "Listen to me. We're alive. We're going to figure out what happened, and we'll find our friends. They're out there somewhere."

Meiryn nearly screamed at him. "How do you *know*?"

"Because I can't believe anything else," he shouted. His mask of certainty and strength crumbled, revealing a fear that rivaled Meiryn's. He was shaking, pale, and struggling to steady his breathing. If he weren't trying to mitigate Meiryn's emotions, she suspected that he would be spiraling into a panic now, too.

Lukas was the only thing keeping her grounded. He was her single sliver of hope in this cobblestone wasteland.

"Come on," he finally said. He pried his gaze away from the scar in the sky. "We need to keep moving."

Meiryn let him take her hand again. Together, they staggered over rocks and planks of wood, pieces broken off from the suspension bridges. They leaned on each other, each nursing their wounds and drawing on each other for strength.

As they passed through hollow streets and scoured the buildings that withstood the storm, Meiryn forced herself to think only of what they saw right before them. Bricks, blood upon the glass, rain pooling on every doorstep, seeping into the floorboards, and a single crow, perched atop the corner of a building about a block away.

A crow. Grey—still alive?

She didn't know. She couldn't let herself think of him, though. If she let her mind stray too far ahead of her own two feet, she would think of Elder, then picture Faun and Reina meeting the same fate. She could not—would not—think of their bodies broken and bleeding on the ground. Until she knew for certain who had lived and who was dead, Meiryn would keep searching.

Fear had no place in her heart anymore. But it linked hands with guilt, which clamped its cold jaws on the back of Meiryn's neck and threatened to squeeze every drop of air from her throat.

She swallowed hard. Forced the breath in through her nostrils, into her lungs, and out between her lips. And still, the taste of blood lingered.

XXXII. REINA

A HIGH-PITCHED TONE blared in Reina's ears, carried by a roar of rushing water. Her face was pressed against wet stones, and slowly, as her senses returned to her, she felt the steady fall of rain drenching her back. She groaned and turned toward the weeping sky.

Two faces blurred into focus when she pried open her eyes. Aaron hovered close, bearing a nasty wound that bled across one side of his face; Korris crouched some feet away, features tight and indurate. The stench of charred flesh filled her nose, and Reina choked on a pitiful cough. She could barely lift her head without the entire world spinning.

"What happened?" she managed to ask. Her throat felt raw, cracked. "Where did he—the dragon, where did it go?" Her mind had gone blank, silent. There was nothing left to suggest Aelythius had ever been there at all.

Aaron shifted his weight. His voice was low, toneless, yet shock paled his face, dilated his pupils. He wouldn't meet her stare. "There was an explosion. It blasted the dragon out of the sky. No one saw where it went."

Reina wracked her memory. All she could recall was light: blinding, cold, and deadly—yet beautifully irresistible all the same.

"Is that it, then?" she asked. "It's over? We're safe?"

Aaron's hands were white-knuckled as he clenched his fists in his lap, and Reina frowned. She tilted her head, willing him to look at her.

"What is it? What's wrong?"

His throat bobbed. Rain trickled down his face like tears, and when he finally lifted his gaze, a familiar sensation gripped her: the tongue-tying paralysis of being caught in a lie; the sinking dread of facing a nearby threat.

"I found Evren with Iliana." Sorrow dulled his voice. "He said that you...that Iliana is dead, because of you."

For a frozen moment, Reina could only gape. Her heart was beating, but she was not breathing. The tremor had returned to her hands. Strength abandoned her arms, and a feeling of utter helplessness crashed into her like a wave.

"No," she stammered. Thoughts were sluggish, her words bustling against one another in some desperate attempt to explain her way through the guilt creeping around her neck like a rope. "I was with her. I was trying to save her, but the huntsmen—that archer..."

Aaron offered no reaction. Her words might as well have been arrows blunting against iron walls.

Her eyes shuttered against the rain. She forced herself upright, grimacing at the low burn in her muscles. "There was nothing I could do," she offered. "I was unarmed. We were outnumbered. Aaron, I had to run. I had to stay safe. Raiko found me, and—"

"You killed him."

Her shoulders dropped. The ringing in her ears grew louder, and her hands twitched at her sides. Disbelief stole her words and replaced them with a weak groan. It was a lie—it had to be. She had been desperate to save herself, but who wouldn't be in that position? Draconis was under siege by a raging dragon. The earth was crumbling, the ocean consuming a once-invincible city. The destruction lay before them: a street with no end, a coastline that breached the border of Draconis, a black hole that choked on seawater.

Survival was a hopeless endeavor, but she would *never* kill anyone to secure it for herself.

Aaron repeated himself with lethal calm. "You killed him."

Reina winced and shook her head, as if she could shrug off the accusation like a ruined cloak. "I didn't touch him," she insisted.

"Athira." The sound of her name came like the sizzle of extinguished flame. Aaron never broke her rigid stare; just pointed behind him.

She followed his finger to where Korris knelt beside a motionless figure. Dark hair was glued against deathly pale skin; water dripped into unseeing eyes.

Raiko. The center of his chest was exposed, the fabric of his shirt singed, as if scorched by fire.

Dread sank in her chest, and Reina looked down at her hands.

Scars like lightning—scars matching the one on Raiko's chest—warped her skin. The tangled knots that she hid at the center of her palms now stretched beyond the joints of her wrists, snaked around her forearms, and reached toward her elbows. Reddened and raw, her skin stung, burned beneath the cold rain that drenched her.

"No," Reina breathed. Bile rose in the back of her throat. Aelythius's silhouette flashed in her mind. "It was that beast. That *monster*. It shot us—"

"And yet here you are. Alive." Aaron dropped his gaze to her arms, and Reina folded them around her ribs.

"It wasn't my fault."

"That woman in the mountains was right," Aaron continued. His tone had not changed. It would have been better if he were shouting, screaming at her. But instead, he made his accusations with unsettling detachment. "You are Drāga."

Reina dragged her cloak around her shoulders to cover her scars. "I don't know what I am."

"You're a murderer."

"*Stop it.*"

Aaron never blinked. Never flinched. He stared at her like she was some peculiar creature from a foreign land. Like she wasn't even human. "You killed my cadre. Endangered everyone who cared for you."

Reina ducked her head against the cold drizzle, but nothing blocked Raiko's body from her periphery. He was dead; somewhere in the wreck of this city, Iliana lay dead—Reina's doing.

It's not my fault. It's not, it's not, it's not.

"Aaron—"

He slammed a fist against the ground, hard enough that his sword clattered at his side. Reina scrambled backward, hitting a wall behind her. She stifled a sob but was given no chance to speak.

"You were supposed to be nothing more than a prisoner," Aaron despaired, "but we treated you like an equal. You wormed your way into our numbers and made a fool of me. I trusted you, Athira. I thought you... I thought..."

Reina swore she saw tears glistening in his eyes.

"You knew, didn't you?" he asked, casting a disgusted look at her hands. "About your connection with that monster. You knew you could wield its power, and you said nothing."

"I knew just as much as you," she insisted. "Believe me, if I knew what I could do, I wouldn't have—"

"Wouldn't have what?" Aaron barked. "Wouldn't have let us waste our time and energy saving you from that woman? You knew something was going to happen here, yet you said *nothing*, and now my friends are dead!"

A shaking, scarred hand muffled her cry. Tears bled into the rain on her cheeks. "Aaron," she begged, "please—"

"I should have killed you the moment I found you in West Glen." His hand fell to the hilt of his sword. "You don't deserve a wisp of the air you breathe. You never did."

How deeply those words stung, yet the anger Reina used as a shield seared even deeper. She straightened her neck and lifted her chin. "Kill me, then. Throw me into the chasm."

She barely heard her voice; could barely discern whether her words were a challenge or a plea. She didn't care enough to know.

A muscle in Aaron's jaw twitched. He slid his gaze along the length of his sword, as if imagining the way her blood would trickle down the blade, sizzle and burn when he called the fire from the hilt. His nostrils flared on an exhale, and he loosened his fists. Bowed his spine. The whites of his eyes were tinged red.

"I owe you a life debt," he whispered.

Finally, Korris broke his silence. "You're not serious?" he demanded, jabbing an accusatory finger at Reina. "She killed half your men, Aaron. Does that mean nothing to you?"

"You will not question me," Aaron roared. But his voice

broke. He glanced at Raiko, and when he faced Reina again, black shadows cradled his eyes. Then he spoke, the words meant only for her ears. "Raiko is dead. Consider his debt to you repaid. But I—" He bit off the rest of his sentence, forcing himself to drag a slow breath into his lungs and push it out. "Gods know I'll regret this until the day I die."

Reina wept silently. Aaron's judgment fell like an axe through her neck.

"Whatever you are, Drāga or otherwise, you have no place here. The secrets you kept, the things you did to obtain this power..." He trailed off and shook his head, then began again with renewed fury. "As repayment of my life debt, I am granting you the freedom you always craved. Take it. Run with it. Squander it. It matters not to me, because there is no place you could go where I will not find you. For as long as this world turns, I will hunt you down until you no longer walk its face.

"Everything you hold dear will become ashes at my fingertips, and you will watch it burn. There is no amount of power you could wield that I will not overcome with my own. If it takes an army to tear you down, then so be it. You will reap the pain you've sown tenfold. Even in death, you will rue the day you ever crossed me."

Rain trickled down the bridge of Reina's nose. She had not moved an inch, nor did she dare to breathe too deeply. Every beat of her wretched heart sent freezing ripples through the rest of her body.

"Aaron," she whispered, treading into deep waters, "it was a mistake. I never meant for any of this to happen."

He gave her a cold look, as hateful as he'd seemed the day his cadre dragged her from the streets of West Glen. "The only mistake was believing we could be a family."

Reina turned to Korris, desperate to find some glimpse of the warmth he'd once shown her yet knowing there would be none. He placed a protective hand on Raiko's arm. An expression of stone met her stare before Korris turned away.

"Go," Aaron muttered. "Evren may find us soon, and if he does, I doubt he would be inclined to spare you as I have done."

Korris sniffed heavily—the only dissent he was allowed.

Reina glanced around them, taking in the ruins of the city. Water gushed over the crippled shore. Darkness crept in from the east. The cries of people shouting for their missing loved ones were distant, but they would only grow louder, thicker, more pained as the night rolled in. The huntsmen would take the city if they hadn't already.

"You're not safe here, either," Reina warned.

Embers sparked in Aaron's eyes. "You dare to threaten me now?"

"No." She willed strength into her voice. "The Hunters Guild is here. They'll kill whoever remains of the Order. You have to leave."

"Draconis belongs to the Order," Aaron growled. "No one can take it from us."

"You have no one to protect you." Reina gave her brother an imploring look. Her hands had started shaking again, and anxiety coiled tight in her chest. "It's over, Aaron."

Aaron closed a fist around his sword. Weak fire spat in the rain, casting garish lights over Raiko's pale face. "It will only be over once you are dead on the end of my sword."

"Please—"

"Go, Athira." Water trickled down his cheek. "Go before I kill you now."

XXXIII. MEIRYN

Meiryn's limp and Lukas's injury slowed their pace. The city seemed to stabilize once the dragon left and the storm calmed, but the pair of them still kept a considerable distance between themselves and the edge of the chasm. Meiryn peered down streets, pressed her face against darkened windows, pounded on locked doors.

No sign of Reina or Faun.

"What if they made it to the gatehouse?" Lukas suggested. "Hundreds of survivors are crowding there. We could have missed her."

Maybe, Meiryn thought. But if their friends were incapacitated somewhere, waiting beneath the rubble to be rescued, she would never forgive herself for abandoning them.

"I need to keep looking," she decided aloud. "If we don't find them anywhere here, then we'll search among the survivors."

Lukas just nodded, jaw set and eyes forward.

They rummaged through brick and mortar, wandering through shelled-out homes and shops littered with hailstones and remnants left behind by scavengers. While Lukas shouted for Faun, Meiryn called Reina's name, hoping that if she couldn't see her, then at least she might summon her out of her hiding place.

They reached the last street that fed into the pit. With Reina still nowhere in sight, Meiryn's final shreds of hope were shriveling. She stopped and turned her back toward the chasm.

"I don't know where she could be." Her voice sounded so frail. "I was prepared to break into Morturrim, but this..." This was far worse. "What if Reina... What if she—"

Lukas reached out to offer comfort, but Meiryn shied away, pretending not to notice the hurt flash across his face as he retracted his hand. He instead cleared his throat and said, somewhat rigidly. "We saw her before the explosions, remember? The prison wasn't even standing then. She escaped somehow. She's here."

"But what if—"

The clattering of bricks interrupted her. Meiryn followed the noise two streets down, Lukas trailing after her hurriedly. Brows furrowed, she kept hope at bay until she rounded a corner.

Reina was clambering over a half-fallen wall, tripping over her rain-soaked boots. Her face was scratched and bleeding.

Meiryn called her name weakly. Reina froze, eyes wide and pitch-black. Her cloak swallowed her when she landed on unsteady feet. She met Meiryn's gaze, opened her mouth to speak—and only emitted a heavy sob.

Meiryn rushed past Lukas as Reina's legs buckled. Meeting her on her knees, Meiryn crushed Reina against her. They were both shaking and weeping. Meiryn shot prayers of gratitude toward the settling clouds. She pulled back slightly—just to see Reina's face, to know that she wasn't a mirage.

"You're alright," Meiryn choked out, smoothing a hand over Reina's hair. "You're alive. You're safe now."

Reina didn't say a word. She couldn't even lift her arms to return Meiryn's embrace. She only wept, her head falling against Meiryn's chest. Meiryn shushed her and bit back her own relieved cries.

Lukas approached warily. Meiryn smiled at him over her shoulder when he knelt a couple of feet behind her. Gently, Meiryn lifted Reina's chin.

"This is Lukas," she introduced, turning Reina's attention to her ally. "He helped me in West Glen. I joined the huntsmen to try and find you."

The color drained from Reina's face. "You—what?"

"It's alright. They aren't bad people." Meiryn's heart ached at the thought of Elder, and it took every effort to keep her focus on Reina. She was here, *alive*; amidst every horror she must have endured, Reina had come out relatively unscathed, and Meiryn would never again curse the gods for their apathy. "Come. It's dangerous here, and we still need to find our allies."

Reina stiffened, but she didn't protest or pull away.

Meiryn did not miss the way Lukas stared at Reina with barely restrained suspicion. She paid him no mind—only cared that Reina was found—and if that was the only victory she took away from this horrible day, then she would be grateful.

Silence accompanied the three of them. The storm had dissipated to a chilly drizzle, and the sound of the ocean faded as they neared the west side of the city. Draconis was widely unmarred here. Buildings still towered like enormous monuments in a cemetery, complemented by the motionless figures sprawled beneath them. As they continued toward the gatehouse, a chorus of angry voices grew loud once again.

Meiryn stopped before they reached the back of the crowd. Her heart sank a little, and she craned her neck. "What's happening now? Why haven't they let anyone through?"

Reina spoke in a hoarse whisper. "The Order may still be trying to keep the people in check."

"The Order has fallen," a proud voice boasted. "Our huntsmen made sure of that."

Meiryn spun. Her mouth split into a relieved smile when she spotted Faun, but the archer's eyes glinted with sudden bloodlust. Reina shoved herself away from Meiryn's side as Faun lunged.

"Stop!" Meiryn cried, throwing herself in Faun's path.

Faun reached for her knives, but Lukas shot forward, restraining her. Faun clawed at open air and screeched, "She's one of them! She's an agent of the Order!"

Meiryn prayed no one had heard Faun's accusation. She stood with both arms spread to keep a wide berth between Reina and Faun, blinking in confusion. "No," she corrected, "she was *captured* by the Order."

Faun roared. Her arm slipped free of Lukas's cage, and she hurled a knife past Meiryn's ear.

Meiryn screamed. Reina dodged the attack but slipped over a broken chunk of brick. Her cloak fell away from her arms when she hit the ground, and Meiryn gasped at the scars that welted her flesh. Red branches of lightning blazed from Reina's arms, as if she had embraced the storming sky.

As if she had wielded the storm dragon's power.

The thought crossed her mind just as Reina pinned a horrified gaze upon Meiryn's identical expression. For a moment, no one said a word.

Then Faun shattered the silence. "I saw her! She was in the woods that night when everything went up in flames. She defended Nona's murderer. That was *her* cadre, *her* companion who set the forest on fire."

Meiryn shook her head. "No. You must have seen someone else." Cold, paralyzing fear plucked her out of her body and dangled her above herself until she felt as if she was observing everything through some shadowy vignette.

"Gods—stop lying to yourself," Faun pressed. "How else do you think I killed that white-haired little snake? *This one* stopped her—likely for *your* sake!"

Reina stifled a sob with a hand over her mouth.

Meiryn wracked her memory. The fight had been so brief, but it came back to her like a gust of freezing wind. "You stopped her... She only listened because she knew you."

A headache pounded against Meiryn's temples, hammering in the truth of Faun's allegations. Her breathing shallowed, and slowly, her hands fell to her sides. She looked at this girl who huddled on the ground, gazing up at her with a silent plea for mercy glistening in the tears she held back.

"Who are you?" Meiryn asked.

The question was barely a whisper, but Reina flinched like it was a knife wound. Her eyes were leaking and bloodshot. Tired and defeated.

It was pitiful—and it was all Meiryn could do to keep from rushing forth and gathering her friend in her arms, soothing her until her tears dried.

But the friend she loved had slipped beyond her reach long ago. Meiryn repeated herself, and the girl before her dragged in a long breath. In a voice as dark as the storm, she said, "My name is Athira Rhysanthe."

Athira. The one the madman had been searching for. Meiryn staggered as if she'd been struck by an arrow.

The girl who was once her friend rushed to speak. She spewed excuses and pleas as easily as she'd woven her lies, and Meiryn's ears rang as her accent slipped into the natural lilt of a northerner. A polished and preened highborn. "I grew up in Verilonne. I am the youngest child of Lord and Lady Rhysanthe. My brothers—"

"You," Meiryn ground out through clenched teeth, "said your name was Reina. You told me your family was gone."

The stranger at her feet wept. "I might as well have been dead to them. That's why I took a false name—to protect myself, and anyone who might have shown me kindness. I was protecting you, Meiryn—"

"Stop." Meiryn's mind folded in on itself, coming undone as she tried to recount the sheer number of lies she'd believed without question. She could barely catch her breath. Could barely stand to look at this person who had once been her entire world. She paced in agitated circles until a thought hit her, and she stopped at Faun's side. "Your brother was in that cadre that took you from West Glen, wasn't he? Was that your plan all along, to be rescued from poverty the moment things got hard?"

"It's not what you think, Meiryn, *please*—"

Meiryn swore so heavily that her voice cracked. She swallowed a thick knot in her throat and fixed a burning stare on Reina's scars, each thought more damning than the last.

Proclamations from Nyrōna and Temaerys resurfaced: all the impossible things they spoke of, the magic they claimed ran through the blood of their ancestors... No human in history had ever wielded magic.

But Temaerys had shot her down: *"None in recorded history."*

They'd reported sightings of a cadre stranded somewhere within the Dragon's Spine. They believed one girl to carry the mark of their ancestors—these Drāga. All this time, Meiryn dismissed the notion that it could have been Reina. She had seen the cadre take her out of West Glen. They strung her over the side of their horse like baggage. But the matter of their whereabouts and what became of them was pure speculation—until now.

Because now, Meiryn knew. "You caused all of this, didn't you? You and that—that *monster*. All the people who died today died because of you."

Faun swore beneath her breath, and Lukas shifted his weight uneasily.

Reina curled her hands into fists. "It's not my fault. I would never—"

"You lied to me," Meiryn seethed. "All these years, I believed you were my friend."

"I *am* your friend." Tears rolled down Reina's cheeks. "I was my brother's prisoner. His cadre hated me."

"That's not how it seemed when they saved you from my arrows," Faun interjected. A smug grin spread on her lips, and her eyes narrowed. "Too bad I'm not that merciful."

Lukas shouted as Faun yanked her last knife from her belt. Without thinking, Meiryn reached up and grabbed Faun's wrist. The knife clattered to the ground between their feet.

Faun bristled, but Meiryn steeled her nerves. "Don't kill her."

"Why. Not."

Because I can't bear to see her hurting. Because she was my friend, and I loved her. Because part of me always will.

Meiryn forced a steady breath. "Because she saved Lukas's life, and yours. Regardless of who she is or where her loyalties lie, that remains true."

"And who's to say that she won't strike once our backs are turned?" Lukas pointed out.

Iron closed around Meiryn's heart. "I was her friend for years. I know how she thinks. I've seen how she acts. When she's scared or hurt, she doesn't fight. She runs." She glared at Reina.

No—that wasn't right. *Athira.*

Meiryn forced herself to see Athira as she saw all highborns: disillusioned with reality; self-preserving and graceless; careless of the lowborn lives with which they toyed.

Meiryn released Faun with a warning glance. She stepped forward, blocking Faun's path so she couldn't strike out again. Athira looked up at her with giant, begging eyes.

"You need to get out of here," Meiryn told her. She lifted her chin and stared down the length of her nose. "I don't care where you go—just get out, before the huntsmen see you."

"Meiryn—"

"*Go!*" Her voice broke, and she yanked Athira to her feet. She shoved her hard, feeling the bond they once shared sever as Athira's back slammed against the wall. Meiryn stared into the face of a stranger and hardened her voice. "Go, Athira."

The name tasted bitter on her tongue.

Meiryn turned away from the heartbreak on Athira's face. She did not watch Athira flee—only heard the quivering breath, the scraping of worn boots against wet cobblestones. Meiryn hugged herself tight and dug her fingers into her arms, refusing to let herself cry.

Faun crouched and retrieved the knife she'd dropped. She ran a fingertip along the blade, and before anyone could stop her, she sent it flying after Athira.

Meiryn spun, blood running cold—but the blade only pinned the end of Athira's cloak against a plank of wood. Meiryn bit back a sob as Athira jolted in a panic. She wrestled herself free with those terrible, scarred hands, then tossed a bewildered look over her shoulder.

Faun panted from exerting her injury, but she bared her teeth. "It'll be a rip in your heart next time."

Athira's lips parted as if to speak, but her eyes flicked to a point beyond them. Lines appeared between her brows. She uttered a word that Meiryn couldn't hear from this distance, but when Faun reached for Lukas's sword, Athira blinked twice and sped out of sight.

Meiryn found what had caught her attention: Grey, bleeding from numerous minor wounds and limping stiffly—but otherwise unharmed. His head was bowed to watch for obstacles in his path, but he looked up when Lukas said his name.

"Six hells," Grey swore, taking them all in at once. Dark shadows limned his bloodshot eyes. His voice sounded hollow, as if he'd been shouting. "All of you managed to survive?"

"Don't sound so displeased," Lukas muttered.

Meiryn stepped forward. "Elder?"

That was all she said—just Elder's name, but it was enough to halt Grey's steps. A look of grief twisted his face, and he gave a tiny shake of his head. Not even the rain had washed Elder's blood from his hands.

"She should not have been here," Grey said.

It would have been easy to sink to her knees then. To let her emotions overwhelm her until she was nothing but a shivering body curled beneath grey skies. But Meiryn felt empty enough. She had shed more tears today than she thought possible, and if she let herself stop, let the thoughts roll in, she might never again rise to her feet.

"The dragon is gone," she said instead.

Grey nodded. "I know. And I found no trace of the Drāga."

The other three of them stiffened, creating a shift in the air that even Grey could not ignore. He glanced between them all, eyes narrowing. "Is there something you wish to tell me?"

"We found her," Meiryn heard herself say. When Grey's expression filled with hope, a surge of unfamiliar rage sparked within Meiryn's heart. She said, with no amount of hesitation, "She's dead. Killed by the dragon."

It was half-true. The person Meiryn thought she knew, the girl she'd spent all this time searching for, was dead. Reina was never real. Reina was a persona fabricated for the sake of hiding someone whom Meiryn had never known.

And I pray I never do.

"How is that possible?" Grey asked. "Drāga are supposed to bond with their dragons—"

"Maybe this one was different." Meiryn shrugged, as if her lies weren't pressing deeper against her heart. "Maybe it only wanted to retaliate against the Order for capturing it, and it didn't care about some mystical connection."

She could feel Faun and Lukas staring into the back of her skull. Could sense Grey weighing her words. And she felt only a stroke of dark triumph when Grey nodded in grim acceptance.

"Then our only victory today lies in the dismantling of the

Order," he said in a brittle voice. "They angered the people when they cast them out of the city, and now the civilians are exacting their revenge. Some of our own are among them."

It was a public execution.

Meiryn tried to picture Athira: she had been wearing a cloak, but was she dressed in the Order's uniform? Would anyone be able to tell what she was, or what she had done?

Did Meiryn even care?

"We could stop them," Grey continued.

"Why? The Order deserves every bit of what's coming to them," Faun spat. She grimaced at a flare of pain in her side but managed a handful of bitter words. "I hope they get the commander, too."

Lukas eyed her carefully. "With the guards dead and the Order disbanded, the people will try to take the city. They're untrained, mostly unarmed. Once news spreads of what's happening, it's only a matter of time before the king sends his soldiers to restore order."

"Hard to restore order when half the city has sunk beneath the sea," Faun crowed. "You said it yourself: this city is ours."

Grey hadn't looked away from Meiryn, and she hadn't processed most of the words exchanged. Her mind was on Athira, on the field where Elder's body lay.

Grey spoke her name, and in that mere utterance, she could have sworn he was asking for her advice. Asking for her to choose mercy.

She lifted her gaze off the ground. Her eyes felt heavy, her body weary, and her heart shredded beyond repair. A gust of wind blew in from the hungering sea. The skies gleamed like amber through a veil of thin clouds as the sun fell over a fractured kingdom. She smelled salt and blood in the air; heard the distant jeers from those who lingered to witness the execution.

Meiryn sighed deeply. She knew Grey looked to her for advice because he hadn't a clue where to go from here. The huntsmen were split between Rook's forces here and those who remained in the forest, completely oblivious to the horrors that their allies had endured—but at Grey's call, they would swarm Draconis. If they acted soon enough, they could overtake it. Defend what still remained and stake their own flag outside the gates before the Kingsguard had a chance to reinstate their hold.

Her throat tightened. "Let the huntsmen decide what to do with the agents. After all, this is their victory."

"It's your victory, too," Faun said. "You survived, in spite of everything, didn't you? You should join them. We'll be feasting tonight."

"On what?" Grey scoffed. "The blood of our enemies?"

Faun flashed a foxlike grin. "We are huntsmen, are we not?"

Lukas sighed. "If that's your idea of a joke," he droned, "then I'd prefer you to remain silent. Besides," he added with a nod toward her wound, "you need to be saving your strength anyway."

Faun opened her mouth, but Grey butted in. "I'd prefer not to stand by and watch our men become cold-blooded killers, but who's stopping them?"

"They're killing our enemies," Faun pointed out.

Grey rounded on her. "Who are just as defenseless as we were. If we slaughter them now, what message does that send?"

"It shows that we are a force to be feared," Faun said. She lifted her chin against Grey's scrutiny. "If we let those agents run, they'll only come back with forces ten times as strong as our own. The citizens of Draconis have lived in subjugation their entire lives. Was it not the purpose of the Hunters Guild to fight against injustice?"

Grey said nothing.

Meiryn's tongue turned to stone in her mouth. Every emotional blow she'd sustained dragged her further into herself, even as Faun's declarations rallied her to arms. "The Silver Order brought this destruction upon themselves, and now Draconis is ours to take. We will earn the trust of the people. Rebuild everything that was taken from them."

"It's not that easy," Grey warned.

"We outnumber the noble ring."

Meiryn's thoughts jumped to what she'd learned of Grey's history, but she couldn't find it in her to care that Faun was trampling over it. Grey, she decided, should just be grateful she didn't expose his secrets to Faun and Lukas now.

"We were strong enough to overtake the Order today," Faun argued. A light sheen of sweat glistened at her brow, but she ignored Lukas's urges to rest. "The Kingsguard won't dare to leave His Royal Majesty's side, so why not train our new allies and build our forces to stand against anyone who gets in our way? We could establish our own rule. Tip the scales."

"The dragon destroyed the Order," Grey corrected, "and what you're talking about is civil war."

"We've been at war for years," Meiryn finally interjected. All eyes bored into her. "It's always been a game of survival for people like us. The highborns may host charity events or pass on their condolences whenever another dragon ravages a coastal village, but I never once saw them take in the destruction for themselves. Our fight isn't against the dragons. It's against the people who promised to protect us, then never gave a damn when we really needed them."

Grey's voice rose. "So instead of rebuilding and protecting our own, you'd rather launch an attack on people who never played a hand in any of this at all?"

"Did you not hear what she just said?" Faun demanded. She started to spit out some nastier retort, but pain twisted her face and severed her words.

Meiryn swept to Faun's side, ushering her to sit. It was exhaustion, Meiryn told herself, that caused Faun to lean against her for support. She guided Faun's hand over her wound and instructed her to keep pressure on it, then addressed Grey again.

"I'm not interested in mindless slaughter," she said, "but you can't stand there and tell me that the huntsmen are wrong for condemning our enemies."

The agents had only themselves to blame for the fury of the civilians they evicted. With the Order felled by the storm dragon, the huntsmen no longer had to live in so much fear. For once, they could step beyond the shadow of the woods.

And if the root of pain and suffering in Ver Signia could be traced all the way to some highborn lord's decree, or even to the king...

Who was Meiryn to stop the huntsmen from chasing down their prey?

"This *is* how we rebuild," Meiryn insisted. She gestured to the ruins around them, sodden and crumbled—but vacant. "We take what our enemies lost in their own arrogance. We forge new alliances to stand stronger against anyone who threatens our campaign for peace."

Faun huffed a breathy chuckle. "You're sounding like a true huntsman now, princess."

Meiryn shushed her, but the tips of her ears warmed at the validation.

Grey, however, only seemed more dubious. He studied Meiryn closely, lifting a bloodied hand to rub a sore spot over his chest. "Do you really think you're advocating for peace if you go down this route? Do you think the huntsmen would stop after just a handful of deaths?"

"They will, if you continue to lead them," Lukas said with no small amount of indignation. He held Grey's stare for a moment before muttering, "They've listened to you all this time. They trust you."

"But can I trust that they won't go behind my back if my orders go against what they want?"

"You should trust that they'll avenge what was lost," Meiryn said. Her throat thickened. "Faun avenged Nona. Don't you want to avenge Elder?"

Rage darkened the pale blue of Grey's eyes to a steely indigo. "I told you—she shouldn't have been here."

His unspoken accusation dangled between them, but Meiryn refused to take the bait. Elder's death, she knew, would haunt them both for the rest of their lives. The guilt was already clashing against her simmering anger. Tossing the blame back and forth would get them nowhere.

"Many things shouldn't have happened today," she said, thinking again of Athira, "but here we are. Alive in a dead city."

A muscle in Grey's jaw twitched.

Faun drew in a ragged breath. "We'll bury our fallen soon enough. The rest of our forces need to be told what happened today."

Lukas nodded in agreement. To Grey, he said, "Send your crow. I'll see how many of us are with the survivors." He caught

Meiryn's eye as he reached out. Then, seeming to remember how she'd recoiled earlier, he let his hand fall. Quietly, he said, "I'm sorry." And then he was gone.

Grey faced the women with crossed arms, and his stare was too scalding for Meiryn to hold. She dropped her gaze and let his words fall like stones into her chest. She couldn't tell whom he addressed now.

"I hope you know what you're signing the Guild up for. Anger alone can only get you so far."

It was Faun who answered. "Enough of your lectures. If you're so against the idea of revenge, why bother summoning the rest of the huntsmen anyway?"

"Because divided we don't stand a chance. And maybe, once they see what's become of this place, they won't want to risk inciting a war anyway."

"They'll fight," Faun pressed, "because this is the moment they've been waiting for. The Silver Order is gone. We're still here, after all these years. How can you not see how that's a good thing?"

Grey said nothing. He was staring at Meiryn—she could feel it, though she kept her head down. If he was waiting for her to protest, he'd be waiting all night. There was nothing left for her to say. Nothing left to drive her except anger and hurt.

"The Guild may grow stronger without the Order standing in opposition, but the road ahead just became much steeper," Grey said. "We now sit on the front lines of every assault from the Nest. None of the Order's equipment still stands, and without the help of even one Drāga, we won't have any way to mitigate the rage of the dragons."

"We don't need to mitigate them." Faun waved her free hand, a motion exerting enough to leave her leaning more heavily against Meiryn. She gave a thin sigh. "We just need to direct them toward Caer Savalier and those ridiculous courtiers."

Grey shook his head and dismissed himself in silence.

Meiryn finally looked up when his footsteps receded from earshot.

Head on Meiryn's shoulder, Faun studied her with a softer form of compassion and sympathy than Meiryn anticipated. "Are you alright?"

Meiryn huffed a laugh. "Is that a serious question? I should be asking you that."

"Right." Faun clenched her jaw. Gone was the brasher tone with which she'd fantasized about the fall of the nobility. "We've all been through a lot. But try not to think of what we lost; think of what we still have to fight for."

What did that amount to, weighted against everything she'd already lost? Reina was not Reina; Elder was dead; the Guild would find Draconis in ruins. She had survived impossible things, yet it hardly felt like a victory.

Reina should have been here at her side. Reina should have been *real*.

Salt stung Meiryn's eyes, and she asked, "Does it get easier?"

Faun read her like an open book. Lips thinning, she shook her head.

Meiryn sobbed once, and Faun slid a tentative arm over her shoulders. Meiryn leaned into her embrace, chest burning as she stifled her cries.

"It never goes away," Faun said thickly, "but you either let it kill you, or you make it your weapon. Nothing is promised, Meiryn. Not our days or our nights; not the childish fantasies of a lifetime spent with the ones we love. So let your anger burn.

Let it turn to hatred if you must—but don't let it consume *you*. Turn it outward. Let your enemies know your rage."

Meiryn curled her palms into fists. Tears dampened her lashes, but she forced herself to take steady breaths. One in. Two out. Three in. Four out... Out. Out.

Turn it outward. My enemies will know my rage.

Athira... Enemy or lost friend? She could not think of it. Not today.

Today she would grieve. She would mourn all that she fought for in vain, all that she lost before she knew it was gone. But when the sun rose tomorrow, her eyes would dry beneath the sun. She would bury memories of today deep within her mind. She would join her allies and turn her focus to the work ahead.

There was much to be done.

XXXIV. REINA

AT THE MOUTH of the tunnel, the people of Draconis had erected gallows from whatever debris and reclaimed wood they could find. They reared and snarled like animals, dragging agents and city guards onto the platform and sliding ropes around their necks.

Their current prisoner was from the Order, distinguished by the silver flames upon his uniform. His nose was broken and leaking blood. On either side of him were two younger acolytes —a boy and a girl, neither of whom could have been any older than fifteen. Both faced the bloodthirsty mob with faces white as the moon.

Reina was so relieved that she didn't recognize any of them that she gaped, too long, with her hood down. The senior agent searched the crowd for salvation, but instead, he found Reina. Their eyes locked.

"You—girl!" he cried, writhing against his bindings. "Do something. Help us!"

His desperation shattered the acolytes' resolve. They burst

into tears and begged for mercy, for their parents, for *anyone* to save them.

Reina panicked. She couldn't help this man. Couldn't help anyone the Guild targeted. The acolytes wailed as she darted past the gallows, but Reina threw her hood over her head as if it would block out their screaming.

Their echoes followed her into the tunnel. They didn't stop shouting until the huntsmen sentenced their prey to death's drop.

Reina flinched at the shadows that chased her. The prisoners performed a grotesque dance, like fish thrashing on dry shores.

The death at Reina's back seemed only to multiply as she fled. Her feet slid in pools of blood. Corpses littered her path: one nailed against the stone carving that once proudly boasted the Order's grasp on Draconis, another laying open and gutted, as if ravaged by an animal.

Lightning cracked in her heart. These huntsmen would tear her limb from limb if they knew who—*what*—she was.

When she broke free of Draconis's suffocating walls, she fell to her knees and heaved up the contents of her stomach. The bile tasted of copper and bitterness, but when her body stopped convulsing and her head stopped spinning, she forced herself to her feet again.

Night shrouded the fields. A cooler wind swept away the rain clouds and left the earth in eerie peace. Even the crickets had ceased their singing. It was as if the entire world beyond Draconis had gone quiet, holding its breath until the storm dragon made its next appearance.

Reina lifted her head, finding a mess of long, streaking clouds webbing from the site of the blast, like some colossal giant had drawn its fingers through the sky. For the first time since the cadre touched Ver Signian soil, she could see the stars. They mocked her with their permanence and impassivity.

The clattering of stones in the passage behind her made her jump. Reina seized her cloak and drew it tighter around herself, ensuring her face was covered. Her legs wobbled at the knees. Her hands hadn't stopped shaking since she'd turned away from Raiko's pale corpse.

Raiko—

She shut her mind to everything that now lay in ruins. There was nothing she could do, nothing that would absolve her of her crimes.

She set her eyes on a distant point ahead of her, and she ran.

ONE WEEK LATER

The water tasted sour, but it was better than dying of thirst. Rivulets trickled down Reina's chin and along her lightning scars. She winced at the sand and dust particles that scratched her throat, then placed a palm flat against her empty stomach. She breathed deeply, as if that would soothe the growling, and in the silence, Meiryn's final words shouted in her mind.

"Go. Get out of here."

Like she was a stray dog.

Reina splashed water over her face and shook the moisture from her hair. She'd not found a trace of Aelythius, though that invisible string still pulled her forward. Her intuition led her back into the Dragon's Spine, but caution kept her close to the river, where the break in the trees could not hide any aerial threat.

She sat back on her heels, watching the night creep over the earth. Shadows bled around her, and Reina examined her hands, as if waiting for that otherworldly light to jump at her fingertips again.

Once, she might have marveled at the power living within her. She might have found it awe-inspiring—a secret ability for just her to nurture. Now, the truth left a bitter taste in the back of her mouth: this power was a curse. Even the dragon who trespassed in her dreams refused to share his magic with her. He'd tried to kill her twice, though somehow, he'd failed.

It would have been a mercy if Aelythius killed her, or if Aaron had exacted his revenge when he found her lying beside Raiko. What right did she have to live when she was the reason Raiko's heart had stopped beating? His, and Iliana's—both of whom had so faithfully trusted her, believed in her.

Did you really think you were one of them? the wretched voice in her mind hissed. It had been haunting her ever since she fled Ver Signia. *They might have cared for you, but you were never one of them.*

Another piece of Reina's heart cracked, but she had no tears left to cry, no patience for pathetic wallowing.

A moonless sky covered her shuffling path along the river's bend and crooks. Mountains stood like giants on either side of her, and the sun was cresting over their peaks when her legs finally gave out. She fell to all fours, hands slipping into the river. Hunger tore at the lining of her stomach, left her shaking and weak. She let the earth carry the weight of her head, straining under all the guilt that wracked it until she could no longer bear it.

Some time passed before she was spotted.

Two voices, muffled beyond the fatigue fogging her brain, exchanged urgent words. She recognized the blurred syllables as Mal'dhi, and her heart ached.

"Raiko?" she called, peering into a blinding sun.

A female voice, familiar yet strained, answered her in accented Vers. "Save your strength, *reksara*. You are safe now."

Warm, callused hands lifted Reina from where she lay. Her arms swung limply, her head lolling against someone's shoulder.

"Nyrōna," a second voice implored. The speaker was male. Angry. He spouted his dissent in rapid Mal'dhi, which the woman sharply silenced. Her response was much gentler, and Reina nestled against her.

The woman spoke again to Reina. "Your troubles are over. No one here will harm you." She embraced her tighter, and Reina felt something hard prod against her cheek.

Her eyes fluttered. She lifted four wandering fingertips and grazed something sharp.

A collar made of fangs and bones wrapped around the woman's neck. Rough dragon hide scratched Reina's skin, and a low growl pierced her mind.

"Despite my efforts, you survived."

Her body went rigid. She searched the skies for the dragon, scented the air for an oncoming storm, but the weather was clear. The heart beating against her ear was steady.

"You tried to kill me," she whispered.

The woman holding her tensed. Her lips moved, but it was Aelythius who answered her accusation. *"You are a thief. An interloper into my memories."*

Reina curled her fist, watching her scars grow white. "I know who you are. You called to me."

"To reclaim what is mine."

She sensed his anger coiling tight. Her words were reduced to incoherent mumbling. "This power is mine now, too. You marked me."

"You would kill yourself if you sought to control it," he hissed.

Defiance sharpened her heart. She spoke now only in her mind, knowing that he would still hear. *I want to learn, to understand.*

The Ashuman woman jostled Reina in her arms, called to her. When Reina did not respond, her tone became frantic. Shadows fell over them, and sunlight dipped behind a rooftop of swaying leaves.

Reina felt herself drifting to another plane of consciousness —one where only she and the dragon existed. The physical world around her melted, and in place of gold-edged leaves and dragonflies, stars hoisted themselves up toward an infinite night sky. Rain fell in light showers, warming her skin. She walked barefoot toward a sleek black silhouette.

Aelythius turned when she approached. His chains were broken, but scars riddled his body. Lightning flared around his horns. *"You dare enter this place again?"*

I have dreamed of this since I was a child. I belong here.

"The gall." He lashed his tail, fangs gleaming as he sneered. *"You are the byproduct of a failed empire. I have survived centuries of slaughter, and your existence is but a footprint in the sand. There could not be a place more unfitting for you."*

Reina paused. She opened her hand, tracing with her eyes the scars that ran along her arms. Reaching within herself, she closed a spectral fist around the string that tied her to Aelythius.

She pulled, and a ball of crackling light glimmered in her palm. It did not shock or sting. It pulsed with her steady breaths, reflecting in the dragon's narrow pupils.

"You think a little light trick changes anything?"

A piece of you lives in me. This changes everything.

Aelythius uttered a growl that resonated into empty space. *"You would not so readily flaunt your strength if you understood the consequences of wielding such power."*

I understand that this power is the reason you kept yourself hidden. I want to know more.

"And killing the one who loved you did not sate your curiosity?" He snapped his jaws, and Reina flinched back, spurring a cloud of stardust at her heels.

The lightning in her hand fizzled and died. She braced herself for that heart-wrenching guilt, but she felt no pain here. It was quiet, neutral. Her body lay somewhere soft, carrying the weight of her regret, her wounds, her fears. But here, she was free from all that. She could describe this disconnection in no other way than a ship anchored in the harbor while she took a rowboat into depthless waters.

She blinked passively. *I never meant to kill anyone. I regret his death.*

"You shall regret far more if you venture down this path," the dragon warned. *"Countless Drāga have come before you. All have fallen."*

Reina nodded. She remembered what she saw, but fear, too, could not reach her here—only an insatiable hunger for knowledge and understanding of the magic inside her, even if it summoned entire armies of foes.

As if her conviction was written on her face, Aelythius emitted a strange hiccupping sound—almost like he was choking. But the cruel lift in his eyes betrayed his laughter. He fixed a scornful gaze on her.

"You spent a lifetime running from danger," he condescended. *"You are not a fighter, nor a survivor. You live only because some god continues to litter your path with pockets of luck. I know the things you've done, the past you try to forget. Am I to believe that you've had a change of heart so suddenly?"*

She grasped for the power she'd summoned mere moments ago, but it evaded her like smoke. Her heart beat erratically. *I could, if you taught me control.*

"You are hardly deserving or worthy."

And yet this power is ours to share. Centuries passed, and still, you appear in my dreams. The Drāga may be gone now, but they trusted that one day, they would walk the earth again. Do you have so little faith in their hope?

Aelythius glowered. *"The Drāga of Old have long since passed. Their beliefs are irrelevant."*

Reina lifted a brow. She sensed the prickling edges of a lie, and boldness—or perhaps a lack of clear judgment—caused her to ask, *What do you believe you are preventing by continuing to refuse me?*

The stars trembled against an invisible gust of wind. Aelythius's eyes sparked dangerously, and he bared those black, leathery wings like the sails of a ship. *"You barely know the cost of things. It would be a waste of time and breath to ensnare you in the battles I fight."*

Battles you have yet to win on your own.

Aelythius roared. Lightning lashed out from the pit of his throat, and Reina wheeled her arms as an invisible force blasted her back into her physical body. She bolted upright, gasping like she was seconds away from drowning.

A door slammed open, and the Ashuman woman from the mountains took three strides to crouch at Reina's bedside.

Reina flinched away from her worrying hands. Her gaze latched onto the dragon bone necklace, but before she could get a word in, the woman blurted in clumsy Vers, "You have returned!"

Her eyes were bright and hopeful—not a trace of resentment or anger to be found, though her arm was heavily bandaged. Behind her stood the male companion whose Mal'dhi had reminded Reina of Raiko. His arms were crossed tight, and he did not step beyond the threshold.

Reina blinked. Her surroundings flooded back on a wave of recognition. She was in the same bed, the same room she'd awoken in the night she was first captured in the Spine. Fresh curtains waved lazily in a gentle breeze, and in the next room, warm candlelight swayed and danced against the wall.

"What is this place?" Reina asked. She rubbed her eyes, then paused. Someone had wrapped her arms in lightweight cloth, all the way to the knuckles of both hands.

"You are safe," the woman assured her, "and that is what matters most. Now, tell me: what was he like? The dragon? You spoke with him, did you not?"

Reina leaned away. "How do you know... Who are you?"

Impatience twitched in the woman's face, but she bowed her head apologetically. "I am Nyrōna. This is my brother, Temaerys. We are like you—Drāga."

At the mere sound of the word, an involuntary shudder passed through Reina.

Temaerys scowled. He gestured to Reina sharply, speaking fluid Mal'dhi that Nyrōna ignored. She knelt at Reina's bedside and opened her hands.

"You are not alone anymore."

"You're Drāga," Reina repeated, still not quite believing it.

But Nyrōna nodded. "There is much for you to learn, but you are still weak. You have traveled far from home, and you spent three days in the Crossroads. Your body needs to heal."

Three full days? It felt like mere minutes.

Reina swallowed, only then feeling a painful dryness in her throat. She grimaced and asked, "What do you mean by 'the Crossroads'?"

At the door, Temaerys dropped his arms and spun away, muttering under his breath. Nyrōna's smile wavered when he slammed the door shut behind him.

"Do not pay him any mind," she said. "He is...slow to warm up to strangers. But you are welcome to call this your home until you are reunited with your dragon." Nyrōna examined Reina carefully, then stood. She was tall and graceful. Her limbs were lean, muscular, like she spent hours training every day. A hostess's grin pulled at her lips, warm but tight with the distance of a stranger. "Rest here. I will return with food and water."

"Wait." Reina grabbed Nyrōna's wrist, experiencing a surge of vertigo at the sudden movement. She waited for the dizziness to fade before asking again, "What is the Crossroads?"

Nyrōna hesitated. She glanced toward the doorway, as if contemplating whether to leave Reina wondering, but then she sighed and knelt again.

"The Crossroads is a place that all *reksari* can access. It is the place where riders can converse freely with their counterparts, but when the conscious mind extracts itself from the body, it leaves your physical form vulnerable."

Reina lowered her gaze. Three days, Nyrōna had reported.

For three days, while Reina argued with a mere image of Aelythius, she'd lain here, prone, at the complete mercy of these people—one of whom had already captured her once.

But Nyrōna had not killed her, yet.

Hoarsely, Reina said, "I did see him there. The dragon, I mean. Aelythius."

Nyrōna looked like she was suppressing her elation. She ducked her head, letting a curtain of earthen-brown hair conceal her face. Still, there was a smile in her voice, along with a touch of buried pain, when she said, "Do not rush yourself. The two of you will be reunited soon enough."

"I don't think that's a good idea."

Nyrōna tensed. "Why not?"

Reina recalled the audacious, reckless demands she'd made. Aelythius was staunch in his rejection, yet she had pushed him until he forced her out of the Crossroads.

She flexed a hand—the one that summoned lightning.

Powerless. Empty.

"I think…" She drew in a ragged breath, imagining the scars beneath her coverings. "I think he would kill me if he saw me again. He never wanted a rider."

And so this tiny seed of power would remain dormant until the end of her days. She might search for him across the continent and never lay eyes on him again. It might as well amount to a wild dream.

But Nyrōna shook her head again. "The bond between a rider and her dragon is a sacred one. Once you have unlocked your gifts, nothing can stop you from watching them grow." She smiled encouragingly and stood to take her leave. "When you have recovered your strength, you will learn more. For now, rest."

She excused herself with a quiet, murmured farewell.

Reina caught strained whispers from the other room: Nyrōna and Temaerys were arguing. They sounded close, like they were standing just beyond the door, but with surprising ease, Reina blocked out the noise.

She tossed the blankets back and ambled on unsteady feet toward the window. Crisp, cool air blew the hair back from her face, and Reina gazed up into the dark night sky. A few lone crickets chirped, preluding the turn of summer into autumn. Leaves swept down from the treetops and littered the space where Aaron slayed the Infernal. She could still hear the screaming, Nyrōna's wailing. Her fingers curled over the windowsill.

She was alone again, but this time, everything had changed. Aaron detested her. Meiryn would never trust her again. And though the dragon had rejected her in every sense of the word, Nyrōna seemed steadfast in her belief that this connection would be restored.

What then? Even if she managed to find Aelythius and convince him to teach her to control this power, what would become of her?

Everything she thought she knew about herself would become false. She would be a stranger to herself, a threat to the world that was never a home. The freedom she craved could only be attained by harnessing the storm lying dormant inside her.

But Aelythius threw her out of the Crossroads.

He was a Tempest, the last of his kind. He was the Rage of the Storm, the Chaos Incarnate. His very existence defied what humans knew to be true about the history of their own world.

And she...

She was only a thief. A coward who lied to save her own skin.

Reina hauled one leg over the windowsill. She was halfway through the window when she paused, tasting the mountain air. Salt filled her eyes as she stared into the blackness of the forest around her.

What good would running do now? If, by some miracle, she unlocked the secrets of her power, she would only paint a target on her back. Aaron would find her and make good on his promise. He would burn everything in his path to get to her. No one she associated with would be safe.

Then you must burn him before he can burn you.

The thought slithered through the cracks of her heart. She perched on the windowsill, one leg dangling over the outside edge, and dried her tears. Dispelling images of the ones she had abandoned, the ones she had betrayed and hurt, she lifted her chin with stubborn defiance.

Aelythius was wrong. She *was* a survivor. She survived by leaving the past behind, by never once looking back. It delivered her from the cages of her childhood, carried her through years of wandering, brought her to this point.

It could take her further. It had to.

Reina opened her hands and peeled back the cloth that covered her scars. Her skin prickled at the cold wind, but she did not tremble. Air flowed steadily through her nostrils and into her lungs, then expelled in deep exhalations. She reached inside herself, searching for that kernel of magic. She could sense it coiling, writhing away from her, but she strained for it until sweat beaded at her brow.

This is my power, she raged silently.

A distant growl shook the walls of her skull, but she ignored it. He refused her, and so would she him.

Threads of lightning danced just beyond her reach—she could *feel* them. She recalled that sensation of weightlessness she experienced in the Crossroads, the ease of summoning light at her fingertips. It was so far away now, but it still existed beneath the layers of doubt and fear.

Aelythius might have shunned her, but he could not rip this shred of magic away from her. It was imprinted upon her skin, woven into the fibers of her being.

Reina tightened her fists. A gentle warmth spread from her elbows, where the scars reached further, all the way into her fingertips. Her heart fluttered.

There you are.

The air around her turned warm. Every hair on her body stood on end, and she grinned when tiny bursts of gold lit up the darkness.

EPILOGUE

THE RAIN FOLLOWED him all the way back to Verilonne. Even with the storm dragon gone and Athira cast from his side, Aaron was plagued by grey skies flickering with lightning.

He watched the rain pelt his bedroom window. From the moment he locked himself away, it had never left. Lady Rhysanthe's garden was flooded: the petals of her magnolias were limp and lackluster as they drifted in the little creek that wound between the hedges.

Pitiful.

He was busy grazing his thumb along the dragon pendant he had recovered from Raiko's body when his ears pricked at the whine of a floorboard. His body tensed, and he felt a twinge of annoyance just before a faint knock sounded at his door.

"Leave me," he called without turning from the window. How many times would he have to turn away these servants? The footsteps did not recede, and Aaron scowled, picking his head up off his fist. "I said *leave*."

The doorknob turned. His father strode in, hands clasped neatly behind his broad back.

Aaron nearly toppled his chair as he scrambled to his feet. Then, remembering his manners, he folded into a deep bow. The pendant dug into his palm. "Lord Rhysanthe," he breathed. "Forgive me, I did not—"

"When I heard of your return, I hardly believed it." Lord Dante Rhysanthe paced the room on silent feet, the gold lining of his boots glistening each time a vein of lightning cracked outside the window. He cast an unimpressed look toward Aaron's unmade bed, then ran a finger over a thin layer of dust that had collected on his wardrobe. "Five years you've been away—and you didn't even bother to notify me of your homecoming. I'd have prepared a feast if I had known."

"My return warrants no such extravagance," Aaron said quickly. He swallowed hard. "And...I was not expecting you, either, my lord."

His father approached. He stopped a foot away and cleared his throat.

Aaron straightened, taking the cue to meet the stare of the man who had never once blinked at anything Aaron did. Even his acceptance into the ranks of the Silver Order was not enough to earn his father's pride.

Lord Rhysanthe had not changed. Every hair on his head was perfectly coiffed, every wrinkle on his clothes ironed out. Eyes as black as midnight, hooded by a protruding brow, guarded any display of emotion. His face was cleanly shaven, and the sharp jawline he'd passed down to his sons still cut like a knife.

"You look taller," the lord observed. "Perhaps carrying the weight of the family's honor no longer burdens you?"

Aaron blinked, confused. "I don't—"

"Do not interrupt me." Lord Rhysanthe circled Aaron with

his chest thrown out and his chin propped high. He sniffed and wrinkled his nose, as if catching a whiff of something unsavory. "It is bad enough that your brother seeks an annulment of his marriage with the Drumond chit. Now I must answer for your involvement in the dissolution of the Silver Order."

Lightning flashed outside; thunder groaned a few tense seconds later. Aaron stared ever forward, feeling himself dissociating a little more every time his father passed in front of him.

Lord Rhysanthe paused and leaned close, until his mouth was a mere inch from Aaron's ear. "Did you lose your tongue along with your dignity? Or are you going to tell me what happened in Draconis, so I do not have to waste time spinning night-tales for every eavesdropper at court?"

Aaron's eyes shuttered at another burst of lightning. This one was closer. Its thunder rocked the roof over their heads, and for a heart-stopping moment, he feared the dragon had come back to finish what it started.

Draconis had only fallen a week ago, but news of its sacking had already traveled across the kingdom and into every corner tavern. Whispers of the Wolf King's return were combated with wild accounts of a shadowy beast coming to exact revenge against the Order's dragon campaign. Even the servants of House Rhysanthe speculated behind closed doors: Aaron heard them chattering when he wandered the halls after hours to keep the nightmares at bay.

Their guesswork was patchy at best. They knew of the dragon only because more huntsmen than agents survived this second assault, but what they didn't know—or perhaps refused to think about—was that it was the Order that first tried to keep the beast contained. Families were displaced and the people were made unhappy, but none of them gave pause to recognize that the Order had imprisoned the very thing that now left the kingdom buzzing with fear and anticipation. No one knew where the dragon went, or what sent it away. No one even guessed that its disappearance might be the result of a single girl's actions.

But Aaron knew, and so did Korris. As far as he knew, they were the only ones who knew what she had done, the powers she wielded.

And if anyone found out that Aaron let her go, it would be his body flailing from the gallows next.

"What happened in Draconis was the result of misjudgment," Aaron said stiffly. "Our forces underestimated the power of the storm dragon, and it awakened without precedent. We were unprepared."

"'Unprepared,'" Lord Rhysanthe echoed with a scoff. He resumed his pacing. "Your lack of preparation could be excused once, but a second time was insulting. A disgrace to everything you agents stand for."

"You were not there."

The air tensed, and Aaron braced himself for a biting remark, a spiteful backhand across the cheek. He should not have spoken so disparagingly.

But Lord Rhysanthe merely said, "It's obvious you are troubled by what happened. Is there anything you wish to discuss? Perhaps it would be good to...ease your mind."

Aaron dissected his father's expression. His brow was drawn tight, giving the impression of concern, but his mouth was crooked, hanging by the thinnest thread of a smirk. He wanted answers, just like everyone else. The hands resting behind his back were empty, yet strong enough to throttle secrets from a loose tongue if he felt he wasn't getting what he wanted.

Aaron's chest deflated with a heavy sigh. "I am grieving. That is all."

Raiko's face flashed in his mind: skin white, eyes gaping, mouth flooded with rainwater.

He cleared his throat on a clap of thunder, dropping his gaze to the floor. "There is nothing I wish to discuss."

"Well," Lord Rhysanthe answered with a cocked head, "the court has questions, and seeing as you are the only one of repute who still lives to testify, you don't have much choice in the matter. Caer Savalier will listen to you, if they won't listen to your pathetic excuse of a commander."

Aaron's ears pricked. "She survived?"

Lord Rhysanthe scowled. "With hardly more than the skin on her own back." He offered nothing more; though questions surfaced, Aaron knew that he would find no answers from his father.

"You can either tell me what happened," the lord continued, "or speak before all of Caer Savalier yourself."

In privacy, the truth could be warped. It was easier to sway one mind than a thousand, but Aaron knew that even if he spoke truthfully in front of the king's city, most would not believe him. He was Ashuman, *malduna*. Nothing was more incriminating than bearing resemblance to the enemy.

"I would need a moment to collect my thoughts," he murmured.

"You had plenty of time for that before I arrived." An impatient edge crept into the lord's voice. His dark shadow tapped its forefinger against the back of the opposite palm. "Surely amidst all that grief, there is a spark."

"'A spark,'" Aaron repeated inquisitively.

"Anger," Lord Rhysanthe urged. "A wish to exact your

revenge against the ones who delivered such a humiliating defeat."

Of course there was. But the pain was still raw. Aaron spent his days in that chair by the window, praying for a break in the clouds to sear through the memory of finding Raiko dead and cold by Athira's side. His heart still burned from that loss. It may well never cease to burn.

"I will speak to the nobles," Aaron decided aloud, "when I am ready."

Contempt curled Lord Rhysanthe's mouth into a twisted grimace. He halted again, dropping his fists by his sides. "Did you not hear me, boy? Caer Savalier wants answers. The king wants answers. This is your chance to lift House Rhysanthe from the ashes of ruin."

So this is what it was about.

"You are an ex-agent of the Silver Order, a survivor of the attack on Draconis," Lord Rhysanthe continued. "These nobles have never known such disaster; it is a distant thought that taints their conversations over high tea. Look at me, boy. You are Aaron Idelius of House Rhysanthe. You are my son, and I will not allow you to revert to your bed-wetting days just because a dragon haunts your dreams. You trained to slay those monsters, did you not?"

"Yes, sir." But it was not the dragon that lurked in Aaron's nightmares.

Lord Rhysanthe narrowed his stare. "Then a public address should be no issue. You will accompany me to Caer Savalier at the end of the week, along with that dolt Alexander."

Aaron suppressed a groan. "Are there not more important things for him to attend to here?"

"Like what?" his father barked. "His wife who despises him

just as much as he dreads her? Don't be stupid. The whole of the family shall back you. Yes, even your mother," he added when Aaron threw him a bewildered look. "Rinh may worm her way out of her duties as easily as your brother, but she has her uses—scarce though they may be."

To Aaron's knowledge, Lady Rhysanthe hardly left her room most days. He'd almost forgotten his mother was here, in this very mansion. She had not sent for him upon his return. Had not even graced him with her appearance.

It should not have surprised him, nor should it have hurt the way it did.

His father finished, "If we are to convince the court that we are worthy of respect, we must appear as a solid unit."

Lord Rhysanthe started to exit, but before he could catch himself, Aaron blurted, "What about Athira?"

Slowly, Lord Rhysanthe released his grip on the doorknob. Lightning lit up a terrifying gleam in his eye. "What about her?"

"The nobles have not forgotten her desertion," Aaron said. "They will note her absence if we make an appearance."

"It's been years since she disappeared," Lord Rhysanthe dismissed. "She might as well be lying dead in a ditch somewhere, rotting with the rats. And even if she somehow still lives, the nobles have more pressing things on their minds. No one will remember her. Unless," he added when Aaron foolishly averted his gaze, "you are trying to tell me something."

Aaron felt his breath catch in his chest. "No, sir."

"Speak."

"There is nothing to say."

The door shuddered under the impact of Lord Rhysanthe's fist. Aaron took one step back before his father descended upon him. One hand clamped around Aaron's neck; the other seized a fistful of his hair and pulled.

"Speak, you fucking coward," the lord seethed. "Or, gods help me, you'll regret the day you slithered out of your mother's womb."

Water burned in the corners of Aaron's eyes. He swallowed against his father's hand. "Athira," he managed in a strained whisper. "She's alive."

Lord Rhysanthe bared a row of white teeth with his smile. "Good. What else?"

Aaron fought back a cough. "She took a different name. To hide herself."

A look of bemusement crossed Lord Rhysanthe's face. He glanced up toward the window, as if expecting to find his wayward daughter trudging up the muddy path of the estate. He blinked at a flash of lightning, and as the thunder rolled, a low chuckle rumbled in his chest. It built into a roaring laugh, and Aaron gasped when his father tossed him away like a childhood toy he'd outgrown.

"A false name," the lord crowed.

Aaron massaged his neck, ducking his head as he dried his tears. He nodded and forced strength into his voice. "My cadre happened upon her by chance. She called herself 'Reina.'"

He chose his next words carefully. "She set an Infernal loose in West Glen. A band of huntsmen sought to recruit her into their ranks, but we had our own orders to capture her and deliver her to Morturrim."

Intrigue sparked in Lord Rhysanthe's eyes. "Is that so?"

Aaron nodded again. His hand trembled around the dragon pendant. "However," he ventured cautiously, "I intended to deliver her here. To Verilonne."

"Oh?"

"I thought, in your possession, she would be less prone to causing trouble. I failed to complete my mission, but it did not matter in the end, because…"

Because things went to shit. Because she wields the power of the storm dragon. Because she killed Raiko.

"Because when Draconis fell, she escaped."

Because I let her go.

Lord Rhysanthe's chest swelled with a deep inhale. He side-stepped Aaron and approached the window, some wisp of a smile still playing on his lips.

"Athira," he murmured, as if testing the weight of her name on his tongue after years of estrangement. "You brave, stupid girl… What are you thinking, running off again?"

Rain streaked across the glass like cracks in a mirror. The wind threatened to peel every shingle off the roof, but neither Lord Rhysanthe nor his second son flinched at the deafening *boom* of thunder that rattled the building all the way down to its foundation.

Aaron watched his father's silhouette with bated breath. He had not moved from where he lay, discarded on the ground, but when Lord Rhysanthe turned, it was all Aaron could do not to flee the room, the mansion, the entire gods-damned estate, with nothing but the clothes on his back.

A look of giddiness lit up the lord's face in an uncharacteristically youthful way. It reminded Aaron of the corpse they found in the crypts—the one whose mouth had been carved into a permanent grin.

But this terror was alive, and it was very, very real.

"My son," Lord Rhysanthe said, "if it's honor you seek to restore, then heed my words: your grieving ends here. From this day forth, you are the hand of justice, the force to bring chaos to its end. First you will speak before Caer Savalier. You will remind them that House Rhysanthe stands resolute. Then, once the nobles are swooning at your words, you will direct our own private forces to find and capture your sister. I shall deal with her myself."

Aaron masked his shock behind a neutral expression. "That would take months. Athira wouldn't risk sheltering anywhere in Ver Signia after all that happened."

And despite all the rage and hurt that coursed through him that final day in Draconis, Aaron was tired—of the chasing; of the fighting; of never coming away victorious. He wanted to forget it all. Everything he built, every little scrap of honor he scrounged up, was blasted away when that storm dragon tore through Draconis.

And now, Athira was free to flock to its side, to grow in whatever abominable power she possessed.

Lord Rhysanthe crossed the room and plucked Aaron's sword from where it leaned against the wall. He examined it, hilt to tip, and light sputtered into the room when he activated the flames. Embers leaped from the hilt and died on the leather of Lord Rhysanthe's boot. The glow of warming steel reflected in his eyes as he extended the sword, hilt-first, toward Aaron.

"Then you know where to start looking."

ACKNOWLEDGMENTS

This project wouldn't have made it this far without the support, encouragement, and feedback of so many people. I can't thank all of you enough.

To my wonderful editor, Erin: thank you for taking a leap with me on such a long manuscript, for your insightful comments and flattering words. Without you, *Unraveled* would be incomplete. I'm beyond thrilled that our books get to sit together on our shelves.

To all the coffee shops I haunted throughout the years—Yellow House (RIP), J&B, Rosalind, White Rhino, Eiland, Pax & Beneficia, Mudleaf, Native, Staycation, and of course, Tre Stelle: thank you for my daily doses of caffeine and for providing such beautiful spaces for my creativity to flow.

To Ash, Semy, and Mia: you were my first trusted readers. I'll always remember how excited you all were when I first met you and told you I was writing a book—and how eager you were to read every scrap I offered, even the unedited pieces. That eagerness and excitement opened up a door for me that helped me grow comfortable with sharing my work with others. Y'all were the catalyst. And y'all are the best.

To Julia and Bryce: though years and miles have distanced us, I still hold you both in such high regards, and I always will. Thank you for hyping me up, for commiserating with me when I needed it, and for being a quiet, constant support in my life.

To Kendalyn and Matt: I am so grateful and lucky to have you both in my corner through everything. You're the best family anyone could ask for.

To Hae-won: you reignited my love for the literary community. You showed me that there are people who still read, who still hunger for new books and ideas, and that they are closer than I realize. Never change, my friend.

To Judy: my first author friend, you are such an inspiration. Meeting you and being blessed by your friendship has done more for me than you'll ever know. Because of you, I learned to let myself feel like I belong within the author community. I'm so proud of what you've done with your writing, and I can't wait to see how far you'll go.

To the one who was with me at the start of this journey, when this book had a different name, different characters, a different story: you know who you are. You were the first to know about this little world of mine, the first who fueled the flame of inspiration. So wherever you are, know that I couldn't have done this without you, either.

And to everyone else whose support, admiration, and intrigue kept me motivated on the bleakest of days, this book is especially for you. You'll never know how honored I am that you expressed even the slightest interest in reading my work.

GLOSSARY & PRONUNCIATION GUIDE

NAMES

Reina: *RAY-na*
Athira: *ah-THEE-rah*
Rhysanthe: *RISE-anth*
Aaron: *AIR-in*
Evren: *EV-rin*
Iliana: *ill-ee-AHN-ah*
Korris: *CORE-iss*
Raiko: *RYE-koh*
Meiryn: *MARE-in*
Faun: *FAWN*
Lukas: *LU-kass*
Corvere: *CORE-veer*
Pyrrha: *PEER-ah*
Nyrōna: *nee-ROH-nah*
Nona: *NOH-nah*
Temaerys: *tem-AIR-iss*
Aelythius: *ay-LITH-ee-us*

PLACES

Ver Signia: *VAIR SIG-nee-ah*
Draconis: *dray-CON-iss*
Verilonne: *VAIR-ih-lonn*
Ashuma: *AH-shoo-mah*

Rhonestiel: *RONE-steel*

<u>VOCABULARY</u>

Malduna: *mal-DOO-na*
A slur used by Ver Signians when speaking derogatorily to or about Ashumans, meaning *trickster* or *enemy*

Kaeli rekks: *KY-lee rex*
Ashuman for *rulers of the sky*, an honorific moniker for dragons

Drāga: *DHRAY-gah (soft D sound, rolled R)*
People of an ancient dynasty now lost from the history books
While bonding with a dragon is an ability unique to the Drāga, not every Drāga has a dragon counterpart

Rhaksha: *RAHK-shah*
Ashuman, translating roughly to *fool* or *oblivious/empty-minded one*

N'benem: *neh-BEN-em*
Ashuman, translating to *good evening*

Amia: *AH-mee-ah*
Ashuman, informal or casual term for *friend*

Mi'amiya: *mee-AH-mee-ah*
Ashuman, more affectionate term for *dear(est) friend*

Dha'katsi: *dah-KAT-zee*
Lacks any direct translation into Ver Signian common tongue

Term of endearment often used by two lovers with a deep affection for one another, but can be used by one as an indirect way to express interest in the other

Skorhui: *SCORE-way*
Ashuman, translating to *shit*

Reksari: *wreck-SAH-ree*
Ashuman, translating to *dragon riders* (plural)
Singular masculine: *reksar*
Singular feminine: *reksara*

ABOUT THE AUTHOR

A lifelong lover of fantasy worlds and complex characters, Kit Aldridge weaves relatable human experiences into imaginative worlds to create her stories. She draws inspiration from film and video game scores, often losing herself in the daydream of a scene rather than putting it down into words. When she is writing, however, you'll find a half-drunk mug of coffee gone cold sitting beside her—or maybe her cat nestled under her chair.

For more information and updates on Kit's writing endeavors, follow her on Instagram @authorkitaldridge or check out her website at www.authorkitaldridge.com.

www.ingramcontent.com/pod-product-compliance
Lightning Source LLC
Chambersburg PA
CBHW061104310726
48974CB00002B/382